CANDLELIGHT
Ecstasy Supreme

"THANK YOU. I KNOW YOU'VE WANTED ME OUT OF THE COUNTRY. I'LL GO.

"I don't know what I supposedly did, but I'm very grateful. I'll oblige you and go immediately."

He just kept staring at her, but Erin kept talking. "I know how terribly annoying this mock marriage must have been. I realize it will cause you a great deal of embarrassment, and again, all I can say is thank you and that I'll never trouble you again."

"Don't be ridiculous," he grated close to her ear, sending a ripple of fear and electricity raging through her. "Shut up before someone hears you. You're not going anywhere—not until it's convenient for me to take you. You fool! Did you really think I could take you from the Russians with theatrics? That marriage was no mockery. Madam, you just became Mrs. Jarod Steele."

A CANDLELIGHT ECSTASY SUPREME

RED MIDNIGHT

Heather Graham

A CANDLELIGHT ECSTASY SUPREME

Published by
Dell Publishing Co., Inc.
1 Dag Hammarskjold Plaza
New York, New York 10017

Dell ® TM 681510, Dell Publishing Co., Inc.

Candlelight Ecstasy Supreme is a trademark of
Dell Publishing Co., Inc.

Candlelight Ecstasy Romance®, 1,203,540, is a registered
trademark of Dell Publishing Co., Inc.

ISBN: 0-440-17431-7

Printed in the United States of America
First printing—March 1984

*For my aunt, Eleanor, who has always been there for me,
and for the Russian people, the ordinary people, who made
our trip so very warm and extraordinary.*

To Our Readers:

Candlelight Ecstasy is delighted to announce the start of a brand-new series—Ecstasy Supremes! Now you can enjoy a romance series unlike all the others—longer and more exciting, filled with more passion, adventure, and intrigue—the stories you've been waiting for.

In months to come we look forward to presenting books by many of your favorite authors and the very finest work from new authors of romantic fiction as well. As always, we are striving to present the unique, absorbing love stories that you enjoy most—the very best love has to offer.

Breathtaking and unforgettable, Ecstasy Supremes will follow in the great romantic tradition you've come to expect *only* from Candlelight Ecstasy.

Your suggestions and comments are always welcome. Please let us hear from you.

Sincerely,

The Editors
Candlelight Romances
1 Dag Hammarskjold Plaza
New York, New York, 10017

RED MIDNIGHT

PROLOGUE

The hallway was long and white, white walls, white tile flooring, evoking complete sterility. The man who walked down the corridor was a dark and compelling contrast. His height of six feet two was amplified by a slender physique, broad shoulders tapering to wire-muscled trimness. His suit was of dove gray and he wore it well, its finely tailored angles emphasizing the toned quality of a body well fit for action. His appearance of casual and understated elegance was deceptive: he could turn on a dime and demolish distance in seconds, endure fearful rigors of cold and heat, and tangle with the best, be it a duel of fists or tongue. Ice-blue eyes that never betrayed an emotion were a point of beauty in a face not particularly handsome but ruggedly arresting. Forty years of character were etched into that strong face, capable of compelling great trust—or great fear. The direct gaze of his extraordinary blue eyes could instill chills that raced inexplicably up the spine. Women shivered deliciously at his glance, wondering later what had been the great attraction while still dreaming about feeling that strange caress of piercing blue again, imagining the vital touch of the enigmatic man behind the eyes—a man who exuded a quiet power that was only a hint of what lay beneath the surface.

His footsteps brought him swiftly and quietly down the long hallway, where the white sterility ended in a mass of silver-gray machinery. From floor to ceiling, wall to wall, disks, reels, keyboards, exhausts, and drives exhibited an overwhelming display of man's ingenuity. In front of the mass of gadgets and technology was a single chair, its metal frame and upholstery gray. The chair awaited the man, and when he was seated, his first action was to slip his hand into a pit below the computer's screen. Cogs whirred, a light flared. The screen above the man lit into action.

HELLO, JAROD STEELE.

Jarod smiled a bit wryly. Even the computer was sociable and courteous. He punched out a return.

GOOD MORNING, CATHERINE I.

He made no effort to add to his greeting, because he knew the next message coming.

THE DATE IS MARCH 2. TIME, 10.03.28 AM. OUTSIDE THE UNITED NATIONS BUILDING THE TEMPERATURE IS 60 DEGREES FAHRENHEIT, 15.6 CELSIUS. NO RAIN IN FORECAST. NICE DAY, SIR, FOR NEW YORK THAT IS, IF YOU KNOW WHAT I MEAN.

Great! Jarod thought, nothing like a highly technical piece of machinery with a sense of humor. But then Catherine I had been programmed by Neils Weir, who was a genius and a little crazy. The Catherine I and her counterpart across the seas were very lovely ladies. Jarod lifted a brow at the screen and waited. It was sometimes incredible. Catherine I would continue a social commentary on his welfare, monitoring his moves by the laws of probability. Within her memory banks Catherine I knew all there was to know about Jarod Steele.

But this morning Catherine had nothing else to say. Jarod started to punch in a thank you for the information, then remembered a bit sheepishly that he was dealing with a computer, nothing more than machinery. Catherine would not be hurt if he didn't express his gratitude. He repunched the keys.

"A" PROMPT, PLEASE. READ FILE. MERGE ALL PERTINENT INFORMATION. FILE NAME HUGHES, SAMUEL, #34ABB277. RETURN.

In a split second the screen was filled with information. When the computer had completed the file, a command request appeared at the top of the screen.

SUPPLY ADDITIONAL DATA, PLEASE.

Jarod touched more keys.

MERGE FILES. HUGHES, SAMUEL, AND PROJECT
MIDNIGHT.

A screen of new information appeared, but Jarod felt an uneasiness in the pit of his stomach as his lips tightened in a grim line. What he now saw was not what he had expected. Where had this new information come from?

Jarod punched in a new question based on the data that had appeared on the screen.

PRESENT LOCATION, SUBJECT HUGHES?

The answer flashed back immediately.

UNKNOWN

Frustrated, discouraged, and now concerned, Jarod sat back in the chair, staring at the screen with a frown lining his forehead in deep furrows as he waited. Suddenly he hunched intently over the keyboard, his long fingers fringed at the joints with lighter tufts of the silvering jet hair on his head, with nails short and bluntly cut but immaculate, coursing over the keys as he filled in further information for assimilation. Then he repeated his question, only to receive the same answer. The nagging question of where the new data on Project Midnight had come from remained a mystery.

Baffled, he leaned back in the chair once more, his blue gaze staring at the computer with reproach, as if once again forgetting that Catherine had no human qualities and couldn't be shamed into answering him. Jarod ran his fingers over his temple, then thoughtfully rubbed a freshly shaved chin. Damn! he thought with disgust. The computer wasn't human, but he was, and he was making mistakes.

Catherine was a fantastic piece of machinery, but she was only machinery. He was seeking intelligent answers based on assumption: unless he asked for assumptions, she could give him nothing but facts. And now with these recent revelations, the matter had become more complicated.

But if you fed her all the pertinent information and requested the probabilities, Jarod thought, a slight smile flickering across his lips.

Jarod quickly punched the new command.

Having given Catherine the new data, he reworded his question.

WHERE IS SUBJECT, HUGHES, SAMUEL?

The answer was the one he had feared. He winced as feelings of both sadness and disgusted resignation at Hughes's probable death made him suddenly tired, very tired. He closed his eyes for a moment and it suddenly became clear to him what might have happened. Sam Hughes had always seemed like such a nice guy around the embassy, but apparently he had got a little more involved in Project Midnight than he should have. He had fallen to the age-old allure of easy riches to be made through treachery. But somewhere along the line he must have panicked. Or maybe he wanted something to hold over the head of someone else, which is what could have accounted for the new information Catherine had acquired. Whatever his reasons, Hughes had fed her with clues, leaving Jarod more confused.

If I could discover what happened, I would have the answer, Jarod thought dryly. But he didn't have any answers, and so Project Midnight had to remain his first concern. Because if he could trust this new data from Hughes something very dangerous was going on—just how dangerous, Sam Hughes had discovered too late.

Jarod reopened his eyes to the screen, and smiled with little humor. Catherine was apologizing for the information she had been forced to supply.

Jarod began to punch keys, stupidly assuring Catherine it wasn't "her" fault. He requested another "A" prompt.

HUGHES'S SPECIFIC ASSIGNMENT, PROJECT MIDNIGHT?

Jarod read the file information again, most of which he already knew. But the tail end of Catherine's listing was useful. A description of someone had been cleverly filtered into the routine information. A description and some kind of a key code. *Mc* . . . the letters *M* and *c,* as in a name . . . Jarod tensed as a creeping sensation came over him. Hughes had added these clues, which pointed toward something happening soon. Jarod was more distressed by this information than by any of Hughes's previous clues. He punched more keys.

VISAS PLEASE, REQUEST FOR RED ZONE, PRECEDING TWO WEEKS.

Catherine efficiently replied.

ADAMA, JOHN
BENTON, THEODORE
DAYTON, ANGELINA
LYDELL, HAROLD
LYDELL, MARIE
MCCABE, ERIN

A look of chilling intensity filled Jarod's ice-blue eyes. He punched the stop key, and zeroed in on the last name, the only Mc in the grouping. He requested the file on her, his well-wired muscles taut as he waited.

SUBJECT, McCABE, ERIN.

Jarod read on, requesting a portrait. He punched in the necessary color key codes to give the proper hues to the graphics.

Once more he leaned back in the chair, his long fingers idly brushing his chin as he looked on.

He had seen her before: most Americans had seen her face and figure. Not even the distorted colors and graphics of the computer image could take away from the elegant beauty of her fine bone structure, her liquid eyes, her full pouting lips. Her face was a classic oval, her cheekbones high, her eyes large, wide, well set apart. Winged brows gave her a look of both delicacy and spirit: she could pose as angel or devil. In her career, he knew, she had appeared as both.

It can't be her, he thought. She can't be Hughes's contact. But she could be. He would have to watch her, and it might prove interesting. It was usually the least suspicious person one needed to suspect.

"What the hell would a woman like that be doing going there anyway?" he wondered aloud. "It's not exactly the place for social butterflies." Damn! he muttered. It looked like trouble either way.

She was going to be his responsibility, just like every American citizen who crossed the border. Even under normal circumstances, he would have noted the name skeptically, bemoaning the fact that he was responsible for watching the antics of this whimsical beauty out for a careless lark. He couldn't think of her visit as a lark. He had to watch her very carefully, because all the clues pointed in her direction. It seemed incredible.

Or was it? What if she were in on Project Midnight?

Such a beautiful face . . . And body, he reminded himself dryly, which only served to increase his irritation. Erin McCabe was packaged merchandise; she was a lie, created by those whose products she advertised. What a damn complication.

It could be her—five feet nine, blond, blue eyes . . .

No, they weren't blue—the computer showed them as blue. They were actually somewhere between blue and gray, a glistening, beguiling silver. He could see the real Erin McCabe, just as he had seen her on the cover of a magazine recently, hovering over the computer image. He hadn't realized until now how closely he had looked at that cover. Yes, her eyes were really silver and her hair was a shade between burnished gold and softest platinum, not that common yellow.

She's packaged merchandise! he reminded himself dryly, and they had packaged her quite well. He gave himself a little shake. She could fit the bill, Jarod thought. Wasn't she just the type? She could look into a man's eyes with that liquid enticement that made the blood race. She was an angel; she was a sensually seductive woman.

Recently divorced, Jarod noticed, arched brow winging as he pondered his subject. Yes, of course. She had been married to a photographer. *Time* had run the story.

Jarod found himself wondering what she would look like without her makeup, without that wealth of gold hair floating about her features with abandoned but dignified beauty. She was very, very elegant.

It's going to be interesting, he consoled himself. Madam Elite is going to be in for a few surprises when she crosses the border.

He moved his fingers to clear the screen, then hesitated, fascinated by the face that so enchanted. She was incredibly beautiful, and he was human and certainly male.

Erin McCabe. Was she as innocent as a man believed when

staring into those silver eyes? Or was she playing the perfect game of treachery? But she was simply too stunning to be so treacherous, to live that type of devious lie.

What a fool you are, Steele, he berated himself.

Impatient, Jarod hit the keys. Catherine, he thought, you're the woman I give my heart to. . . . Never any trouble . . . never any back talk! . . . Of course, I doubt you'd be much in a bikini. . . .

But a computer also couldn't feel; it couldn't be soft and fragile; it couldn't falter when confronted with a smile of sunshine and a will of steel.

"Yes, Catherine," Jarod murmured. "You are the only woman in the world for me. . . ."

He cleared the screen, and checked out.

THANK YOU, CATHERINE.

YOU'RE WELCOME.

He retraced his footsteps down the long hall, his dark, silvering head slightly bent in meditation, his hands thrust in his pockets. The blue ice of his lowered eyes seared to a cold flame with his contemplations.

There was a static aura to this man. He was dangerous, compelling. He played for high stakes. He was cunning; he was cautious, tenacious, vibrantly involved. And at the moment, very angry. People so seldom recognized the games they played. Perhaps Samuel Hughes had, but apparently too late. And now he had Erin McCabe to worry about. Devil or angel.

If she were just vacationing, why the hell couldn't she vacation in Paris or Madrid?

In Jarod's eyes, the woman already had a few strikes against her. Was she devious beyond belief? Was she simply a pawn in a great board game? Or was she merely getting in his way when things far more important than the welfare of a foolish model were at stake?

He hadn't met her, but he knew her type. If he had his way, she'd be sent packing so fast she wouldn't need to open a suitcase.

Strange, though, he couldn't shake the image of her face—the computer image, or that which he had discovered he knew so well superimposed over the graphics in his mind's eye. She was incredibly, incredibly beautiful . . . incredibly, incredibly sensuous.

19

Damn butterfly, Jarod thought with annoyance. That he thought of her as alluring and desirable infuriated him. He was entranced by her image, just as any man would be. That was natural. He could usually afford to humor himself for following normal male tendencies. But this was different. He couldn't afford to humor himself where Erin McCabe was concerned. She was not just a suspect, but at the moment the only suspect.

I

Heads turned when she walked into the room, and not because she was recognized. Her hair was pulled into a severe chignon, and her navy business suit, though expertly tailored to the trim lines of her form, was strictly conservative, offset only by a wide silk ascot that hinted at an inability to hide completely her femininity. Finely etched matching gold bracelets on her wrists—her trademark, a personal whimsy—might have identified her as one of the world's most seductive models, but at the moment they were concealed by the sleeves of the shirt and blazer.

Heads turned because in three-inch heels she was a sleek six feet, and she carried her height with grace. No severity of hair style could hide the exquisite angles of her china fine features, nor the unaffected assurance that made her seem to glide across the room.

As she walked into the handsome lunchroom of the St. Regis that afternoon, Erin McCabe was totally unaware of the appreciative glances she received. She spoke quietly with the maître d' for a moment, then her quicksilver eyes began to seek a certain face as she followed the man to a table in the sunshine-lit rear of the room. Seeing her friend Mary Terrell waving, she smiled, her brows raised in anticipation and query.

Mary laughed and nodded as Erin was seated, then lifted a glass of wine and waited until Erin's was poured to clink a toast.

"You're all set!" Mary said excitedly. "Two weeks from today you fly out of JFK for Oslo. That first week you can do whatever you want, but Erin, you must be at the train station in Helsinki on time on the fourteenth. Russian trains are never late and they leave on time!"

Erin laughed and sipped her wine as she accepted the black leather visa and passport Mary handed her. "Mary, I'm always on

21

time. Oh, Mary!" Her famous silver eyes blazed enthusiasm and warmth. "I do appreciate this so much! It's going to be wonderful."

Mary grimaced. "I hope so, Erin. I still wish you'd reconsider. Think of Paris in the springtime! The Côte d'Azur, Nice, Monte Carlo—London is beautiful in the spring—"

"Mary," Erin murmured, shaking her head with a smiling determination, "I've been to all the above—"

"Jeez. Hard life!" Mary interrupted dryly, but immediately regretted her outburst. She might be the one person in the world who was fully aware that Erin McCabe *had* endured a hard life. No, not for all the beauty and glamor and travel could Mary really envy her childhood friend. She had watched Erin bury both her father and mother and then her beloved fiancé, a victim of a cerebral hemorrhage at twenty-two. She had seen Erin leave college to support her aging parents until their deaths, and give up her simple dream of becoming a teacher of social sciences and government.

Mary had also watched Erin rise to the top of the modeling field, work she had chosen when she was desperate for income, work which had become habit. And then Mary had shared her friend's happiness when she had fallen in love with Marc Helmsly, the handsome, charming, world-renowned photographer. She had laughed and cried at the wedding that had made front-page headlines, so pleased that Erin had finally found happiness.

She had also been the one to receive Erin on her doorstep in the dead of night three months after the fabulous wedding, an Erin in shock, so profoundly hurt and disillusioned that to this day Mary didn't really understand fully all that had happened.

Marc Helmsly had spoken to the papers; he had labeled Erin a beautiful and charming woman unable to accept the commitments and responsibilities of marriage.

Erin had made little comment. She had pursed trembling lips that would never falter again; her silver-blue gaze had become opaque, forever hiding her secrets and emotions. Her words to the press had been simple and noncommittal: she and Mr. Helmsly had made a terrible mistake—their differences were irreconcilable.

That had been six months ago. Erin had gone back to work, more beautiful than before, her unique and stunning eyes touched by a new, haunting enigma. Those eyes of deep, seductive silver seemed on camera to hold all the intoxicating mystique of the ages.

And of course, there were always the gold bracelets. No matter what the product or costume, Erin wore the bracelets that had come from the one person who had come to mean the world to her. But it had been only since the breakup with Marc that she had nervously played with the bracelets. When agitated, she absently slid them in circles around her wrists.

Mary knew why Erin had become so attached to the bracelets in the first place, and she shrewdly assumed she now knew why Erin—unknowingly—used the bracelets like another woman might chew her nails. She wished she could help, but she really couldn't. Certain things had to take time to work themselves out.

Erin was ready for a vacation: Mary was well aware of that fact, and certainly agreeable. She knew that the glamor of Erin's work was only the finished product. Erin spent hours and hours doing the same thing over and over to perfection in the photographer's eye. She silently endured the elements and grueling hours. It had been good for her, it had kept her from thinking.

But the divorce was final now, and Erin had firmly cleared her schedule. A change of scenery was needed.

"Think of it, Mary," Erin was laughing. "If I ever do get to teach, I'll actually know what I'm talking about! The history fascinates me—everything about the U.S.S.R. is so relevant and vital to the times we live in! And Mary, you've been there! I remember when Ye Journey Shoppe first became a qualified Intourist office. You and Ted went, and you told me what a wonderful time you had."

"Erin," Mary protested with a frown, "Ted and I went with a tour. We had a Russian-speaking American guide—as well as the government Intourist guides—with us all the way. You're going all alone, by train! I've warned you that you're not going to find the majority of the citizens on the streets speaking English like in Oslo or Stockholm."

"I know, I know," Erin soothed her friend with patience. "I have the book you gave me, and I've been reading up on rules and regulations and language! Trust me, Mary, I'll be okay. Contrary to popular opinion, I do have a mind, a rather quick one at that. You're not letting an illiterate waif loose in the big bad streets!" Erin laughed. "I've survived New York for twenty-eight years! Surely, I must have acquired a certain amount of survival savvy."

Mary smiled. "I just worry about you, Erin."

Erin clutched Mary's fingers on the snowy white tablecloth. "I know that, Mary, and I appreciate it. But I'll be fine. I'll never discuss politics or religion or government. I'll steer clear of anything that looks remotely military, and I'll never take a picture without permission. I won't cross the border with anything that could be called subversive literature. And"—Erin hesitated a moment—"I'll be so absorbed by the uniqueness of my surroundings that I'll be able to forget the past. Mary, I need this!"

Mary felt a little clutch in her throat. Ever since that night Erin had called her in tears, asking desperately if she could come over, she had closed herself in. She had needed to talk that night but she hadn't been completely coherent. Mary understood Erin's total disillusionment but not exactly what had happened. And after her fit of rambling tears and a night's sleep, Erin had sweetly thanked Mary and begged that they not discuss her marriage—or the reasons for its dissolution—anymore.

Mary had agreed reluctantly, fearing that the short-lived marriage had done Erin serious damage. In all this time she hadn't had so much as a lunch date with a man.

But they had been through that round of discussion before. Erin would answer coldly that she simply wasn't interested in dating, and had no desire ever to marry again. She had her work; she planned to go back to school. That was enough for her.

"Jeans," Mary said aloud.

Erin smiled with amusement and query. "Pardon?"

"Jeans," Mary repeated. "Remember, it's illegal to sell your jeans."

Erin laughed, and Mary had to admit that the sound was free and real after a long time when she had barely smiled naturally.

"Mary! Of all things. I don't think I'm going to run around trying to sell my jeans! We'd better order," she said, picking up her menu and turning her interest to the entrees. "I think I'll have the beef Wellington. What about you?"

Mary grimaced. "No—I'll have the spinach salad. Some friend you are," she moaned. "Models are always supposed to be dieting—and here I am, the green eater. It's disgusting. I gain weight just by looking at food!"

"Mary," Erin protested, "your weight is all in the right places! Ted always says he wants a woman he can hold on to!"

24

Mary grinned slowly. "Oh, what the hell. I'll have the beef Wellington. For Ted."

Their waiter came to take their orders. Erin lowered her lashes and smiled as Mary ordered the Beef wellington, chocolate mousse —and a Diet Pepsi.

Erin entered her small apartment off Central Park that night with a long sigh, slipping off her heels and edging them beneath the antique deacon's bench in the entryway. The cool tile welcomed her weary nylon-covered feet, as did the soft pile of beige carpeting as she moved into the living room and tossed both shoulder and tote bags on the old sofa she had just had recovered in soft brown corduroy. She hesitated a minute, then decided that if she gave in to temptation and tossed her body along with the bags on the sofa she would never get up again. And she sorely needed a cup of tea.

Erin walked into the kitchen with its cheerful pale yellow accents —a complement to the earth tones of her apartment—and filled the kettle. While she waited for the water to boil, she glanced idly around. Handsome copperware and plants hung from high decking above the island range; the overpass gave view to the comfortable living room and the plate-glass windows that let out to a small balcony—and a view of the city far below. Her home was coming along, she thought with pleasure. For years she had collected antique furniture, delighting in refinishing it herself. She knew the period of each piece she collected, and loved to envision the lives of the previous owners. It was a hobby, it was a relaxation. It was a way of reminding herself that she had come within a stone's throw of finishing her studies and that one day she would go back.

The divorce had cost her many of her most prized possessions. She had moved her belongings into Marc's penthouse before the wedding, and when she had moved out, the last thing on her shattered mind had been material objects. But she had had this place six months now, time enough to fill it with pictures and plants, time enough to make it home.

The kettle whistled. Erin made her cup of tea and took it out to the sofa, where she curled into a corner to sip it while watching the moon through the plate-glass windows. A long sigh escaped her. She had spent the day dancing across Fifth Avenue countless times in fur coats. She shook her head at the incomprehensible genius of the advertising agencies. Did dancing in the street make women crave thick fur coats? Surely, winter was enough in itself to get that point across.

She shook her head again, wondering why she was still modeling. She was always telling herself that she would go back to college and get her degree.

She had always meant to get out of modeling, but somehow the time had just kept passing. She had forgotten about everything else when she had fallen in love with Marc. And, she admitted dryly, the more time passed, the harder it became to leave this life-style behind. She was accustomed to writing checks on a whim, purchasing things when they caught her eye. Her apartment alone was beyond a teacher's salary—far beyond a student's income. But since the breakup of her marriage she had begun to take steps in the right direction. More and more of her income was finding its way into a savings account. This trip to Russia was diminishing the savings account, but it was necessary for her sanity, and it was a part of the circuitous road toward her dream.

A soft scratching at the door interrupted Erin's thoughts, and she uncurled her long legs from the sofa. With a smile on her face she opened her door to the perpetrator of the sound—a sleek gray Persian tom with the unpretentious name of Bill. "What are you up to, huh, Bill? A little scrounging-around-town time?" Erin stooped to collect the highly independent animal into her arms and stroked his silken coat until Bill decided he had had enough of such coddling. His purr became a protesting meow and she set him back down. "You know, Bill, you don't live here. You have an owner who feeds you and cares for you! But I always was a sucker for a pretty face. I bought you a can of sardines just the other day."

I sure as hell was a sucker for a pretty face, Erin thought with a stab of chilling pain as she led the cat into the kitchen. A total fool. But I really wasn't so terribly foolish, she defended herself. Marc wasn't just pretty, his appeal had been devastating. Tall, suave, and sleek. Omar Sharif eyes. Many women had fallen head over heels in love with him before Erin, and many would do so in the future.

He had always been charming; he was athletic and rugged. For the first time in her life Erin had been enchanted beyond control.

How was I to know? she tormented herself with the same question she had asked a million times. But she should have known. Her job

26

had given her exposure to the sophisticated world of fame and wealth. She had been verbally warned, but she had been sure Marc's ex-mistress was merely jealous, and she listened with kind patience only to the hints given.

Yes, she should have had a certain sophistication. But she hadn't. She had lived too long with tragedy not to welcome happiness with open arms. But oh, God, Marc himself had given her warnings. Yet she had never thought anything about his comments regarding other women. Marc was a photographer. She had always assumed he would have a normal, professional interest in other beautiful women.

When she thought of it now, her naiveté seemed mere stupidity. But her parents had been so loving, so traditional . . . it had simply never occurred to her that marriage could be based on any other values. She hadn't believed any of the rumors that had begun before their honeymoon ended. Her mind must have truly been in a cloud. Remembering wasn't good for her. She could feel the blood draining from her face as she thought of the night when she had been so cruelly slapped in the face with the truth. The night when she had walked into her own home to find another man, a friend of Marc's, an acquaintance of hers . . . a photographer . . . waiting for her.

He laughed disbelievingly at her when she asked him to leave.

She was shaking as she tried to lift the lid of the sardines with the key supplied. She froze. She would never, never, forget that night. She had been so shocked, and then so panicked, struggling desperately as he kept chuckling and telling her how much he loved a spirited woman. And she had so stupidly kept calling for Marc, Marc who was with another woman, who thought she knew the score . . . Marc, who really wouldn't have cared.

Finally breaking free, she had run from her own home in tears and dishabille, begging for a dime from a man on the street to make that call to Mary, praying that she would be there. . . .

Bill broke through Erin's remembrances with a yowl. Erin started, then smiled and apologized. "Sorry, Bill. Sardines coming right up."

Of course, she wasn't a child. When faced with the facts she had simply accepted them. Marc had never had any intention of changing his life. He might have loved her in his way, but there hadn't been a single second when he had even considered a conventional marriage.

She had spoken to him only once after that night, and he had been truly mystified. Surely she knew . . . surely she accepted his life-style . . . she did, after all, move in the same fast lane. He had been very apologetic about his friend. Marc believed in the old Live and Let Live. He would never have forced Erin into anything.

But the physical force of the situation had been shattering, more shattering than even she had realized at the time. Shock had given way to pain, and she had wondered just what she had been lacking. She was supposed to be one of the most beautiful women in the world, yet she wasn't woman enough to hold her husband. Yes, her ego had been badly bruised. But she had been able to go beyond that and understand that no one woman would ever be enough for Marc. Yet she hadn't been able to get past the terror of that night.

Erin shuddered and felt her involuntary movement become a whole race of shivers. *I was so pathetically naïve. I can't make matters worse and start blaming myself.* She stretched her fingers and forced them to stop trembling with the sheer strength of will-power.

No, she couldn't blame herself. Definitely not! But neither could she shake the aftereffects. "Do you know, Bill," she murmured, her voice growing level and strong as she awarded the feline his long-awaited sardines, "I really am doing well. At first I flinched every time a makeup man or stylist tried to touch me. I've gotten over all that. And guess what, Bill? I am going to Russia! I'm going to see the Kremlin and Red Square and the Hermitage and all the palaces and study myself silly. I have a week in Scandinavia, then a full week in Moscow, and a full week in Leningrad. What do you think? No comment, eh? Well, I think it's going to be just great! But do you know what? Mary keeps warning me about language problems, so I'm going to do a little studying right now."

Erin absently fingered her bracelets with a little smile. They had been a gift from fiancé Jodie, and since the day she had received them she had never taken them off. Now they had become some kind of special link with a world of normality where there were still people who loved one another, and only one another. . . .

Once more curled on the sofa, with Bill not too independent to enjoy his own comfortable curl at her feet, Erin began a serious study of the language book, frowning as she realized she wouldn't recognize anything she learned anyway—the alphabet was entirely different. "Oh, well," she murmured, scratching the cat's ears, "I managed okay in Arabic when we did that junior wear spread in Morocco. I guess I'll survive this!"

Cat and woman both fell silent as the moon rose to its peak. Erin found herself yawning, although it was still early. She thought about dinner, but the beef Wellington was still with her and she decided to forgo another meal. She was tired, and she had an early morning call. More dancing in mink coats.

Erin rose and stretched. "Sorry, Bill, but it's out time. Spakoi nai no chee. That's Russian for good-night. A bit long, I'll admit, but I suppose it gets the point across. I don't want Casey coming home at three to pound down my door and retrieve you and wind up telling me all about her hot date for three hours! And believe me, Bill, Casey might do just that! She has Wednesdays off you know."

Bill was most put out, but Erin stuck to her guns and closed her door on him. She showered, washing her hair to assure its silkiness and freshness for the morning session, and slid between the cool sheets of her bed.

Half the time she hated trying to sleep. She kept envisioning scenes of her own loss of more than innocence. But tonight she fell immediately into a deep slumber before she even knew it. And if she dreamed at all, it was about colorful domes, gilded skylines, and regal palaces.

The next two weeks sped by for Erin. There was a rush to finish all her commitments, and although she blamed her own anxiousness, every shot seemed to take longer than the one before. She didn't have a day that ended before seven, and even her Sundays were taken to assure deadlines. Casey cornered her on the Monday two nights before her flight, and feeling guilty that she had avoided her friend for so long, Erin forced herself to sit politely through an hour and a half of conversation about Bob Masters, the newest man in Casey's life. It was amusing to listen to the petite brunette who didn't have a qualm in the world about saying whatever came to mind and was not particularly hampered by morals. Yet Erin still tried to cut her short. In her heart she was more than happy about her friend's pleasure, but she was also envious in a very painful way.

29

She didn't think she'd ever dream of an affair or a man again, unless she dreamed of Marc, and the images would turn into a nightmare. Her problem wasn't a unique one, she knew, but that knowledge couldn't change her feelings. That was why she so vehemently disagreed with Mary's caring suggestions that she seek help from a professional. A counselor couldn't tell her anything she didn't already know; time was her only possible cure, and the promise of the time away—spent so very differently!—had already eased her mind considerably.

"Casey," Erin interrupted, when her friend's comments became almost embarrassingly graphic, "I leave in two days and I still need a heavy coat. If you'd like, you're welcome to come shopping with me. We have just enough time to make Bloomingdale's before closing—if we rush."

"Imagine!" Casey declared. "You model minks all day and you don't own one!"

"I don't care to own a mink," Erin replied with a wry grimace. "I always think about how tiny and cute they are alive."

"Wish I had that hangup," Casey grumbled. "Well, come on, I'll keep you company."

Once they got to Bloomingdale's—fifteen minutes before closing time—it wasn't difficult to locate a coat; Erin was far more concerned with warmth than style. After Erin had made her purchase of scotchguarded suede, Casey suggested an Irish coffee in a nearby pub and Erin somewhat reluctantly agreed. Casey was going to continue her spiel about Bob, but Erin knew Casey would miss her—and Casey was also going to look after her apartment and her plants. Tonight she owed her a little humoring.

"I have to admit," Casey mumbled as she licked a swizzle stick clean of whipped cream, "I'm glad you're taking your vacation now. Bob thinks you're the next best thing to Venus hitting the earth, so I'm not sure I want him to meet you just yet!"

Erin shrugged. "Don't be silly, Casey. You don't have to worry about his meeting me. I'm not in the dating mood at the moment, and I'd surely never date a friend's man!"

Casey looked at her curiously. "You're still in love with Helmsly, aren't you?"

It was all Erin could do to keep from gagging. "No, Casey," she said with great control and patience. "I'm not still in love with Marc."

Her tone seemed to strike a note of remorse in Casey, but for all the wrong reasons. Casey bit her lip and lowered her lashes in nervous misery. "Oh, Erin, I'm so sorry. I know you must keep telling yourself that, and don't you worry, soon enough it will be true. It must be so hard for you! Being rejected by a man like Marc Helmsly, just where does one go from there? But there are other men, Erin . . ."

Erin wasn't sure whether to laugh, scream, or cry. If anyone else had offered such off-base solace, she would surely have been offended and furious. But Casey was Casey, and Erin was well aware that all she meant was the best.

"Casey," Erin said softly, controlling a growing agitation, "please don't worry. When I feel the need, I'll worry for myself about reentering the dating world!" Erin suddenly rose. The day had been long—too long—and she still had too much to do in too little time; she had a five o'clock call in the morning. And just talking about Marc had made her nervous, in a hurry to retreat to the security of home. "Come on, Casey," she prodded. "Let's get home. It's late."

"Ummm. I guess so." Casey yawned as she collected her handbag and trenchcoat. Erin began to thread her way quickly through the pub, excusing herself hastily. She knew Casey. Even if Casey were in love, she would lag behind to flirt if the right man was available, and Erin would be stuck whistling away more time.

"Are you coming, Case?" Erin turned her head to watch her friend.

With a twisted brow and pursed lips, Casey replied, "Yes, yes! I'm right behind you."

Erin turned to watch where she was going just in time to collide with what felt like a brick wall near the door. Except it wasn't a brick wall. Not unless walls were wearing charcoal gray suits and blue silk shirts these days . . . blue silk shirts and fine pinstriped ties literally doused in vodka or gin or whatever it was she had just managed to spill all over the man with the force of her collision.

"Oh, Lord!" Erin gasped, stepping back. "I am sorry!"

She looked at the damage she had done and then glanced at his face, only to step back another half step. She had never seen such eyes, blue and piercing and relentless, set in a grim face of ruggedly angled granite. Damn, Erin thought, I did crash into brick.

The strangest tickle of chills raced down her spine, chills that touched like mercury until they felt like a wave of electric heat.

"I'm sorry," she repeated as he continued to stare at her, only reaching into his breast pocket for a handkerchief to brush at his shirt and jacket after she apologized again. He recognized her, she realized, as a subtle change took place in his icefire gaze, but it wasn't the recognition she was accustomed to. He seemed totally unimpressed, and actually irritated!

"It's all right," he said curtly. So this, Jarod thought, is Erin McCabe up close. Beautiful, yes, that she is, but—graceful?

The irritation suddenly left the stranger's face. His left brow raised slightly, and one corner of a firm mouth curled as if with an inner amusement.

"Really, I'm terribly sorry—let me pay for the cleaning—"

"It's all right!" he repeated, and though low, his tone was a velvety murmur that Erin suspected few ever challenged. But her own lack of coordination served to irritate her. She wouldn't have been the recipient of such a tone if she'd been paying attention, and she would have been paying attention if it weren't so late, if Casey hadn't made her nervous, if she didn't have a five o'clock call. . . . She opened her mouth to insist, but his tone was final.

He turned, and the strange interlude was over. Erin gave herself a mental shake. She felt as if she had suddenly been released, and yet she had never been held. With a touch of bemusement she hurried on toward the door and the night air, forgetting the incident entirely as she saw a taxi she was determined to flag down. At this hour, if she didn't attract the cab, they could wait hours for another one.

"Oh, thank you!" Erin gasped as she crawled into the cab and shimmied over for Casey to join her. Breathlessly, she gave the address of their apartment building and leaned back into the seat with a sigh, closing her eyes.

"He was gorgeous, in the weirdest way!" Casey began muttering. "I mean, he isn't handsome—not like Christopher Reeve or Michael York or Richard Chamberlain—but there's something about him. Those eyes . . . so compelling! Or maybe it was his chin—I love a strong jawline. He certainly wears his clothes well."

Erin slowly and warily opened her eyes. "Casey—who or what are you talking about?"

"Him!" Casey supplied incredulously. "Come on, Erin, you're the one who stumbled into him!"

"Oh," Erin muttered, frowning as she tried to recall the face. Surprisingly, she found it easy. It is his eyes, she thought. But she certainly wasn't going to say so and add fuel to Casey's fire. Besides which, his attitude was a little blunt. No, crude. She had certainly apologized.

"Suave but ruggedly tough," Casey was continuing. "A man's man. And a lady's man! Maybe he does look a little like Christopher Reeve. Those blue, blue eyes, and that dark hair! Except his has some silver streaks here and there. He must be a little older. I think I'm in love."

"Really?" Erin queried with cryptic amusement. "What happened to Bob?"

"Well, I love Bob!" Casey said demurely. "But good heavens, Erin, that certainly doesn't mean I don't have eyes anymore!"

Casey continued to chatter. Erin closed her eyes again, praying they would soon reach home. Her head was pounding, she needed to sleep, and she was so eager for her trip that her work days already seemed merciless. Casey was a wonderful friend, but Erin was afraid she'd scream and throttle her if she listened much longer.

Nor did the remaining two days before Erin's trip improve any. On the morning before her flight, she found herself finishing up a commercial after being warned by her agent that failure to do so might result in a lawsuit. With barely an hour to spare, she nervously gave up all attempts to hail a cab and pulled her little Mazda out of the garage, deciding that at least she could park it at JFK. As luck would have it—she seemed to be following Murphy's law to a T, everything possible was going wrong—she, who never inched over fifty-five, was stopped for speeding. The policeman, apparently charmed by her nervousness, magnanimously decreed he would not give her a ticket but a warning. However, as his "warning" escalated into a full-scale lecture, Erin began to wish he had given her a ticket.

By the time she had acquired long-term parking for her car, she was next to positive she was going to miss her flight. But the Scandinavian Air Systems baggage attendant informed her that she still had a chance to make it if she hurried. With renewed hope spurring a revival of energy, Erin began to tear through the airport toward the Scandinavian Air gate.

But Murphy's law still applied. As she quickened her pace with the appropriate gate in view, she discovered herself blocked—too late to prevent her from plummeting straight into a pair of broad, darkly suited shoulders and from sending the tall stranger to which they were attached stumbling forward for several feet before he regained his balance. Erin teetered to regain her own balance, watching in horror as the contents of the file folder the man had been holding billowed about him in wild disarray, scattering papers about his feet as they wafted back to the ground.

"Oh, Lord!" Erin gasped. "I am sorry!"

The stranger turned to her slowly, brows raised, piercing blue eyes registering both irritation and amusement. Erin's jaw lowered in weak astonishment and she gasped once more. "You!"

It was the same man. The same jet hair with silver-streaked temples, the same ruggedly hewn bone structure angled around the same hawklike nose, full grim mouth, and impenetrable icefire eyes.

Graceful? Jarod queried himself once more with incredulity. Definitely not. Erin McCabe was apparently a grade-A klutz.

"Yes, me," he replied dryly, bending to retrieve his papers.

Erin saw the man wince slightly at the smudges that marred his crisp white pages. Of course, she thought a bit resentfully. His appearance was fastidiously neat—surely he would never allow business correspondence to be anything but. She stooped to help him, bemoaning the fact that she would surely miss her flight, her resentment blossoming to irrational anger. If he hadn't stepped before her, she wouldn't have collided with him, wouldn't now be scurrying around on the floor while her plane readied for takeoff.

"You know," he began to mutter, accepting a handful of papers and grimacing with reproach at the dirt that smudged them, making her feel like an errant adolescent, "there are, miss, a good ten million people milling about New York. Do you think you could possibly select one of the other nine million, nine hundred and ninety-nine thousand, nine hundred and ninety-nine with whom to collide next time?"

Erin flushed and angrily grabbed several more straying sheets of paper.

"Stop!" he groaned. "You're cleaning the damned floor with them!"

"I said I was sorry!" Erin snapped.

"Fine, you're sorry! Now please, just leave. I'd rather do this myself!"

Erin sat back on her heels, biting her lip. She wanted to help: she still had a minute chance of catching her flight.

"Go!" the man barked.

Erin was on her feet. He was rude and ridiculously arrogant, and for such an individual she certainly wasn't going to miss her flight.

"I am sorry," she said tightly. "And I certainly shall make sure we don't collide again."

Jarod watched her leave as he retrieved the bulk of his papers, thinking he should have had them clipped. Hell, if he'd known Erin McCabe wasn't on the plane yet, he wouldn't have been idly studying them to begin with. The woman was a walking disaster.

Woman! Today she looked like a slender waif. Too slender, he thought. With her blond hair loose and just waving over her shoulders, her silver eyes wide and luminous, her thin form clad in a beige corduroy pantsuit, she looked more like an adventurous teenager than one of the nation's top models.

He smiled slightly as he watched her hurry in near panic. Pity she didn't know her plane wouldn't be leaving, not without him aboard. Jarod glanced down at his smudge-encrusted papers with a spurt of annoyance and uncharacteristic vengefulness. Pain in the . . .

His smile became grim. Good, let her worry about making her flight.

Erin was easily able to forget her unpleasant interlude as she discovered to her vast relief that she still had time to board the 747. When she was actually seated, she closed her eyes with grateful exhaustion, then reopened them to check the time on her pendant watch. The plane was leaving late, and for once in her life she was exceedingly grateful for the delay. She closed her eyes once more and sank her head back comfortably against the headrest, irrationally wishing then that the delay would last no longer. In her state of nervousness she was craving to be up in the air, lighting a cigarette, sipping on a long, cool vodka and tonic with heavy, heavy lime. She had actually made it! The next three weeks were hers, no work, no schedules, just the delightful fascination of new places and faces.

When she closed her eyes again, a frown knit her brow and a vision of ice-blue eyes set into a strong, arresting face suddenly chilled her memory and sent those strange, seemingly hot and cold shivers racing along her spine. Her eyes flew back open so that she could erase the vivid recall. Why did he return to her mind with such startling clarity? she wondered. In her haste, she had totally forgotten him. Why remember him now? Two freak incidents, both distasteful, should be forgotten. Still, Erin felt a squirming discomfort. She was so seldom blatantly uncoordinated, why the coincidence of both times occurring with the same rude and cold individual?

Coincidence?

He's following me! Erin thought with a shade of panic. But she quickly brushed aside the notion with an inward chuckle. This man was certainly not following her. He had been totally indifferent toward her. If anything, he had been down right hostile! No, he wasn't following her: happenstance was happenstance. And if she were remembering him, it was merely because he had the gift of making one feel impaled and touched by the force of those remarkable eyes.

Immersed in her thoughts and finally relaxed and comfortable in the plush space of her first-class seat, Erin didn't notice that the stranger peculiarly filling her mind walked right past her. She noticed a scent, a very pleasant, woodsy and masculine scent, but she thought nothing of it. It belonged to the stranger, she knew: she must have brushed his suit while picking up his papers.

You'll never see him again, she told herself, so don't worry about him. After all, she amended silently, I wasn't rude. Any harm I caused him was purely accidental. He was rude.

Yet still, as the mammoth plane shuddered, its engines thundering to takeoff, she was transfixed with her memory of the man. Why? she kept wondering. And then a shudder went through her with the force of those that riddled the giant jet. Because thoughts of him were not unpleasant, the heated chills that had coursed her spine had been exciting. The sense memory of his after-shave combined with a very masculine scent was nice.

Erin smiled to herself. It was strange, but the very rude man had made her feel very good about herself. Very normal. She laughed slightly aloud. He would probably resent it highly, but he touched chords she had thought silent forever.

Her smile faded. Thinking about the stranger made her think of Marc, and she didn't want to think of either of them.

The Fasten Seat Belt and No Smoking signs went off, and a pretty stewardess gave a safety speech. Erin kicked off her shoes, curled her feet beneath her, and lit a cigarette. Moments later the stewardess brought her a tall vodka and tonic. The seat beside her was empty, giving her the freedom of being in her own little world, which was nice since the flight was a long one, almost seven hours in the air.

Very comfortable, Erin squashed out the nerve-settling nicotine and slowly continued to sip at her drink as she drew out her guidebook on Russia. Determined to think of nothing else, she studiously considered what she wanted to see, managing to clear her mind of all the pain in her past.

Time passed easily. After a champagne dinner was served, Erin allowed her book to drop to her lap as her eyes closed. She drifted into a doze as light and free as the white clouds they passed above.

It was late in the night when Jarod passed by her. While she slept peacefully, he was in turmoil.

In sleep she appeared entirely guileless. Her lips were curled in a small sweet smile, her slender elegant hands were curled beneath her chin. Her toes, covered in nylon, the nails painted the same fashionable maroon color as those on her long fingers, just peeked out from their curled position beneath her.

She was tall, Jarod noticed, hardly petite and delicate, and a klutz, he reminded himself. But as he stared at her, he strangely found himself touched by long-forgotten feelings. She looked like an angel . . . a rather sexy angel. Looks, he was well aware, could be highly deceptive.

He shrugged with accustomed professional indifference. Only time would tell if he dealt with heaven or hell.

He shifted to return to his seat, then paused, uncertain as to why. He leaned close to her face and whispered, "You should wake up, Miss McCabe, you'll be able to see the fringes of the northern lights soon."

She stirred slightly. Jarod straightened and moved away with sleek silence.

II

Oslo was refreshing, Stockholm was marvelous with its Old Town and flavorful history, and even Helsinki, with its island of restored homes from another era, was utterly fascinating. Erin found the Scandinavians wonderfully polite, courteous, and helpful—and the majority of the people Erin met spoke English very well, sparing her from constantly having to comb through her language books.

But to Erin, her trip was just beginning—and perfectly so. Her week among the cultured and sophisticated Scandinavians had been just what she needed. As she stood in the Helsinki train station at the appointed time—"I'm EARLY!" she wrote in a quick postcard to Mary—she was sure she hadn't felt better in years.

A sense of high excitement seemed to make her adrenaline race, and she felt incredibly alive. It was probably the cold weather, she advised herself, but whatever, it was marvelous. A faint mist hovered over the tracks, a pleasant tenor announced arrivals and departures in an impressive range of languages, whistles shrieked, and vital industry seemed to be taking place all over.

Her silver eyes alive with exhilaration, Erin watched everything that took place around her, wondering about the lives of the colorful people who came and went, some sad as they left loved ones, others laughing and glowing as they greeted husbands, wives, children, and lovers.

A soft smile curving her lips, Erin consulted her pendant watch. Her train was due to leave in thirty minutes, but it had yet to come in. Deciding to trust leaving her baggage on the platform, she adjusted the strap of her shoulder bag and returned to the station to post her card to Mary. She chuckled wryly as a copy of *The New York Times* caught her eye. She decided to buy the paper and a small stalk of brilliantly yellow bananas that were extraordinarily appealing. The cost of the fruit was ridiculously high: importing bananas to the winter bleakness of Finland must be a costly venture. "I don't even usually like bananas!" she murmured to herself as she paid the pleasant clerk the Finnish equivalent of four dollars for three of the captivating fruit. "I have to come to Finland to develop a penchant for bananas."

The Finnish concierge smiled at Erin, apparently aware she was dealing with an American. "You are crossing our border to the U.S.S.R.?"

"Yes," Erin smiled in return.

"Then you must be sure to consume your purchase before you reach the border," the woman advised. "Agriculture!" she reminded Erin. "The Soviets can be very . . . sticky . . . about such things."

"Thank you," Erin murmured. Yes, of course, she knew she couldn't bring fruit—or dirt, grass, trees, vegetables, etc.—into Russia. Her smile became a little sick. She'd have to eat all three bananas within the next few hours.

"Your train!" the clerk said, pointing toward the tracks.

Resembling a large green sea monster, the train labeled *Moscoba* was hissing and chugging its way to a stop. A whistle shrieked, and the train went silent except for the softest whisper of air.

"Thank you," Erin murmured again.

"It will be an interesting trip!" the friendly clerk commented. "You will probably have a couchette next to another American—or Briton. They like to keep the English-speaking peoples together. Cornered off, yes? You understand?"

Erin nodded as she turned to hurry back to the platform. She didn't understand at all, and she wasn't terribly sure she wanted to. For the first time, she was feeling hesitant. Had she been a little foolish to rush into the U.S.S.R. by unconventional means, all alone? No, she scoffed at herself. She wasn't doing anything that adventuresome! College students did this type of thing all the time, and surely other Americans traveled into Moscow by train from Helsinki—otherwise the clerk wouldn't have known that they were usually put together.

The *Moscoba* suddenly issued a deafening shriek. Startled, Erin shoved her three bananas into her bag and hurried for her luggage, placing a firm grip around each of her bags as she followed a small stream of people into the train. She had no difficulty boarding; a porter politely showed her to a delightful couchette—handsomely furnished with Victorian-style wood. The Russian government might be based on a concept of a classless society, Erin thought, but "class" could certainly still be purchased. Mary had rattled off something to her about deluxe first class, which she and the majority of tourists visiting the country traveled by, the "soft" class, which was the second in comfort, and the "hard" class, which translated to economy.

The train lurched, seeming to heave a deep breath as it chugged into action. Erin threw her window open wide and allowed the wind to course through her hair as she watched the Helsinki train station slowly become miniature. Curiously she looked ahead at the approaching landscape, but it was winter bleak and barren. After a while she felt her face becoming numb, and she pulled her head back in. The trip was a long one; the train would not pull into the Moscow station until morning. Erin knew she couldn't spend all that time staring out windows, but for the moment she was willing to allow her sense of excitement to rule her actions. She opened the door to her couchette and moved across the small hallway to stare out on the other side, then laughed at herself as she saw more barren-looking snow. It might be approaching spring in New York, but here winter still held a solid grip.

Staring at the endless snow and lifeless stick trees suddenly brought the snap of unwelcome pain. It had been a winter like this when Jodie died. There had been a severe snowstorm and the ground had been so frozen that they had been forced to delay the funeral for a couple of days.

Erin moved in from the window, shaking herself as if she could dispel memory. She could remember her parents with great love but little pain; Julie and Howard McCabe had become parents very late in life, both near fifty when Erin was born. They had lived long and happily, always considering themselves double-blessed with their little daughter so late in life. Both Julie and Howard had died of natural causes, easily, in their sleep, within months of one another. Her parents had been so in love, and so proud and independent, that after the pain of loss Erin had been grateful that they had died so very gently with their dignity intact. She could never imagine her self-sufficient father forced to rely upon a machine for a life he would no longer care to live.

40

But Jodie . . . Jodie had been a shock. He had always been there for Erin, a friend for so long, gentle and patient, never pressing their relationship. Their love had been a soft one, built mutually with time and respect. They had carefully planned their marriage; Erin would continue working until Jodie acquired his degree, and then they would switch roles. Jodie never doubted Erin; his serene pride and trust were the virtues of a young man secure in himself, secure in the woman he loved.

As long as she lived, Erin would never forget the day he had been due home. Christmas vacation. Jodie had stayed in the background after her parents' death, understanding how the loss of her parents so close together had left her in need of a special time to mourn without the complications and pressures of pushing her relationship with him. It had been Erin who had suddenly realized she had kept Jodie waiting long enough. On the day he was to arrive she had purchased the most stunning of nightgowns and a bottle of the finest champagne. She had laughed and smiled all day, imagining the night and Jodie's pleasure when he found her fully determined to seduce him and satisfy all the longings they had held back for so long.

Jodie never came home. His roommate had brokenly tried to explain how he had been laughing in the passenger seat on their drive to Manhattan one minute, dead the next. A strong, healthy, twenty-two-year-old man who had his whole life to look forward to.

It had taken Erin a long, long time to quit hating God and herself and everyone else who lived. But with time and the tender care of good friends like Mary and Ted, Erin had learned acceptance. At first she had turned catatonically to work, rising in her field because she was not only extraordinarily photogenic but extraordinarily professional and cooperative. And she had learned to live again, to enjoy the camaraderie of new friends and old, to enjoy her life. She had finally opened to the possibility of romance again, and just when loneliness had made her prime taking for a sophisticated male, Marc Helmsly had walked into her life.

It was strange, Erin thought now as she stood in the hall, feeling a little weak. Marc, she was sure, had really cared for her. He had just misread her. He hadn't understood that he was not only not dealing with a sophisticate—but had wound up with a pathetically inept innocent! He should have figured it out rather quickly, Erin

41

thought bitterly. No, not Marc. He had probably thought himself the great leader, giving her a crash course in freedom and an "open" marriage.

It didn't really matter. It was over. And in retrospect, she could only blame her own persistence in refusing to see and accept the truth of that last night. If Marc—and his friend—had been dealing with a more sophisticated woman, things wouldn't have come to that point.

Damn, Erin thought with irritation, what the hell was she doing? The past was the past, and she was on a personal quest, fulfilling a dream she had had since she was a child. She should be imagining herself as an old—but charming and elegant, please!—teacher or professor, enchanting her government students with her quiet tales of her personal experiences in the Soviet Union. She was a very level-headed individual, and she took a certain amount of pride in positive willpower. She simply wasn't going to waste time brooding.

Erin rotated on her heel to return to her couchette, then paused in midswing as she noticed the door next to her own was open. Remembering that the friendly concierge in Helsinki had advised her that her nearest traveling companions would most probably be English-speaking, Erin impulsively took a look into the couchette.

The compartment was empty, but displayed sure signs of occupancy. A dark leather briefcase sat ajar on the bed and a heavy suitcase in complementary leather was shoved beneath it. A garment bag hung in the small open closet, and an array of toiletries was neatly set above the sink, very masculine toiletries, Erin noticed quickly as she assessed the shaving cream, deodorant, and after-shave. Masculine and expensive, she thought wryly. The after-shave was one she knew; Ted loved it and she often gave it to him as his Christmas gift, since neither he nor Mary would think to endanger their household budget by such a purchase. She seemed to remember someone else wearing it too . . . recently . . .

So my next-door neighbor is a finicky male, she thought, withdrawing from the compartment with a shade of guilt as she realized she had actually been prying. Not really, not if the dummy had left his door standing wide open.

Erin moved on into her own couchette and curled comfortably onto her bunk with her book. "Zdra stvooite," she whispered aloud, grimacing as the attempt at pronunciation twisted on her tongue. "Damn," she muttered. All that for a simple hello.

She frowned suddenly as she heard footsteps and then conversation in the hallway. A slender brow raised in consternation. Her next-door neighbor was definitely male—no one could mistake the deep velvet tones—but he most certainly wasn't American. The Russian language was rolling off his tongue in double time. Strange, the voice sounded vaguely familiar. She shook her head, returning her attention to her book. The voice couldn't be familiar. She had no acquaintances well versed in the Russian language. She forgot the sound of voices, until moments later when she was startled by a knock at her door.

She began thumbing the pages of her book to find a translation for "Come in," but unable to find anything remotely similar, she shrugged and called, "Come in."

The porter who had shown her to her couchette opened the door with a gnomelike grin, nodding and bowing slightly. "Will you have tea?" he inquired.

"Oh, yes, thank you," Erin murmured. He bowed again. Erin lifted her torso automatically to bow in return. They continued the friendly procedure until the man bowed himself back out of her cabin, only to reappear shortly with Russian tea served in a glass set in a silver filigree holder. Erin thanked him, discovered she was supposed to pay, discerned that he would accept Danish kroner, and once more thanked him.

It was Erin's first taste of real Russian tea and she found it absolutely delicious. She was also relaxed and thirsty. Erin drank the glass of tea quickly, too quickly, then decided she wanted another one.

She remembered that the porter had said something and motioned toward the front of the coach when he had shown her to her couchette. Balancing herself against the jostling of the train, Erin collected a handful of her Danish money and her glass in the little silver holder that so fascinated her and made her way toward what she assumed had to be the porter's couchette.

She was shortly congragulating herself for being correct as she found the first door open, the porter relaxing over a newspaper she couldn't begin to read although she did recognize the characters. He glanced up immediately and smiled brilliantly at Erin. "I'd like more tea, please," she murmured, handing him her glass.

He rose immediately. "Yes, yes," he murmured. "Please. You go back, and I will bring."

Erin shook her head with a little smile. "Thank you, that isn't necessary." She pointed toward his paper. "You relax." The small man looked as if he were about to argue further so Erin gave him her most professional smile. "Please," she murmured very softly. "I can take it myself perfectly well!"

Apparently, she thought wryly, the smile did the trick. The balding Russian sighed with an enchanted grimace and accepted the glass to fill from an immaculate silver samovar. Erin stuffed the kroners into his hand and decided to try out a Russian thank you.

"Spasee ba," she murmured.

"Ah, very good!" he congratulated her with pleasure. And then once again he was bowing, and Erin was automatically bowing in return.

Afraid they were about to go through another five-minute interlude of curtsies, Erin began to back down the length of the hall as she bowed, making each bow a little shorter. She frowned as the porter suddenly began waving at her, apparently losing his command of English as he attempted to warn her of something. She raised a curious brow in question, but the answer came too late. She backed into something warm and extremely solid. The tea sloshed from her glass, barely missing her shoes. Feeling an idiotic sense of "oh, no!" she turned around slowly, her eyes ridiculously remaining downward.

Her sense of déjà vu was instant and debilitating. As she stared at a pair of trim leather boots—black boots, spotlessly polished— she felt a riddling of electricity insinuate itself hotly along her spine. She looked up slowly, over long legs, trim hips framed by an expertly tailored black jacket . . . over the broad, brick-wall chest clad handsomely and masculinely in crisp off-white cotton, tapered black vest and jacket. Her eyes continued up to a long, well-corded neck. She could look no further.

It simply can't be, she told herself. Twice in New York might be coincidence, but she was halfway around the world now. That kind of coincidence was simply impossible.

Erin noticed vaguely that a pulse beat erratically within the

44

strong tanned throat that held her eyes. Dreading the sight she was sure she was about to encounter, she had to forcefully urge her eyes to look further upward.

And as she had known, she encountered the rage of a blue firestorm.

"You!" she croaked incredulously. "I don't believe it!"

The brow twisted sardonically, the jawline shifted. "I think that should be my line," he said dryly, very obviously straining to hold an explosive temper in check. "Good Lord, woman, I'm beginning to believe you must be some sort of a secret weapon. The ultimate cold-war tactic. One week with you, and Moscow will be promising anything."

"Don't be absurd!" Erin snapped, totally unnerved by the man's appearance. It was impossible, she wanted to shriek, she couldn't be running—literally—into him in this many places. A bar yes, maybe even an airport in the same city—but in a train to Moscow?

"Well?" he suddenly demanded.

"Well what?" Erin muttered blankly.

"No apology this time?"

Apology, Erin wondered rebelliously. No, somehow this was all his fault.

Erin unconsciously took a step backwards. "I do believe that, this time, you barged into me."

"Oh? I don't recall walking backwards."

Erin flushed uncomfortably. He had a marvelous knack for putting her awkwardly on the defensive, something she was unaccustomed to feeling.

"Why are you following me?" she demanded curtly.

"Following you?" he inquired in sardonic disbelief. "My dear Miss McCabe, trust me. For the sake of my clothing, possessions, person, and sanity, you are the last woman in the world I would consider following."

Erin twisted her bottom lip and bit into it with irritation. "You really must be the last of the great gallants," she snapped back.

"So sorry, Miss McCabe," he continued with his cutting sarcasm as he gazed down at her, "but this isn't New York. You will not find a multitude of lovesick fans following in your footsteps, willing to give all and forgive anything! You're entering the Soviet Union."

Erin stiffened with automatic indignation, fighting for control over a temper seldom so aroused. "I do not expect people to fall all over me and 'forgive anything' here or anywhere else, Mr. . . . ." He didn't supply a name and she continued with barely concealed hostility. "And I know very well where I am going, thank you. You wish an apology? I'm very sorry I barged into you. But think of it this way—at least I didn't get your suit this time!"

He stared at her curiously for a moment, a fathomless light in those eyes which never failed to touch her with the heat of blue fire.

"True, Miss McCabe, it was kind of you to douse the train rug rather than my clothing. Do you take care to ruin only one suit per man?"

He is incredible! Erin thought. Rude didn't come anywhere near an adequate description.

"I don't make a habit of ruining anything!" she declared, her voice low and smooth but clearly heated. "Please, sir, do allow me to make amends so that you needn't feel so persecuted! I'll be quite happy to reimburse you for any loss I caused!"

"All right," he said unexpectedly. "I'll take a check."

Outraged, and admittedly unnerved, by his reply, Erin hesitated. The stranger, who was unfortunately no longer quite so strange, bowed ever so slightly and stepped back so that she might precede him down the hallway.

Erin uneasily passed him by, tangibly aware that he followed her footsteps. She could feel more than the power of his incredibly searing stare as it sizzled her back; she could feel a heat emanating from the man, a force that seemed untamed . . . primitive . . . something very raw and masculine and elemental despite the civilized and sophisticated suavity of his very contemporary and apparently restrained appearance.

The alluring scent of his after-shave seemed especially seductive when combined with his own brand of potent masculinity. Yet Erin wasn't quite so sure she was appreciating it anymore. This man was making a wreck out of her; she was righteously infuriated, while nervous as a cat. He made her feel as if blood raced in mercury streams, as if each nerve ending were raw and exposed. She realized she was tense with excitement, quaking with ridiculous, but undeniable, subliminal fear.

She wanted to touch him; she wanted to run. And she wanted to break his neck! Never had she met a man so devoid of common courtesy—with such utterly galling nerve!

This is all absurd, she assured herself. She would write him a check for his suit, he would leave, she would avoid him until the train arrived in Moscow, she would never see him again.

Erin stopped at the door to her couchette, about to ask him to please wait just a minute in the hall. She never had the chance. He glanced into her features with a fathomless expression, twisted the handle, and ushered her into the couchette ahead of him. He followed behind her, silently closing the door and leaning against it.

Erin moved on in, trying to appear nonchalant as she reached for her purse. "Who do I make this out to?" she inquired, adding too quickly with the need to keep talking, "Or else I do have a few American Express traveler's checks. I'm afraid I have little left in any Scandinavian currency, and I'm sure you must know I haven't any kopecks or rubles yet—my money was deposited in a Moscow bank to be retrieved upon arrival."

"A check from your personal account will be just fine," he interrupted with an obvious trace of amusement.

Erin picked up her checkbook and glanced at him with a dry assessment spurred by his tone. She lifted a brow and made no attempt to disguise a certain sarcasm as she said, "My dear sir, I'm afraid I must have a name if I'm to write a check."

"Jarod," he said, "Steele. *E* at the end."

Erin began to scribble his name. Steele, she thought bitterly. Good name for the man. He was apparently as unyielding as the metal. The only more fitting name for the man would be Brick Wall.

She hesitated over an amount, and glanced at the understated quality of his garments, her gaze not reaching to his eyes, but starting from just below and sweeping downward. He didn't appear heavy, she thought, more tall and trim, yet she had the strange feeling that the agile body beneath the suit was supple, wiry, and tautly muscled.

From the far corner of her vision, she sensed another twinge of his detached amusement in the hiking of an arched brow. "Shall I turn around, Miss McCabe?"

"I don't believe that will be necessary," Erin replied without humor. She affixed an amount to the check and handed it to him, oddly stretching her arm out as far as possible rather than approach him too closely. "Will that be adequate?"

He didn't glance at the check. His stare of fire and ice locked with hers. "Most adequate."

Erin felt encompassed by his look, as if his eyes had a hypnotically magnetic strength all their own. Was it seconds, or did minutes pass by? She only knew that as he watched her—with interest? or a very strange disinterest?—she felt as if waves of heat assailed her in a curious backlash. Her legs felt like lava. She began to pray he would leave before her knees buckled beneath her.

And then, amidst the practical joke her composure seemed to be playing with her, she came to a very chilling realization. Jarod Steele hadn't moved; he had remained very still against the door. But for all his apparent lassitude, he had very thoroughly scanned her couchette.

He slipped her check into his pocket and inclined his head in a courtesy that she felt was mocking rather than respectful. "Spasee ba, Miss McCabe," he murmured, the ghost of a thin smile curling the corners of his lips. "Do sveedah nya."

He left the couchette, quietly closing the door behind him. Erin's knees did give; luckily she sank down to her neatly made bunk. Jarod Steele, she thought. What a strange individual. And what a strange effect he had on me. No, not just me, she amended wryly. She was sure he had this effect on everyone, male or female.

Erin glanced at her fingers: they were trembling. She stretched them before her, then clenched them into fists. This was just too much coincidence, she thought. To run into the same person twice in New York City with its throngs of humanity was absurd enough, but to run into the same person while traveling on a train from Helsinki to Moscow? And obviously he knew who she was.

And yet, why would he be following her? (She was the perpetrator of the actual collisions!) It was very apparent he did not find her particularly appealing; if anything, he seemed to dislike her, or at very least find her intolerably irritating.

Erin frowned and suddenly jumped from the bed, trying to recall the Russian words he had spoken. "Do sveeda nya?" she murmured to herself, hoping she could find the pronunciation equivalent in her tourist manual. Her fingers began an industrious thumbing through the pages until she found the translation.

"Till we meet again," she murmured ponderously. Erin tapped a finger against her chin. "We won't meet again, Mr. Steele," she murmured. "Not if I can help it."

But she would see him again, she thought wryly. They were on the same train. She could avoid him only if she spent the remainder of the trip locked in her couchette.

Erin tossed her book aside and stretched out on her bunk, slipping off her low-heeled leather boots and hugging her pillow. She was thoroughly annoyed with herself for finding Jarod Steele an incomprehensibly compelling man—especially since it had been ages since she had found the male of the species even remotely interesting. Maybe, she thought ruefully and tried to tell herself convincingly, she was merely being feminine and finding him fascinating simply because of his lack of reaction to her. She had many male friends, and all were gallant because they were friends. Nine out of every ten males she encountered socially or professionally were also gallant; their motives were highly suspect, but they were courteous nevertheless. Most had exotic sexual fantasies about the seductive Erin McCabe, and she found their innuendos both amusing and painful. Only she really knew that "Erin McCabe" was truly a myth, more fantasy than any man would ever imagine. She couldn't go beyond a good-night kiss without feeling the chills of terror that froze her into something more glacially cold than dry ice.

Erin unconsciously began to play with the gold bands around her wrists. Jarod Steele was different. She wasn't even sure he had noticed that she was female. No, she corrected herself. He did know she was female. She had the feeling he had been irritated enough to have given her a good slug if she had been a man. No, that too was unfair. She had a feeling that Mr. Steele would at all times have ultimate control over a very fierce temper. If he ever lashed out, it would be either because he had been provoked beyond human endurance, or because he allowed himself to do so after calculated thought.

Who was Jarod Steele anyway? she wondered. A New Yorker with a flair for what sounded like a perfect command of an unusual language for an American to master? He had to be some type of businessman, she decided. But what type of business did Americans carry out in Moscow? Damned if I know, she mused vaguely, caught in the midst of a yawn. Despite the flow of adrenaline set off by the unusual stranger Jarod Steele, the lulling motion of the train was having its effect on a body that had eschewed sleep for sightseeing for seven days and nights.

She must have dozed, because the next thing Erin consciously noted was that the monotonous motion of the train was beginning to slow down. She bolted from the bunk and looked eagerly out of her window, seeing nothing but blackness. Then a dim light became steadily brighter as the train approached a small station. She heard and felt the screeching tug as the *Moscoba* ambled to a full stop, then saw passengers hastily detraining. Curiously, she ran a hand over her tussled hair, straightened her skirt, and hopped about as she hurriedly tried to fumble back into her boots. Then she swiftly ventured into the hallway, her curiosity at a peak.

Erin was just in time to see Jarod Steele leaving his couchette—dressed now in gray tweed. He lifted a brow in cryptic acknowledgment, then proceeded down the hallway in the wake of a few others departing the train.

For the moment Erin forgot he was a self-proclaimed enemy. "Mr. Steele!" she called after him compulsively.

He paused, turning slowly back to face her, his blue icefire gaze as fathomless as ever, the wry twist of his mouth a shade cynical.

"Please," she found herself mumbling nervously, "would you mind telling me where we are?" Erin knew he had the answer; whatever his business might be, it was evident he was no stranger to the U.S.S.R.

He stared at her for a moment, as if he were debating something behind the amused guard of his countenance. Then he sighed, like a man resigned to an unpleasant task, and brought himself back to her with a firm, long-legged stride. "We're at the final stop in Finland before we cross the border," he informed her. "There's a decent restaurant here. If you want something to eat before morning, this is your last chance."

Erin hesitated. She was starving, but suddenly fearful of leaving the relative security of the train for the unfamiliar darkness of an unknown town. And she certainly wasn't going to attempt to inflict her company upon Jarod Steele, not when he seemed to consider her presence similar to that of a swarm of locusts.

Besides, warning bells were shrilling in her mind. One way or another, she sensed that his quiet power was very dangerous. His

50

very control reeked of vital masculinity, the leashed force and vibrant heat of the sun.

While afraid of that dangerous power, Erin found herself shivering with excitement when he was near, trusting in his strength for a security that didn't exist.

She wanted to dislike him, but he compelled her interest. She was gradually discovering that she was at a complete loss because she didn't know how to handle him—she who had always known how to courteously handle people of either sex. And what was worse, she didn't know how to handle herself.

There was valor in dignified retreat, she reminded herself, biting her lip with irritation as she found herself taking a step backwards. "Thank you, Mr. Steele," she began to murmur.

His arm shot out and secured her elbow in a grip that was both light and firm, a sure hint of the steel evoked by his name. And like a clash of steel, his touch aroused her senses. Quicksilver flashes of both fire and ice trailed in feathered brushes from her nape to the small of her back, over and over again.

"Get your coat and come along, Miss McCabe," he said with a spurt of velvet patience. "You already look sadly undernourished. I would be shirking my duty to allow an American tourist to starve, even if we're not quite in my realm of jurisdiction as of yet."

Startled, Erin ignored his less than complimentary appraisal and quizzically met his amused stare. "Jurisdiction?" she murmured. "Just what are you, Mr. Steele?"

"A troubleshooter," he said briefly, escorting her quickly to her couchette for her coat, then off the train with a proprietary expertise.

Erin frowned. She would not be answered so briefly when her confusion was so vast. "A troubleshooter? Are you with the U.S. government? With the American embassy in Moscow?"

He hesitated only slightly and shrugged. "Well, I'm an American, and I'm assigned to the United States embassy. Actually though, I work for the United Nations."

Incongruously, Erin took one look at her escort's steel and granite features and began to laugh.

"What's so amusing, Miss McCabe?" he demanded sharply.

"Nothing!" she murmured, then felt a tensing of the strong fingers that held her and the relentless demand of his stare. She

attempted to sober herself and stuttered an explanation. "I mean
. . . I mean . . . you! United Nations! Peace and harmony and
diplomacy . . ." Her voice trailed away. Apparently he didn't appreciate the ironic humor of the situation. Erin cleared her throat
uneasily and escaped his hold to descend the coach steps to the
steam-fogged platform. The shock of the frigid night air set her
shivering, and she suddenly discovered a warm arm around her
shoulder, enveloping her against the heat of her accidental companion.

She was warmed, but her shivers didn't cease. She had the strange
feeling she had been offered the dangerously explosive heat of a
deceptively dormant volcano.

III

It couldn't have been more than fifteen degrees Fahrenheit on the platform, but the frigid weather didn't seem to bother Jarod Steele as he quickly led Erin to the restaurant's door.

The restaurant itself was cozy and warm. It was also loud and smoky, but the boisterousness was encouraging to Erin. She glanced around in fascination, glad she had chosen to enter Russia by train. The people and scenery of this Finnish border stop offered the kind of experience she would have missed on a route tour.

"Miss McCabe?"

Erin noted a resurgence of impatience in her unwilling escort's tone. A none-too-gentle tug on the arm informed her that he was not as fascinated as she and in a hurry to secure a table. Propelled would be the only way to describe his leading her as he chose a table, curtly seated her, and sat across from her.

"What would you like?" he inquired. "I'm afraid you'll find little to resemble alfalfa or bean sprouts."

"What?"

He grinned. "Aren't you continually dieting, Miss McCabe?"

Erin sighed, determined to be patient. "No, Mr. Steele, I hate to disillusion you, but I never diet. I'm afraid my appetite somewhat resembles that of a trucker."

He hiked up a rather dubious brow, but dropped that particular vein of discussion. "What would you like?" he inquired.

He knew damned well she couldn't read the menu. It was written in three languages, but English was not one of them. Her recognition of Russian characters was nonexistent, her Finnish was little better, and she could make out about approximately three of the words that were in French.

"What do you suggest?" she inquired lightly.

53

"The lamb stew is good."

"Lamb stew sounds fine."

Bread and butter appeared on the table quickly; a harried waitress hastily took their order. Only moments later their food arrived in deep steaming bowls along with two glasses of curiously dark liquid.

"It's a native Finnish beer, served warm, Miss McCabe. You seemed willing to sample all that was native, so I took the liberty of ordering two."

Erin smiled with very dry sweetness. "Thank you."

The warm beer wasn't bad, and the stew was delicious. She didn't realize just how ravenous she was until she glanced up to find Jarod Steele staring at her, the amusement in his eyes warm and genuine for once rather than cynical. "You do have the appetite of a trucker —a small one at least."

Erin flushed slightly and sipped at her beer. "I warned you," she murmured.

"It just seems rather incredible. You're little more than skin and bones."

"High metabolism," Erin shrugged.

Jarod leaned back in his chair, pushing his plate aside as he reached into his breast pocket for a pack of cigarettes. He offered one to Erin, which she accepted, and he politely lit them both. Then he continued with his nerve-tingling stare through the cloud of smoke.

"To what, Miss McCabe," he finally queried, "does the U.S.S.R. owe the honor of your presence?"

Exposed nerve endings seemed to grate throughout Erin's body. If she were ever lulled into believing he considered her human, she would be an idiot.

Erin returned his stare with no change of countenance. She inhaled and exhaled slowly. "I thought you said you were with the United Nations, Mr. Steele," she murmured softly, arching a slender brow with innocence. "Not the KGB."

"Clever, Miss McCabe," he acknowledged with a slight inclination of his head, "but hardly an answer."

"I didn't care for the phrasing of the question."

"Do forgive me. I'll start over. What is one of America's favorite faces doing wandering around eastern Europe alone? Moscow by train from Finland is not one of the leading advertisements in your general tourist office. One would have thought Erin McCabe would opt for Paris or Monte Carlo—Morocco, perhaps—but the Soviet Union? In late winter?"

Erin patiently inhaled on her cigarette once more. "I'm fascinated by history, Mr. Steele, pure and simple. Russia has always intrigued me. A friend of mine owns a tourist agency and she helped me plan this trip."

"Oh," was his reply, short, apparently innocent. Yet it was the most irritating use of the word Erin had ever heard. It implied a multitude of things, among them blatant cynicism. She was about to snap out her annoyance, but their waitress seemed to have timed her return trip to collect their check as if attuned to Jarod Steele's convenience. Erin felt her annoyance with him fade as she belatedly winced with a more strident annoyance directed at herself. She had nothing with her, and she didn't want a man like Steele paying her way even for a phone call.

"I'm sorry," she said crisply as the waitress disappeared with Jarod's money. "I left my bag on the train. I'll reimburse you as soon as we're aboard."

"I don't wish to be reimbursed," he practically snapped as he stood, moving behind her to assist her up with such smooth agility that she had no choice but to politely accept his overture. His hand was upon her elbow once more—was the touch even more proprietary now?—and once more she felt herself propelled along, stormed by command, but so dazed by the electricity that never failed to spark that she couldn't think to protest his natural assumption of authority and assert herself.

"Russian trains leave on time," he said curtly as her glance at the restaurant's door must have nakedly displayed a rebellion against his rough haste. Then the door was open and they were hit with a blast of excruciating cold.

Even if he disliked her, Erin mused between the painful and almost deafening chattering of her teeth, there was something simply too basically male about Jarod Steele for him not to immediately assume the role of protector. She suddenly found herself no longer escorted but swept into a secure hold against the strength and heat of his body as he carried her the several feet to the train.

"That—that wa—wasn't necessary," she stuttered, still shivering in uncontrollable spasms as he brought her back into the relative warmth of the train's hallway. He merely lifted a brow, and Erin fell silent. It hadn't been necessary, but it had been damned convenient. He had saved them an eternity of seconds with his swift action.

"You're easier to carry than drag along," he replied, setting her down before the door to her couchette. Blue icefire eyes met her rather wide ones. "Good-night, Miss McCabe."

"Good-night," she replied, thoroughly irritated by the tremor in her voice. "Thank you for dinner," she managed more nonchalantly.

"The pleasure was mine."

Somehow, Erin didn't think so. Her eyes met his with that cryptic challenge, but he merely smiled and turned, disappearing into the door of his own couchette. Erin stepped inside and closed her door, leaning against it as he had earlier. She felt breathless and weak and disoriented—and all because a man who evidently disliked her had held her in his arms.

"This is certainly a little ridiculous," she chastised herself aloud in a soft murmur. But she couldn't shake her strange feelings. Where his arms had touched she could still feel the heat; the alluring scent that was after-shave and all male lingered around her.

She suddenly realized she was quivering from head to toe. She felt as if there were a glittering prize sitting before her, and if she just reached out it could be hers. But she couldn't reach out because she was scared to death.

How absurd, she thought, shaking herself. There was nothing to reach out and grab. She was going to get some sleep, and she wasn't going to think about the strange Mr. Steele.

Carrying out her resolution didn't prove to be at all difficult. She followed her mechanical night-time routine, brushing her teeth, washing her face, and industriously combing out her hair, then slid into a warm emerald flannel gown and hurriedly brought her cold toes beneath the crisp sheets and heavy blanket on the bunk. The feeling was wonderfully warm and cozy. She might have been thinking about Jarod Steele, but she didn't do so for long.

Her sleep was very deep; it took some time to interrupt. Erin began to frown from the hazy depths of oblivion, to open her eyes with a start. Above her stood a man, an extremely poker-faced man, in an immaculate and tight-fitting uniform of red and gray. He was impatiently rattling off words in what she was beginning to recognize as Russian. Apparently he had been attempting to wake her for several minutes. His irritation was becoming evident.

Erin bolted to a sitting position in the bunk. The border, she thought, we've come to the border. He wants my papers.

Erin smiled, but the man's face didn't lose its severity. Her smile turning to an inward grimace, Erin slid her bare feet from the bunk, remembering ruefully that Mary had warned her that crossing the Soviet border would be a no-nonsense affair.

"Please!" she murmured, padding quickly to her purse and extracting the papers she assumed he wanted. He accepted them, glanced over them quickly with an astute eye, and pocketed them, shaking his head as Erin reached to retrieve them, halting with surprise. The slate-eyed man motioned for her to sit, and Erin numbly did so.

She watched the man as he began to comb through her couchette. He appeared to be about thirty, in the peak of fitness and health, and his manner was a strange combination of civility and determination.

Wonderful, Erin thought. He is most courteously scaring the hell out of me.

He emptied the contents of her purse and neatly replaced them. Her luggage was next. To give the man credit, he was careful to see that her neatly arranged stacks of lingerie, sweaters, dresses, skirts, shirts, and jeans were just as neat as when he had begun his search. Erin folded her hands and stared blankly at her fingers to hide her nervousness, only to glance back up and find the guard staring at her with chilling reproach and accusation—the bananas she had craved in Helsinki and then summarily forgotten, held high in his hands.

Oh, hell! Erin thought sickly, berating herself for such sound stupidity. Bananas. I'm about to be in some kind of trouble over a stupid yellow fruit I don't even like. Did they put you in jail for bananas? she wondered, fighting a wave of panic. Surely not. . . .

"I'm sorry," she began to murmur, lacing her fingers together and clenching them tightly. "I knew—I was aware I couldn't bring fruit into the country. I meant to eat them, you see, and then I forgot all about them. Couldn't we just put them in the garbage?"

The slate stare of the young guard didn't change. He began to approach Erin and it was all she could do to keep from screaming. But he meant her no harm—of the physical variety at least! He merely reached for her hand and brought her to her feet, positioning her near the cabin door. "Please," he said as he motioned her to remain there. She had the feeling it was the one word he knew in English.

The man was more than thorough. Her bedding was ransacked, the closets and cabinets. Nothing was left unturned. Even the window shade was checked; it rattled as he spun it carefully, filling the night with a sharp, discordant sound.

Had the discovery of the bananas initiated further search, she wondered, or was this customary? Mary, she thought belatedly, you were right, I should have come with a tour. . . .

Her heart seemed to catch in her throat as he turned back to her. She didn't need a translator to tell her he was still, for some enigmatic reason, dissatisfied. He caught her arm—once more his grip polite but very, very professionally cold, and proceeded to open her couchette door. Where is he taking me? Erin wondered desperately. She felt as if she would fall in another second, she was so damned scared. If only she knew what was going on.

Clad only in her flannel gown, her hair mussed and wild from sleep, she felt the beginnings of panic settle in, and she automatically began to work a bracelet around her left wrist. The harsh, alien man beside her, now barking orders in a glacial voice she couldn't begin to comprehend, became a terrifying entity.

No, she told herself, don't give way to fear. This is probably customary. He is not being cruel, merely professional. I have done nothing. I am guilty of nothing but stupidity, and buying bananas. She would laugh about it one day. It would be an adventure to tell. But right now she was about to lose control and fall to the floor in panic-stricken tears.

"Spasee' ba! Ne noo' zhna!"

The crisply authoritative Russian comments came from her recent dinner companion. His appearance in the hallway halted the border guard; the two men proceeded to engage in a rapid-fire exchange that left her standing between them, riddled with confusion. She was amazed to see the border guard actually smile.

He is human, Erin thought a little bitterly. As soon as Jarod had appeared, the man had become human.

The Russian was laughing. Delivering her into Steele's hands, he tipped his hat.

Jarod began to speak again, his hands upon her shoulders as they both faced the guard. Erin felt the smoothness of his palm as it moved caressingly up her neck. Thumb and forefingers absently cradled her cheek and chin in an astounding display of tenderness.

Too stunned to do anything else, Erin stood stock still. A vague part of her mind was warning her she had been safer with the young Russian guard. Jarod Steele's touch was doing nothing to repair the weakness in her legs. If anything, she felt more immersed in quicksand; the heat and pressure of his powerful chest and long-sinewed legs behind her was dizzying and engulfing. She was once more keenly aware of the scent of elemental strength and masculinity.

The border guard made a last comment to Jarod and turned crisply to continue onward to the next compartment.

"You'll have to come into my couchette," Jarod said quietly, releasing his hold and prodding her gently. "Our friend will be back in a minute to lock the doors until the rest of the train is searched."

For once, his tone was merely gentle. But at this point, had he shouted the order, Erin would have meekly complied.

She moved uneasily into Jarod's couchette, noticing from the disheveled bedding that he, too, had been hastily aroused from sleep. Unwilling to allow her vision or mind to dwell upon the rumpled sheets and blankets, she wandered nervously to the unshaded window—apparently the guard hadn't seen fit to rake his couchette apart—and stared out into the blackness of the night. It was thick forest land that set the boundary separating Finland from the U.S.S.R.

The loud retort of a bolt clanging shut on Jarod's door was so unnerving that Erin literally jumped and spun around to face Jarod with wide eyes.

"Relax, Miss McCabe," Jarod said, gentle amusement tinging his voice of husky velvet. "This is all quite in order, I assure you."

"Oh," Erin murmured, swallowing and lowering her eyes. She was calming down enough to panic again. It had taken her until now to realize that her strange rescuer was dressed in nothing but a brown velour robe, one that bared long, heavily muscled and thickly haired calves, ridiculously appealing feet—of all things!—and a shade too much of a taut, muscled chest, clearly outlined in the loose V of the robe as was another attractive swatch of coarse, curled dark hair. A few of those were also turning silver, Erin noticed; she was suddenly swamped with the obsession to reach out and touch, feel that silver within deepest black.

Unconsciously she began to play with her bracelets. She was beginning to feel claustrophobic, and the cabin seemed to shrink, making her aware of the larger-than-life presence of Jarod Steele. Her heart was beating at a deafening pace, and she was finding it difficult to breathe. His energy, his virility, permeated space and air. His icefire gaze, even when amused, seemed to have the ability to pin her down, to strip her of both clothing and soul, and it terrified her.

"Relax," he repeated very quietly, leaning against his door and reaching into the pocket of his robe for cigarettes and lighter. He shook two from the packet and lit both, finally leaving his stance to walk over to Erin and put it into her trembling fingers. She didn't like him so near, but the cigarette helped. She inhaled deeply, then returned her vision to the blackness of the night.

Erin finally managed to clear her throat and talk. "I don't think I understand," she murmured, not looking at him as she questioned him. "You mean all that was customary? Where was he taking me?"

"It was customary that he search your couchette and belongings. Rules and regulations on what may enter the country are very strict." He hesitated a moment and then continued. "He was taking you to a female guard to be searched. He must have decided you looked suspicious—and you were trying to bring fruit into the country."

"I wasn't!" Erin protested. "I forgot I had the stinking bananas! And I can hardly believe I look suspicious!"

She felt Jarod's eyes on her in calculation as he exhaled a long plume of smoke. "A young woman traveling into the Soviet Union alone? Eschewing the more normal, controlled routes and entering through Finland? A young, attractive, American woman. . . . He wasn't quite sure what you were up to. Neither am I."

"Up to?" Erin exclaimed incredulously. "I'm not up to anything! It was my understanding that more and more Americans were visiting the U.S.S.R."

Jarod shrugged, his nonchalance belied by his astute and assessing stare. "Who's to say, Miss McCabe? Fragile-looking women usually travel with tours."

"I'm hardly fragile," Erin retorted.

A dark handsome brow arched in amused mockery. "I'll accept that, Miss McCabe. Sometimes I get the distinct impression that any fragility of yours would be comparable to that of a boa constrictor."

Erin felt an instant grinding of her teeth, a tensing of her fingers. It was incredible that this same man had come to her rescue, touched her with the lightest stroke of tenderness, instilling quicksilver in her veins.

Erin directed her own most piercing silver-frost stare into his eyes. "Would you mind telling me, Mr. Steele, just why you dislike me?"

He appeared mildly surprised; his reply held a similar note, as if he were discovering something new himself. "I don't dislike you, Miss McCabe. I'd just as soon not be terribly near you when you drink. You're rather hard on a wardrobe, you know. But I certainly don't dislike you."

Erin turned back to the window. She hesitated a moment. "I suppose I should thank you, Mr. Steele, for saving me a great deal of unpleasantness."

She felt rather than saw his shrug. "I dare say that nothing too dire would have happened. They would have asked you a few questions, frisked you a bit, and allowed you to return to your cabin. That is, unless you are hiding something."

"Don't be absurd!" Erin protested angrily. "How many times must I tell you? I'm simply a tourist, trying to do something a little off the beaten track, trying to really see a little of the countryside and the people!"

Despite her anger, she was shivering again. Frisked you up a bit. Jarod Steele couldn't possibly imagine what a nightmare that would have been for her.

Thankfully, his astute gaze was no longer focused on her. He had moved toward the ledge above the shelf and was pouring a clear liquid from a bottle into the two glasses on the wood shelf over the ornate sink.

"How long are you staying, Miss McCabe?" he inquired with what could have been interpreted as a normal, polite querying tone.

"Two weeks," she replied briefly, then added, "one in Moscow, then one in Leningrad. Then"—she couldn't prevent a bitterness slipping in—"you'll be pleased to hear I'll be leaving the country."

He turned back to her, his expression noncommittal, his blue gaze fathomless as he handed her one of the glasses of clear liquid. Then he ruined the effect of his gallantry by carefully stepping back. "I carry only one robe, Miss McCabe, and I'd just as soon not have it drenched."

Erin closed her eyes for a moment of control and pursed her lips.

Jarod lifted his glass to her. "Drink up, Miss McCabe. Welcome to the U.S.S.R.—with a taste of the country's finest."

"What is it?" Erin inquired suspiciously.

He laughed, and it was as if she could feel the sound. It was low and smooth and throaty, very male, very seductive.

"Vodka, Miss McCabe. What else?"

Her nerves compelled her to take a sip, and then she was gasping. The liquid burned like a brushfire.

Jarod rescued her glass first, patted her back second. "I should have warned you, Miss McCabe. This is their equivalent of our moonshine—very powerful stuff."

"I won't argue with you there," Erin finally managed to mutter.

He chuckled again, that warm sound that seemed to fill her senses. "You should sit down and relax—and sip slowly," he advised. "It will still be some time before they finish checking the train."

Unable to think of a sensible reason to refuse, Erin attempted to sit with the comfortable nonchalance that seemed to rule her companion's every movement. But he isn't casual, she thought, he isn't casual at all. He's as sharp as a whip. Those eyes of his burn while they freeze. They seem to see everything. . . .

Erin curled into the far corner of the bunk, leaning against the wooden footboard and tucking her bare feet beneath her, as if by hiding them she could regain a certain dignity.

He smiled at her, but she had the feeling that his smile was absent, that it hid something else.

"What?" she demanded irritably. Had she gone from the frying pan into the fire? Or straight from one fire into another fire? She was absurdly nervous; it was as if she could still feel the incredible heat of his body from the bed, as if the innocent bunk held a sensuous

62

threat by mere alliance to the man. A man, she reminded herself, who found her no more sexual than the "skin and bones" he considered her to be.

"Pardon?" he inquired with a frown.

"What is that stare for now?"

He shrugged, then apparently decided to give her an honest answer. "You're right, Miss McCabe, I'll be glad to see you out of the country. I would just as soon not think about you gallivanting around Soviet Asia."

"Oh really?" Erin inquired with a smoldering irritation. "What on earth is it to you where I go?"

"Ignorant English-speaking parties are the basis of my concern."

Erin stood. "Mr. Steele, I am not ignorant. I realize that you seem to think very little of my profession, but I beg to inform you, models are not necessarily ignorant, uneducated, or stupid! I've studied the Soviet Union very carefully, I planned my trip with even greater care. Thank you for the help you've given me. Please remember it was offered, not requested—and excuse me, I'll try not to cause you any more concern!"

Her pride was wrapped about her like a cloak. Erin was regally straight, her chin tilted high. With distinct care she set down her barely tasted vodka and whirled for the door, her exit an almost perfect display of dignity.

Except that the door was still bolted—from the outside.

Erin closed her eyes and lowered her head, her fingers tense around the knob. She knew without turning that Jarod Steele was silently laughing, and if she could have viciously kicked herself, she would have done so.

She finally turned, leaning against the door, her silver gaze one that would quell most men, her sigh aggravated and yet resigned with a very blatant effort at self-control.

"How much longer will I be locked in here?"

Jarod made little attempt to hide the amusement that twitched the corners of lips capable of appearing full and sensual one minute, hard and grim and white thin the next.

"It depends," he said.

"On what?"

"On how many other criminals they find trying to smuggle bananas into the country."

"Not amusing, Mr. Steele."

"But true, Miss McCabe."

They were at an impasse, each staring at the other. Oddly enough, it was Jarod this time who broke the silence with irritation. "Would you please light somewhere, Miss McCabe? You remind me of a damned butterfly flitting about."

Erin took a deep breath and lowered her eyes, then moved to regain her curled position on the bunk near the footboard. She did so simply because his tone had been much more of a demand than a request and she didn't think she was up to a battle with this man over something so idiotic and she was very, very afraid that he might touch her again.

"Tell me," she demanded in return, "what did you tell the guard to get him to let me go? He even forgot about the bananas."

"I have diplomatic immunity, Miss McCabe. I'm allowed to bring certain things into the country which a tourist isn't."

"Yes, but I had the bananas."

"I told him you were my fiancée."

Although his expression remained carefully neutral, Jarod was stunned by the reaction his statement drew. She didn't move, she didn't even blink, but he had never seen another human being literally turn almost paper white. For some reason, that irritated him. No, he thought, I'm not just irritated, I'm bordering on being furious.

It was illogical, unreasonable, but he still found himself lashing out. "Don't be alarmed, Miss McCabe. You're not obligated in any way. It was simply the first thing that came to mind. You needn't worry. I don't plan ever to marry again, so if the story should happen to get anywhere, it won't harm either of us."

She was still silent; her paper-white coloring was becoming even more ashen than before.

"Dammit, woman! Would you have preferred I allowed the guards a body search?"

That finally brought forth a response. "No!" she rasped, and he felt a relenting of his temper—and a new surge of curiosity.

And a surge of something else, something which had lain dormant in him a long time. Tenderness. A warming flush of emotion he didn't want or need. He was supposed to be watching the woman, not falling for her lures—if they were lures. Her expression had been

64

one of pure panic. Surely such a drastic physical change could not be part of an act.

Whatever, she could certainly have an effect upon the male senses. He had touched her tonight and she had felt like silk. He had felt the stirring of his blood created by the essence of her cologne, by the clean sweet fragrance of her hair. Skin and bones, he reminded himself.

He had had many women since his wife's death; if he hadn't been able to give emotion, he had certainly given courtesy and pleasure. But those who had attracted him to interludes of pure physical need had been extremely shapely as well as attractive and knowledgeable. Erin McCabe was more than thin . . . she was like lifting air.

And yet he had discovered tonight that her compact body was beguiling and seductive. The artificial light of the cabin had drawn a clear silhouette beneath the thin flannel of her gown. Clear enough for him to realize that mystically enchanting hollows lay within the surprising curves of her hips, that her breasts, though not voluptuous, were high and firm and soft.

I want her, he realized, somewhat stunned that he had reached such a point of raw desire. But desire itself was natural; it was a normal physical accompaniment to being a healthy male. He was simply startled that he had joined the throngs he thought he ridiculed and discovered that he was finding Erin McCabe not just a packaged illusion of seduction, but shockingly sensual in a way that was quietly innate, simply a part of her very feminine existence.

His desire didn't bother him. It was physical; it was controllable. That she seemed to be able to touch his emotions was something that didn't particularly please him. He didn't believe he would ever love another woman—and even if all the gentler of his emotions did not lay in the past with Cara, he sure as hell didn't believe in love—or strong liking—at first sight. No, it was merely the panic he had sensed in Erin. He hadn't become completely inhuman; he had seen a hint of that look earlier when he had lifted her in his arms. And he had seen it fade to something like trust. Surely that was what had touched his ego, he thought wryly, and that in itself now made him feel that need to protect her. It had brought him from his cabin tonight, it had made him determined to save her from the guard.

Territorial feelings, my man, he told himself. No good. No, no good at all.

Don't trust me, Erin. Because I don't trust you. I can't trust you, I can't afford to. I still don't know if you're real, or one of the finest actresses ever created. And, madam, I am not a man who will be taken.

Still, he couldn't handle the ghostly pallor that haunted her beautifully sculpted features. He retrieved the glass she had so pointedly set down and walked over to her, pressing it into cold fingers.

"Drink it!" he commanded, his tone not harsh, but one that denoted unquestionable authority.

She complied, swallowing the contents of the glass with only a small shudder. "Thank you," she murmured. Her color began to regain a rosy hue, yet she remained very still, her only movement that of a subconscious twiddling with one of the gold bracelets she never seemed to remove.

Odd, he thought, she had been wearing them even to sleep.

"Look, Miss McCabe," he found himself saying very gently, "this may still take some time. Relax, or you'll wind up half asleep on your first morning in Moscow."

Even more curious than the soothing words that seemed to be slipping out of his mouth were his actions. He noticed that she was shivering. He ripped out the neat folds of his blanket to secure it lightly around her. Did he imagine it, or did she flinch slightly, then smile as if in rueful self-chastisement.

"Thanks," she said very huskily. "I was rather cold."

He didn't return her smile; he knew his expression was rather grim. But he was next handing her the pillow and gruffly telling her she might as well be comfortable. She hesitated a second, chewing her lower lip, then whispered another thanks.

Jarod restlessly moved to the window, lit another cigarette, and stared out at the thick forest in its barren winter guise—barely visible in the darkness of night. They were checking the train very thoroughly tonight. He knew the efficiency of the border guards: they were looking for something . . . or someone. . . .

"My name is Erin."

Jarod jolted back to the present at the sound of her soft, drowsy voice. "What?" he murmured.

Her eyes were cold, her head rested upon the bunched pillow as if she could remain awake by keeping her body folded in an upright position. "Erin," she repeated, and he smiled a little as he realized the gulped vodka and the late hour were combining to soften her defenses. "You keep calling me Miss McCabe. Since I'm sitting in your couchette in a nightgown, I think we could consider it proper to be on a first-name basis."

Jarod inhaled and exhaled, his smile increasing. She still hadn't opened her eyes; she was mumbling and half asleep. Like a web of spun gold her hair fluttered in disarray over her shoulders and forehead; her lips were slightly parted, slightly curled.

He left the window to glance down at her at closer range. The rise and fall of her breathing was slow and even.

"All right," he murmured softly. "Good-night . . . Erin."

She didn't reply. Jarod walked back to the window pensively, finished his cigarette, glanced back at his sleeping companion, then mumbled, "Oh, what the hell!" and poured himself another shot of the vodka. It had worked for her.

He yawned and stretched, then reached upward to pull the top bunk down to a sleeping position. He automatically started to cast off his robe, remembered what he wore—or rather didn't wear—beneath it, and resecured the tie around his midriff. He gripped the bunk to swing himself upward, then paused again, glancing at the woman. She was going to wake up with one hell of a pain in the neck.

Gingerly he touched her, swinging the pillow beneath her head as he slowly lowered her frame until she was recumbent on the sheets. Remembering how she had curled her feet beneath her, he carefully tucked the blanket warmly around them. She barely stirred the entire time; only one hand, slender and elegant and beautifully manicured, lifted slightly, then fell back to the sheets. Again Jarod noticed the gold bracelets and he frowned as he pulled himself up to the top bunk.

Why the bracelets? he wondered, forcing himself to think back to all the occasions when he had seen her in either magazines or commercials. Had she always worn them? No, he didn't think so. It would be something to look into. Very, very curious. . . .

No more curious than tonight, he thought with irritation. Invite the enemy in—set them by the fire, pour them a drink. Great going, Steele, really great.

She couldn't be the enemy. Not the slender creature sleeping so peacefully on the bunk below. while he was lying up here, unable to sleep because she was sleeping down there.

Idiot, he charged himself. Hell. He couldn't remember the last time he had been so beguiled, so tempted to discover just how silken skin fitted over well-formed bones.

Jarod shifted, staring sightlessly up at the paneled ceiling of the couchette. He stretched his fingers, clenched them, stretched them again.

It was going to be a long, long night.

As he lay there, eyes open, a whistle sounded. The deep green train hissed back into action and treaded her way across the Russian border.

IV

As Erin's eyes flickered to open, she became immediately aware that bright sunlight was streaming through the opened window. The train, she realized gratefully, was still chugging; she hadn't slept through her actual arrival in Moscow!

She knew where she was without the rustle of Jarod's movements to remind her of the evening. Damn, she must have gone out like a light! But then she had been so nervous and frightened, it was easily understandable that she had been extremely exhausted.

She blinked the fuzziness of waking from her eyes and covertly turned her gaze to her host. He stood before the mirror and sink, cursing softly as he shaved against the continual lurch of the train. He wore only a pair of well-pressed black trousers, and she was treated to her first view of the supple corded back, the trim waist, and—reflected in the mirror—the full curly-haired broad chest she had only caught a hint of the night before. He really wasn't thin at all, she found herself thinking. He only appeared so because of his height, because his form was so very toned and trim.

He turned to her then, shaving foam still flecking his face. "Good morning, Miss McCabe . . . Erin." He corrected with a small smile. "I was about to wake you. We reach Moscow in thirty minutes."

"Oh!" Erin murmured, swinging her feet over the bunk. "I'd better get ready."

"Thirty minutes worth of makeup?" he inquired, swinging around to splash his face clean over the sink. Grabbing a hand towel he ruggedly dried his face and tossed back the silver-streaked jet lock that fell over his forehead. "Come, come, Miss McCabe, don't you want to disillusion me again? Aren't you going to tell me you can be ready in less than ten minutes?"

"Look whose talking!" Erin charged. "You've obviously been getting ready yourself for a while!"

"The curse of being male!" he groaned. "Believe me, if I didn't have to go through this torture every morning, I wouldn't."

"Grow a beard," Erin advised.

"I did once," he laughed, "but it was solid silver. Very depressing!"

Erin smiled in return, somewhat surprised by his good humor. "I hadn't thought you the type to worry much about age," she murmured. She really should be moving, but she was enjoying the light banter with him, feeling both comfortable and pleasantly scintillated as he unself-consciously went about the act of dressing.

"I don't worry about age," he replied, reaching for an immaculately pressed blue shirt and sliding it over nicely curved biceps. "I simply don't encourage anything before its time!" A tie was next stripped from a hanger. Jarod Steele had no difficulty dealing with it. He was a man accustomed to caring for himself with no-nonsense expertise. His was not a practiced perfection; it was natural to him, something of which he probably wasn't even aware. "I ordered you some tea," he said, smiling still to take away the sting of his next half-serious, half-ribbing words, "but will you mind keeping your distance? I'm running out of suits."

Erin flushed and shot him a glance of reproach. "Yes, Mr. Steele," she replied with her own lips curving slightly, "I'll keep my distance." She stood with a half bounce, retrieved the tea in its filigreed holder from the sink side shelf, and carefully—actually gracefully—sidled past him to the door of the couchette. "I'll keep a big distance—that of a door away! If I don't get moving, I won't even have ten minutes!" Erin paused at the door, her smile turning to a frown. "Oh—what do I do now?" she queried. "You're Russian friend took my visa and passport last night."

"I have both," he assured her.

"You do?"

"The porter brought them to me this morning."

"Oh." Despite herself, Erin was flushing again. She barely knew the porter; she would probably never see him again. Why should she care what he thought about her sleeping arrangements?

Jarod obviously ascertained far more from her simple "oh" than she had intended. Cryptic amusement shone freely in his eyes.

"What a lovely flush from a divorcée!" he chuckled. "But don't worry, Erin, the Soviets are also living in the twentieth century. They believe in love and sex and all that stuff. I sincerely doubt a soul would think a thing about your spending a night with your . . . ah . . . fiancé."

"But you're not my fiancé, Mr. Steele," Erin said softly. "And like you, I certainly intend never, never to marry again."

Her words, Erin knew, held a strange timbre, but she couldn't help that. She slid out the door and closed it behind her, rushing quickly into her own couchette. She was running out of time; she hurriedly scrubbed her face, brushed her teeth, and dressed in a warm wool outfit. Whatever time she had left would have to do for her makeup!

But as she sipped her tea—cold now but at least something for the morning!—and brushed some shadow on her lids and mascara on her lashes, she found the time to again ponder her recent companion. She kept thinking of the wonderful very clean and yet very masculine smell of him, a scent that was as ruggedly pleasant as the feel of his suits, as the feel of the strong smooth palms that had so tenderly grazed her face for those fleeting moments last night.

"I don't dislike you, Miss McCabe." She could hear the strange echo of his words, recall the magnetic touch of fire and ice when he gazed upon her. He had mentioned he would never marry again; obviously he had been married at one time. Good, bright conclusion, Erin! she told herself. Was he also divorced? she wondered. Or a widower? Something had left him capable of being very, very cold.

And yet he wasn't cold. He was as searing as a tempest flame. One had only to stand near him, to see his sharply chiseled face across a room, feel the dagger pierce of his gaze, to know that.

He knows I'm divorced, Erin thought. Yet that meant little. Her divorce had been shamefully capitalized upon by more than just the trade media. But he doesn't know why, she thought morosely to herself.

No one knew why, just she and Marc—and that one other party. Not even Mary knew completely. Anger and humiliation had kept her silent. Marc had never intended her harm, and it was doubtful he had ever realized just how much harm he had caused her.

"Oh, Mr. Steele," she murmured to her mirror. "I think I'm very glad you seem to consider me an overrated toothpick! You must be some kind of sorcerer. You compel me, you hypnotize me. You make me feel things I never thought I would feel . . . that I didn't believe really existed.

"And of all people, Mr. Steele, you are one man before whom I don't care to make a fool of myself . . . before whom I couldn't bear humiliation. Yes, Mr. Steele, I'm glad you have no expectations to have shattered."

Erin brought her lipstick line halfway across her cheek as the train suddenly shrieked out a long low whistle and began its steady screech to a stop. Grimacing, she rubbed her cheek clean and hurried to the window, clapping her hands together with pleasure. A light snow was falling; even the train station looked magical.

"Imagining scenes from *Dr. Zhivago*?"

Erin spun around at the sound of Jarod's voice but didn't bother to dignify his taunt with a reply. She lifted a wry brow in his direction as she shrugged into her new coat and gathered her belongings.

"I'll take your bag," he informed her.

"I can manage," Erin murmured in protest. "Remember, Mr. Steele—I'm the lady who is as fragile as a boa constrictor."

"But the key word is lady, isn't it?" he inquired with a slight smile. "I want to see you safely in the hands of your Intourist agent."

Erin shrugged. He already had her suitcase in hand. There wasn't much she could do, since she doubted her ability to wrest it from his grasp.

The railway station was very busy, and Erin found herself, as usual, fascinated by the industry going on around her. Her ears were filled by the sound of the Russian language; her eyes were constantly flitting from people to newsstands to tiny shops to people again.

"Miss McCabe!"

Startled by the sharp call of her escort, Erin hurried along. Mary had told her that an agent from Intourist—the government agency that handled all travel to the Soviet Union—would be there to meet her. She hadn't thought to inquire at the time how she would actually find her agent, so at the moment she had to be grateful that Jarod obviously knew where to take her.

He stopped so suddenly that she plowed into the expanse of his back, righting herself as he turned to her with a lifted brow and a deep sigh of patience and resignation. "Well, you stopped!" she murmured, only to fall silent as she realized they were before a third party.

"Ivan Shirmanov," Jarod greeted the young man. He said something in Russian, from which Erin recognized only her own name.

The young man nodded, then turned to Erin. "Welcome to the U.S.S.R., Miss McCabe. If you are ready, I will take you to your hotel."

"Thank you, and yes, I'm ready," Erin said, accepting the hand offered her. The Russian's grip was brisk but firm and warm. His pronunciation was perfect, English-accented rather than American. She would learn later that the King's English was taught in the majority of the schools.

Jarod was turning Erin's suitcase over to Ivan. His sharp gaze suddenly turned to her. "Enjoy your stay, Erin," he said quietly. "The embassy is on Chaikovsky Street should you need anything."

To Erin's vast surprise he took her hand in his and lightly touched it to his lips. His eyes, as they rose to meet hers, were more enigmatic than ever. They were crystal, they were ice. They were that incredible and intangible imprisonment of blue fire.

"Thank you," Erin mumbled, nervously retrieving her hand. She adjusted the shoulder strap of her handbag over her shoulder and fought to dispel the hold of his eyes, then turned to follow Ivan, who was already briskly leaving the station.

"Oh, Miss McCabe?"

Erin turned back. With his customary half grin of irritating amusement, Jarod Steele was reaching out to hand her something. Luckily, she noticed from the corner of her eye that Ivan had paused to wait for her.

Somewhat warily, Erin reapproached Jarod. "Your passport and visa," he told her wryly. "You'll need them when you check in at the hotel."

"Thank you," Erin said crisply, accepting her papers.

"Not at all," he murmured dryly. "Do sveedah nyah."

It was he who turned this time, his long-legged stride quickly taking him into the crowd. Erin watched as the silver-touched jet of his head became distant—its height above the throng of others remaining distinct.

"You are a friend of Mr. Steele?" Ivan broke her mesmerization with the polite question.

Erin chuckled a bit dryly. "Do you know, Ivan, I'm not really sure."

The young man frowned, apparently worried that his question might have been out of line. Erin quickly gave him a brilliant smile. "This is really marvelous, Ivan, being met like this. I can see where I might have been terribly lost."

Moments later she was ushered into a small economy car and they were moving into very hectic traffic despite the fact that it had been Erin's understanding that automobiles were luxuries to the majority of the Soviet people. The car they were in, Ivan explained, belonged to the Intourist agency.

"We really do not need automobiles, Miss McCabe," Ivan continued cheerily. "Our metro is fabulous. You must see it while you are here!"

"I've read about the metro," Erin said enthusiastically, "and I wouldn't miss it for the world!"

Ivan glanced at her and then returned his eyes to the road, a smile curving into his lips. "You are a good tourist, Miss McCabe! You seem to know a great deal about us!"

"Not a great deal, I'm afraid," Erin muttered. "But I am fascinated by the history and the country. It's all so vast!"

Apparently she had touched him with her enthusiasm. His job, she knew, was simply to see her to her hotel. But Ivan detoured around the city, showing her the world-famous circus, several of the ancient cathedrals, and so many monuments that she lost count. As they approached her hotel, the Rossia, he pointed down the street.

"You're lucky," he told her, smiling. "The Rossia sits right off Red Square. You can walk to the Kremlin and St. Basil's and Lenin's tomb. You must be sure to see the changing of the guard at the tomb. It is an awesome sight. Do so at midnight, Miss McCabe. It is especially exciting at that time with the lights creating magic on the square."

"Midnight!" Erin laughed. "I shall be there!"

Uniformed bellboys appeared to take her luggage, and Ivan escorted her into the hotel lobby. He helped her cut through the red tape of registration and then smiled politely to her once more. "I leave you here, Miss McCabe."

74

"Will I see you again?"

"It isn't likely," Ivan replied, then shrugged. "But then we never know. That is why we always say 'Do sveedah nyah!'"

Erin laughed and thanked Ivan, but the sound of the phrase had brought her mind back to Jarod Steele. Would she meet him again? Probably not. She hoped not.

What a lie. She did want to see him again, just to figure out what his fascination was. No, no, no, no, Erin thought, clenching her fingers together as she followed the bellboy to her room. She couldn't handle Jarod Steele. He was a furnace, and she would find herself consumed in flame.

"Oh, how lovely!" She interrupted her own thoughts as the door to her "room" was pushed open. It was actually a suite, a ridiculously large one with a quaint and gracious bedroom, luxurious sitting room complete with piano, and a private office. The feeling of Old World charm was warm and endearing. Erin made a mental note to thank Mary profusely for the deluxe-class accommodations as she thanked the bellboy, who was grinning with pleasure at her obvious endorsement of the premises.

With a few words of spattered English—and a very few words of spattered Russian—Erin and the bellboy managed enough of a conversation for her to ascertain that breakfast would still be served in the dining room for another hour. Erin unpacked a few things, ran a brush through her hair, and started off.

The Rossia was an Intourist hotel and therefore specifically designed to cater to foreigners. Erin didn't have much difficulty locating the dining room, nor did she have difficulty with the menu, as it was printed in seven languages—English among them. She chose the buffet, and happily dived into ham and eggs and rolls, as well as a number of less familiar dishes, several made with fish and potatoes. Russian coffee, she decided, left quite a lot to be desired, but it would certainly keep her wide awake for the tour of the Kremlin and Red Square which she had elected for the day. Besides, she was still thinking about Jarod Steele. Having known him, she thought dryly, his presence seemed to hover, and she was very determined to keep her mind and appreciation just as Russian as possible.

Why the hell do I keep wondering about that man, she asked herself with irritation as she resolutely sipped a second cup of coffee in hopes that she would acquire a taste for the strong brew. She was reading things that simply weren't there into his last words. Do sveedah nyah. The phrase was a polite exit line, nothing more. But it was hard not to think about a man when one had spent the night in his couchette . . . accidentally.

Oh, yeah, of course, accidentally. And platonically. No, nothing about Jarod Steele was platonic. His eyes could caress and sear the flesh like a perceptible touch, strip it, bare it; his voice could do things that were far from decent to the blood. And damn him, the worst thing about him was that he was impossible to forget, even if she wasn't even sure whether or not she liked the man.

Erin left the open and airy dining room with its attractive display of windows and plants to explore the crimson carpeted and crystal chandeliered elegance of the Rossia's hallways. The hotel was marvelous, but she didn't dare spend too much time discovering its amenities. She was due to meet her Intourist guide for the day in the lobby at eleven, and she had learned that the Soviets were punctual.

This time she was met by a young woman whom she judged to be about her own age. Tanya, as she introduced herself, immediately aroused Erin's admiration. She was very attractive, with sable hair and deep, expressive hazel eyes. Her manner was friendly yet assured. There didn't seem to be such a thing as a cultural gap between the two women. Both seemed aware, as so often happens when people meet for the first time, that they would warm to one another immediately.

As they stood in Red Square and Erin's eyes wandered from Lenin's tomb to the thick red walls of the Kremlin to the intricate architecture of St. Basil's Cathedral, Tanya explained that much of the contemporary life-style of the Soviet peoples stemmed from the thirteenth century, when Russia was invaded by the bloodthirsty Mongol hordes of Genghis Khan. The Mongols left behind them mountains of skulls and miles and miles of smoked-out cities. For the following two centuries the Russian people fought to free themselves from the yoke of the Mongols, thereby missing much of the Renaissance and Reformation that were taking place in Europe. Not until the time of Ivan the Terrible—the first czar—were the Mongols subdued, and then Russia continued under the rule of the czars until 1917.

"In this century we have also been plagued by war," Tanya continued. "Our own revolution, World War One, and World War Two—to name our main conflicts." She paused suddenly. "Why are you here, Miss McCabe?"

Erin laughed, thinking she should tape-record her answer to the continually asked question. Yet from Tanya the query didn't bother her. Erin hesitated, then answered with far more depth than she had given Jarod Steele.

"When I was very young, Tanya, our president Kennedy was in office. I was in grammar school during the Cuban missile crisis, and I can still remember the drills in which we crawled under our desks. I was terrified of war, and as I grew up, I was determined to study Russian history and try to understand our power balance across the world. That, in a nutshell, is why I'm here. I discovered an American could see the U.S.S.R.—and here I am."

Tanya smiled slowly. "I think I shall truly enjoy taking you through our history, Miss McCabe. I, too, was always terrified of another war," she murmured. "Many Soviet people are, and you will understand that when you travel to Leningrad. But for now—"

Erin was next taken to St. Basil's, where she studied the many priceless icons while Tanya colorfully related the history of the cathedral built between 1555 and 1560 by Ivan the Terrible. She shuddered with a true understanding of the "Terrible" in Ivan's name as she heard how he made certain each of his architects died so that their expertise could not be reproduced.

When they left the cathedral, Tanya pointed out the common grave in the Kremlin wall of the revolutionaries killed in 1917. Then they were just in time to see a changing of the guard at Lenin's tomb. The ramrod-stiff goose steps of the crisply uniformed military guard sent shivers racing along Erin's spine.

"You look a little horrified," Tanya murmured.

"No," Erin protested. "I heard it was an awesome sight—in fact, I promised the agent who brought me to the hotel that I would be sure to come at midnight."

Tanya smiled. "You must try to understand, Erin, that we have bred backbone to survive. Many of our leaders have been ruthless men; they have taken the path of heartless purges and rigid isolationism. But we have been burned out and massacred many times. Twenty million Soviet citizens lost their lives in World War Two.

77

I admit, we are a people who often put bullets before bread." She shrugged eloquently. "We have far to go; perhaps that may soon change."

So awed had Erin been by the guards, then so touched by Tanya's speech, that she screamed as a hand descended upon her shoulder.

"I am so sorry, Miss McCabe, I have startled you. It *is* Miss McCabe, is it not?"

The accented query came from a tall man of about fifty, handsome in a tall and austere way, clad in a heavy wool coat and a fur pillbox hat. At Erin's stunned nod his lined faced creased further into a smile. "Forgive me. I knew you were in the country and I was most eager to make your acquaintance."

Tanya took that moment to intercede, her voice a bit awed. "Miss Erin McCabe, you will please meet Mr. Sergei Alexandrovich."

Still bewildered, Erin extended a hand. "Mr. Alexandrovich, how do you do?"

If she had been bewildered, total confusion was to follow. The Russian had barely replied before Erin felt another hand descend upon her shoulder. The vital and masculine scent she had come to know so well told her "do sveedah nyah" had come sooner than she expected from the man who had the uncanny ability to appear in the most absurd places at the most absurd time.

"Erin! How is the sightseeing going? And how on earth did you happen to run into Sergei already?"

Erin turned and discovered Jarod staring at her with crystal eyes alight with good humor. He touched her as if she were a long lost and valued friend.

"Hello, Tanya," he murmured to her guide. Then he addressed himself to the Russian man. "I'll be damned, Sergei, you do have a knack for routing out your more beautiful visitors."

Erin's eyes darted to the Russian. He was affably grinning as he replied to Jarod. "Ah, but I didn't seek out Miss McCabe simply because she is beautiful, my friend. I came to find her because I heard news from the border today that *you* were entering the country with a fiancée and I simply had to resolve the curiosity that was plaguing me!"

"Oh, no!" Erin murmured, horrified by the turn of events. Surely Mr. Aloof and Contemptuous Steele was going to be furious that his ruse to help her out had put him in such an embarrassing position with a man who was obviously more than an acquaintance. "But Mr. Alexandrovich—" she began, determined to set the record straight.

The fingers curling into her shoulder tightened, almost causing her to gasp as Jarod interrupted her. "My Lord, Sergei, I have to hand it to you. You have one hell of a grapevine."

"Ah, yes," Sergei replied, still smiling pleasantly and observing well all that he saw. "But then you did come in with a very rare beauty, and you, my friend, are most certainly one of our favorite Americans."

"Flattery, Sergei," Jarod laughed. How could he appear so pleasant when he was practically breaking her collarbone? Erin wondered. She was thoroughly stunned when he continued with, "Well, Sergei, you wished to meet my fiancée. You have done so. What do you think?"

The Russian's deep brown gaze focused with warmth and apparent humor on Erin. "I think, my friend," he said with soft appreciation, "that you will not have to try very hard to find happiness. And I think, too, Jarod Steele, that although you have been so very secretive, you must still bring this exquisitely lovely creature to the dinner at my apartment this evening." Erin once more found her hand gallantly enveloped by the Russian's. "You will come, Miss McCabe, won't you?"

"I . . ." Erin began to murmur, wondering desperately why Jarod didn't come to her aid. Why didn't he simply tell the truth? Surely this man, whoever he was, would forgive Jarod's ruse to help her over the border. "I'd be delighted, Mr. Alexandrovich, but Jarod and I haven't had much time yet to discuss anything . . ." She allowed her voice to trail away with one of her best smiles. She didn't wish to offend the Russian, but she did want Jarod to clear up the mess he had created.

"No problem, darling," Jarod said with disgusting calm. "It's a small dinner, not an affair of state. I should have mentioned it to you earlier. Sergei, Erin certainly shall attend with me. You see, we had been intending to keep our engagement a secret awhile longer. I'm afraid when I mentioned it to Nicolai at the border that I forgot to mention that fact."

"Marvelous," Sergei responded, true enthusiasm shining in his dark eyes. "Then I am the first to congratulate you!"

"Oh, that you are," Erin murmured, managing to maintain her smile through bitterly clenched teeth. A sharp strengthening of the fingers around her shoulder blade informed her Jarod didn't appreciate her dry comment.

Evidently finished with the business of dinner, Sergei turned to Tanya, who was a little overwhelmed to find her tourist such a subject of attention. "So," he said, "how far has the tour gone?"

"St. Basil's, sir," Tanya murmured, collecting herself quickly. "We have discussed some history—"

"But not yet viewed Lenin or entered the Kremlin walls?"

"No."

"Then we shall begin together."

Erin was at long last relieved of Jarod's hold as Sergei Alexandrovich politely slipped his arm through hers and started toward the black marble mausoleum before the red brick wall which was the shrine and tomb of the revered Lenin. Lines of people waited to enter; the viewing of their great leader was a pilgrimage taken very often by many of the Soviet people as well as by the burgeoning tourist trade. But apparently Sergei was important. He was greeted with the utmost propriety, and he and Erin—with Jarod and Tanya close behind—were led immediately to the front.

Moments later Erin was viewing the face of the great Soviet leader of the Revolution, specially preserved and shielded by the crystal of his sarcophagus. The experience was chilling—as awesome as that of watching the guards change before the tomb.

"You shiver," Sergei commented as they returned to the crisp and cold daylight. "You do not approve?"

"Well . . ."

"Speak honestly, Miss McCabe."

Erin laughed, strangely touched by the dark eyes of her escort. "Okay, honestly, Mr. Alexandrovich, I'm not much on open coffins to begin with!"

"Ahhh . . . but he is magnificently preserved, don't you think?"

"That I will agree with."

"Our scientists spend three to four days each week assuring that he will last the century and more. But you are right, Miss McCabe—viewing the dead can be a morbid experience. Come, I shall take you into the Kremlin."

Within the triangular high brick walls of the Kremlin were ancient towers and palaces and the buildings that housed the Soviet government.

Erin quickly discovered that she was being given much more than the average tour. She was treated to many palaces and the museums therein, a recital on the furs and jewels that had belonged to the czars, and a discourse on the many fine bells that were a pride of the Kremlin, and she was escorted into a number of the guarded contemporary buildings.

Her mock engagement, she thought wryly, was proving to be beneficial to her in many areas. But why, she wondered, was Jarod taking it so far? The benefits were hers. What possible good could come his way?

And yet, from a certain standpoint, Erin was also enjoying a new view of Jarod Steele. He was capable of being a very charming companion. As part of their foursome, he appeared to be as pleasantly involved in touring as Sergei; his knowledge was no less complete. It was he who explained to "Darling" that wood walls had stood upon the site as early as 1156—the present brick had been installed between 1462 and 1505. His smile and his touch were excruciatingly pleasant.

He must be about to bust a gut! Erin thought with a certain amount of vindictive relish. Attempting to chastise herself for such thoughts of vengeance, she simply gave up. Mr. Jarod Steele had laughed at her discomfort one too many times for her not to appreciate his at this moment.

But just how uncomfortable was he? She was discovering that Jarod could handle her with apparent intimate affection and yet not think a thing of it while she still felt the mercury chills from the slightest brush of his fingers.

The group parted before St. Basil's where Erin and Tanya had begun the day. Erin was more convinced than ever that Sergei Alexandrovich was definitely important when he informed Tanya that since Miss McCabe seemed to so enjoy her, he would arrange with her supervisor to have her guide Erin for the remainder of her stay in Moscow. Tanya seemed awed. Erin was aware that Tanya was dying to know just who she was to deserve such attention.

No one, Tanya, Erin thought. This is as startling to me as it is to you.

Sergei offered to drop Tanya off at the Intourist office, and Erin and Jarod were finally left alone.

"You can let go now," Erin said dryly. Jarod still had his arm around her waist.

His response was none too complimentary; he dropped his arm as if he had touched a hot potato.

"Come on," he said briefly. "I'll take you back to your hotel."

His stride was long and hurried. Erin was breathing so hard that she was unable to question him until they reached the long carpeted hall that led to her suite. Then, panting, she began in spurts.

"You really should tell me what's going on. Who is Sergei Alexandrovich? And why did you let him believe in this farce? Just because a nasty border guard—"

He stopped and spun before her door—so quickly that, as was becoming usual, she plowed into his broad chest. His hands caught her shoulders; his eyes became the blue icefire that she knew far better than the gentler look she had seen during the day.

"There isn't a damn thing 'nasty' about Nicholai. He was simply performing his duty. This is his country, madam, not yours, and you shouldn't be here to begin with. I've warned you this is the U.S.S.R. —not the Côte d'Azur. Sergei Alexandrovich is a top party adviser. His expertise coincides with mine. He works with English-speaking tourists and handles the fiascos created by those who foolishly or purposely break Soviet laws."

Erin felt tears sting her eyes at his icy rough treatment. It was an especially difficult pill to swallow after his forced—but dear God, almost believable—gentle amicability of the day. Why do I care, she wondered? I know him for what he is. And she would never allow him to see that a thing he said or did daunted her.

"Then please, Mr. Steele," she bit out as he released her to slip her room key from her grasp and slide it into the bolt, "would you mind telling me why you are allowing this ridiculous charade to continue? I am leaving the city in one week, the country in two. Isn't it going to be a bit embarrassing when two mature adults break off an engagement that quickly?"

He paused for a moment, dropping the room key back into her hand. His eyes rose to meet hers, crystal blue, glacially challenging. How on earth was it possible, Erin wondered, for eyes to appear so deathly cold while also giving the impression that they burned with all the intensity of hell? "Are you suffering from this, Miss McCabe? I would think a woman who tells me she is fascinated with history and people would sincerely appreciate this opportunity to come closer to the reality of the situation."

Erin was determined to hold her own. "Mr. Steele," she sighed with a great deal of patience, "I do appreciate this opportunity, and of course I'm not suffering, but—"

"Good," he interrupted curtly, "then let me do the rest of the worrying."

"But—"

Jarod had pushed the door open and ushered her in. As soon as she had entered and spoken, she felt his hand come from behind her and clamp firmly over her mouth. Before she could protest, he had spun her around until she nestled hard against his chest, painstakingly aware of the heat that radiated like a furnace, of the vital thundering of his heart, of her own.

Terror hit her in wave upon wave. If she had been free, if she hadn't been frozen in panic, she would have screamed and screamed; her mind went back in a bolt of memory so strident it was crushing; it took her back.

He must have sensed a fear deeper than the obvious. He must have known, instinctively, something about her; he was aware he should have warned her before he had so roughly subdued her.

"Trust me, Erin." His voice was a whisper of silk. "Go along with whatever I do. Please! Trust me, trust me. . . ."

Trust him. She was incapable of trust. He didn't understand . . .

Jarod had expected the microphone. It was, in fact, rather insultingly blatant. But were they also being filmed? He felt her shaking and realized it was rather understandable. She was being half attacked, but her fear of him was going beyond that, he thought with a jolt. She could really panic, she could create a hell of a mess.

"Erin . . . !" He put all the assurance he could into the whisper. She stared at him, her lips parted to speak.

He shook his head at her in warning, then began to ease his hold on her mouth. But he didn't simply release her; the action became a display of tenderness so provocative it left Erin stunned and trembling within his arms. His fingers moved caressingly over her lips, shaping them, parting them, finding the moistness within and sliding over them once again with a touch tantalizingly damp.

Erin held perfectly still, hardly able to breathe. It registered dully in her mind that his performance had been such that, had they been seen, it would have appeared that it had all been done in passion, rather than with a firm determination to shut her up.

There was certainly a motive behind his actions, a calculated motive. What the hell was going on? she wondered desperately. Why was he doing all this, whispering so only she could hear, acting out this charade which was so devastating to her?

Her realization that he had a motive did nothing to alleviate the devastating effect upon her. Instinct flared; her first panicked thought was to fight, but the force of his arms and that intangible strength in his eyes held her mesmerized even as an instinct more shattering overwhelmed that which had surfaced first. She was dimly aware that his heat was transferring, transfusing to her. The mercury aroused by his touch riddled through her in tiny laps of flame that dizzily tintillated, leaving her weak, breathless, and pliant as she suddenly found herself lifted into his strong arms and carried through the suite into the bedroom.

A tidal wave of panic resurged as her body hit the softness of the mattress. But he was stretched beside her, a powerful leg draped over hers, even as she attempted to bolt. His hand slid into her hair, soothing and caressing as his head burrowed beside hers and his whisper found her ear. "Stop it, Erin," he murmured, so softly that it was but a breath of air searing a new jolt of tingling flame against the sensitive flesh of her throat and lobe. "I'm not going to hurt you. I simply don't want our relationship doubted. . . . Nod if you understand."

She didn't understand; she hadn't understood a damned thing since she had incredibly collided with him on the train.

But she couldn't talk; she couldn't move; she was still struggling just to breathe. It was as if her insides had crumbled. She had no strength, no consistency. She was terrified, she was trembling and burning, alive with anticipation, feeling the heat of him, encompassed by the scent of him, aware—oh, so terribly aware—of the power that stretched beside her, of the fingertips that threaded her hair, of the lips, breathing seduction against flesh with nerves stripped bare.

"Erinnnn . . ." he whispered.

She felt her head move in a jerky nod.

The prize was sitting before her again and she was panicked. Something cried out to her that she had to fight. But still she stayed quiet, shaking now like the leaves blown by winter winds. She closed her eyes, she swallowed, and then she simultaneously felt several things . . . the agonizingly soft caress of his fingers over her cheek down the column of her throat, his mouth moving sensually from her ear to her lips, touching them, grazing them with his teeth, parting them and firing to deep and demanding passion.

His body pressed ever closer to hers. She could feel the crush of her breasts against the rock-hard and yet giving strength below the fabric of his shirt and jacket. The clothing was there, between them, and yet it was as if the burning touch of their bodies had melted the barriers that separated them.

His hands began to move, subtly trailing a path beneath her open coat, discovering the firm mounds of her breasts, fondling, grazing the nipples sensuously through the fabric until they hardened to his touch, seeming to stretch for more.

A gasp caught in Erin's throat, smothered by the increasing plunder and demand of his tongue, intimately seeking deeper and deeper, cajoling, compelling, hungrily commanding response.

Erin still fought the panic. She trembled as if tiny earthquakes riddled her slender frame. But also still within her was that instinct which overwhelmed all others . . . primitive, essential. Her hands rose, her fingers dug into the fabric of his shoulders. But they didn't ward him away. They simply gripped to help her ride out the storm and she realized dimly, very dimly, that she was reaching out to him, arching to his hands, against his hips, against the sinewed length of his thighs.

She felt the movement of his hands again, firm, assured, but gliding with persuasion even as they sought new discoveries. They hovered over the conclave of her hip and abdomen, trailed lower over her thigh, beneath the hem of her skirt, upward, over the ultrasensitive flesh of her upper thigh once more.

Erin felt another gasp rising, but it wasn't that at all. It was a moan, a whimper, a cry deep within her throat. It was fear overridden by need, the shuddering of terror compounded by the deliciousness of trailing fire that swamped her system.

This is necessary, Steele? Jarod could hear the mocking voice screeching within him. An act was an act, but who was he kidding? Come on, Steele, ease up. . . .

What had happened to him? He had started to touch her and the blood had boiled in his veins; his pulse had risen to thunder. Tempest winds had begun in his head, and he had discovered himself in the grip of a maelstrom, seized by a desire as strong and potent as an incoming tide.

Business, Steele, this is business. . . .

His mouth lifted slowly from hers. The torment of feeling her legs pressed against his ended as his fingers touched upon her lips once more, seemingly fascinated with the touch of dampness upon them.

Erin opened her eyes slowly to feel a freeze steal over her body. Jarod touched her, but he didn't glance at her. His face was still near hers—within an inch—but his eyes, always astute, always piercing with the dagger sharpness of crystal, were assessing the room.

Oh, God, Erin thought sickly, all that. All that just for I Spy to check out the room.

Something cataclysmic had happened to her body; something devastating to her life. And he who had been the catalyst hadn't been truly involved; his simple mechanical expertise had seduced her into a loss of barriers that she could have sworn were impregnable.

She thought of all she had allowed him, of her quivering, innate response. She wanted to die, or at the very least, drop through a hole in the world and reappear a hemisphere a way.

She wanted him away from her. She wanted freedom from the deceit of the intoxicating heat and strength and security of his powerfully wired frame. Freedom from the hard thighs that touched with hypocritical demand against hers . . . freedom from the arms that held her, that so easily solicited trust and the most incredible, elemental, sexual need.

Of all the men in the world, why did Jarod Steele have to be the one with such overwhelming sexuality that he could still her defenses without effort, without thought?

She was angry, and she wanted to be angry. She wished she had the strength to push his rugged body from her and onto the floor.

But she also had to admit to another of the fears that plagued her, one that went deeper than ego. Had he been disappointed? Had he already discovered that Erin McCabe was not mystery and passionate beauty but very simply a woman working with a great handicap, frightened, unsure?

She opened her eyes to discover that this time his gaze was upon her, thoughtful, pondering, totally enigmatic, and for once, not cold at all. The fire heat was in them, they seemed almost indigo, but it was still a heat she couldn't begin to read, an indigo that was illusive.

The gentle touch of his fingers as he brushed stray wisps of hair from her forehead and lightly caressed her cheeks was also absent. His smile was almost a shrug; he inclined his head toward the top far corner of the room as he touched his own finger in a barely perceptible shushing action to his own lips.

Erin twisted slightly to see the object of his silent inclination. High in the wall, with no effort at concealment, was a microphone. Erin caught and held her breath and returned her eyes to Jarod's.

He shook his head as if she shouldn't worry, but his warning only stirred new fears. Everything he did was so subtle. Was there also a camera in the room? Why else the kiss . . . the warnings . . . his proximity still?

Why didn't he move? Please, move! she thought silently. Surely he could hear the erratic pulsing of her heart, the pants that were still her effort at breathing. He had touched her; he knew that she responded to him physically. Why didn't he move and save her further humiliation?

Instead, his lips moved over hers again as long strong fingers massaged the tendrils of hair at her temples, the curves of her cheekbones. His kiss was very light this time, yet it seemed to linger. When he lifted his head once more, that enigmatic, wondering indigo was still thawing the usual ice of his stare.

But then it had always been fire. Icefire. A cold that burned with raging intensity no matter what the veneer of polish and civility.

He spoke loudly as he slipped his body from hers and the bed with agility. "Damn, it's hard to leave, darling. Perhaps we should make this a short engagement . . . very short. I can't seem to work with you around and yet not with me. . . . Oh, well, let me get out of here while I can. I'll be back at eight. Oh—dinners at Sergei's are always very formal. Love you, darling. . . ."

His voice was a caress, it was husky, it was velvet. It was astoundingly believable . . . and she couldn't even respond. She could only watch him with all that had been hers just moments—or had it been eons?—before hopelessly, irrevocably shattered.

INTERLUDE

The hall here was the same, long and white and sterile. And at its end the picture was also the same, floor-to-ceiling machinery, reels and disks and memories and drives.

It might have been the same place.

It wasn't. It was miles and miles and miles away.

This lady had been dubbed Catherine the Great.

He slipped his hand into the pit, waited for the whirring and lights of the computer, and leaned back in the chair.

GOOD EVENING, JAROD STEELE.

GOOD EVENING, CATHERINE II.

His mood was hardly at its best, and he hurriedly punched out keys.

PLEASE SPARE ME A WEATHER REPORT. I AM WELL AWARE THAT IT IS FREEZING AND MISERABLE.

Catherine II whirred a second; her drive lights blinked.

TESTY, TESTY, JAROD STEELE.

Jarod scowled. He needed this from a computer.

NO UNSOLICITED DATA PLEASE.

RUN A PROGRAM. FILE: PROJECT MIDNIGHT

Jarod read the program, scanning the file for any little thing he might have missed. The information hadn't changed any; he hadn't really expected it to.

Somewhere along the line, Samuel Hughes had panicked. Perhaps he had known he had played his cards too far, or perhaps he had been so supremely confident that he had taken a perverse pleasure in filing information right beneath the noses of the U.N., the U.S.A., and Great Britain. And most likely he had somehow fed equivalent information to a Soviet counterpart.

A newcomer was involved, but whether the newcomer was actually in on the espionage, or merely a patsy to be used, Jarod didn't know.

Code name Mc.

The Mc didn't necessarily have to belong to a name, but none of the computer or cipher experts had been able to come up with anything else.

Mc.

McCabe.

And Sergei was also showing a tremendous interest in Erin.
. . .

We should be working on this together, Jarod thought. For once we are both determined to put an end to this dangerous double-dealing.

Perhaps they were working together, but they were also encircling one another warily.

FILE PLEASE: ERIN MCCABE

Jarod found himself scanning the words very carefully, propelled now by a driven curiosity that he had not had when he had first read the data from Catherine I. The file contained little on her personal life; no reason for the dissolution of her short-lived marriage. No mention of the bracelets.

Jarod began to fill in all that had happened since the train, finding that his observations could hardly be called objective. Annoyed with his own wordage, he added:

SUBJECT A BIT OF A KLUTZ, BUT SURPRISINGLY AWARE OF MUCH; DRESSES WELL FOR CLIMATE, SEEMS UP ON HISTORY AND CONTEMPORARY AFFAIRS. GRACIOUS PERSON; OFTEN RESERVED, IS ABLE TO HIDE EMOTIONS. ATTRACTIVE, BUT OVERLY SLENDER. SKIN AND BONES.

Jarod was startled as Catherine II whirred her motors after the last—giving him a double-check query on information filed.

Jarod typed irritably:

Yes. I said skin and bones. Why the double check?

Probability law: a man who becomes so intensely involved in a hotel room does not consider the object of his involvement "skin and bones."

Stunned, Jarod stared at the screen with his jaw somewhat slack. He snapped back quickly.

Where was that information acquired?

Filtered from Katerina at Justice Building in Kremlin.

"Damn!" Jarod murmured aloud. His suspicions had been well founded. Erin's movements were being taped as well as recorded. It didn't necessarily mean anything. The Soviet government monitored tourists frequently, doing random checks, something like the IRS. But if Catherine was managing to hone in on Katerina, was Katerina also tuning in to Catherine?

Has Katerina access to our files?

No. Code has not yet been broken.

Jarod breathed a small sigh of relief. He desperately wanted to ferret this one out himself before an incident was created.

Return to file. And for your information, Madame the Great, hotel incident was in the line of duty. Subject needed to be quieted.

Catherine's whirr sounded like soft feminine laughter.

Oh, really, Jarod Steele? A simple peck on the cheek would have sufficed.

Oh shut up, Catherine. You know damned well

His fingers went still. Yes, the Catherine systems knew all about Jarod Steele. All about Cara Steele. Knew well that his wife's death had devastated him, lost him years of his life, then put him where he was today, married to his job, the perfect candidate for a position that demanded all from one who had ceased to care about much else.

SCRATCH ENTRY, CATHERINE. NEW QUERY. THE SOVIETS BELIEVE THAT MISS MCCABE AND I ARE ENGAGED?

MOST CERTAINLY, JAROD STEELE. VERY CONVINCING PERFORMANCE. VERY, VERY CONVINCING PERFORMANCE.

THAT WILL DO!

Jarod typed in INTERRUPTION.
Catherine's whirring motors went still.
Jarod sat very still, sighed, then began typing again.

ALL RIGHT, CATHERINE, MISS MCCABE IS BLESSED WITH ONE OF THE NICEST ARRANGEMENTS OF SKIN AND BONES I HAVE YET TO COME ACROSS. SHE IS AN EXCEPTIONALLY ALLURING WOMAN, AND YES, I FIND HER UNDENIABLY SEDUCTIVE—YOU'RE THE COMPUTER HERE, NOT ME. I DIDN'T SWEAR OFF ALL PHYSICAL RESPONSES WHEN I TOOK THE JOB, AND I MUST STICK WITH MCCABE. EVERY POSITION CARRIES CERTAIN BENEFITS!

Catherine's lights blinked and she whirred, filling the screen with an innocent question.

DID I SAY ANYTHING, JAROD STEELE?

"Oh, Christ!" Jarod muttered aloud in disgust. "I'm explaining myself to a computer!"
He punched the keys.

WHAT DID I TELL YOU ABOUT UNSOLICITED OPINIONS? LET'S GET BACK TO FACTS AND BASICS.

Jarod proceeded to fill in information about Erin, focusing upon the strange panic he so oftened sensed from her when she was touched, on the look he had seen in her eyes when he had lifted her into the train. He mentioned the ever-present bracelets again, ended input, and typed out:

LAWS OF PROBABILITY: WHY?

Catherine barely whirred; her lights blinked but once.

COME, COME, JAROD STEELE. THIS DOES NOT TAKE A DE-
GREE IN PSYCHOLOGY OF THE HUMAN MIND OR EVEN BASIC
BEHAVIOR 101. SUBJECT HAS BEEN HURT SOMEWHERE
ALONG THE LINE. BRACELETS? PERHAPS THEY HAVE SENTI-
MENTAL VALUE. MOST LOGICAL EXPLANATION.

Jarod assimilated the information on the screen with arched
brows, then tapped keys without even thinking.

CAN'T I EVER GET A SIMPLE, STRAIGHT ANSWER FROM YOU?

IT IS NOT LIKELY. I AM PROGRAMMED TO RESPOND ON A
THINK LEVEL.

"Great," Jarod muttered. "When all else goes like hell, you can
count on a wise-cracking pile of nuts and bolts and screws." He
typed out:

SIGNING OUT, CATHERINE II.

Catherine whirred a moment, then taunted:

HAVE A NICE NIGHT, JAROD STEELE. A NICE, NICE NIGHT.

He stood and watched as the computer went still, then turned to
walk down the long white hall. "I'll tell you one thing," he muttered
bitterly, "if I do have a nice night, I'm going to be damned sure it
doesn't appear on anyone's files!"

V

Jarod returned before Erin had completed dressing. She was wandering around in her stockings when the knock sounded on the door, and she threw her teal blue velvet dress over her head, barely zipped it, and ran to answer the summons.

"Just a moment," she murmured as he entered, "I need my shoes."

"Take your time, darling," he replied in a husky drawl. "You look absolutely stunning."

Erin lowered her lashes and pursed her lips as she turned to leave him in the salon. She knew damned well the man didn't think her stunning. Anything pleasant he said was for the benefit of others.

She didn't want him hovering in her room long; his presence and the clean manly scent of him was a reminder of the afternoon—a period of time she had tried long and hard to forget while soaking in the tub until her skin pruned. She was no longer thrilled to know that a man could have an effect upon her—not when the man was Jarod Steele. She had never, never in her life experienced the unpleasantness of feeling so used.

"I'm ready," she said distinctly in the entryway, sliding by him even as he reached for her shoulder. She opened the door herself and exited hurriedly out into the hall.

He joined her, brows raised sardonically as he locked her door. Despite her efforts to elude him once more, he slipped an arm around her waist and pulled her close, leaning slightly to whisper in her ear.

"You're being watched as well recorded," he whispered, adding as if he spoke to a child, "Hidden cameras as well as mikes."

She felt herself go white, but she was so stunned that she didn't reply until they had left the sumptuous lobby of the Rossia behind and she had been courteously seated in the passenger side of a small Mazda.

Then the explosion of her words was a shriek. "I'm being watched?"

She was answered with a hard sardonic glance from her companion before he returned his eyes to the road. "Yes, watched, as in *Candid Camera*."

"Why? By whom?" Erin stuttered, shrinking within. She had known Jarod's behavior had been for the benefit of someone other than herself, but she had been thinking only in terms of being heard. So the little interlude that had created such a devastating effect upon her body and soul had also been witnessed, as had her every movement . . . dressing, undressing, bathing . . .

"Why?" she repeated again in a furious hiss.

Jarod shrugged, apparently rather callously unaware of her discomfort. "Sometimes they work like the IRS," he said, "singling out a percentage of tourists just so that all are aware that they could be monitored. Sometimes they watch people because they believe they are hiding something."

"Oh, hell!" Erin muttered, covering her face with both hands and then raking her fingers through her hair. "Dammit! How dare they! What an incredible breach of privacy."

Jarod interrupted curtly. "You're in the wrong place for a speech on civil rights, you know."

Erin fell silent for a second, a shiver of fury catapulting within her. "Damn *you*!" she hissed. "Ever since I first came across you I have had nothing but trouble. I've been harassed, maligned—"

"Oh, come on, Erin!" Jarod ejaculated in impatient interruption. "Nothing has happened to you that isn't part of the game. If you can't stand the consequences, you shouldn't be here."

"I simply can't believe that these are normal consequences. You're going to try and tell me that the 'normal' tourist rates an assault by you in her hotel room?"

His jaw tightened, but his eyes didn't flicker from the road. "Assault, huh? Come on, now, Miss McCabe, you're a big girl, and you've been around. Don't insult either of us with such a description."

"Don't insult . . . ?" She repeated, a white blaze of anger creeping over her. "Don't *you* insult my intelligence, Steele! You took that little scenario a hell of a lot further than you had to!"

"Come off it, Erin." He cast her one of his dry glances, which seemed to label her as both an ineffectual child and a scarlet woman all rolled into one irritating package. "Would you like an apology? I'm terribly sorry—I must have lost my head. I mean, after all, the Erin McCabe . . ."

"Oh, go to hell," Erin muttered in reply to his amused sarcasm.

She felt a freeze settle over her while inside she still felt hot as if a geyser churned in her stomach. She was sick, angry, frustrated, and confused—and determined that the motorized brick wall beside her become aware of nothing. Holding her fingers with grim determination so that they wouldn't tremble, she reached into her small black evening bag for a cigarette and managed to light it without burning her nose. She exhaled with a slow breath that she hoped would bring her an outward calm so that she might reply to his last statement, only to find herself startled when he nonchalantly spoke himself.

"Light one of those for me, will you? They're not menthol, are they?"

Erin shook her head and floundered for a second cigarette. She lit it and slipped it between his waiting fingers, a little unnerved by the small gesture. How many times had he done this for her? It felt so strange. They could hardly be termed friends, and they had easily shared many things which usually came only with intimate relationships. She had dined with him, slept near him, watched him dress. And that afternoon, mockery or no, she had lain in his arms, felt his strength, the very, very, intimate contours of his body. And in return, he knew her almost as well as the one man who had been her husband.

She was sinking, she thought, sinking into a quagmire. She didn't want the frightening attraction, nor did she want the things that were coming along with it. For no decent reason she could think of, she trusted Jarod Steele. She admired him, she felt he was a man who would put his honor above all else; he would think, he would reason, he would act with cunning but only on principle. He was an enigma she couldn't begin to fathom. At times so gentle; at times so hard.

Erin inhaled and exhaled once more, trying not to rest her eyes upon the long wire-strong fingers that rested upon the steering wheel. "Whatever today was," she said coolly, "I would appreciate its not occurring again."

She felt the shrug of his broad shoulders beside her. His icefire gaze turned briefly to her. "That's rather up to you, Erin. If you can learn discretion—that is, if you can learn to keep your mouth shut—I don't foresee any difficulties in the future."

Totally aggravated, Erin pounded her palm against her forehead. "Why should I need to keep my mouth shut? I keep telling you, I'm a tourist, nothing more! I didn't ask for this fiasco. You're the one determined to carry out a ridiculous charade."

"Would you please shut u—shush." He grimaced as he suddenly twisted the wheel and brought them to a halt before a tall and imposing brick structure. "We're here."

He was around to her door before she could reply, courteously helping her from the car. "Behave tonight, okay? This isn't the norm for American tourists. It will be one of those experiences you can tell your grandchildren about. Surely you appreciate the opportunity."

Erin smiled sweetly. "Yes, darling. I'm here, aren't I?"

One of his brows arched in acknowledgment. "I never doubted your mind for a moment, my dear."

The building apparently housed a number of complexes. They were both silent as he led her to the proper door and rang the buzzer. Then he smiled at her with a slight cynical curve to his lips. "You do look stunning tonight, Miss McCabe. Absolutely stunning."

Before Erin could wonder at the surprising compliment, the door opened and they were greeted by their courteous and cordial host himself.

Dinner did prove to be a fascinating affair. In attendance along with herself and Jarod were two members of the American legation, Joe Mahoney, an elderly gentlemen who seemed to be a distinguished career diplomat, and a younger, extraordinarily good-looking man, Gil Sayer, whom Erin ascertained to be the older gentleman's assistant and one day possible replacement. Two female secretaries, one British, one American, and Sergei's dark and exotically beautiful wife rounded out the party.

One would never have suspected that a terrible housing shortage existed in Moscow from an evening with Sergei Alexandrovich. His apartment covered two floors of what Erin learned was a very elite street. Although tasteful, it was almost as splendid as some of the palaces she had visited within the Kremlin walls. Drinks were served in an elegant Victorian salon, and dinner was laid out upon a massive oak table covered in finest Irish linen and decked with fine crystal and china and heavy silver tableware. A three-tiered chandelier lit a vast display of national delicacies: various caviars and salmons, borsch with cabbage and meat, chicken croquettes a la Kiev, Caucasian mutton shashlik, kefir yogurt, and many others.

Erin was eager to sample everything, and dining became extremely pleasant when she discovered herself seated between the two American diplomats, Joe Mahoney and Gil Sayer.

The older man was charming. He entertained her through the meal with anecdotes about his difficulties in his first years of foreign service after warming her with a surge of natural flattery. He had never thought an aging diplomat like himself would be enjoying a dinner next to a young and lovely model. He seemed to be surprised by but extremely pleased with her engagement to Jarod Steele.

"Steele is a good man," Mahoney told her, and she sensed the pride in his voice. "This is a bit of a shock to us, but a very nice one. We never thought to see him really happy again, not after Cara died."

Erin almost broke a tooth on her spoon. "His wife?" she managed to inquire with a soft tone.

"Yes, the first Mrs. Steele. She was such a lovely little thing, so very gentle and sweet and soft-spoken. Such a contrast to Jarod! He's always been a bit of the lion, hard as his name, as rugged and relentless. But every bit as reliable and talented. They were quite a pair, a sword and a sheath. Cara had the ability to bring out all that was gentle and tender in any man. She was a great loss . . . a very great loss . . . I am sorry, my dear!" Joe suddenly interrupted himself. "I didn't mean to go on so. It's just that Jarod must love you very, very much to be considering marriage once more."

How Erin didn't choke she would never know. She managed a thank you and a smile for the kindly man with the shimmering white hair and took a long sip of burgundy, her mind racing. At least she understood why Jarod had apparently sworn off women.

Well, not sworn off them. His expertise stated clearly that he still enjoyed the physical aspects of the feminine gender.

Her thoughts were interrupted by the man to her left. Gil Sayer caught her eye as she glanced up from the rim of her wine glass. His smile was almost hesitant, and again she was struck by his incredible good looks. A blue-eyed blond, he possessed the perfect aquiline nose, perfect teeth, perfect facial structure—perfect everything. *He* should be modeling, not I, Erin thought fleetingly. Or else starring in a beach boy movie somewhere.

"I apologize for staring," he said, "but since I first discovered you were coming to the U.S.S.R., I started creating fantasies about meeting you. Now I've met you. As the fiancée of an associate, but meeting you nevertheless. And it is a fantasy."

Erin chuckled. "Thank you. That was a very lovely speech."

"For a very lovely lady."

"Thank you again, Mr. Sayer," Erin murmured. "It's easy to place you as a diplomat!"

"Gil, please. I'd like to be on a first-name basis with Erin McCabe."

"Gil," Erin acknowledged with a soft smile. She sipped her wine, watching the young man. "You knew I was coming to the U.S.S.R.? Since when?"

"Oh, we always know whose coming and going," Gil replied with a handsome grin. "Visa applications, you see. We receive all the listings."

"Oh," Erin murmured. For some reason, that seemed important. Why, she wasn't sure.

It wasn't until they adjourned to the salon for coffee that Erin once more found herself near Jarod. She was seated in a wingback chair near the pleasantly burning fire; he stood by the mantel to her left. Pity, she thought briefly, that Gil Sayer hadn't been the American she had had her continual run-ins with. He was carefully solicitous.

Yet even as she covertly watched the two men, she had to admit Jarod the more attractive, despite Gil's superb looks. Gil lacked something that Jarod had in abundance. What it was Erin couldn't discern. Jarod moved with complete self-confidence, lithe and smooth like a tiger. His face was not near so perfect, but its character was indelibly stamped. And of course no one, no one, possessed the compelling strength of Jarod's icefire eyes.

Gil was younger, by several years, Erin decided. Perhaps in time he would have the same firmness of jaw, aura of raw assurance. No, age would never make a Jarod Steele of the man. But it was still a pity her mock engagement wasn't with the handsome blond. He was constant flattery instead of continual mockery, and at the moment her ego could stand the flattery. And she wouldn't feel as if her senses had erupted in a tempest of ice and blue fire.

"So, Miss McCabe"—Erin started as Sergei addressed her—"what do you think of our capital?"

Erin watched her host cautiously from the shade of slightly lowered lashes. Was the question as innocent as it sounded? Or was she constantly enduring some sort of test? Sergei appeared to be the perfect congenial friend. He sat with one leg casually crossed over the other, an arm dangling easily over the arm of his chair, the other stretched casually before him as he idly swirled the amber liquid in his liqueur glass. Erin realized suddenly that although comparisons would never be made between Gil and Jarod, they would certainly be made between Jarod and Sergei. The men shared a common thread. They were toned, rugged physical specimens, and there was a clearly denoted aura of cunning danger beneath their thin veneers of gallantry. Or at least, Jarod was capable of Sergei's gallantry.

Yet with both men she also felt as if their civility was worn as a cloak, easily shunted when necessary. But even with all facades cast aside, both men, despite their cultural differences, would act by conscience, a strange combination of ruthlessness ruled by honor and justice. Oh, brother, am I getting carried away, she thought.

"Erin?"

Joe Mahoney's quiet prompting reminded her that she was supposed to be answering the question. She cast a quick glance toward Jarod, only to find him watching her with his customary raised brow and anticipatory, mocking half smile.

I *am* being tested. Everyone in the room seems tense, as if my simple answer were really going to mean something.

"I have been very impressed by Moscow," Erin said honestly. "It's beautiful, artistic, historic, and—modern. The people have been charming."

"Eloquent," Sergei chuckled, glancing at Jarod. The look exchanged between the two seemed strange. "Miss McCabe, you will make a wonderful wife for a man in Jarod's position. Let's push you a bit further. How does our capital compare with yours?"

"First of all, Mr. Alexandrovich," Erin said wryly, "I will remind you that I'm a New Yorker—and nothing compares with New York! As to capitals . . . Washington in the springtime is an incredible place . . . the flowers blossoming, the cherry trees blooming . . . it's very, very lovely. But we haven't your ancient history. Again, I don't think one could actually compare the two. They are different, both outstanding."

"Ahh, what a diplomat," Sergei murmured. "Sincere and honest —and you haven't said a word." His eyes suddenly turned to Jarod. "You've neglected this gem of yours, comrade. Where is her customary engagement ring?"

Erin was startled by the sudden question. Involuntarily her fingers curled into a ball.

Jarod, however, took the question in stride. She felt his presence as he moved against the rear of her chair, reaching to set one hand upon her throat and shoulder, the other upon her left hand, lifting it, idly running his fingers over hers. "You're right, Sergei," he drawled nonchalantly. "I'm afraid I have neglected Erin. But we really haven't had time yet to select rings."

"Perhaps I can solve your problem," Sergei said. He waved a hand in the air and a maid Erin hadn't even noticed in the room before disappeared to put in an almost immediate reappearance with a small velvet jewel case in her hand. Sergei flicked the case open with a deft hand, rose, and walked over to Jarod. Again she sensed something between the two men, and when she twisted to view the contents of the box, it was all she could do to withhold a gasp.

The ring was exquisite. Nestled in an oxidized antique setting, it was composed of one perfect pear-shaped diamond of a minimum of two dazzling carats. The prisms, caught by the light, were blinding, seeming to pick up every color of the rainbow with exceptionally brilliant blues and golds. Drawing her eyes from the box to Jarod's with confusion, Erin was further baffled to make an extraordinary discovery: Jarod had seen the ring before. He was not at all surprised by its appearance.

There was an anticipation in the room. All eyes were focused on

Jarod. It seemed as if everyone held their breath while waiting for Jarod's reply.

Tell him, Erin thought desperately. Tell him the truth. Let's stop this before it gets any further out of hand.

Jarod, apparently oblivious to the air of strain, slowly removed the ring from its case and slid it onto Erin's damp and limp finger. It was just a shade loose.

"It's perfect, Sergei. Erin has the long slender fingers to be able to wear it," Jarod said casually. "Thank you, Sergei."

Erin had to speak up. "Yes, thank you, it's very lovely, but I really can't accept—"

Jarod's fingers dug into her shoulder just as Sergei interrupted her. "Don't worry, Miss McCabe. The ring rightfully belongs to Jarod."

Belongs to Jarod? What kind of a game were they playing? But if she opened her mouth in protest again, her only sound would be a scream. Jarod's warning viselike grip was becoming painful.

I'm going to go home a cripple, she thought mournfully. First he half shattered her collarbone; now he was working on her shoulder. . . . And she could feel the terrible weight of the ring.

Sergei suddenly stood, putting an end to the conversation. "Come. We shall all play tour guide and take Miss McCabe via the metro to Red Square. She really must see it by night."

"I would enjoy that," Erin murmured, "but it's really not necessary for you all to ruin your evening. You work all day. I know my way from the hotel to Red Square. I was intending to go to the square to see the changing of the guard at midnight anyway."

Suddenly she felt the strangest tension. Nothing was said, nothing was done. But this time she was sure an exchange passed peculiarly between Jarod and Sergei. It was subtle; it was controlled. But it was there. Did Gil, too, look strange? She was imagining things. Mahoney even looked as if he waited for something, someone to speak.

It was Jarod who spoke. "Erin and I had been intending to see the square tonight, Sergei; it will be pleasant to go together."

No, Erin thought, *we* hadn't been intending to see the square; I had intended to be alone.

"Lovely," Sergei intoned. "Let us go."

The metro was beautiful. Not a gum wrapper or cigarette butt marred the floor. Exquisite chandeliers hung from the arched ceilings, and fine art adorned the walls. A speck of graffiti or garbage could not be found. "Art," Sergei explained, "belongs to the people. And we solve the welfare problem here by making a man work for the income he receives from the government. That is how we keep such cleanliness."

Erin nodded with a vague smile. They did seem to have an answer for welfare. But she would take the smut and grime of New York City any day over the microphones and cameras in her room.

Red Square was magnificent at night. With the glow of lights, it truly earned its name. Bunted against the cold and held tight against Jarod's side, Erin viewed the bubbled steeples of St. Basil's, magical and fanciful in the red glow. Snow lay on the ground and small flurries fell. She had never felt quite so strange.

Nor quite so imprisoned. Since the ring incident at Sergei's, Jarod had barely released his hold on her. Bars, she thought. His fingers, hands, and arms were bars . . . bars of steel. She was almost hysterical. His determination to keep her close to him was fantastic, and she was powerless to stop it.

"Midnight approaches," Sergei said with a smile.

And then, as the clock struck and the guards began their chilling goose steps before Lenin's tomb, Erin felt herself swept back behind the others, spun into Jarod's arms in a strange grip, both tender and fierce. She caught one look at the blue intensity of the stormfire in his eyes, and then his lips came down upon hers hard, encompassing, overwhelming.

Erin brought her hands against his chest to push him away. She automatically went rigid against him, but her efforts were futile against the tide of his lashing wave. Her lips were parted, joined, melded to his; the brandishing sear of his tongue was a ravishment of sensual demand, a flame of heat so intense she lost all will, all thought.

The slender hands that had clawed against his chest clung to it now merely to keep her from falling. Only the hand that spanned over the small of her back and that which held her at her nape kept her upright. She was held so close that despite their heavy winter coats she could feel the grinding bone of his hips, the hard muscles of his thighs, all that was unmistakably masculine about him. Her system went to war.

With the red glow of the square bathing them, the night became ethereal. Despite the rigid hold of the fingers that confined her, they moved, caressing, massaging, sending those electric laps of quivering heat along her spine. Jarod's scent swirled around her and around her. She could barely breathe, but each breath was him. Her body buckled; her mind seemed to explode until it was riddled by the wildfire of the red glowing midnight. His lips seemed to move and move and move . . . drawing away her soul . . . turning her blood into something that was alive and hot and racing to a deep secret core of her stomach to knot it with a burning need. And yet the defenses were there, tearing her apart . . . making the flame of desire even more agonizing.

Yet, as if from far away, she realized that with this man she simply responded. Her fingers began to move in little ripples over his chest. Her lips were parted of their own accord; she was seeking to know his mouth, the heady recesses, as he knew hers. She found the opening of his coat . . . of his black velvet jacket, and as flakes of snow fell upon her, she began to know what it was like to feel like a furnace of craving flesh and blood.

And it was a simple kiss in the red glow of midnight.

Midnight madness. . . .

She was oblivious to those around them, oblivious to everything. Beneath only the thin fabric of his shirt she could feel the taut muscles of his chest, and they were alive and vibrant and giving to her touch. She could feel a rampant pounding; and it wasn't just the surge of her heart but his too. A guttural moan sounded, and it had come from him.

"Lord," someone laughed. "If this was an engagement party, I can bet the wedding is going to be something!"

The kiss broke; Jarod seemed just fine, grinning at the taunt from Gil. Erin felt her face flush as red as the square. She wanted to kill him.

Sergei laughed next. "Ahh, Miss McCabe! Please! No embarrassment. Love is universal. Many a woman has found herself caught within the glow of the square. It is not all pageantry and severity, Miss McCabe."

Erin tried smiling, but she was still only standing because of Jarod's support. And she didn't want his support; more than anything, she simply wanted to be away from him, from the responses he elicited, from the panic that would surely come if things went any further.

For once, he seemed attuned to her desires. In a daze she heard him thanking Sergei for the evening, and then she, too, was saying good-bye and expressing her thank yous. A certain amount of strength was returning to her watery legs. She replied graciously to Sergei's comment that they would meet again, accepted a kiss on the cheek from Joe Mahoney and a firm, enveloping handshake from Gil Sayer. His light blue gaze upon her was very kind and very gentle . . . and envious. His voice was a bit throaty. "If you ever need anything, Erin, anything at all, and Jarod isn't available, I'll be there. Call me. For anything."

Erin thanked him and nodded.

"You can pick up the car for me," Jarod interrupted dryly. "I'll just walk Erin to her room and take the metro home. You and Joe came together, right?"

With transportation disposed of, Jarod and Erin began a silent trek for the Rossia. This time, Erin didn't let his long-legged stride keep her quiet long—she knew there would be no talking later. She had to forget that she still quivered from what had transpired between them and had to create a shell as tough as his.

"Jarod—I really can't wear this ring. It simply isn't right. What did Sergei mean that it was yours anyway?"

"The ring is mine," Jarod said briefly. "Don't worry about it."

"I have to worry about it! Jarod, I don't like any of this, and I've about had it! Everyone behaves as if they've seen a ghost when I mention the word midnight, and then when the hour actually comes along, it's as if a full moon came up and you became a werewolf in seconds."

"Werewolf! Miss McCabe, a flatterer you're not."

"Yes, but an animal you are," Erin muttered beneath her breath.

He heard her, and surprisingly, she had struck a chord. He stopped dead, wrenching her around before him. She saw the glistening of crystal fire in his eyes and heard the grate of his teeth as his jawline tightened. An apology formed on her lips; she hadn't really meant it, he simply scared her so that she was compelled to reinforce her wall of defenses.

I should be grateful, Erin thought. I should accept what he has given me, a knowledge that I can respond, will someday respond.

Like him, I should be able to take this for what it is, blink, and forget about it. A simple physical draw between two adults compounded by whatever game it is he's playing.

But she felt somehow terribly, terribly used. Because she knew now that he loved a dead woman, that she was nothing more than a body he had discovered he could enjoy. She was a substitute taken with no more thought than a—

"Animal?" Apparently control had won out over temper. His query was sardonic, his half grin touched his lips. "Perhaps, Miss McCabe. Biologically, we're all animals, aren't we? And I might add, my darling, that if the vixen in you continues to respond to the fox in me, we just might discover how animalistic we both might be."

She felt as if she were sinking again. The world appeared to blacken. His words, spoken with amusement in husky velvet, were somehow a threat.

She had to fight to surface before the panic became engulfing. "I think, Mr. Steele," she enunciated, "that I requested no repeats of that type of performance." Drawing her dignity about her like a cloak, she stepped past him. "Besides," she added over her shoulder, not at all sure where the rush of words came from, "I called you a wolf, not a fox."

His laughter followed her, but didn't ease her nervousness as he caught up in a step and slipped an arm around her waist.

"What was that for, anyway?" Erin demanded, afraid of silence.

"What was what for?"

"You know damned well what I'm talking about. Midnight. As soon as the first strike of the clock sounded . . ."

He was staring at her as they walked and she broke off, unable to continue. But her eyes didn't falter, they challenged his with silver demand.

"You tell me, Erin."

"Oh, Lord," she moaned. "I never do know what you're talking about."

"Don't you?"

"Oh, please, don't start that!"

He shrugged, and she could read nothing in the rugged contours of the face of the tall, powerful man beside her.

"Chalk it up to midnight, then," he murmured, and then conversation between them ceased as they reached the hotel.

As they neared her room Erin began to twist at the ring on her finger. "Listen, Steele," she muttered as he unlocked her door and stepped aside, "I don't understand what the story is with this thing, and I really don't care. But I can't accept it or wear it." Damn! Of all things, the ring wouldn't come off her finger. When Jarod had slipped it on, it had been loose. Now it wouldn't slide over her knuckle.

"Leave the damned thing alone!" Jarod snapped irritably. "It really is mine and it really isn't important." None too graciously, he prodded her inside the open door. For a terrified moment Erin believed he meant to follow her. But he didn't. He handed her the key, and then his voice rose. "Listen, darling, this is all so ridiculous, this hotel bit. Pack tonight and check out in the morning. It will be much more convenient if you simply stay at my place."

Erin opened her mouth in stunned protest, but the narrowing of his eyes reminded her that every word she said would be heard. Why should I play his game, she wondered. But she remained silent and slowly closed her mouth. His fingers feathered over her cheek, leaving shivering, molten flame in their wake, and then he turned to leave her.

Erin watched as his fur-clad broad shoulders disappeared; despite herself she remembered how marvelously trim and sleekly male his body appeared in the well-tailored velvet jacket under his overcoat.

Then she closed the door, and when she would have leaned against it trembling, she reminded herself she could be seen.

She changed by slipping her nightgown over her head before shimmying from her dress. Then she turned out the lights and lay in her bed wide awake, her thoughts racing in a nightmare tempest. There were so many unanswered questions. It was a maze, one ridiculous thing leading to another. But one refrain repeated itself above all others, and it began a pounding screech in her head: I have to get away. I have to get away.

They watched her. Why did they watch her? They saw everything. But who was "they"? Why, why, why?

And she had been so blissfully ignorant. Moving about, shedding her clothing with little thought, bathing.

And then there was Jarod. Dear God, the outrage was such that even now she wanted to scream. She felt violated. How could this be happening?

It wasn't a place to query civil rights, he had warned her. This was normal.

It wasn't normal to her. Long ago she had walked out on humiliation. And now there was this. Things going on that she didn't understand. Fear and humiliation and . . . Jarod's strange effect upon her. Trust me, he had said. And she kept trusting him, even as he manipulated her. Even as she came back to this, lying in the dark, wondering why they watched her, wondering what midnight meant, feeling the darkness close in on her, ready to explode.

It was simple. She had stumbled into an insane asylum, and she was taking the first exit as soon as she could.

She lay there for hours and hours without sleeping, and the panicked beat in her head became louder and louder. She tossed and turned, burned and froze all night. And became very determined to escape this nightmare she found herself caught up in.

Very very early the next morning she went down for coffee. And in her determination, she remembered Gil Sayer's thoughtful offer of help.

With the red tape over the simplest movement in the U.S.S.R., she was going to have to be very careful how she worded her request.

Praying and crossing her fingers, she put through a call to the embassy. Relief made her giddy when Gil answered the phone.

She was never quite sure what she actually said. She managed to convince Gil that although she adored Jarod he could be just a bit overbearing (that was rather easy to get across) and that she needed to slip out to Paris. "You know Jarod," she said cheerfully. "Anything out of line and he's an eagle-eyed worrier! I'd just like to manage to arrange this surprise. I can't let you in on the details yet, but I promise I will!"

It worked, it all worked. Gil came himself to see her to the airport, and she was finally sitting in a craft of the Aeroflot line listening to flight procedures in Russian, German, Spanish, and French.

What went wrong where, she would never really understand. The humming engines suddenly ceased to growl and the plane went still.

She had settled down with a magazine; she looked up to see two grim, uniformed guards coming down the aisle.

They were coming for her. Somehow she managed not to fall apart as they forcefully escorted her off the plane. Her demands were crisp and clear and polite even as she trembled from head to toe. But if she had screamed and cried and pleaded, the results would have been no different. She was politely ignored.

Terror built inside her as she was led to an official-looking vehicle and seated beside a stone-faced guard. It continued to rise as they rode through the streets of Moscow. Where are they taking me? she wondered desperately. Why?

Visions floated through her mind. This was Russia. You weren't necessarily innocent until proven guilty. But guilty of what? Innocent of what? Where the hell were they taking her? Jail? Oh, dear God. . . .

Her imagination began to play havoc with her. She pictured a blindfold, a firing squad. . . . No, no, no, no! Don't be ridiculous, Erin. It is a civilized country. There is just some misunderstanding.

But she felt as if her heart had permanently lodged into her throat as the seemingly never-ending drive continued. Just when she thought she would lose all control and burst into tears, they drove into the driveway of the hotel Rossia.

She thought she would faint with the relief. She wasn't being taken to jail, they weren't going to throw her in front of a firing squad. But neither were they just dropping her off, she realized quickly. Very politely—they really were such wonderful, stone-faced, polite people—the two uniformed men assisted her from the car—and back to her room. A man on either side.

As if I could run, she thought wryly. She felt like laughing as she imagined herself suddenly throwing them both off and bolting down the hall. Sure. Bolting down the hall—and then what? A helicopter would appear out of nowhere, as one always did in the movies, to rescue her.

Tears kept forming in her eyes. As the door to the room she had thought she had just checked out of was cordially opened for her, she made one last attempt with the guards.

"Please . . . spasee ba . . ."

The younger of the two men faltered. He looked confused for a moment, as if struggling for words.

"You wait. Wait. Understand?"

No, she didn't understand at all. But she was ushered into the room. The door was closed behind her and she knew she would find it locked from the other side if she tried to open it, just as she knew that a guard would be hovering on either side of the door.

The tears that had continually threatened finally fell. What on earth have I done?

The deluxe-class room suddenly closed in around her. It wasn't a room anymore; it might as well consist of iron bars.

Get ahold of yourself, Erin, she muttered.

She tried to calmly light a cigarette. Tears were still damp on her cheeks. She had to flick the lighter several times before she could create a flame. Even then her fingers shook so badly she could barely take a drag. She started pacing the room. Time became eternity as she tortured her mind over and over again. Why? Why? Why? And what was going to happen now?

Jarod had been stunned when he tuned into Catherine II and heard first that Erin had planned to run and second that she had been taken off the plane by Sergei's men. He was both furious and alarmed. What did Sergei have on her?

Nothing, probably nothing. Was Sergei in the same quandary he was in? Wondering if Erin was really a suspect, or merely an innocent pawn. Damn! If only he had a few answers. . . .

He couldn't believe she was guilty, but it was still possible. He had to get her back under his control.

He left the computer room and hurried into his office, taking deep breaths and clenching and unclenching his fists as he planned his phone call. Finally he asked his secretary to get him through.

He had to plead an emergency. Hell, it was an emergency. *He* had to be the one watching Erin McCabe; he had to be the one to discover what was happening first. And if she was innocent, she needed to be protected.

That's an emotional response, he reminded himself with impatience. Emotional, but true. . . .

His phone call went through. He heard Sergei's voice and spoke Russian in return.

"What's this, Sergei? I hear you dragged my fiancée off a plane. For what?"

Sergei hesitated a long time. "I think we both know, don't we, Jarod?"

110

"Do we? Did you find anything on her?"

More hesitation. "No."

No. Jarod breathed a long sigh of relief.

"But I think Miss McCabe should remain our guest for a while, don't you, Jarod? We haven't searched her person—"

"Dammit, Sergei!" His indignation was more than acting. "Listen, Sergei, leave her alone. You've got her at the hotel?"

"Yes."

"I'll be right there. You can't really suspect her of anything, and damn it all, Sergei, she's *my* fiancée. I'll take care of things, I promise you."

"Jarod," Sergei replied slowly, "I havn't even had a chance to speak with her yet."

"Christ, Sergei! Trust me, will you? I told you, I'll take care of things. She'll be with me."

Jarod prayed silently as he waited.

"Make sure you keep her, Jarod. You do seem to be having problems with this woman to whom you are . . . engaged."

"I'll handle things," Jarod promised grimly.

He hung up the receiver and drummed his fingers on the desk. A second later he had his secretary putting through more phone calls.

An entire pack of half-smoked cigarettes littered the ashtrays. She had cried, she had sat in shell-shocked silence. And now she was pacing the room again, trying not to cry again, ready to scream, beat on the walls, or tear her hair out.

The door finally opened and then she heard his voice. Husky, velvety, authoritative. And for the first time since meeting him, the sound filled her with abject gratitude.

Jarod. Oh, thank God! When she so desperately needed him, Jarod had come for her.

"Oh, Jarod!" she gasped as she saw him, his tall frame and undeniable presence an aura of power and security that overwhelmed her.

But she caught her words in her throat. His eyes as they caught hers were pure blue ice; she had never seen the rugged contours of his face more grim. She swallowed and stood silent as he came to her, gripping her hand in a vise of frigid steel.

"Jarod, what did I do? What's going on? Why—"

"Just shut up and go along with everything," he hissed quietly.

Erin could do nothing but nod, and realized that he had not come alone. Joe Mahoney was with him and one of the secretaries from the dinner at Sergei's the night before. (Had that been less than twenty-four hours ago? It felt like years.)

And there was a third man, dressed in the robes of a priest. He positioned her beside Jarod, then began speaking in Russian. He paused and glared at her, and Jarod tightened his grip on her hand.

"Say yes," he whispered in another hiss.

Erin nodded, forming a yes that didn't create a sound.

Jarod said something; the strange ritual continued.

Not even Joe Mahoney would meet her eyes. The entire proceeding was tense and cold and miserable. It seemed the Russian man would go on speaking interminably.

She could only lay it down to the shock of the situation that it took her so long to realize they were going through a mock marriage ceremony, but it wasn't until Jarod took her hand and slipped a plain gold band over the diamond that she did understand. By then it made no difference. She hadn't been in a jail, but she had been just as surely held in a nightmare. Whatever ruse he had constructed to free her from this terror of not knowing, of waiting, of being scared half to death was fine.

And then it all ended. Jarod made a quick, terse phone call. The two guards deserted her door. She was so relieved she felt as if she were intoxicated, stumbling, weak.

"Thank you," she managed to gasp to Jarod, still grim, still meeting her with his glacial stare. She didn't care. "Oh, thank you. I know you've wanted me out of the country—I'll go. I don't know what I supposedly did, but I'm very grateful. I'll oblige you and go immediately."

He just kept staring at her, so Erin kept talking, her words gushing out like a waterfall. "I really appreciate everything. I know how terribly annoying this mock marriage must have been. I realize it will cause you a great deal of embarrassment, and again, all I can say is thank you and that I'll never trouble you again."

He clenched his hand around her wrist; she almost screamed out. "Don't be ridiculous," he grated close to her ear in a sizzling whisper that made her hot and then cold and clammy again, a ripple of fear and electricity raging along each vertebra of her spine. "Shut up before someone hears you. You're not going anywhere—not until it's convenient for me to take you. You little fool! Did you really think I could take you from the Soviets with theatrics? That marriage was no mockery, madam. You just became Mrs. Jarod Steele."

VI

The building was old, but the apartment had been done in a contemporary style. The downstairs consisted of a kitchen—large and airy, bright and inviting with soft yellow tiles—a formal dining room, a music room, and a living room or salon that reminded her of a friend's ranch house in Denver. There was a warm brick fireplace, a cowhide rug over earthen tile, and a couch in leather with complementing chairs beside it. The drapes were in mellow orange and beige, the coffee table was hewn from maple. As yet, she hadn't seen the upstairs.

Despite his hard demeanor, apparently Jarod wasn't completely immune to the depth of her shock. From the impromptu wedding he had brought her here; he had placed her before the fireplace and stoked up a flame. He had made coffee, and she could dimly appreciate that the coffee was excellent.

From nervous emotion which had left her stuttering word after word in shaky quivers, she had gone completely still. Cold seemed to have invaded her extremities; she was numb. Even her mind felt numb. She hadn't said a word since they had entered the apartment. She now sipped her coffee jerkily, as if she were a mannequin performing a task.

Finally she managed to open her mouth, and her single word was an agony of torment and confusion. "Why?"

He straightened from the fireplace, watched her as he picked up his mug of coffee, took a sip, returned it to the maple table, and took one of the chairs beside the couch. His glare was cool, distant, and yet probing. With elbows casually upon the arm rests, he folded his hands together, the forefingers straight, idly held beneath his chin.

"Because Ivan Shirmanov was arrested last night."

"Who?" Erin said blankly, a frown creasing her brow with further bewilderment.

"Ivan Shirmanov, the Intourist guide who picked you up at the train station."

"For what?"

"Treason."

If she had been cold before, she was colder now. Breathing seemed so terribly difficult. "But what on earth has that to do with me?" she demanded, barely keeping her tone from becoming a screeching wail.

"Perhaps nothing," Jarod replied, his eyes still watchful and yet strangely distant. "Any tourist with whom Ivan made contact in the last week is being questioned."

"You mean they were just going to question me?"

At his nod Erin rushed on. "Then why the wedding? Why? I have nothing to hide! Why didn't you just explain things to me? I could have handled myself if I just understood what was going on."

"Erin." His interruption was quiet—too quiet. It held a razor's edge. He hadn't moved, and yet she had the uncanny feeling that if she were to rise he would pounce upon her in a split second. His condemning and unyielding stare was fast wearing on her nerves, but she still fell silent at his statement of her name.

"I have certain friends within the KGB. And a few . . . other . . . ways of knowing things. I don't think the Russians would have listened politely and let you go. They have reason to believe you might be a spy."

"What?" It wasn't really spoken; it formed on her lips.

He raised a cryptic brow and smiled. "That surprises you?"

"Oh, please! Dear God, don't start that stuff on me now!" Erin exclaimed, her voice rising hysterically. She tried to set her mug down; the liquid spilled all over the table. Jarod finally rose to haunch down beside her and help her sop it up with his handkerchief.

"Don't, don't!" Erin hissed. "I'll get it." But as she tried to wrest the handkerchief from his hand, she dumped the remaining coffee over his sleeve.

He rather painfully went still, staring at her with resignation and reproach. "Damn! You really are an occupational hazard."

"Oh, go to hell!" Erin spat out, tossing the handkerchief down.

"How can you worry about a coffee spill at a time like this! Talk to me! Tell me what the hell is going on!"

He stood again, tight features portraying a tense and controlled anger as he jerked out of his jacket. "All right, Erin. We'll take this at face value. You don't know a thing. But information is coming into and leaving the country—all linked by ciphers indicating that you might be involved in espionage."

"Me! Ciphers!"

"Codes, Erin!" he snapped, ripping away his tie and working on the buttons of his shirt. "Key codes—numbers—easily passed. A sign, a word, a motion. The key that links everything else together. They think you might have been leaving the country with that key."

Erin gasped. "I wasn't!"

He said nothing else at the moment, but started up the short staircase to the second level, his chest bare, his stained clothing left upon the tile where it had fallen. He reappeared a moment later, buttoning up a new and crisply ironed shirt. His attention was focused on his dressing. For a moment Erin felt as if she weren't even there. He was getting ready to leave, she realized, and she was still floundering in darkness.

"Jarod!" Erin stood with hands clenched tightly at her sides. "What information? Please! Talk to me. I swear to God I don't know what's going on. I still don't understand why we had to go through that ceremony."

He continued to button his sleeves, staring at her coldly. "I don't know what the information is yet. I'm going to have to keep working with Catherine to try and break the code. There was only one way for me to protect you and watch you myself—diplomatic immunity. As long as a country is among the so-called civilized, foreign ministers cannot be detained or searched. Nor can their wives."

Erin sank back to the couch. "Oh, God," she murmured.

She felt him as he paused behind her, shrugging into a fresh jacket. "I don't suppose you could help me with that code?"

It was the finishing straw. They were in a mess which hadn't even fully registered in her mind yet and he was still going on about codes.

Her fingers curled around the empty mug, she threw it against the fireplace with a flaming rage, rising and swirling to face him. "What do I have to do to convince you?" she grated. "Son of a bitch, Steele!

You have to be worse than the Russians, worse than the KGB—or else you should be with them."

His face went white beneath the tan, his hands shot out over the back of the sofa for her wrists.

Not my wrists, Erin thought desperately, not my wrists.

"Don't ever talk to me like that again," he muttered darkly, his icy eyes suddenly searing. "Or else I will be sorely tempted to turn you over to the real KGB—and Siberia is still cold, lady. Very, very cold."

She couldn't even answer him, she didn't really hear him. My wrists, she thought, my wrists. . . . Panic took hold of her, she felt the loosening of his hold and she twisted to strike out with animal fear, catching him squarely across the cheek.

The sharp sound, the red staining of his flesh, brought Erin back to a modicum of control and reason. She watched with horror as emotions filtered through his eyes; as his facial features, already tight, hardened muscle by muscle. For a wild second she was terrified that he would retaliate, and she hadn't even meant to strike him—he couldn't know what he had done.

But he didn't retaliate. He blinked once, fathomless. Cold blue ice reigned, and he took a step backwards.

"I have to leave," he said simply. "Please do us both a favor and sit tight here today. The kitchen is fairly well stocked, there are all kinds of books and magazines upstairs in my room. Towels are in the hallway closet if you want a shower. I'll be back about six."

Erin swallowed sickly. She wanted to apologize; she didn't think it would make any difference, she couldn't explain. But more than anything, she didn't want him to leave, not yet. She didn't know what was going to happen.

"Wait, Jarod, please!" she murmured. He lifted a brow to her and she awkwardly continued. "What do we do now? I mean, you said that marriage was real. When will I be able to get out? How do we go about getting out of this?"

He paused, hesitating a second. "I'm afraid it will be a while before I can get you out of the country. This is all getting sticky. We can jeopardize everything if you attempt to waltz out now, and I won't have my position jeopardized." He shrugged. "When you are back in the States, you can arrange for a divorce. It shouldn't be too difficult."

117

Oh, God, Erin thought desperately. Oh, God, oh, God, oh, God. She had to swallow again to speak, and even then her voice was as weak as she felt her legs becoming.

"How soon do you think that will be?"

His reply was another shrug. "Two months? I'm not really sure."

Her knees gave. Thank God she was still by the couch.

Her reaction irritated him. "Listen, Erin, I'm really sorry I so inconvenienced you by saving your neck. But you will have to be inconvenienced. What is at stake here is far more a priority than the leisure and working life of a model—even Erin McCabe."

Steele, Erin thought, hysteria rising within her. My name just became Steele. But he certainly didn't seem to register that fact. Of course not, it was only a part of the game plan. He certainly didn't really consider her his wife.

An icy strength suddenly returned to her veins. She tilted her head to look at him, silver flashing in her eyes. "I wasn't thinking only of myself, Jarod, believe it or not. I do appreciate what you've done—I realize you can't possibly run around marrying all your suspects. I'm sorry for what this may cause you—I'm a divorcée already. A bit notorious. A marriage to and then divorce from me can hardly be advantageous to your career."

He blinked, and his blink hid something, a streak of emotion, that she almost caught. But it was gone. "Don't worry, Erin. I was never the material for a presidential candidacy anyway. And no, I can't marry every suspect, but you needn't feel overly obligated. I didn't particularly do it for you, but because I *will* get to the bottom of Project Midnight."

Cold, hard, to the point. Why waste time on feelings? He had never pretended any, unless a certain desire, another "occupational hazard," could be stretched and called emotion.

"Project Midnight?" she heard herself say.

"Umm," he murmured, watching her. "Perhaps I'll tell you about it someday."

He turned then, striding for the door.

"Jarod!" she called again.

He turned to her once more, impatience showing.

"What . . ." She had to moisten her lips. "What am I supposed to do for two months . . . here . . ." Her voice trailed away.

"Do you knit?" he inquired politely.

118

"No."

"Then I suppose you have plenty of time to learn." He sighed suddenly.

When he turned to leave once more, she didn't call him back.

It was strange being in Jarod's apartment. She remained before the fire at first, smoking cigarette after cigarette, rising only to refill her coffee cup until she had drained the pot. All she managed to do was make herself more nervous.

And she still couldn't believe all that had happened; everything was so much worse than she had ever believed could be possible. The enigma had deepened, only now the enigma had a name, Project Midnight. Somehow she had become a player in a high-stakes game, and she hadn't even known she had ever rolled the dice.

She had twisted furiously at her bracelets subconsciously, then realized she was also twisting at the mysterious diamond and the gold band that encircled her finger above it. I'm married to him, she thought incredulously. But the fact had no substance; it simply wasn't credible. She couldn't be Mrs. Jarod Steele; Jarod Steele was a hard man she would never understand.

"I'm surprised he left me alone in his apartment," she murmured bitterly. "There mustn't be any family jewels around; surely I would steal them!"

Two months! The thought hit her with a walloping panic. Tears filled her eyes; she had a decent life back in New York; good work, good friends. But here she was, stuck in the home of a man who seemed to despise her the majority of the time. She couldn't possibly stay here with him.

But she would have to. She was supposed to be his wife—was his wife. He would never let her go. Her feelings meant nothing next to Project Midnight. She had heard of marriage for money, but never for a cipher!

I can't stay here, I really can't. I don't believe this, any of this, it can't be real. . . . But it was real. She could see the warm earth tones of the living room, feel the leather of the couch, hear the crackle of the fire. . . .

Lost and overwhelmed, Erin finally began pacing the apartment. The music room drew her, and she idly ran her fingers over the keys of the grand piano. The chords sounded ominous and she left off.

In the far corner of the room was an instrument that somewhat resembled a guitar. It was large and deeply bowled. She plucked out a chord, and the sound was sweet. A balalaika, she thought, frowning as she strained to remember the display at one of the Kremlin museums. It was an old Russian instrument.

She jumped half a mile when she heard the ringing of a phone. It was several seconds before she realized she should answer it. Then it occurred to her that she had no idea where the phone was.

She forced herself into action and raced for the living room. No phone. Of course, idiot, I've been sitting in there for hours—I would have seen the phone.

The kitchen. It was, she was sure, sitting on the overpass counter.

She was right, but by the time she reached the receiver, the ringing had been going on for quite some time and she was panting and breathless.

"Hello?"

"Erin?" It was Jarod's voice; it was sharp. "Are you all right?"

She took a deep breath—he had almost sounded concerned. "Yes, I'm fine. I—uh—couldn't find the phone."

"Oh." He fell silent for so long that she began to believe they had been cut off.

"Jarod? Are you there?"

"Yes. I called to apologize for . . . our argument."

She wondered from his use of words if she were supposed to be careful of what she said on the phone. "It's all right," she said softly.

"Things will work out," he told her. "I left you rather abruptly. I'm going to take off early and we'll go out to dinner." He hesitated a moment again. "Feel at home in the apartment."

Did that mean she shouldn't fear cameras or mikes? Probably; he had that special immunity, and she sincerely doubted he would allow such an intrusion into his life no matter where he was.

"I—I will."

"Be ready about five. We have a lot to discuss."

"Yes," Erin murmured.

He hung up without a good-bye. Erin very slowly returned the receiver to its cradle.

The apology from him had been startling at the very least. It hinted of something human within the burning ice. Then she started to shiver again. She was better off a bitter enemy of the man. Friendship could mean catastrophe.

She was his wife now and destined to play the role.

She slowly looked up from the phone. There was a clock on the far wall; it was moving past three.

She should have been in Paris in the little pension overlooking Montmartre. Russia should have been behind her. Memories of Jarod Steele should have been fading into a strange past.

After three! If she were going out she had better get moving.

For the first time, she treaded her way up the staircase. There were only two rooms on the second level, an office and a bedroom, also in earthtones . . . deep chocolate drapes matching the bedspread. An array of masculine toiletries stood upon the one handsome dresser. There were no closets, only an old-fashioned wardrobe.

And I'm going to have to live here. What on earth are we going to do? We'll constantly be at one another's throats, she thought miserably.

Surely he would give her the bedroom and take the couch. Don't count on that, she told herself wryly. He wasn't the most gallant gentleman she had ever come across. That wasn't fair either. Whatever his motives, he had a tendency to be there, authoritative, offering certain security, when she discovered she needed him.

But was he really helping her? Or merely assisting her to jump from the frying pan to the fire? She just might have been better off in jail.

No. She was logical enough to realize that, whatever happened between her and Jarod Steele, she was better off with him. She had heard of Americans who had been imprisoned in other countries for years, and she was wise enough to realize she might have been given a long stay in Siberia.

She thought of young Ivan. Treason. She didn't envy him; she felt tremors of terror arcing through her again. She didn't want to think of Ivan. And if she didn't hurry, she wouldn't have time for the one luxury offered her at the moment. A bath. A long hot bubble bath with the supreme luxury of knowing she wouldn't be watched.

Her suitcase sat upon the bed. She discovered as she opened it that the lining was gone. She closed her eyes for a second, and then reopened them. She wouldn't have time to wash her hair, so she clipped it high above her head. And then she reached for her bubble bath and robe. On second thought she raced back to the kitchen. There was wine in the refrigerator—what respectable U.N. delegate would be without it? With a long stemmed glass in her hand, she returned upstairs, ran water in the tub in the spacious bath off the bedroom, poured in a ton of bubbles, sank in the heat, and finally, finally, found that she could begin to relax. . . .

Jarod stared at Catherine's screen, but he wasn't really seeing the information printed. He was chewing at his thumbnail. He stopped in self-disgust. He never chewed his nails.

Catherine couldn't break the cipher. It was a number; the key number, and it made perfect sense that the computer couldn't come up with it. Whoever was supposed to be on the receiving line would have the key number.

He could start trying every possible numerical combination, but numbers were infinite, possible sequences were infinite. . . .

Why the hell had he mentioned Project Midnight to her, he suddenly wondered. They were words that almost everyone recognized, but words neither side ever spoke. They were part of the circle waltz that played on and on, ignored on purpose in the eternal quest for rational diplomacy.

Because she isn't guilty, he answered himself, and she deserves some answers. But it would be almost impossible to explain to her the workings of that fragile waltz.

Jarod sighed and rubbed his temples. The code exchanges were taking place at midnight. He knew it; Sergei knew it. Right in Red Square, blatantly before the seat of Soviet power. But none of them knew how.

Last night he had been there. So had Sergei. Nothing tangible had come about.

But Erin couldn't be on the giving or the receiving end. She couldn't have heard anything or seen anything. By making a spectacle of them both, he had seen to that.

But Erin had still been used.

Why did he keep accusing her? he wondered. He knew damned well that she hadn't been guilty. He had been angry; an anger that almost overwhelmed him. She hadn't trusted him; she had tried to slip away from him. She had called another man for help. She had

122

taken him completely off guard, left him feeling like an untrained idiot.

She had forced his hand. He had married her when he had sworn he would never marry again. No one would ever know what that had cost him. He could forget, he could function, he could need; he could even be courteous and charming . . . but marriage was Cara. Gentle Cara with her beautiful, tender smile. The soft voice that was never raised in anger. Rippling fingers that soothed away the tensions of the day. Warm hazel eyes that offered trust and love as she listened to all he said, voiced an opinion, cared to sort the workings of his mind.

He could never call another woman wife. But now he had a wife. That she was a woman he wanted only served to make his sense of betrayal to the beauty of Cara's memory worse.

But at the same time, he felt sorry for her. Erin was nothing like Cara. She was independent, assured, cool as crystal. Her tongue was capable of dagger sharpness; she could draw a cloak of dignity about her that was almost impregnable. She had substance; she could endure. . . . And she was exquisitely beautiful.

She hadn't deserved all that had happened; he was sure of that. Almost sure. And so he had forced the apology, and so he was going to do his best to make it easy for her. It wasn't her fault she had become his wife.

It was Project Midnight. Double-dealing was no new thing; it went on continuously. But this was a case he fully intended to end. Each piece of information imparted to either side was another flame upon the fire; as often as not, the information was exaggerated or blatantly untrue. But the balance of the world's two greatest powers was precarious; neither side ever trusted the motives of the other. And in Project Midnight nuclear armament was involved. Already the secrets passed had created devastating insecurities between negotiators; talks had been delayed, abandoned, now picked up again.

Sergei wanted it stopped, as did he. But distrust and insecurity had already run so deep, they couldn't even accept one another at face value; the waltz continued.

Jarod stared at the screen to see that Catherine was asking him for a command. He shook his head; he had already tried every command he knew.

He should stay and work, but he was beating his head against a brick wall.

I'M GOING HOME, CATHERINE. MAYBE I CAN SOLVE A
FEW PROBLEMS THERE.

He moved to check out of the computer; Catherine displayed a huge

CONGRATULATIONS

"Funny," Jarod muttered a bit bitterly. But he was thinking of Erin as he walked the long hallway, thinking of her the short drive home. He was sure she was a pawn, nothing more, but he was torn between resenting the infinite problems she had caused him and a sorrow that she had been dragged into the whole thing.

And then he was thinking that he still didn't really know. Throughout history the mightiest of kings, princes, and lawmakers had fallen prey to the guiles of a beautiful, innocent face. He could be taking Mata Hari to dinner for all he knew.

He knocked at his door and then scowled at himself with irritation. It was his home. She was the intruder, unwillingly, but still the intruder. He inserted his key in the lock and entered, discovering with a quick scan that she wasn't downstairs. Casting aside his coat he strode quietly up the staircase.

Her suitcase lay open upon the bed, and a soft trickle of water alerted him to movement within the bathroom. Without thinking he walked toward the open door and stopped within its frame.

Her head rested upon the ridge of the deep old-fashioned tub, her eyes closed. Pins held her golden hair in alluring curls above the water, only the tips of certain tendrils dampened. A mist of soft steam rose above the mountains of white bubbles that formed around her. A quarter-full wine glass rested on the rear tile of the tub; its contents had probably induced the relaxed, half smile that tinged her lips. Light tan knee caps were visible above the bubbles, and dark against the clouded mystery of white were the roseate peaks of her breasts. A long slender arm, slick and glistening with the moist heat of the bath, dangled from the side, the diamond and wedding band displayed brilliantly and beautifully against the long manicured fingers that were without doubt the most elegant he had ever seen. Even now the bracelets held her wrists.

Her lashes, darkest honey against her cheeks, were a startling contrast to the creaminess of her complexion. Again, he knew he had never seen such skin before; it was spun silk to touch.

And it was easy, very, very easy to understand why Erin McCabe had become the epitome of elegance, beauty—and sensuality—to millions throughout the civilized world.

Watching her was arousing: the trickle of a droplet of water down the slender white column of her throat, the swell of her breasts, not large, but firm and high and full, tantalizing as her breathing slipped their level lower, higher, lower in the water, the adjustment of a leg, the bubbles sluicing down a slender thigh . . .

She looked like an angel, a creature of ultimate golden beauty, sent to embody all the delights of heaven. No, no woman with a body that promised such earthly delights could be classified as angel. But she was golden and beautiful and so unbelievably perfect and ethereal, surely the loveliness that was the ideal and pride of any god or gods.

He wasn't sure of his feelings for her. They ranged between bitterness and an instinctive protective tenderness. But be she angel or devil, innocent or Mata Hari, he did know one thing. He had never wanted a woman more. And at this particular moment, this particular woman, who was making the liquids of his body rise and steam with the heat of the mist, was his wife.

As if his overwhelming need had actually reached out and touched her, making her aware of his presence, her eyes suddenly flew open wide with alarm. She blinked upon seeing him and sat up. She then realized she had deprived her breasts of the shield of the eternally popping bubbles, and sank back down, trying to appear nonchalant and undaunted while also attempting to swirl the remaining field of misted white around herself.

Despite the feelings gripping him in a surge of intense heat, despite the blood that seemed to rush and pound within his head, he had to laugh at her efforts.

Her eyes closed for a split second of annoyance and she demanded irritably, and a little breathlessly, "What are you doing here?" Her eyes, narrowed against the honey fluff of her lashes, were sheer, glittering silver.

"What am I doing here?" he queried with a brow lifted high. "I live here."

125

"Yes, but you said five—"

He crossed his arms over his chest, leaning against the frame of the door—thoroughly enjoying her determination to wish the situation away.

"I didn't think I needed to stick to an appointment time to enter my own apartment."

She flushed slightly. "You don't, of course, but I didn't mean the apartment, I know it's your apartment, that you come and go . . . I mean the room, I mean I don't mean the room." She finally stopped, drawing a deep breath, her anger partially directed at herself with rueful disdain for her own stuttering. "I mean, don't you think it's rather rude for you to stand there staring at me in the bathtub?"

"Not at all. You're the one who left the door wide open."

"Yes, but—oh, never mind! Would you mind closing the door for me?"

His smile warned her immediately that she had not phrased her wishes correctly at all. Dark lashes half fell to hide amused eyes as he inclined his head as if in acquiescence, and then he very amicably closed the door—with himself inside.

Erin felt a silver shivering race along her spine despite the heat of her bath. That he was amused at her expense again was evident.

But something else was also evident. He wasn't playing games and the rippling lash of needs, fears, and confusions that washed over her in those few seconds of his appearance was engulfing. She wasn't stunned; she was an adult. The tension had sparked between them from the very beginning. But she had never really known what he would expect of their marriage until this minute, until he finally raised his eyelids fully, exposing her to the deepest blue fire she had ever seen. It had always been impossible to know what he really felt. She had always thought his passion, his tenderness, his slightest move a calculation, easily perpetrated for his own motives.

But there were no motives now. Just the two of them and a message that burned blue fire, caught and held, challenged, demanded.

He didn't move. He had leaned against the door, arms once more crossed over his chest, his brow still slightly raised as he waited, apparently casual, apparently negligent.

If only she could fight her awareness of him. The scent that came to her now, clean, woodsy, and crisp; the sight of his fingers, long and lean, idly tapping against the rough texture of his tailored jacket; his face, lean, contoured, craggy, but like his scent, all very individual, all strong, all virile, all male were assailing her.

I can't, she thought, the panicked warning washing over her, I can't, I can't. . . .

She struggled to speak in a level voice. "That wasn't quite what I had in mind," she muttered dryly. "But since you wish to be inside, perhaps you would hand me a towel and I can then be outside."

He shrugged, secured a huge terry towel from an ornate lion's head rack, and stepped toward her. But he held the towel just out of her reach.

She knew, without a second's thought, that there would be just one way of securing it. Gritting her teeth, Erin stood. But as she rose from the water, a new heat flared through her body. It was as moist and steaming as that which she had left behind; it caused her to quiver even as she reached out.

Instead of handing her the towel, Jarod slipped it around her shoulders and used it to pull her close against his chest. The rough feel of his jacket fabric against her bare breasts was so startling and sensual that her knees threatened to give beneath her.

"Jarod—" she gasped out.

"We are married," he murmured, stilling her protest.

"But . . ." They both knew all the buts. The main one being that the marriage was a fraud, a fraud Erin sensed that he resented. He was in love with the wife he had lost. Yet even that full knowledge did little for her now. She could feel the span of his hand, warm and firm over the towel against the small of her back, the light touch of his finger upon her cheek. "Your suit," Erin murmured stupidly, bringing her hands between them.

"I've ceased worrying about my suits around you," he returned softly. The soft caress of his fingers left her cheeks, threaded into her hair, where he dislodged the pins, sending the cascade of shimmering damp gold around her shoulders.

Damn, was she beautiful. A silver-eyed mystery. Slender but so enticingly curved, so warm and alive. He allowed his hand to wind into the sleek softness of her hair, tilting her head back. And he kept staring into her silver eyes. Sun and moonlight, silk and satin, tanned and rose cream, igniting to a furnace beneath his touch.

He pressed her closer, pulling her to his hips, letting her feel just what she did to him. And as he spurred his own desires into spiraling heights with the intimate pressure of her, he dropped the towel, availing his hands of the sleek line that was her back, the trim contour that was her waist.

She quivered without protesting; the silver that clashed with blue fire misted until just the lure of her eyes was irresistably sensual. And then he touched his lips to hers. They were wet and full and parted, waiting, knowing. Her tongue readily met his. He slipped his hands low to her buttocks, fluttering lightly over them, moving around to course smoothly over her lower abdomen, pause, relishing the deep curves of her hips, rising high to cup and caress the full, swelling mounds of her breasts.

His own fevered need kept him momentarily from realizing that she had gone dead still. The warm darting tongue that had so eagerly, so beguilingly, intoxicatingly responded to the seeking quest of his had suddenly retreated; the sweet pressure of her golden creamy body attempted a retreat.

"Jarod, no!" she shrieked, and the sound of her voice and the pressure of her hands took him off guard. It was with shock that he stared at her at first; shock because it had all been there. A need and desire to soar fully to match his own.

"Erin," he began in soft confusion, his touch going very gentle. Her silver eyes were wild; they were a storm of tempest he couldn't discern. "Erin—" he began to repeat.

"No!" she hissed firmly, wrenching from him with a spinning force that swept her past him at such a speed that his balance was lost; his customary agility deserted him.

He careened into the bubblebath before he could right himself, and then the explosive degree of his desire fused with the deepest fury he had ever experienced. He was livid. He was out of control.

It took him only split seconds to regain his balance, to stride after her with cougarlike speed despite his thoroughly drenched clothing.

She saw his eyes, and panic lit hers. She attempted to wrench the spread from the bed to clothe herself. "Wait, Jarod, please—"

But there was no mercy to be found in his eyes. He continued after her despite her hands raised in supplication before her.

"A 'no' at the beginning would have been honored, Erin," he hissed, his approach slow but as sure as that of a cat circling its prey. "But not after that, honey. I'm not sure what Erin McCabe is accustomed to getting away with, but madam, you don't play that way with me."

He was coming close, too close. She had wanted to explain, but the terror hit her. It was blinding; it ruled away any form of logic or common sense. She knew that even now Jarod would never hurt her, but the thought simply failed to register over her overwhelming terror.

She struck out, catching him first fully against one cheek, then flailing madly with her nails clawing.

"Dammit, you little bitch—"

She was absolutely no match for Jarod. It took him two seconds to duck beneath her wild blows and catch her in her midriff with his shoulder, another second to send her sprawling backwards upon the bed with his own weight hovering over her.

And then, even as she still struggled in half insanity to rise, he caught her wrists in the iron vise of his fingers.

"Oh, dear God!" she shrieked then, falling still in a horrified numbness. "Oh, dear God, please, Jarod, not my *wrists*!"

He, too, went dead still, stunned and touched to the very core of his being by the pathetic depth of the raw pleading and beseechingness in her voice. Silent tears raced down her cheeks like the cascade of a waterfall from her tightly clenched eyes and she quivered against him in gigantic spasms.

"Please!" she gasped again, "oh, please . . ."

He released her instantly, leaning beside her, all anger toward her eradicated in a fury against the unknown he was slowly discovering. He touched her cheek very very tenderly, his fingers wiping away the moisture. She had almost left him; her eyes were so glazed and blank. With calmness, with gentleness—but with unbreachable firmness—he spoke. "Erin, you are going to talk to me. *Now*."

VII

She couldn't say or do anything. It was a ridiculous scene; she naked, quaking upon the bed, Jarod stretched beside her in his drenched tailored suit.

He wasn't going to hurt her. She had always known that no matter what the provocation, he would hold back. But just as surely, he would demand answers, as he was demanding them now, and there would be no place to hide. But she couldn't talk to him. God! Of all people, she couldn't to him. Her past was locked away. She didn't want to open the Pandora's box of the past. She couldn't. A paralyzing force had enveloped her. She knew she breathed, she knew she saw dimly through a shroud of mist, but his voice penetrated through it. "Erin."

Still she couldn't move. And then she felt him reach for her arm. Cold permeated her; the numbness, the paralysis, were too much to fight. The effort would be futile. His grasp was careful, very gentle, but like his voice, firm. He soothed her palm with a fingertip. Erin barely noticed; she had slipped away somewhere, aware that she waited, but not aware of what she waited for.

"Something went very wrong somewhere," he said softly, moving to circle his fingers around a bracelet.

Not there, Erin thought vaguely. The bracelets were memories of what was good. . . .

Apparently Jarod realized quickly that the root of her problem lay in something far deeper than a penchant for favorite jewelry. He was silent for several seconds as he lay beside her. And then she heard his voice again, a crisp sheath of whispered velvet. Persistent. "Something happened with someone. Was it your husband?"

She didn't speak, she didn't nod. She still couldn't focus on his

130

rugged features; she couldn't, oh, dear, no, couldn't, raise her eyes to meet that deadly icefire of his.

Yet somehow he had received an affirmative answer. She heard and felt the rasp of his indrawn breath; the shudder that swept his form in an infinite wrath.

"I'll kill him," he said tersely.

He sounded as if he meant it. That thought finally broke through the perimeters of her mind. Jarod's anger was all the more deadly because it was always so controlled. But it wasn't an icy wrath; it was a flame.

"No," she managed, though little sound came from her lips. "It wasn't exactly Marc . . . and I was as much to blame."

"I don't believe that." Erin felt his touch as he removed her bracelets. "The bracelets really aren't any mystery, are they?" It was a question that didn't require an answer. "But you're panicked by having your wrists held. . . ."

She began a slow descent back toward reality from the corner of her refuge as he gently held her hands before him, then very tenderly kissed her wrists one at a time. He moved away from her, shedding his wet jacket.

Her eyes were still dazed, he thought, and yet she was coming back to him. He was struck afresh by the purity of her beauty as she lay there, silver eyes wide, liquid and vulnerable in her perfect stillness. Her hair appeared as the softest web of spun gold, the curls like a riot of sun beneath the fine sculpture of her pale face. Her lips were slightly parted as she breathed, an effort that created an almost indiscernible heave of her bare breasts, high and coral-rose-tipped above a slender torso in which the delineation of each rib created haunting shadows, falling low to the inward and equally haunting hollow of her abdomen. She was slender, so very slender, but he had never fully realized that her slenderness could hold such alluring, rounded, and beguilingly angled shapeliness.

One knee was slightly lifted and tilted inward; her entire length was golden and glistened flawlessly. He ached to reach out and touch her, feel the silk of that skin, the softness of her secret places, the touch of her shimmering hair.

His entire body was rigid with instinctive reaction to his senses, but even as he wanted her with a torture that was agony, he knew that this moment was fragile, infinitessimally delicate. He held her

131

future in his hands. She was the embodiment of exquisite loveliness, but all that lay unnurtured within her, her sweet sensuality, untapped passion, could be forever buried if he didn't handle her with the greatest of care. She was as soft and tender and vulnerable as the new petals of a storm-tossed rose. He knew that they had come to a crucial point in her life and that he would have to lead her past it. He held her as he might that storm-tossed flower, and he knew that his greatest restraint and most gentle moves could bring the most beautiful and softest of roses to full bloom.

He gathered her into his arms, holding her, soothing back her straying curls of gold with gentle fingers that hinted of comfort, not passion.

He should have known, he thought belatedly. He should have realized she harbored a terrible hurt and fear. She was not coy, not a game-playing temptress. All that she had ever offered him had been real; the passions, the sensuality, the warmth, the giving he had sensed within the heat and natural rhythms of her body against his.

The temptress in her was warm and alive. This golden seductress was a woman born to love naturally . . . beautifully.

None of it had ever been a lie.

At that moment, nothing existed for Jarod except the two of them. The reasons they had come together, the life he lived, suspicions, doubts, and mistrusts ceased to be. They simply weren't relative to the fragile now.

He didn't even stop to think of his own feelings, to question them, or ponder them. He didn't think of love; his was a deep-rooted humanity. And he was outraged. The care of this exquisite golden beauty had become his. She bore the title of his wife. He craved to have her as his lover as well; he wanted to purge her wounds.

Again he picked up a slender wrist with infinite tenderness, pressing his lips against it.

"If you don't release things, Erin," he said softly, "they grow and they fester inside. I can't make you, but I would very much like you to talk to me."

She was silent for a moment, her golden head bowed low against his chest. He waited. It was a tiny movement, very tiny, but she nodded.

Standing up, with her in his arms, he swept the cover from the bed and wrapped it around her. He made his way down the stairs, cradled her into the corner of the couch, and stoked the dying fire. He disappeared into the kitchen and returned with two glasses of wine, pressing hers into her fingers, then lifting her to bring her back against his body again. He asked nothing of her now and she knew it; his desire was simply to be there, to offer safe harbor, to give her the much-needed security she craved.

"Were you in love with him?"

Erin nodded again. She took a long sip of her wine, gratefully feeling the liquid wash away even more of the numbness.

"I lost a fiancé once when I was very young," she murmured. "I hadn't believed I would ever love again." She came up with a dry little smile. "My bracelets were a gift from Jodie. They were just very special, and they became my trademark. It always amused me a little to know that people thought them such a mystery."

"Go on, Erin," Jarod prodded softly.

"I . . . I had learned about loving from Jodie. Our marriage was all planned out, our values were the same . . . old-fashioned, I guess."

"You were never lovers?"

She blushed and bit her lip. "No . . . Jodie died before . . ." Her voice trailed away and came back thinly. "And then Marc came along. I was very flattered that he should care for me, so much to insist upon marriage."

"And so you married him very quickly." It was more statement than question, but again Erin nodded against his chest. It wasn't so terribly hard to talk; it was becoming amazingly easy. And it was absurd that a man like Jarod Steele, living by a cold code of principle and efficiency, could offer such understanding and compassion and not turn away. Not be repulsed, but want to understand even more.

And she needed to make him understand; she owed him an explanation. And so far, she had done nothing but give him cryptic half-truths.

"Marc isn't a cruel man," she found herself explaining. "Marc never hurt me—purposely or physically I mean. He . . ." She started chewing upon her lips again. "I think he was disappointed from the start. He was accustomed to worldly women. He had thought for sure I would be one. Until the night of our marriage, I guess he didn't realize—"

"That you were a virgin?"

Erin couldn't meet his eyes. "Yes," she murmured, barely coherently. "As I said, he wasn't cruel, and he didn't intentionally hurt me. But the night was miserable. I . . . I tried to pretend . . . I tried to give the responses he wanted, but all I ever wanted was for it to end. And he just kept assuring me that it would get better."

Her color had risen. It was getting easier to talk, but her explanations still seemed so poor. She started speaking again quickly. "I was touched at first that Marc cared enough about me to be so patient. But I should have known from the beginning. Lord knows, there were enough women around to give me the hints." She finally managed to meet Jarod's eyes. "My being a failure meant little to Marc, because I don't think a day passed when he didn't see another woman. But I never believed the hints. I just kept believing Marc that things would get better, because even though Jodie and I hadn't been together, I had wanted to be with him."

"Erin," Jarod interrupted softly. "There was nothing wrong with you. He simply wasn't the right man." Not a man at all, he thought furiously. "But there's more to this, Erin. I want to know what makes you so terrified to have your wrists held."

She hesitated a long moment, but he allowed her to do so. Again, she started so softly that he could barely hear her. "I didn't believe that Marc saw other women. I . . . I did love him. And I . . . was simply unbelievably naïve. Anyway, I came home after work one day to find a friend of his—another photographer I had worked with once or twice—drinking brandy in my living room. I was surprised, but I assumed Marc had let him in, which he had. I greeted him cordially—and asked him where Marc was. He started laughing and winked at me and told me Marc would be busy for a while. I still didn't get it. I tried to carry on a casual conversation and I offered to make him another drink"—she stopped, took a breath, and rushed on—"and all of a sudden he was behind me, kissing my nape, slipping his arms around me. I was shocked, and I demanded to know where he got the nerve to do such a thing in Marc's own house. He started laughing and said something about what the hell did I think Marc was doing. He accused me of being a tease: he and I both knew damned well Marc wouldn't give a damn. Everyone knew that Marc and I had an open marriage. I was so stunned and incredulous. I was easy prey when he started after me again. But then I started fighting him and he just kept laughing, telling me how he loved my little game, how the fight gave the finale all the more gusto.

"He got me down and he held my wrists and I couldn't break the hold. I'd never been so powerless, so terrified, in my life. And humiliated. He was going to be able to do whatever he wanted to me and my own husband had put me in that position.

"I don't know how long he held me. He thought I was playing all along . . . and so I finally got a chance to kick him. He was so surprised and in so much pain that he released me and . . . and I ran. Out into the street. I went to a friend's house, and I never returned. I did talk to Marc once after the incident. He couldn't believe that I had ever thought he intended our marriage to include fidelity. I should have known the score."

"Bastard!" Jarod rasped, and she felt the fury within him. His hands had grown tense. With an effort they relaxed, and he smoothed the golden tendrils of her hair against her temple. "And so you're still afraid. . . . Oh Erin, don't be afraid! Your fiancé was more the norm. You were not at fault in any way. You are beautiful and giving, and if Helmsly had had a single iota of sensitivity he would have discovered it all. And I guarantee you, Erin, any normal man would cherish you and want to kill before allowing another man to touch you." He broke off a bit gruffly and enveloped her into his arms.

"You poor thing," he murmured against her hair, his whisper then changing to assure her that everything was all right, that things would be okay, that she should cry if she needed to.

But she didn't cry. She shivered and shivered until the shivering stopped. Outside the day had become night; only the warm orange glow of the fire touched them, and it was warm, and it was secure, as was the feel of the arms of the man around her.

And as he held her, the outrage continued in his mind. He didn't speak the thought aloud again, but he was certain that if he were ever to meet the man—or men! Helmsly was guilty of emotional cruelty, the other of attempted rape—who had taken such a tender crystalline beauty and made a mockery of the innocent and loving sensuality she had offered—he would surely be tempted to kill . . . or cripple. . . . At the very, very least, rearrange a nose and jawline.

He merely held her for a long, long time. And then he tilted her

135

chin upward, bringing her silver stare to meet his. He should leave her alone, he thought briefly. If he were really honorable, he would leave her alone. But he wasn't quite that honorable. He was a man, and the vital male within was roaring that the wrong done to her needed to be purged.

And it was just as true that the real crime would be to leave her believing that her sensuality was anything but extremely natural and healthy.

"Erin," he said softly. "You're very beautiful. I don't believe I've ever seen a more beautiful woman. A sexual experience between a man and a woman should be just as beautiful—and can be. I want to make love to you, I want you to know that it can be wonderful. But I won't force you. You angered me before because I didn't understand. I believe you know exactly what you do to me, and I believe a part of you is very eager to learn exactly what I can do to you. But the choices are all yours."

She returned his stare, seeking something in his eyes. Then she seemed to find a new strength. Wrapping the bedspread about herself she pushed away from him and stood, walking to the fireplace.

"I . . . I don't know what I expected you to want from this marriage. I suppose I did wonder . . . and I am very grateful. I would very much like to please you—"

"Dammit!" he suddenly roared out. "I don't want you in my bed out of gratitude, woman!"

She felt him spring to his feet, felt him behind her even before he whirled her to face him. But her explanation was already rising to her lips as her eyes widened to the confrontation with his.

"No, no!" she murmured vehemently. "That wasn't quite what I meant." Suddenly she felt herself blushing to the roots of her hair. "You know I don't mean that," she said very softly. "I know you must know that I respond to you . . ." She left off, not floundering from his piercing stare, but chewing worriedly upon her lower lip.

"You're thinking that our marriage is meaningless."

She straightened suddenly, and her chin tilted. He was very certain he had never seen finer dignity, heard such sweet honesty.

"No, Jarod. I'm fully aware that undying love and devotion are not the necessary ingredients for an affair. And I don't condemn a physical relationship between consenting adults. I . . . I want to go to bed with you."

She slipped from his grasp and stared at the fire again. For a second she was silent, then she glanced to him with a rueful smile, then back to the fire.

"I have a friend, Jarod, a very lively and refreshing woman named Casey. She's great. So open and honest it's sometimes shocking! But I envy Casey often. She can tell me how very much she enjoys a man she cares about in bed. She takes great pleasure from receiving pleasure and from giving it in return.

"Jarod, I'm afraid that you're going to find me a tremendous disappointment. I never got a thing out of sex; it was painful and humiliating. I can tell you would want a woman to give all and receive all. I—I can't even imagine the . . . ecstasy Casey tells me about."

He was so relieved he wanted to laugh, but he didn't dare. He slipped his hands over her shoulders instead, smiling softly down into her luminous silver eyes. He lowered his lips to hers, barely touching them, allowing the tip of his tongue to circle the line of her lips, then bringing that moist inducement along her cheek to the hollow of her throat, to the lobe of her ear, his breath warm as he explored the cavity within.

She began to quiver again, but it wasn't with the horror of memory.

He pulled away to look at her. Her breathing was quickened and labored; her lips, moist from his kiss, remained parted slightly. Her form was very pliant against his.

"Did you enjoy that?" he asked with a tender smile.

She moistened her lips with the tip of her tongue; they seemed to dry so quickly. "Yes," she murmured huskily. "But you know that, you know that I respond to you. Its just that at a point I always panic." She lowered her eyes. "The feeling is there with you, Jarod, I just—"

"Then trust the feeling," he told her. He bent and scooped her into his arms. "Trust me, Erin, and I will move very slowly. I will stop whenever you wish, but if you will let me, I'll try to show you just how ultimately beautiful it can be. I will take from you, but I'll give you that ecstasy you've been envying."

She suddenly found she couldn't speak. She could only meet the incredible fiery hold of his eyes. She nodded. He had received his answer.

His strong sure strides moved once more to take them both back up the staircase they had descended what seemed like years before.

He laid her carefully on the bed, unwrapping the spread from about her as if she were a gift of precious and delicate crystal. He leaned over to brush his lips with hers. "How are you doing?" he murmured huskily.

"Fine," was her whispered reply.

He straightened, holding her eyes, and undid the buttons on his cuffs and down the front of his shirt. For a second Erin was sure he would neatly hang up the shirt. But he mumbled, "What the hell," more to himself than to her, and the shirt hit the floor in a rumpled heap.

Excitement tensed within Erin even as she watched him disrobe. She lay still, just as he had left her, shivering within. His physique was prominent in her memory before he undressed. It was so easy to recall the simple pleasure she had felt awakening in his couchette on the train.

He was so beautifully built, so sturdy and supple, sinewed and yet lean. She longed to reach out and touch the rippling muscles of his shoulders and arms. And she prayed that she could.

He cast off his shoes and socks, keeping her gaze locked to his and adding a buildup of the tension that was tangible within the room. He kept his hold on her eyes as he stepped from his pants and briefs, watching her reaction to this new view of his long, long legs, hard thighs, strong and well-shaped calves thickly netted by coarse dark hair. Tantalizing tufts of hair as enticing to touch as that which splayed across his chest, narrowed and disappeared at his waist, returned thickly again low on his abdomen, creating a fascinating frame for the vital extent of the masculine desire he had controlled so long.

A shuddering shock wave gripped Erin; she was afraid, she was eager. She was amazed and pleased that she could so excite this unique man, and was engulfed by the slow burning fever that was both torturous and delicious as it flamed low in the depths of her abdomen and took wings of flight to slowly spread in a wave of heat.

He lay down beside her, his head propped on an elbow. Unwittingly, Erin's nervous fingers moved to grip the spread closer to her body. He stopped her with a simple touch upon her hands. "No," he said softly, a tender smile curling the corners of his lips. "I

138

wonder if you have any idea of how incredibly beautiful you are."
His words were accompanied by the feather light touch of his fingers
moving along the length of her arm, the silken gold above, the pale,
sensitive ivory beneath.

"That's very nice of you to say," Erin heard herself babble. She
felt compelled to talk, words seemed to trip on her tongue. "I mean,
especially when you believe I'm sort of a spy."

His smile deepened, his dark fringed lids half closed, and the
expression in his blue gaze was shielded from her. "But I don't think
you are a spy," he murmured lightly. "And at this time, I would
just as soon not discuss it."

"Oh," Erin whispered, trying to hide a touch of miserable confusion. He didn't wish to talk; she was chattering like a magpie. But
then she had warned him she was scared and so nervous. "I won't
say anything else."

He chuckled softly. "Come here, angel-witch, and talk all you
like. I want to hear you talk." He drew her into his arms, pressing
her length against his. She was on fire, he thought, as her flesh
seared his. And her fire was adding fuel to his. "Tell me what you
feel, Erin. Tell me what's good," he prompted huskily.

As suddenly as it had come, the compulsion to talk was gone. She
swallowed, meeting the ocean blue of his stare in confusion. It all
felt wonderful; the crisp hairs of his chest teasing the softness of her
breasts, that feather touch of his fingers as they now stroked low
over her spine, hips and buttocks.

"Tell me, Erin," he persisted in a voice of raw velvet that ignited
the passion within her just as the silken touch of his hands did.

She couldn't meet the demand of his eyes. She buried her head
into his shoulder and groaned, aware that he felt her quivering, the
erratic pounding of her heart. And so was she aware of his need,
strong and full and dizzyingly stimulating as he touched against her
bare thighs.

With one hand he caressed her nape through the wealth of her
hair, with the other he continued to graze her flesh softly from her
spine to her firm and shapely rear.

"Then I'll talk to you, Erin," he murmured. "You are exquisite
from the tip of your silken head to your beautiful toes. When I feel
your breasts press against me, I'm afraid the wanting will drive me
mad. And when I feel your hips fitting to mine, I shake as if I'll

139

explode with the want of knowing them further, of filling you, being one with you, claiming you as entirely mine. . . ."

His whispers had been a hot moist singe that tantalized the very sensitive area of her throat and neck and lower ear. It was wonderful, the feel was wonderful, he could touch her with that breath of air for an eternity. But it wasn't just the sensitive parts of her body that felt his soft lovemaking. The heated coil which had begun to unravel within her was spreading. Flame upon flame licked over her from the center of her abdomen so low and achingly deep. The feeling was overwhelming. Her fear, and the fear of being afraid, evaporated into thin mist. This man could be firm and unyielding, but he would never, never hurt her. She had always sensed his strength by his self-control. His passions could rage like wildfire, but they would stay in check until they could be matched.

Suddenly he shifted, bringing her back upon the bed, himself over her. His eyes held no hint of ice as they blazed into hers; they were a windswept storm; a blue so intense they were deepest, hottest of all flames.

Yet still he was in perfect control, still he held back. His touch, ever so feather light, grazed over her breasts. "I want to consume you," he continued in a ragged whisper. "I want to know you, to feel you, taste the sweet salt of your flesh . . . that sweet fragrance that is only yours . . ."

His lips touched upon her again, as light as air. He held himself above her with one arm, then watched her as he caressed her body with his right hand, moving slowly, another whisper touch, exploring her, the hollows of her shoulders, cupping her breasts, stroking her belly and lower and lower, teasing until she was sure she would go mad. A moan escaped her, and he watched her as her breathing quickened. She was barely aware that she writhed now with a burning ache escalating higher and higher, the ache itself so good, yet so torturous in its reach for appeasement.

He smiled at her; it was tender, it was tense. He shifted, allowing his lips to follow after the trail that still seared from the taunting caress of his fingers. He kissed her, he marveled at her, he used the tip of his tongue to lap over her flesh in little spurts that made her writhe and clench her fingers into his shoulders, unconsciously clawing.

His mouth moved over her breasts, sensuously circling one and

140

then the other. He stroked the hard-tipped peaks with his tongue, then grazed over them with his teeth, sending bolts of streaking fire through her system.

"Ohhhhh . . . !" she cried aloud, her fingers kneading into his shoulders. He lifted his head, massaging the tender mounds that rose with the arch of her back to fill his hands.

"Shall I stop?" he queried with a drawling deviltry.

She implored him with her eyes, but he wouldn't yield his stand. "Tell me, Erin, shall I stop?"

He brought the smooth palm of his hand in rotating circles down her body as he waited for her answer, the lightness leaving his touch as it became more demanding. He brought his taunting circles to her thigh, finding the soft inner flesh.

"Erin?"

"No!" she gasped out, inadvertently raking her fingers into his hair. "No . . . no . . . don't stop."

His mouth, warm and demanding, returned to her breasts, caressing each with the subtle touch of gentle care finally giving way to passion. His lips were greedy, tugging in a suctioning motion that made the electric currents playing havoc within her become electric shafts that sent her into convulsive shudder after shudder.

His lips returned to hers, hungrily, his tongue plummeting deep to quickly withdraw, leaving her senses spinning, her respiration ragged. And then, of all things, he shifted, and he was kissing her toes, moving a slow, slow pattern up the silken sheerness of her legs, barely touching one second, teeth nipping lightly the next. He moved higher and higher, his hands caressing her along with his lips, seeking full discovery as if she were a paradise of verdant land to be explored as a priceless treasure.

A strangled cry escaped her as his taunting touched upon the center of the searing heat that enveloped her. She bolted up, her fingers digging into his hair, but he eased her back.

"Is it good, Erin?" he murmured. "Tell me."

"Oh, yes," she gasped, and then she was talking as she had never imagined she could talk, telling him over and over that yes, it was good, and please, please, please.

But at this point he had no mercy. He pulled her over, and continued his kisses along her spine, her shoulders, her hips, until she was half sobbing in her pleas. And then once more she was facing him as he brought his weight above hers, hovering there as he met her eyes with his own so dark they were indigo in the night, his features tense.

"Now touch me, Erin," he commanded, and she hadn't a single thought of not complying, and the flesh that she touched left her feeling that she skirted the rim of a volcano. And then she touched a vital pulse that was thunder, soaring with the warmth of life, of need.

His weight lowered, his knee wedged her giving thighs, bringing them together. He held there a moment, their bodies just brushing, and the torment was exquisite.

"Erin?" Even now there was a query in his voice.

But she was past pleading. Her arms encircled his neck and she arched high against him, her pressing, writhing slender form giving him all the answer she would now give. Her lips came to his, her teeth bit gently into his lower lip, her tongue imparted her urgency as she became the one to demand.

Even now he was excruciatingly slow, coming to her until she was sure she would pitch into the black abyss with sheer ecstasy as he filled her.

Nothing could be better . . . nothing could touch her more . . . nothing could take her higher. But he did.

As her needs matched his he unleashed all that he had held back, taking her in a wild thirst that could not be slaked. The tempo had been slow; it fevered into a rhythm that was a tempest, a beautiful matched tempest. Her writhing undulation matched his, she arched to him continually with instinctive knowledge of his satin thrusts, barely conscious of all that she gave.

And somewhere, back in his mind, he was thinking of rose petals. So fragrant, soft, perfect, beautiful. Opening to the sun, as she had opened to him, ever more beautiful. Her slender legs held his; she had indeed found full bloom, her feminine demands as delightfully chaotic as his own, her lure and need amazingly, erotically, sensually passionate. In his arms she had found abandon.

He had created a wildcat, a witch, a vixen, and she was incredible. Then even that thought was swept away. The raw need to find ultimate release brought his fever to a pitch. He slipped his hands beneath her, firmly gripping the shapely mounds of her buttocks, holding her to him with a devastating dominance.

The pinnacle that had long been anticipated, the crest of the agony and delirious rapture, came explosively. The volcano erupted, and tremor after tremor of shattering ecstasy washed over Erin in moments so sweet they were blinding; a goodness, a rightness, that touched so deeply she almost slipped into the abyss with the splendor of the climax. And even as the feelings slowly ebbed, bringing her back, new senses just as wonderful swamped over her. The liquid heat of him still inside her filled her with a part of him.

And it was wonderful to be held in comfort, held in the glow of aftermath, bathed in the feeling of complete contentment. Still she felt the stroke of his fingers, light now, over the sheen of her back. It made her feel as if she belonged to the man, as if she were sheltered within his strength. It was so secure, so, so comfortable.

A rasping sound began to fade, and Erin realized that they were just beginning to breathe normally once more. She began to wonder if she could meet his eyes despite the wonderful need to cling to his hard body after all the things she had whispered, after the abandoned urgings her body had willfully conveyed to his.

But suddenly he was leaning above her; his extraordinary eyes were brilliant with blue tenderness, his lips held a very male smile of gentle amusement and pleasure.

"Erin," he teased, "I think I should tell you that you didn't disappoint me one bit—you astounded me! I don't think I have ever made love with a woman so perfectly, wildly, sensually pleasing before in my life."

Erin blushed, her lids lowered, her lashes shadowing her cheeks with sunlit honey.

"You're gorgeous in shades of pink!" he chuckled softly. "Tell me, were the feelings there? Do you think you're still going to have to envy your friend Casey?"

A slow smile filtered into Erin's lips. He knew damned well just what she had been feeling. He had made her tell him even though her urgent hungers had been clearly . . . clearly! . . . evident. He had felt them all.

She opened her eyes to him. "I truly doubt that even Casey has ever experienced anything as wonderful as—" she cut herself off quickly. You. That was the word. It had all been Jarod. But she couldn't say that to him. She had discovered he could be gentle, caring. Giving, so completely giving. She hadn't known just how

143

fully he had checked his own desires until she had met the storm-swept need of him inside her. But though they were lovers now, there were certain things that shouldn't be said. She wasn't terribly sure that they were friends.

He is my husband, she thought. But that was a foreign thought. Unrelated. Because he could be kind did not mean that he despised marriage any the less, that he had forgotton the true wife he had lost.

"Tonight," she said honestly. "Oh, Jarod, wonderful can't describe it. There aren't words for the feeling. . . . Thank you."

He wrapped his arms around her, holding her very close. "Thank you," he said, and his words were deeply husky and shockingly humble. Suddenly Erin didn't want to move. She wanted to stay where she was and forget there was a world, stay caught within the magical fantasy of the night and beat of his heart against her cheek.

She closed her eyes and opened them. It was dark, but the glow from the bathroom, which had allowed them the aesthetic pleasure of seeing one another, still filtered over the room.

They hadn't had dinner, she thought, but she wasn't hungry. Not now. Or if she was hungry, it was for a second chance to stimulate and then appease the appetites she had just learned existed.

God, she thought, in silent prayer, what Jarod had done for her tonight. She hadn't believed, she hadn't dared dream, that ecstasy existed, but Jarod had given it to her. And in that simple giving, he had dimmed all the horrors of the past. He had taken the pain away, absolved the humiliation. And as her body was healed, so now was her soul.

Yet as her heart accepted these things with gratitude, she was learning that she had been wrong before. Jarod Steele could hurt her, because she had just discovered how she needed him. She was caught in a web, living a life that was farce.

Morning would come, and she would have to resign herself to all the inevitable confusion, accept the fact that Jarod was an expert lover but that he didn't give love itself. She was an inconvenience, a burden he had taken upon himself because of determination and the will to win.

No, she told herself, don't think now. Just savor this. . . .

"We missed dinner," he murmured. "Are you hungry?"

She met his gaze and shook her head. But her silver eyes were wide and bare. They told him that she was hungry with fascination, with the incredible joy of the world he had created.

He chuckled, softly, huskily. "Oh, honey," he whispered, taking the time to thread his fingers into the golden strands of her hair with a possessive pleasure. "I think forgetting about dinner is just fine for both of us. Because I am hungry. Very hungry. Starving . . ."

Morning would come. But for now, the contentment and satiation of fulfillment could not be left alone. Fantastic discoveries had been made; they had explored . . . and explored . . . studied and analyzed . . . enjoyed . . . and explored further and further . . . deeper and deeper. . . .

This time her senses, attuned now to him, pulsed at his slightest touch. She could meet his lips with slow, savoring seeking.

Morning would come, but the beauty of this unique moment in the endless eternity of time was hers, with this man.

Blue ice . . .

Raging blue fire . . .

And his fire was hers.

As he tenderly began to make love to her again, she vaguely realized that, somewhere within the city, a chorus of clocks was chiming out the strokes of midnight.

INTERLUDE

Dear Mary,

Greetings from the U.S.S.R.! (Sorry—no palm-tree cards available!)

How are things in the old Big Apple? Believe it or not, I miss home and the insane traffic and the early spring slush and the horns blaring loud enough to deafen.

But anyway, without travelers, you couldn't have a travel agency!

How is your other half of business and home? Give Ted my love.

Anyway, the country is fascinating. I have thoroughly enjoyed everything that I've seen. I have a marvelous guide named Tanya, who has been with me all week. I have learned more from her than I could learn from a million books!

I wanted to let you know that my trip will be extended a bit, and since I know how you—and that charmingly overprotective husband of yours—worry about me, I wanted to let you know that I'm just fine. This is going to be a surprise, I know, but I've remarried. (An American, not a Russian—don't go panicking on me!)

His name is Jarod Steele and he's attached to the U.S. Embassy through the U.N. Actually I met him in the States— call Casey and she'll fill you in on our first encounter! We simply kept colliding, and though I know this has been hasty, it might have been one of those inevitable tricks of destiny. I was literally swept off my feet—never knew what was happening until it was too late. . . .

* * *

Erin stopped writing with a wince. She bit on the nub of her pen. What an incredible fabrication. But she couldn't tell Mary the truth. It seemed that no one knew the truth about anything except for her and Jarod.

And she didn't think Jarod would appreciate her giving lengthy explanations to anyone. And so for the time being she had to convince Mary that her life was moving along beautifully. Besides, Mary and Ted would be horrified if they knew she was embroiled in a strange web of lies and deceit and confusion. She stopped chewing on the pen and started writing again.

> Jarod is an incredible man. (Again, I will refer you to the opinion of our mutual friend Casey, "the male connoisseur"!) He has the capacity for great kindness, and has done wonderful, wonderful things for me. . . .

Again Erin lifted her pen from the paper. Jarod. What could she say about him? He is a magnet, a flame; he draws, he demands. His passions are insatiable; he is like living in the center of a storm, and yet he is the most controlled man I have ever met. His eyes can be blue fire, and they can be coldest, driest ice. Behind them he hides his feelings, if he has any. I live with him, I sleep with him; I do not know him.

She thought of what she could have added in her letter.

> For the next two months I will be his wife. But he does not think of me as a wife; his wife is dead. I became a responsibility of his, because of things I don't understand. He is still not sure whether or not he harbors a spy, although I think he really believes me innocent.
>
> When he holds me it is so wonderful I almost lose consciousness, I enter a paradise. But outside of that room, his room, our room, he is cool and abrupt. He is polite, but distant. He speaks, and he expects his words to be honored without question. I am not always sure—at times when we are physically engaged— whether he actually realizes I'm there or not. He is constantly working; I've called him several times to discover he spends a great deal of time with a mysterious "Catherine."

* * *

Oh, God! Erin thought, if she could only write the truth, speak out. If only she could tell Mary what was in her heart.

> *I'm falling in love with this man, and I mean nothing to him! I am comfort at night, wild, exhilarating passion, but beyond that I am a guest he tolerates with cordiality.*
>
> *I fear his temper, I know it can be explosive. I think I am a strong person, but he can sweep me away like a tidal wave. And I'm frightened, I'm caged. He can hurt me far worse than I've ever been hurt before, because I don't believe I've ever loved like this. But we both know the facts; if he deems me innocent, as soon as he is free to get me out of the U.S.S.R. our pretense at love will be over. He expects me to file for a divorce, because he doesn't believe in marriage. Not since Cara died. She had his love. I have his desires. . . .*
>
> *And I do try to be so adult, so mature. I act as cool as he. I can't pretend that I wish to be anywhere but in his bed, but I do pretend that I accept our situation as that of two knowledgeable adults, mature enough to accept our needs for what they are.*

Erin bit through the plastic shell of her pen. Scowling at herself, she picked up the pieces and discarded them before the ink could create a disaster. Jarod had gone to Kiev. She didn't expect him back until tomorrow, but she worked at his desk and wanted to leave it as organized and immaculate as he did. She didn't want to give him any cause to find her bothersome.

She picked up another pen.

> Mary, I know this is brief, but I just wanted to let you know that everything is wonderful and I'm very happy. . . .

Wonderful! Oh, Erin! You're married to a man who still thinks you might be capable of espionage! He watches you, he monitors you, and you still don't know what's going on, what Project Midnight is, why your engagement ring came from a Russian official. He orders you to stay in the apartment when he is gone, unless you are out with Tanya. Although he often ignores you, he knows your every move. If one step were out of line, he would pounce on you.

148

You never see him during the day; you sit down to dinner like polite strangers.

Yet every time he touches you, you melt like heated silver. Like an absolute idiot, you fell in love with a man with no wish to love you back. And you cling to him with your senses lost, your willpower nonexistent.

Oh, Erin, how could you let such a thing happen to you after all you've struggled to achieve for yourself? You are no innocent, no young child to become infatuated and believe in fairy tales. You have to break away.

And it wouldn't be a loss, because he had given her so much. He had given her back her own belief in love. But she knew what she tried to hide in her subconscious; she would be just as crippled, because another man would never, never compare to Jarod Steele. . . .

It was growing late. She picked up her pen again.

> Miss you and Ted very much. Please believe that I am fine and happy and don't worry about me a second! Tell Casey I'll write her soon, and I promise a much longer account when I get the time to really sit down!
>
> > All my love,
> > Erin

Erin carefully folded her letter and left it in a sealed envelope on the right hand corner of Jarod's desk. She was about to leave the desk when another thought struck her and she reached for the telephone. It was growing late, but she hoped Tanya would still be up.

She chewed her lip as she waited for the call to go through. In moments of sanity during the day following that first delirious night together, Erin had begun to worry about the consequences of "adult behavior." Consequences which could be disastrous in her situation.

"Tanya!" She breathed a little more easily when the Russian woman answered and assured Erin she hadn't woken her.

Erin chattered idly for a second and zeroed in on what she hoped would sound like a casually asked question.

"Have you managed to get me a doctor's appointment yet?"

"I believe I have a date for you—"

"Great! Next week?"

"I'm afraid not. In several weeks. Our medicine is socialized, you know, and emergencies always come first."

Erin bit her lip unhappily.

"Erin—if you asked Jarod, I'm sure he could do something."

"I, uh, Jarod isn't here," Erin said hastily. "And he's so terribly busy right now I hate to bother him with trivia."

She could hear Tanya's pause. Trivia? They were husband and wife.

"I'm surprised you didn't take care of this in the States," Tanya murmured.

"Ahh . . ." Erin murmured weakly. "Bad planning on my part. Do the best you can to push it for me, will you, Tanya?"

"Sure," Tanya promised. "But you should be all right—"

Erin knew what she was thinking. Tanya had reluctantly done some shopping for her in the local drugstore so that she would have a modicum of protection.

"I don't like to rely on such methods," Erin murmured nervously.

"I assure you, our products—"

"Tanya! I believe in your products!" Dear God, she hadn't meant to offend her Russian friend. "I wouldn't like to rely on such methods in the States!"

Tanya chuckled softly, appeased. "Erin, you really should speak with Jarod—"

Erin knew it troubled Tanya that she always avoided the issue, but she could do nothing else. "Maybe," she said evasively, "but in the meantime keep pushing for me, will you?"

Tanya agreed, and they said their good-nights. Erin rose and stretched and left the den to walk into the bedroom.

It was her anniversary, she thought dryly. She had been married to a man who had been a total stranger for two full weeks. What a great record. Her first marriage had been for three months, her second would be for two months.

In her long flannel gown she tried to settle down to sleep. But she found herself staring at the moonglow entering in through the window.

She tossed and turned for hours of misery before she slept. It was the first night he had been away. Good God, what was going to happen when they split for good? If this were her torture now . . .

You're a fool, Erin, you have to find some strength, some cool, cool authority of your own. . . .

But as she fought for sleep, she only knew that she ached with missing him beside her, burned for his touch.

In another city, far into the Russian interior, Jarod Steele also lay awake and he was angered by his sleeplessness, angered by the need he felt for the woman he supposed rested easily in his bed.

She had gotten beneath his skin, bewitched him, enchanted him. She was like no other woman. A cool, assured beauty, an inferno, a wildfire in his arms.

He had awakened her, he had elicited her magic. He could close his eyes and think of her, of the boldness she had learned, of the lazy, seductive cast of her half-closed silver eyes as she padded softly to him with her long-legged walk of effortless grace. Putting her arms around him, drawing taunting strokes over his back and chest, she teased and teased and increased the fevered ardor until they were together again, her lithe body fulfilling all promises.

He stood up in a cold sweat and walked to the window. He was in Kiev on business. Erin McCabe—no, Steele, he reminded himself dryly—was just another woman, a beautiful woman, a sensual, passionate woman . . . but just a woman.

In a few months she would be gone, out of his life. He would form liaisons with other women went he felt the need.

Or would he be able to? he mocked himself. A widow he had known in the city had issued him veiled invitations tonight; he had politely and subtly refused. . . . Because I'm married, he told himself. Supposedly madly in love, a newlywed. That wasn't it. No sane man could hold Erin and then seek another. . . .

Damn her! his thoughts hissed. She created fires in his blood as no other woman before her, not even Cara. But Cara had been love, the folly, the recklessness, the wonder of youth. And Cara was gone. Love, tenderness, and the extreme heartache and extreme wonder of youth were gone, tenderly buried, cherished in memory.

But he wanted Erin. He had come to feel that somehow she was his; the ragged depth of fierce possession he felt for her was startling.

Jarod glanced at his watch and groaned. It was midnight; his day would start at five A.M.

Damn her, he thought. Damn her and her guileless silver eyes. Eyes that seduced, eyes that could deceive.

He still didn't know if he had bedded a devil or an angel . . .

It didn't matter in the heat of her midnight fires.

VIII

By the time she woke up on Saturday morning, Erin was edgy and miserable. I'm acting like a wife, she told herself dryly as her agitated movements caused her to spill half the coffee she was pouring.

Wrapped in one of his velour robes, Erin took her coffee into the living room and prodded at the dying fire. Moscow was cold. She wondered if spring would ever come to the city.

Sitting tired and morose, Erin couldn't control the fury that bubbled within her. He had been due home by dinner time last night at the latest. She had tried with her meager culinary skills to accomplish a beautiful rack of lamb. And at twelve thirty her beautiful rack of lamb had hit the garbage.

He could have called. Kiev. She wasn't even sure of where the city was—somewhere inland. As usual, she had no idea of what he was doing. He had given her some type of explanation about seeking out all those whom Ivan had seen near the time of his arrest.

This damned Project Midnight business. He lived for his work. Or did he? she wondered suddenly, her imagination taking bitter flight. She knew she hadn't interrupted Jarod in the middle of a love affair; the man had no necessity to love. But there were other types of affairs, and it had been evident all along that their marriage was an inconvenience. No real marriage. He might not have been in love—he hadn't intended to ever remarry—but there might be a woman he did care for. . . .

Catherine. He was always working with Catherine. Perhaps his business trip to Kiev hadn't been business at all. Perhaps he wanted to be with this Catherine and he couldn't do so in Moscow—not when he had married the "fiancée" he had supposedly brought over from the States. And what right would she have to say anything? None. She had no rights at all where Jarod was concerned. No right

153

whatsoever to be so furious now. But she was. Her rack of lamb in the garbage was enough to whip her temper into full steam.

He should have called out of common courtesy—and it was the more unusual because Jarod was courteous even when distant. But he had made her sit and sit. She wasn't even supposed to leave the apartment without Tanya, and he couldn't bother with a call.

She had to get out, she was going crazy. And she would also be damned if she sat around at his beck and call while he disappeared for days on end—possibly with Catherine!

That was a sobering thought. One that reminded her that she had to cut loose. When they had started out, she had thought she could be adult. Handle the sexual relationship. But she hadn't been in love with him at the time. Or if she had been, she hadn't known it. And like an absolute idiot she had become dependent on him. Which was why she was so angry now . . . and hurt.

She had to reassert herself. Remember that she was Erin McCabe. With a fascinating life stretching ahead of her when she did return to the States in such a relatively short amount of time.

The phone started ringing and she leaped to her feet with anticipation. It would be Jarod. He would have an apology and an explanation.

It wasn't Jarod, and her disappointment was so vast that tears sprang to her eyes.

"Erin?" Gil Sayer's voice was anxious.

She swallowed, her fingers tightening around the wire, but her voice was level and cheerful. "Yes, Gil, I'm here. How are you?"

"Fine, thanks," he laughed, "but actually I called to ask you that question. I heard that Jarod was held over in Kiev. I thought you might be feeling a little lost in the city without him so I thought I'd call and offer my services! I don't believe you've been to the circus yet. How about letting me take you?"

Why not, indeed? Erin wondered. Gil was with the American embassy. She doubted she could get into much trouble with him. Jarod certainly couldn't care—and if he did, the hell with him.

"Thanks, Gil! That sounds wonderful. I have been going a little crazy cooped up in here. I've been doing some history trips with Tanya, but she's been in Leningrad visiting her family for the last week. I'd love to get out!"

"Great," Gil said with flattering enthusiasm. "I'll be there in an hour?"

"Perfect."

It did turn out to be a perfect day. The Moscow circus was world-famous, and it was soon easy to see why. The performers were highly skilled, eliciting oohs and aahs from the audience with their death-daring feats. But even more wonderful than the exciting trapeze and wild-animal acts were the clowns.

Language barriers did not exist within the antics of the clowns. They were a delight, as were the people around Erin. All laughing, passing little snacks back and forth, warm and friendly despite the fact she didn't understand a word being said. Gil translated for her occasionally, and she discovered that the Soviet people were fascinated by her; the circus was certainly a place where barriers were broken. By the time they left, she had received several chastisements from the "bubushkas," or older matrons, who weren't in the least shy about telling her she needed to put some flesh on her bones. Gil told her that that was why they had passed the candy in the first place.

"Oh, Gil," she murmured, her silver eyes sparkling as they left the circus behind, "I've had an absolutely lovely time! Thank you for taking me. You've been a life saver!"

He blushed slightly, and Erin thought what a charming person he was—so handsome, and so completely charming, always there to try and help her.

She started thinking once more that it was a pity she hadn't wound up playing farcical wife to him. How much easier it would have been. He was never cold, never distant. He never watched her with that callous speculation in his eyes. He, at least, really didn't think she was a spy. And she wasn't in love with him. Yes, it would have been much, much easier if she had found herself beside Gil Sayer on the Moscow train.

Gil set a comfortably friendly arm around her shoulder. "Shall we have some tea?"

"Lovely!" Erin agreed.

Over hot Russian tea and pastries Erin felt the bond tighten between herself and Gil. He was a career diplomat, she learned, originally from North Dakota. He was only three years older than she, and an antique buff as well. They chatted almost an hour before he asked about Jarod.

"I believe I went into a form of shock when I heard Jarod had crossed the border with a fiancée in tow—and that fiancée being Erin McCabe. Jarod has never lacked for feminine companionship, but marriage! I don't believe a one of us thought he would ever marry again! And then to hear he was marrying you! The fantasies of my last few years lay in ruins at my feet! Where did you meet Jarod?"

Caught off guard, Erin fumbled in her purse for a cigarette. Gil reached across the table to light it for her. "We, ah, met in New York. In a little pub. We kind of collided with one another, and well, from there, things just seemed to happen."

"I wish things like you would just happen to me," Gil said wistfully, lightly touching her hand with his unbelievably smooth fingertips.

"Thank you again, Gil. You're always very sweet."

He grimaced. "Sweet was never quite what I had in mind for being to you, Erin, but . . . you are Jarod's wife. I guess I have to settle for sweet. But if steely Steele ever gets to be too much for you, Erin, you call me anyway."

A little catch seemed to form in her throat. Gil's eyes were so giving, so vulnerable. He really cared for her. But that caring was painful. And it also touched off a chord of nervousness she couldn't quite comprehend. He was no Jarod Steele. No enigma of brick. He could be easily touched, easily hurt.

Suddenly uncomfortable, Erin withdrew her hand and stubbed out her cigarette with a rueful smile. "I think I'd better get home, Gil, but it has been a lovely, lovely day."

He smiled and stood, then silently escorted her from the restaurant. During the drive home he chatted amicably about various buildings they passed. It wasn't until they reached the door to Jarod's apartment that she caught the strange wistful look in his eyes again, and she wondered—no matter how charming and flattering Gil was—if she had been wise to spend the day with him. His concern was marvelous for her ego, and she did need friends here, but she didn't want him hurt.

"Thanks again, Gil," she said softly, touching his shoulders lightly as she kissed his cheek. "It was a wonderful day."

"Yes—" Erin suddenly heard in deep velvet from behind her. She whirled in time to see the frost in Jarod's eyes as he stood in the hallway, a frost that belied the pleasant tone of his voice. "I'll add my thanks to that, Gil. I appreciate your taking the time to entertain my wife. Won't you come in and have a drink?"

"Thanks, Jarod," Gil agreed, stepping into the hallway behind Erin. "When did you get back? Joe said you were going to be tied up in Kiev for a while longer."

"I got back about an hour ago," Jarod said, leading the way to the kitchen. "Kiev was a waste of time."

He had barely acknowledged her presence, but Erin had followed along in his wake. Now his dagger cold gaze was on her. "Erin?"

"What?" She almost jumped.

His smile alerted her to the fact that he knew he had unnerved her—and that he was pleased with her discomfort. Bastard, she thought seethingly. He waltzed in when he pleased, but he was angry with her, very angry, even though she was aware that Gil didn't realize it.

"What would you like to drink?"

"Oh, ah, nothing at the moment," she said, keeping the distance of the counter between them.

His infuriatingly cryptic brow raised, the smooth velvet of his tone continued, "Darling, you wouldn't have us drinking alone, would you? You just might discover you really wish you had a drink."

Erin raised a defiant brow in return. I'll never need a drink to deal with you, she thought, and the thought shone in her eyes.

"I really don't care for anything, thank you, Jarod," she said firmly.

He shrugged. "As you wish, darling. Gil?"

"Bourbon, please."

Erin felt as if she had once again been forgotten as she followed the two men into the living room. She was surprised when they began an open discussion about Project Midnight.

"I don't know why you drive so hard at it, Jarod," Gil said, seating himself comfortably on the sofa. "You're not going to stop the espionage—both governments are continually at it." He caught Erin's eyes and laughed. "You look as if you're in shock, Erin. Project Midnight is no top secret—everyone knows it exists."

157

"Oh," she murmured, taking one of the chairs by the sofa.

Jarod had chosen to stand by the mantel. He appeared very rugged in a pullover, Erin found herself reflecting, and then the fact that she was appreciating anything about him at all in her present mood annoyed her.

Except that although he appeared very casual and very comfortable, the host in his own home, he seemed even more tense than usual. It wasn't a visible tension. It was in the aura of leashed strength that he always wore about him, the surety that he could drop that cloak of negligent ease at a second's notice. It was in his eyes, in the firm square of his jaw. Not even an easy smile could hide it when she knew it was there.

He glanced at her now, rolling the cubes of ice, then glanced back to Gil.

"We all know the espionage goes on, and yes, a lot of it is sanctioned by the governments. But not this, Gil. These bits and pieces and half truths are going to cause some serious problems. There is too much distrust, to begin with. This character winds up selling to both sides because neither can resist. Then they wonder. They don't know what is and isn't truth. And they both keep building more defenses, and one day the defenses are going to go so far something is going to crack."

"Oh, come on, Jarod," Gil protested. "You're an American, or at least—"

"That's not the point we're talking here," Jarod interrupted, leaving Erin to wonder what the "at least" meant. "It isn't going to matter what nationality any man claims if this sparks off something that goes too far."

"They both just want to keep a balance of power."

Jarod shrugged. "That could be true. But I work for the U.N., Gil. And there are a lot of countries within the U.N. who would find themselves being battlegrounds if things came to a head. The U.N. wants peace. It's my job to see that nothing—especially some penny-ante double-dealer—upsets all the negotiations that keep a lid on that precarious peace."

Gil shrugged, sipping his bourbon. "I still think you worry too much about this thing."

"Do I?" Jarod queried softly. "Well, the Russians seem awfully worried too, Gil, which worries me all over again. I think it would all go much better if I were to find this person or persons before Sergei does, don't you think? Eighty years in Sing Sing would look a lot better than what the Russians will offer. And God only knows what Sergei could draw out of a man . . . or woman."

Gil shrugged again, draining his glass. His smile was careless and his eyes were slightly sparkling. "You're the big-time stuff, Jarod, not me. The bible pushers and souvenir hunters are the hottest thing I handle!"

Jarod knelt down and tossed a log on the fire, using the poker to set it into the heart of the flame. "Samuel Hughes is dead," he said suddenly.

Erin felt a chill race along her spine, even though she had little idea of what they were talking about—or who they were talking about.

Gil set his empty glass upon a side table. "I think you suspected for a long time that he was playing both sides, Jarod. I can't imagine that—that Sam being taken by the Russians could be too much of a surprise to you."

Jarod was silent for a minute. "We can't be sure the Russians had anything to do with it. Sergei denies knowing anything about Sam."

"The Russians always deny everything."

"I don't think Sergei would in this instance."

"I don't mean to cast doubt," Gil said uneasily. "I know how close you are—"

"You also know that that has no bearing whatsoever upon our working relationship," Jarod said. He was calm as ever, staring at the flames that caught upon the new log. "You're a fool, Gil, if you think you can generalize about the Russian people. Sergei is an honorable man—his sense of justice is outstanding. I'm quite sure he wouldn't be lying about this—the Kremlin is as concerned as the U.N."

"Maybe not. But just what are you getting at, Jarod? If Sam wasn't taken by the Russians—"

"Then he was taken by someone else," Jarod interrupted softly.

"Our side?"

"I wouldn't exactly say 'our side.' Let's say that I'm really worried, Gil. And I really hope that I am the one to get to the bottom of this first. I hate to think of the consequences otherwise."

Erin glanced sharply from one man to the other. It almost sounded as if Jarod were warning Gil. Jarod was being conversational, merely discussing the situation with Gil. Yet the tone in his voice seemed to suggest that a subtle warning had been given, that a trap was closing in, that truth at the moment would be preferable to . . . to what? Surely Jarod didn't suspect Gil of anything!

No, at least Gil didn't take it that way. "I hope so, too, Jarod," he said with a sigh. Then dismissively he smiled and stood. "I guess I'd better get going." He smiled over to Erin, who had been sitting silently through their entire discourse. "Your bride is going to wind up resenting me! I sit here like an interloper when you've just returned. Erin, take care."

Erin forgot her dilemma over the strange conversation as she was reminded that she was about to be left alone with Jarod—a Jarod she knew to be in an explosive mood despite his cordial appearance. Nervously she uncurled her feet to stand, but Jarod rose at that moment, stopping her with a quelling glance. "I'll see Gil out, Erin. Stay where you are."

Erin bristled at his tone, but decided against an open argument in front of Gil. "Thanks again," she said softly to their guest.

She stared at the fire herself as she waited uneasily for Jarod to return to the living room. Why was she waiting like a child about to be disciplined? she wondered. She owed Jarod no explanations. She stood and walked into the kitchen, searching the refrigerator for the iced tea she had made just before leaving.

"Where the hell are you?"

Erin was startled by the open fury in his snarl, but determined to hold her ground. "In the kitchen."

A second later he was at the entryway, his cutting gaze upon her.

Erin returned his stare with irritation. "What is the matter with you?" she demanded.

"I think I asked you explicitly not to go anywhere with anyone except for Tanya."

"I was asked to the circus," Erin said evenly. "I had no idea where to contact you and no idea when you were coming back."

"You knew damned well I'd be here soon."

Erin arched a delicate brow. "Sorry, I didn't see it that way. I thought you'd be back for dinner last night. You might have been gone another week. You didn't bother to call."

"Erin, I was on business. Which is beside the point. I don't want you out again unless I know exactly where you are. If you were to stumble into trouble again—which you have an aptitude for doing —I mightn't get there in time to bail you out."

His tone was extremely hard and tense; his eyes retained that ice, that autocratic shield that reduced her to a wayward child. She felt a little ill. She had never really known this man, never really had any part of him. The caring he gave her, the intimate nights, were based solely on their physical desires. She had fallen in love with him and it had been foolish because he was hard and she could never really enter into his heart, his mind, or his soul.

Her fingers tensed around her glass. "Don't be absurd, Jarod. I was out with a diplomat from the American embassy. I'm sure Gil could have very competently handled any difficulties for me."

He was silent for a second, and then he began a slow, soundless walk toward her, pausing not a foot away. She could feel his body heat; her mind and senses reeled beneath the continual impact of his pleasant male scent.

"I'm going to repeat myself once, Erin. I do not want you out with Gil Sayer again."

Inadvertently Erin took a step backwards. "I really think this has gone far enough, Jarod. I do appreciate everything you've done for me, but I don't intend to follow orders from you when they make no sense. I can understand that I must stay here until you can afford the time to take me out of the country, and I can fully comprehend how allowing anyone else to know that our marriage is a joke could make your position uncomfortable, but—"

"Joke!" he spat out furiously. "Madam, if you consider such a thing a joke, you deserve to be beaten."

Erin paled, but again held her ground. "I apologize, Mr. Steele, for my term. Charade would have been a better choice of word. But my postion stands. I'm an adult, with reasonable intelligence. I didn't go off wandering the streets—I went out with an American official! I'm sorry, Jarod, but I can't be a prisoner while you go off wherever it is you go. Gil was being kind—"

"Kind!" Jarod's interruption was an explosion this time. A pulse beat erratically in a blue vein along the corded column of his neck. "Don't be any more foolish than you are, Erin," he said harshly. "Gil Sayer is interested in one thing and one thing only. Surely you have the sense to realize that. Or perhaps that's what you want."

For a moment she gaped at him in disbelief, then her voice returned with a surge of fury that pounded in her head. "Steele," she said hotly, "you have incredible nerve. And you're capable of being the most insulting human being I've ever met. It may surprise you, and I'm sure it does, but there are people who think of me in more than a physical light. I do have friends. But if I'd have spent the entire afternoon in a hotel room with Gil Sayer, I really don't see where you would have the right to criticize. I can't see where *your* interest lies on any level above his, and at least Gil Sayer isn't constantly quizzing me and assuming that he has the right to issue orders like a drill sergeant."

It was his turn to pause, but he didn't intend to give any ground. His arms crossed slowly over his chest and his icy gaze narrowed dangerously. "I have certain rights, Mrs. Steele, because at this moment you are my wife. And as such, you will not carry on any type of affair with Gil Sayer—platonic or otherwise. You are my responsibility, Erin, and until this thing ends, you will listen to me. Do I make myself clear?"

Erin fought hard not to blink or give away the trembling that assailed her. "What commendable authority, Jarod," she drawled slowly. "I really do think you missed your calling. You should be a Russian—the head of the KGB. You—"

"You—" he interrupted, stepping toward her once more and gripping her shoulders in a barely controlled white fury, "should definitely learn to hold your tongue. I'm not asking you, Erin, I'm telling you. I don't want you near Gil Sayer again—and I mean it. Disobey me, and you'll not only get to see how you think a Russian agent would treat you, but you'll also get to see a taste of an outraged husband. Now how are we doing? Do I make myself clear?"

"Let go of me, Jarod."

"Certainly, Mrs. Steele, just as soon as I have an answer."

It was rather futile to stand there and argue, Erin decided. She could feel the strength in his tense hold, the ruthless command in his eyes as they pinioned hers. The trembling within her was rampant; sooner or later he was going to realize that he did have the power and the superior strength—and that he could reduce her strongest stance at will. She tilted her chin in a last effort at dignity while she fought the humiliating urge to cry. All the tenderness between them had departed; she had been ridiculous at the beginning of their marriage, deceiving herself with the belief that there was something between them, that she did have a special part of Jarod Steele.

"I sincerely doubt that any occasion will arise again in which I would find myself escorted by Mr. Sayer," she said coolly.

His hold on her eased. "See that there isn't, Erin," he warned.

He turned sharply on his heels and left her standing in the kitchen torn between outrage and tears—and wondering what the night would bring.

Erin had become accustomed to doing the little things in the house, to preparing their meals and straightening out the apartment. There was seldom much to straighten: Jarod was as neat in habit as he was in dress, and a middle-aged Russian woman came in twice a week to do the major cleaning.

But today she was determined not to do a thing. It was spiteful, and she knew it, but she was deeply hurt and couldn't help feeling spiteful. She wasn't sure what she had been expecting when Jarod returned—but she supposed she had fantasized that he would have an apology and a good explanation. She had imagined that he would miss her, that he would greet her with his lips half curled in a smile, that he would have begged her pardon so that she would return to his arms; and she would run to him, of course.

Instead, he had come down upon her like lead. And it was rather difficult to forgive and rush into someone's arms when no forgiveness was requested—no explanation at all given!—and no arms outstretched.

I keep wanting to make this more than it is, she warned herself. But despite her arguments toward mature behavior, she was hurt. And her instinct decreed that he should be hurt in return.

He had retired to his den when he left her. She fixed herself a sandwich and took her food and tea to the music room, where she stayed, nursing her wounded dignity and pride.

He didn't make a reappearance until late. As soon as she heard his footsteps on the stairs, Erin tensed, wondering what his reaction would be to her complete withdrawal from her responsibilities. Her heart began a little thump when she knew that he sought her out, but she forced her eyes to remain on the book she had held open on the same page for most of the late afternoon and early evening.

His brows were raised in query as he glanced into the music room and saw her feet curled beneath her on the far chair.

"Were you planning dinner?" he inquired flatly with no telltale emotion as he stretched his shoulders.

Erin looked up slowly from her book, meeting his eyes with hers just as clear. "No, I wasn't. I ate earlier."

"You're being a little childish, aren't you?" he inquired, his tone irritatingly blasé.

"I'm not being anything," Erin replied as nonchalantly as she could manage, turning a page of her book as if she looked with great interest to the next. "It just seems a little foolish for me to plan anything when I have no idea what your plans are."

"Oh," he replied. "Well, in the future, should I be upstairs all day, you can assume that I'll be here all evening—unless I inform you otherwise."

Erin continued staring at her book. He turned and left her. Moments later she heard his movements in the kitchen, and then a delectable and pleasing aroma faintly radiated through the apartment.

Tears stung the back of her eyelids, but she impatiently blinked them away. She was a fool to think that anything she did or didn't do would have much effect upon Jarod. He was an independent man, accustomed to taking care of himself. And apparently their argument hadn't meant a thing to him. He had behaved as if he had forgotten all about it and as if she should have done the same with nothing being solved.

She couldn't forget the anger with which he had lashed out at her, nor could she forget the things he had said in chastisement, even if she wanted to. And maybe it was good. The ties had to be broken. All of the ties.

She sat staring sightlessly at her book for a while longer, then closed it and stood with firm resolution. She walked into the dining room, waiting for him to look up, knowing that he was aware of her presence. He continued to read the Russian paper he held in his hand as he ate.

"Jarod," Erin said, forcefully controlling her irritation.

He looked up with polite interest.

She suddenly felt tongue-tied. She didn't want to say what she had to say, but she knew it was best. And maybe, in a far corner of her heart, she was praying that he would protest, that he would suddenly tell her that he had fallen in love with her and needed her for the rest of his life.

"I believe we've taken this thing a bit too far," she said stiffly. "I don't care to keep this business relationship personal any longer. I realize this isn't a tremendous apartment, and I have no wish to seriously inconvenience you, but I want to make separate sleeping arrangements. I'll be happy to take either the couch or the den."

Erin felt enveloped in tension, as if she had set the timer of a bomb and was incapable of moving away from the sight of the coming explosion.

But there was no explosion. He set his paper and fork down and crossed his arms over his chest, one of his brows ever so slightly lifted as he smiled at her. "That won't be necessary. I'll be perfectly comfortable in the den."

"Fine, thank you," Erin said, feeling as if she were very far away.

He returned his gaze to his paper. Stupidly, Erin remained staring at him, wondering at the numbness that filled her.

He glanced back up again, blue eyes as brilliantly sharp and unfathomable as marble. "Was there something else?"

"No," Erin murmured.

His eyes immediately returned to his paper. Tightening her jaw against the curt dismissal, Erin turned and slowly moved her way up the staircase.

It wasn't until she was in bed, sheets tensely pulled to her chin, that she accepted how badly she had slashed at her own nose. Or had she taken the only sensible course? He wasn't a cruel person, he simply didn't care. He called out demands, but it was all business; he had never pretended he would really give any of himself.

Erin went rigid with both fear and anticipation as she felt the doorknob twisting. She had locked the door, and that determined decision now led him into a spat of oaths.

"Erin—open it now! I don't mind turning my room over to you, but if it isn't presuming too much," he drawled sarcastically, "I'd like to have access to my own clothing."

Erin swallowed. She jumped from the bed, opened the door without glancing his way, then crawled back beneath the sheets, turning from him and closing her eyes, feeling both miserable and ridiculous.

She heard him moving about briskly, then sensed that he stood over her. She slowly met his eyes, forcing her own to remain steady and coolly opaque.

"I take it you would just as soon I move out of my own home—"

"Don't be ridiculous," Erin interrupted, mustering a fine line of disdain in defense. "I fully realize what an absurdity that would be."

"That's big of you," he returned dryly.

Erin blinked and swallowed, but didn't allow the frost in her gaze to waver. Why did he have to challenge her so, she wondered. He seemed to tower over her as he stood there, and he had never appeared more virile, more confidently male than he did now, clad in the blue pullover, hands on hips, eyes highlighted to a deathly piercing degree by the blue in the sweater. She wanted to reach out, to apologize for being foolish and jealous and hurt, but she couldn't. If they were to live together on the terms they had fallen into before, he owed her certain considerations he had no intention of giving.

And he had brought out a few things himself. There was only one thing Gil Sayer was after, he had said. Apparently it was the only interest he had himself. That and using her in his search for Project Midnight.

"But," he continued, the warning ringing clearly through his soft tones, "I will remind you that this is my apartment, my home. Whatever little triumphs you take, you take because I give them to you. I don't have the time, patience, or inclination to play games with you, Erin. Do what you like within this house—it makes no difference to me. But I meant what I said earlier—don't push me. I don't want you out of here with anyone without my knowledge, and I especially do not want you around Sayer. I don't think you fully accept this, Erin, but you are my wife. And any reactions I might have to your actions are going to be those of a husband."

As quietly as he had come, he turned to leave, pausing once at the door, and actually smiling as he turned back to her.

"One more thing, Erin. Don't ever lock a door against me in my own home again. You wouldn't appreciate seeing just how 'Russian' I am capable of being."

Erin didn't think she could bear his eyes cutting into her any longer, but she couldn't seem to tear her own away. Still caught in

166

his gaze, she twisted, turning her back on him so that she could finally close her eyes.

He walked out. The slam of the door behind him was shattering; she could almost hear the splintering of wood.

She lay awake shivering miserably for hours, wondering how she had made such a disaster of what had once been a decent and livable relationship. I didn't do it, she kept telling herself, or if I did, it had to be done. If he had cared at all . . . but he didn't. The fact was that she had fallen in love with him; he wasn't in love with her, and she couldn't make him be.

So all that had had happened was for the best. It would make her inevitable departure so much easier. It would still the dreams and the nightmares, it would make her life at home plausible.

Damn! How she wished she had never come to Russia! How had things happened so quickly? Where did I go wrong? she wondered desperately. And her continual answer was that none of it had been her fault, and that she really couldn't have done anything differently.

None of it helped any. She tossed and turned for most of the night. She was awake when she heard Jarod slam out of the apartment; she was awake at two A.M. when he came back in, and she lay there waiting, still hoping, craving, that he would come to her, that they could both apologize. But he didn't come back to the room, and then her tossing became worse as she wondered where he had gone and with whom.

The pain was terrible. It seemed to tear apart her insides like the twist of a knife. It burned, it tortured. She couldn't bear the thought of him with another woman. Holding another woman. Touching . . . his fingers, so strong, so feather-light tender. . . .

With a deep groan she buried her head in the pillow until it was dawn again and exhaustedly she finally went to sleep.

IX

He glanced up from his papers as she entered the room and eyed her warily. When she came to him like this, looking prim and proper, her manner frigidly dignified, he knew he was in for another bombshell.

He felt himself tense as she took the chair opposite his desk, her elegant fingers folded upon her lap, the shade of her nails a dark red contrast against the golden ivory of her skin.

Damn her, he thought for the zillionth time. Damn her, damn her. . . .

He had been eager to see her, so eager, when he returned from Kiev. A group of kids trying to bring in a truckload of religious literature had held him up in Kiev. He shouldn't have had to be involved, but he had been there, and the American consulate in Kiev had called upon him. He had been unavoidably detained, and in all that time he had grown more and more anxious to come home.

His apartment had become a home because she was there, making meals and anxiously awaiting his approval, quietly keeping things straightened in his wake, even repairing a tear in one of his favorite shirts.

They didn't discuss much. Sometimes they were painfully polite. But when he would finish his work in the den for the day, she would be there, a fragrance of softness and wildflowers in his bed, a touch of satin, a soft breeze that could whip into a torrid tempest when he took her into his arms.

His thirst should have been slaked. But the more he drank of her, the more his need arose. He would be satisfied, filled to contentment unlike any he had ever known. But then he would burn again because she was an addiction. The silver in her eyes bewitched him, the curve of her lithe slender form beside his was fast becoming a narcotic habit he had no desire to break. Which was strange, because he had always believed the excitement would end. He had wanted women with a determined fever before, and that compulsion to possess had been there, but it had always passed. Except with Cara, and he had been lost in love at that time. With Cara he hadn't known that driving passion; she had been so fragile, their love so tender.

With Erin the excitement didn't end. It continued to spiral. He could leave her one minute, turn back to her, and find himself fascinated with the sheer glow of her skin, with the way her long back dipped at the waistline in a provocative curve. Then he would feel the laps of fire touching, igniting a rage of desire within him once again.

But when he had finally returned, tired and disgusted, she hadn't been there. He had made all the calls he could think of and paced the room with fear and anxiety over her welfare until cold beads of sweat broke out all over his brow. Then she had waltzed in with Gil Sayer, and stretched to kiss his cheek with her silver eyes dazzling. He had wanted to break her neck. The rage that filled him had been explosive, barely, barely held in check.

He had never liked Sayer, never trusted him. He was overly subservient to any superior, to the Americans, to the Russians. There was just something slimy about his behavior, something that scented of a rat. And Erin had been with him, fawning over him, taken by the blond beach boy good looks, the profusion of flattery.

It had been all Jarod could do to keep himself from flattening Gil against the wall and dumping him out on the street like garbage. He, a man who deplored the use of violence in any form, an agent of the largest peace organization in the world, had wanted to take Sayer apart limb by limb.

But it was still a violent and at times a savage world he lived in. Possession had been threatened, and his responses were those of a primitive ancestor. He had wanted to stomp Sayer, and he longed to wrest Erin into his arms, shake her until that defiant light faded from the silver of her eyes, and take her right there in the kitchen until she cried out that it was only he she could desire.

Fool. He had been her experiment; a venture back into the world. And now that she had discovered that rapturous world, she was apparently eager to experiment with men she found seductive herself. Not while she was his wife. She could withdraw from him, turn her imperious little back on him, and he would tolerate it, for the time. There was no woman living he would beg or force. But he'd be damned if she'd go elsewhere. He did hold the power to subdue her.

Their relationship could no longer be considered polite. He had been back for five days, and for five days they had carefully skirted one another. They ate separately, they picked up after themselves, and Erin never stayed in the same room with him.

Jarod spent as much time away as he could. Hours in the Kremlin, hours at the embassy, hours and hours with Catherine, trying to break the code, trying to discover where the information was coming from, how it was being transmitted, and why it was so destructive.

And ever since last week he had been trying to investigate Sayer. It had been Sayer who had put Erin on the plane the day she had wound up in Sergei's custody. And he was the man Erin would have tolerated with pleasure as a marriage partner.

He knew that he couldn't allow his emotions to tie in with his work. He tried to think that he was controlling them, that pure logic led his investigation. It didn't, in spite of the logical pieces of information about Sayer that pinpointed him as a possible double agent. He had access to certain installations, he could come and go freely, he had friends among the Soviets and Americans alike. And Jarod truly doubted Gil would have any compunctions about using anyone. . . .

"Jarod!"

He snapped back from the intensity of his brooding to remember that Erin had broken her silent cold war to come in and speak with him as if they had made an appointment.

"What?" he demanded curtly, hating the hostile glaze to the shimmering silver of her eyes as she met his gaze. His tone became very harsh as he remembered their last conversation. "I wish the personal side of our relationship to come to an end."

"What?" he snapped again impatiently. "I'm busy, Erin. If you have something to say, please say it."

"Yes," she hissed in return, her body perfectly still and her back straight as she sat. "I wanted to speak to you about my getting out of the U.S.S.R. It seems ridiculous that I must still remain here, making us both so tense and miserable. Or excuse me—you haven't really seemed to notice, but I am tense and miserable, and I'm sure you must at least want your bedroom back. It would only take you a few hours to fly me out of the country, not that much of an inconvenience—"

Jarod tossed his pencil down on the desk so hard that it snapped and half bounced to the floor. He walked away from her, staring out to the street below from the small window. "A few hours would not inconvenience me, Mrs. Steele, but what your leaving the country at this time would do to my credibility would be very inconvenient indeed. Don't you understand yet why you were taken off that plane? Or perhaps you don't realize who ordered you brought back. Sergei Alexandrovich ordered you held, Erin. He can be a nice, nice man, my love, but he could also talk a nun into renouncing her vows. Do you know what I had to do to get you in my American hands that day? Or do you care? I'm afraid you'll have to hear anyway. My neck went on the block. Sergei trusted me when I didn't know whether the hell to trust you or not. He was a little suspicious that my loving fiancée was taking off into the wild blue yonder to begin with, and I had to swear to be responsible for you. There were a number of times after that in which I had to lie through my teeth about the marriage making sense because we were so desperately in love—"

"But I never asked you to lie for me!" Erin exclaimed irritably. "And I certainly never asked you to marry me—"

"Do you know, Erin," he said, his jaw so tensed she was afraid he would crack his own teeth, "sometimes you sound so incredibly dense its difficult to believe that you function in this world as a businesswoman. The Soviets do not like spies—who are spying against them. But we're not dealing with the norm here: countries will hold captured spies to make trades. The person—or persons—we're all chasing like lunatics now is—or are—a mercenary or mercenaries. Information sold to the highest bidder. Damaging information. Both countries keep buying it, but both countries are getting wise. And the selling of nuclear secrets is considered to be high treason. I might also remind you that in the United States high treason is still a crime and those convicted could very easily find themselves executed. So if you find yourself being inconvenienced now because I made the mistake of assuming you would do just about anything to keep your high-fashion rear end safe, that is just too bad. When I can get you out of here credibly—and when I'm damned sure there's no reason to detain you any longer—I will get you out."

She stood, her eyes like silver rapiers, turned with inimitable grace and dignity, and walked out without a word.

Jarod stared after her, wondering why he was shaking furiously. Why had he been so cruel? And why had he lied?

Well, he thought, stooping to pick up the broken piece of the pencil, he hadn't actually lied, but neither had he told the whole truth.

He could get her out of the country. He didn't believe there was a single reason to detain her any longer. And neither did Sergei. He had never seen the slightest evidence that Erin could possibly be involved in anything. If someone had merely intended to use Erin, they had probably realized by now it would be absolutely impossible with both Sergei and himself on to the possibility.

And his story about incompatability was going to have to be the same no matter when she left. True, the longer she stayed, the easier it was going to be. No matter what, he was going to appear to be either a liar or a lovesick fool. But there were few men, Russian or American, who would care to question him. He could silence almost anyone with a glance.

He should let her go. It was driving him mad to watch her silently moving around his home, dressing with understated elegance when she left on her sightseeing trips with Tanya, curling up in jeans and sweatshirt before the fire, slipping downstairs in a softly feminine flannel robe to fix herself a cup of tea before disappearing behind *his* bedroom door for the night.

But now, when he allowed himself to watch her covertly, brooding as he did so, he no longer thought of skin and bones. He could mentally strip her of jeans, dress, or gown, and know with agonizing certainty just what he would bare to his view and touch. His fingers would itch and burn to feel the silk of her skin and golden hair.

The small end of the pencil he had retrieved suddenly snapped in his hand. He looked down at it ruefully. I am not a cruel man, he thought reflectively. What am I doing? And exactly who is it that I am punishing, Erin or myself?

172

It was that night that Erin first heard the balalaika music. It was soft and plaintive, beautiful and wistful. It began at eleven, and ended at exactly eleven thirty, when she heard the outer door to the apartment opening and closing. He had gone again.

Despite her best efforts at sleep, she lay awake until she heard the opening and closing of the door once more, and knew that he had returned. It was still an agony to wonder where he went, but she closed her eyes to the possibilities.

He had, at least, come home.

Erin was surprised to find him at the dining room table sipping coffee when she came down in the morning. He was usually gone before she awoke.

He glanced at her immediately, taking in her dove-gray wool skirt suit and neat chignon with cool, enigmatic eyes.

"The coffee is fresh," he informed her. "Pour yourself a cup and come back here, please. I need to talk to you."

Erin didn't reply but walked into the kitchen to pour herself a cup of coffee. She hated his politely aloof tone. It made her feel like a personal secretary.

Erin sat down at the table across from him and stared at him as she sipped her coffee. Why didn't he ever look tired? she wondered resentfully. He couldn't get more than five or six hours of sleep a night, yet the granite composure of his rugged features never changed.

His eyes were crystal sharp, and as usual, not even the sharp business suit he wore could take away from that primitive sexual appeal he exuded.

No, it's just me, she thought. I'm letting all this get to me. He isn't extraordinary; he's a normal man.

A normal man who still, despite the wall of ice between them, could touch her to a sizzling warmth with his voice, a look, a brush of his body against hers.

"Where are you going today?" he demanded, lighting a cigarette and pushing the pack across the table toward her.

Erin was glad his basic courtesy still extended to his making such gestures. Reaching for the pack and extracting a cigarette gave her time to think, to replace the coloring that had faded from her face at the unexpected question.

She accepted his light and leaned back in her chair exhaling. "Out with Tanya, of course," she murmured, meeting his gaze with her composure regained and her silver eyes wide with mock innocence. "Where else am I allowed to go?"

He didn't fall for the bait. "I know you're going out with Tanya. Where?"

Erin shrugged uneasily. "Probably to the GUM department store, and to the Kremlin and to the Armory. We didn't set anything too definite. Why? I didn't realize I was supposed to give you an hour-by-hour agenda."

"You're not. I would simply like you to make sure you're back here by four or five. We're having a dinner party."

Erin frowned. "We are? Tonight? You should have mentioned it earlier. There isn't too much in the house—"

"I wasn't expecting you to cook," Jarod interrupted dryly. "Just be back in time to shower and change and act like a hostess."

Erin lowered her lashes and sipped her coffee. His tone stung; no, he didn't expect anything of her. All she had to do was follow house rules and not twist at the prison bars he had erected around her and everything was fine.

"Who is coming?"

"It will be small. Sergei and his wife, Joe Mahoney, Gil, and Tanya."

"Are we having this dinner party for any special reason?"

"Certainly. We've been married three weeks. It's time we did a little entertaining."

They both fell silent. Had she been summarily dismissed? Erin wondered bitterly.

She raised her eyes to meet his again. "Is that all?"

"For the moment."

Erin stubbed out her cigarette, picked up her coffee cup, and went on into the kitchen. Yes, sir, she thought bleakly. I'll take care of this immediately. No problem. Except a secretary usually got a pat on the head. A nice lunch out. A bonus at Christmas. And two weeks summer vacation.

I am really going to go crazy, Erin thought, hands clasping the ridge of the counter in front of the sink as she stared blankly at the spigots. I've done this myself, I know, but how different could it have been?

The doorbell rang as she stood there, and she heard Jarod opening the door and greeting Tanya warmly. Their conversation suddenly turned to Russian and Erin's fingers tightened. Please, Tanya, she prayed silently, don't tell him where we're really going.

Erin hastily grabbed her purse and coat and hurried into the hallway. The less time Jarod had to query Tanya the better off she was going to be.

"Good morning," she called cheerfully.

"Good morning," Tanya returned. "Ready?"

"Yes, yes, I am," Erin smiled. She turned hesitantly to Jarod. "Ah . . . good-bye, darling."

"Have a nice day," he responded cordially. He took a step toward her. His blue eyes touched upon her for a second, his arms came around her, and his lips brushed hers. "See you later," he murmured huskily.

The loving husband, Erin thought bitterly. But then she, too, had done her part.

But she could feel the touch of his lips on hers as she moved out into the cold with Tanya. Tears unaccountably stung in her eyes. How had things gone so terribly, terribly wrong? They had been lovers, almost friends; there had been times they had laughed together. And why was it still so damned cold? It was May, the snow should be gone, spring should be here. . . .

Erin chatted idly with Tanya as they got into her small economy car, but once they were seated and moving into traffic, she felt the need to assure herself. She had come close to the Russian woman during her time in the Soviet Union, and she sensed that she could trust her—on a friendship level that went beyond cultural differences and the strange invasions of privacy Erin had learned existed within the country.

"You didn't tell Jarod where we were going, did you?"

Tanya glanced at Erin and then returned her eyes to the road. "No, I didn't tell him." She fell silent for a moment, and then asked the question bothering her. "But I still don't know why you would not talk to your husband. It is a natural thing. He could have gotten you this appointment long ago!"

Erin shrugged uncomfortably. Why hadn't she been able to speak with Jarod in those first pleasant days of her marriage? Because we were lovers, she thought, but still strangers. She simply couldn't have calmly discussed birth control with him, and she had taken certain precautions. Now she finally had her appointment—when it didn't seem so terribly necessary. But she was in love with Jarod, and she didn't trust herself. If he just touched her, she might not have the strength to refuse to reach out in return.

Sensibly, logically, maturely—it could only be to her own best interests to be prepared should anything happen again. It was frightening to realize she had first been so caught up in emotion and then in whirlwind abandon that her head had been in the clouds and she had not thought of the possible consequences until later. Of course, then she had protected herself, but the precautions had left her terribly uneasy. She couldn't take any more chances.

Erin realized suddenly that Tanya was waiting for a reply.

"Jarod is very busy," Erin murmured. "It's as I told you before: I don't like to bother him with . . . with problems I can handle myself."

Tanya said nothing, and Erin knew her answer sounded as feeble as it had the night they had spoken on the phone. She knew that the Russian woman was still wondering why Erin hadn't taken care of this in the States. Erin could think of no feasible explanation, so she gave none. It would be impossible to say that her first marriage had left her in terror of anything so small as a kiss; impossible to say that it had taken a trip to the Soviet Union and a strange meeting with a dark and mysterious man to break the spell of fear and, in a devastating detour into tenderness, teach her that things could be shatteringly beautiful.

The doctor's office was near GUM, the state department store. Erin breathed a sigh of relief. She could shop after the appointment and Jarod would have no questions.

I'm being paranoid, she warned herself. If she went out with Tanya, Jarod never questioned her anyway. In fact, the trust he had in Tanya was almost annoying.

The doctor's office was like a doctor's office anywhere—except that Erin needed Tanya to interpret for her as the doctor asked his questions. She found it irritatingly difficult to answer the simplest question without stuttering. His exam was as crisp and clean and professional as the sterile white of the office. And it was thorough. Erin breathed a sigh of relief on leaving; she had been sure the

176

doctor would discover a tiny malfunction within her body and detain her.

Tanya laughed as they left the office. "You look as if you have just walked out of the Siberian snows!"

Erin flushed. "I always hate doctors' appointments."

"So do I," Tanya admitted. "Let's stop somewhere and have a drink and then we shall purchase something at GUM to ease that guilty conscious of yours."

"My conscious isn't guilty!" Erin protested.

Tanya lightly quirked her brows, saying nothing until they were seated in a pleasant lunch establishment. It wasn't a tourist restaurant, and therefore Erin had to rely upon her guide's translations. After they had ordered drinks and sandwiches, Erin once more found Tanya gazing at her speculatively. She grimaced and suddenly blurted out, "Erin, you do know that I am your friend."

Erin smiled quizzically. "Thank you, Tanya. I believe that."

Tanya took a sip of dark Russian beer. "I know that you are alone here—except for your husband, of course. But there are things a woman doesn't always wish to discuss with a man. I feel that you are having a problem with your marriage, and I would like to help in any way that I can. I think so very much of both you and Jarod." Tanya smiled warmly. "I have three married sisters, and I have the feeling that newlywed difficulties are very similar, be we Russians or Americans."

Erin grimaced. "I'll bet you're right, Tanya." How she hated lying to this woman, who really was her only friend in the Soviet Union. But she couldn't tell the truth, any of it. "There really isn't anything wrong, Tanya. We, ah, simply weren't expecting to get married in the Soviet Union, and I don't like to bother Jarod with anything now because he is so very busy."

Erin sensed that Tanya didn't believe her, but the Russian woman pressed no further. Tanya shrugged and went on to talk about her family, amusing Erin with stories about her nephews and nieces. When they finished lunch, they went on to pick up a few items at the department store and then Tanya brought Erin home, assuring her she would return for the dinner party.

Erin heard Jarod's movements in the den as she mounted the staircase, but she would have gone on straight to the bedroom if he

177

hadn't called her. She paused in the doorway as he clipped out her name.

"Did you have a nice day?" he inquired, the blue of his eyes very penetrating upon her. Why did she feel as if he could see straight through flesh and dig into her soul?

"Yes," she replied. "It was fine. We went to lunch and poked around the GUM."

He nodded absently. "I've arranged your transport out. We'll leave here on the first of June."

Erin felt as if a cold shaft had hit her, as if she would buckle in the doorway. But she didn't buckle, she didn't move, she didn't even blink. "That's fine. Thank you."

"I wanted to let you know in case you had agents or managers or anyone to contact."

"Thank you." She suddenly remembered the letter she had left on his desk to Mary before his disastrous return from Kiev. "Oh, Jarod—" she began.

"I mailed your letter the day I saw it," he told her before she could go further.

"Thank you," Erin murmured again.

His eyes had returned to his desk. She walked on into the bedroom, fighting the urge to burst into tears. She was glad to know her departure date. She wanted to go home, she wanted to end this torture. And she would never see him again.

It seemed as if her mind waged silent battles, then went numb as she showered and dressed for the party. She chose a navy velvet gown to wear, one with long sleeves and a Chinese collar. Elegant and conservative. Jarod, she thought, would approve.

When she emerged from the bedroom she discovered the apartment full of activity. A plump cook as wide as she was short was busy in the kitchen creating things that smelled divine, and two younger women were setting the dining room table with shimmering silver and crystal. Erin didn't see Jarod, so she smiled tentatively at the women, poured herself a glass of wine, and slipped into the music room—out of the way. She found herself glancing at the balalaika and wondering again at the man who could play the old instrument so beautifully. Then her glance fell to the diamond she wore—the diamond given to her by both Jarod and Sergei. It seemed to mock her as it brilliantly dazzled.

Suddenly determined, Erin set her wine down and marched into the kitchen, excusing herself to the amicably grinning cook. She squeezed a portion of dish soap over her hand and began to work at the ring, which refused to slide over her knuckle. She became so engrossed that she didn't hear Jarod come up behind her.

"What are you doing?" he demanded, startling her.

She flew around, splaying him with soap and water. And of course he was already dressed, in velvet. His eyes closed, and a long sigh of resigned control escaped him.

"I'm sorry—" Erin began.

"Just hand me a towel, please."

Erin groped for the hand towel and passed it to him. Luckily, no real damage was done. He brushed his shirt and jacket quickly with the terry cloth and it was apparent they would dry without staining. Erin kept staring at him, annoyed that she was once more appearing like the disaster that waited to happen. "You startled me," she accused.

"I asked you what you were doing."

"I . . . uh . . ." Erin stumbled for only a minute, then noticed that the hired cook was watching them uncomfortably. She stiffened. "Could we talk in the music room, please."

He inclined his head toward her sardonically. "Certainly."

Erin retrieved her wine glass as soon as they entered the room. She took a sip, then spun to face him. "I insist upon giving this ring back to Sergei. I'm leaving in a little over a month, and it isn't right that I take—"

"Oh, dammit, that again!" Jarod interrupted irritably. "Will you please listen and try to understand? The ring is mine, and it means nothing. While you are here, I prefer that you wear it. When you return home, do whatever you please: keep it, dump it, sell it, or give it away. Just please don't bring it up again!"

Erin was too startled by his vehemence to give an immediate reply, and by that time he was going on. "I'd like this party to break up at about eleven—I have to go out after. I'd appreciate it if you would help see that things go smoothly so that our guests will leave by then."

He turned then as the doorbell rang.

Without thinking, Erin called after him. "Jarod?"

Her voice was soft; he turned back to her.

"Where—where are you going?"

He hesitated, and she felt as if he sought something from within her with his eyes. "I have business on the square," he said quietly. "I'll be home right after."

He left her behind to open the door.

The dinner went very smoothly. The plump little cook had created a mouth-watering concoction of beef in pastry that was nothing short of delicious, and the talk was casual. But as they progressed to coffee and brandy, Erin noticed that Jarod seemed to be watching. Watching what, she wasn't sure. But she had come to know him somewhat. She knew the keen alertness that was ever alive in his gaze despite his casual stance. She knew he could be engaged in one conversation while listening to another, that his solicitous, tender touches throughout the evening were all a part of his design, whatever that design was. Did he feel her? she wondered. And she felt ever so slightly ill because she could feel him so intensely, the gentle graze of his velvet against her cheek, the scent that had long ago lured her, the touch of his eyes, his hands upon her shoulders.

He was talked into playing the balalaika in accompaniment to Tanya at the piano after coffee. Erin had heard him play before, but had never seen him. She marveled at his ease with the instrument, at the lightness of his strong fingers upon the strings. He was such a contrast of qualities, but each of his contrasts further emmeshed Erin in the man.

She glanced at the clock after the musicians declined to do another number to find to her horror that it was already half past ten. Jarod had asked her to help ease their company out by eleven—and she was determined to show him that she was capable. She picked up several of the empty snifters and liqueur glasses to bring them to the kitchen, hoping someone would realize that she was cleaning up because it was late.

"Can I help you?"

Erin glanced up from the sink where she had deposited the glasses to see Gil's eager gaze upon her. He was such an amazingly pleasant person, Erin thought. Always willing to help, always anxious to please. She smiled at him. Jarod didn't want her out with Gil, but Jarod had asked Gil into the house. Surely he couldn't find fault with her for being pleasant in return to a guest in her own home.

"Thanks, Gil," she smiled.

He disappeared and returned to hand her some empty coffee cups and saucers. "You look tired," he said compassionately. "Is that why you're trying to chase us all out?"

"I'm not—" Erin protested, and then she laughed. "All right," she whispered conspiratorially. "I am trying to chase you all out, but not because I'm tired. Jarod has to take care of some quick business late tonight."

"Ohhh . . ." Gill whispered back. "Out on Red Square, huh?"

Gil must be working on the same stuff, Erin thought, pleased to hear his words. It meant that Jarod really was working, that he wasn't leaving her for another woman—at least, not tonight.

Erin nodded with a half smile.

Gil winked. "I'll help you!" he whispered.

True to his promise, Gil returned to the music room and yawned deeply, then apologized profusely and said he must leave. He thanked both Jarod and Erin—kissing her hand elegantly—and led the others into also voicing their thanks and following him out of the door.

Finding herself nervous and alone with Jarod, Erin once more set about cleaning up the refuse of the party, collecting glasses and cups and emptying ashtrays. The cook and serving girls had left right after the last dessert dish had been picked up, and it seemed the only logical thing to do.

His fingers slipped around her arm as she bent to collect a demitasse cup. "Don't bother," he said softly, whirling her around and meeting her wide surprised eyes. "Sonia will be back in the morning and she likes her job. If you leave things too clean, she won't have anything to do." Even he, who knew both the strengths and delicacies of her beauty, was a bit awed by his wife in the navy velvet gown. It heightened the conflict of angel and devil he had always sensed within her. It was conservative, it was concealing, but the velvet clung to her slender curves in a hugging softness of sheer sensuality.

He had been smiling; he stiffened. "Go up and get some sleep," he ordered gruffly.

He had been too close; he could have easily read the things in her eyes, heard the pounding of her heart. She had to move, quickly, before he could sense the things she never wanted him to know.

Erin nodded wordlessly and jerked her arm from his grasp.

His call stopped her at the stairway. "Thank you for this evening. Everything went smoothly. And"—he hesitated only a second—"you were exquisitely lovely."

He spun around before she could reply. Erin watched while he took his overcoat from the hall closet and slipped into it. He didn't glance her way again, but opened the door and disappeared into the night.

She stood at the foot of the staircase biting her lip for a long while, despising the way she clung to his words. "You were exquisitely lovely." Finally she turned and trudged slowly up the stairs, shedding her velvet gown and slipping into a flannel nightdress. She was tired, bone weary, but she seemed doomed to sleeplessness. So she was awake when he returned hours later.

She automatically tensed when the door to the bedroom opened, and she instinctively kept her eyes closed as he walked to the side of the bed. He made no sound, but he stood there, staring at her.

Although he always gave so little away, she was becoming attuned to his moods and emotions. She could always feel his presence, and the radiating heat she felt now was chilling. He certainly hadn't come because he thought her lovely. He was angry. Lividly angry. She could feel it as he stood there, a hot, tangible, palpitating presence.

She tried not to move, not to curl away in instinctive and innocent fear. Jarod would not harm her, but she sensed that he wanted to. That he wanted to waken her, shake her, challenge her. Why? she wondered desperately. Why?

It seemed that he stood there for an eternity, watching her. Erin prayed that he believed she slept. She willed herself not to move, not to jerk. She felt him turn. As silently as he had come, he had gone with his uncanny quiet, and she was left to lie awake for hours more, wondering what on God's earth she could have possibly done. . . .

INTERLUDE

The snow was absurdly deep for this time of the year. Flurries of an hour ago had become flakes, and Red Square was covered in a blanket of white.

His footsteps crunched upon the new snow as he walked, a lone, dark figure in a navy wool topcoat and typical furred hat. He paused before the square near St. Basil's. To the right he could see Lenin's tomb before the red brick Kremlin walls. The guards stood like statues, motionless in the snow.

Why had he come tonight? he wondered, blowing on his gloved hands as if he could add warmth beneath the leather. Instinct. Something in the air of the streets; an aura of tension that had invaded the embassy today, alerted his bloodstream. He was still sure the action took place on Red Square, beneath the noses of them all. At midnight.

In the distance, clocks began to strike the chimes of midnight. He watched as the Kremlin gates opened, as a new vanguard goose-stepped its way to the marble mausoleum.

He waited, tensed. But there was nothing out of the ordinary. Nothing he could see. Nothing he could feel. Nothing, not a damn thing he could hear.

The high-stepped, awesome, and militaristic changing of the guard was complete, and still nothing had happened. He was a fool. A lone figure standing in the snow, freezing like an ass.

The first sound came so quickly he didn't realize what it was. A sound like the whip of the wind, or the instant zzz of a mosquito. Except that there weren't any mosquitos in the frigid capital this May.

The instant of paralyzing numbness was over. Before the next zzz

183

whistled by, he had dropped and rolled in the snow, finding cover behind a workmen's scaffolding. He lifted his head, his blue eyes scanning the frosted terrain, for in the orange glow of the lights was a figure, running. Keeping low he leaped back to his feet, shouting.

Whistles shrieked through the night as he tore after the disappearing form. He was not a lone figure anymore; the square had come alive with racing men in uniforms.

Jarod ran with the pulsing of his blood pounding in his temples. He searched every possible avenue of escape; every nook and cranny near the high brick walls. But despite his efforts, and those of the ultra efficient, productively trained officers, the form had disappeared.

He was breathing heavily, dusting the snow from his fur cap upon his knee, as his long strides brought him disgustedly back to the square. He stopped dead as he saw the man waiting for him, his eyes taking on a guarded mist that shrouded emotion as the snow did the ground.

"Well, my friend, you must be on to something," Sergei said with quirked brows. "Someone taking potshots at you in the snow—that someone must be frightened of your knowledge, Jarod."

"I haven't got a damned thing, Sergei," Jarod said tiredly. "If I did, there wouldn't be someone there taking potshots at me in the snow." He accepted a cigarette from Alexandrovich and watched as the smoke joined the mist of his breath. "Thanks for the quick action, Sergei. My thanks to your men. It is no fault of theirs that we lost this wraith."

Sergei shrugged. "Murder is a crime in the Soviet Union, too, my friend."

"Unless it's sanctioned?"

Again Sergei shrugged. "From you, Jarod, I will not take offense."

They both fell silent, the flames of their cigarettes flaring against the glow and the darkness.

"How come you happened to be here?" Jarod asked.

Sergei laughed. "Feeling, my friend. The same as you. Gut feeling. And I didn't want anything happening to you, Jarod."

"Thanks, Sergei, but I can take care of myself."

Sergei characteristically raised his shoulders again. "No man can

184

always take care of himself, Jarod. And this is my country."

"Yeah." Jarod dropped his cigarette to the snow, and out of habit, crushed out the flame. He jammed his gloved hands into his pockets.

"I'm heading home. I'm freezing, I've got snow inside my clothes."

Sergei chuckled. "If I were you, Steele, I would be home now. Very warm in my bed. Only a fool or a fanatic leaves a woman like that."

Jarod moved off, cursing silently beneath his breath. "Maybe I'm a bit of both," he shouted aloud over his shoulder.

Sergei's deep laughter grew in the night. "Maybe, friend, maybe!" He watched as the tall dark figure diminished. "I'll pick you up in the morning myself, and see you to the airport for that Leningrad trip."

A hand lifted in the air assured him he had been heard. Still chuckling, Sergei Alexandrovich walked off through the snow.

When Jarod reached the apartment, he couldn't quell the temptation to look at her. He entered the room with no real attempt to be silent. But she slept like an angel. Her gold hair spread over the pillow in a haloed web, hair that compelled one to touch, hair that held a man in a web of seductive fascination.

She was the only one who had known where he would be tonight. A devil in an angel's guise?

He wanted to wake her, to shake her, to demand that she tell him the truth, the complete truth. Who had she spoken with, who did she see? Had she whispered to someone at the party, or had she waited until the door closed behind him and made a phone call? Had she known?

He ground his teeth hard. She had only been used, she had only been used. He wanted to think that, believe that, so badly. But suspicions were rising again along with his alarm. He had cleared her in his own mind and now . . .

Now I really cannot let you go, he thought with bitter irony.

He pushed his hands farther into his pockets, the fingers curling inward. Damn, did he want to wake her. Jerk her out of the bed. Shock her from her cool composure. . . . And take her into his arms. Rake his fingers through her golden field of hair. Force her silver eyes to his. Dare her cool innocence, her denial, her dignity. Let her know that the denial was a lie. Prove that he could strip away her pretense, find the woman he had created. Feel himself within her again. Feel warm, the fever burning away the cold, the reckless, unchecked passion that could erase the world.

He stared at her a moment longer, closed his eyes tightly and swallowed, and retraced his footsteps out of the room.

X

"Wake up. Now. I leave in ten minutes and I have to talk to you first."

Erin blinked groggily, not really believing that he was standing over her again, already clad in his coat, his gloves in his hands.

She shook her head, astonished by the rudeness of his tone and trying desperately to clear the sleep from her mind.

"What?" she mumbled in confusion. "You're leaving again? Where—where are you going?"

"Leningrad," he said briefly, reaching for her hand and pulling her from the bed. "I have a cup of coffee poured for you downstairs. You have to hurry up. I let you sleep as late as possible."

"What a gentleman," Erin murmured sarcastically. She twisted her hand from his grasp. "Let me wash my face—"

"You have sixty seconds."

She stared at him with ill-concealed outrage but stepped cautiously around him and into the bathroom, where she rinsed away some of the fog of her deep sleep.

"Erin!"

"I'm coming!"

She followed him down the staircase and into the dining room. He thrust a coffee cup into her hand and she sipped at it. "How long will you be gone?"

"Overnight. And I mean overnight. I'll be back by noon tomorrow. And while I'm gone, you will not leave the apartment. I mean that, too, Erin. There's going to be a guard outside, and should you choose to disobey my orders, I want to warn you that you will be returned bodily to the apartment."

Erin gaped at him, astounded and infuriated.

"Why?" was all she could manage to gasp.

187

Jarod stepped past her, carrying his suitcase to the hall. He opened the door, looked out in the corridor, then returned to her briefly.

"Who did you talk to last night?"

Erin's eyes narrowed dangerously and her fingers curled into claws within her hands. "Jarod, you know damned well who I talked to last night. We had a dinner here. I talked to all our guests. Mr. and Mrs. Alexandrovich. Tanya. Joe Mahoney. Gil Sayer. I also spoke to the cook and the two girls who served dinner, but I'm not sure that counts because I don't believe they understood a single word I said."

"No one else?"

"No one else."

"Who did you tell I was leaving last night?"

Erin inhaled sharply, but rigidly held her composure. Something had obviously happened. But she couldn't be at fault, she hadn't said anything to anyone. . . .

Yes, she had, she had told Gil. But she was certain Gil was guilty of nothing. And it was evident that Jarod disliked Gil to begin with, whether he behaved politely toward the man or not. She couldn't tell Jarod she had spoken to Gil. Jarod was angrier than she had ever seen him, and she felt it was only the tip of the iceberg. Gil would be hanged in Jarod's book without a trial, and whatever it was, Gil couldn't be involved.

"I didn't tell anyone."

Jarod was silent for a moment, but the blue daggers that riveted her to a standstill told her she was a liar.

Indignation suddenly flared within her. He didn't give a damn about her, but he was raising a stink over this whole Gil Sayer thing. Because he was possessive, because he didn't want his pride and ego marred. . . . And he was acting like a jailer.

"Don't leave the apartment," he warned her again.

"Go to hell!" Erin flared. "You may have one of your paid dragoons outside now, but it won't last, Jarod. I've had it. There's a phone here, and I'll get hold of someone at the embassy. I am getting out. Out! I don't care any longer about appearances, I didn't create this fiasco! I was willing to try things your way; I was willing to give up two months of my life. But that was when you could behave like a halfway decent person. You are insufferable. You belong at the head of the Soviet purges. As I've told you before, you should be a damned communist, you make a marvelous Russian, you have a—"

"Stop it, Erin!"

His words were a roar, but she couldn't heed them. She was torn in two, feeling cleanly knifed in half. She loved him, and the more that the feeling ingrained itself within her heart, the more he seemed to turn from her. She loved him, and she hated him with a terrible intensity because of that love.

"I will not stop! And you will not tell me I can't see or talk to Gil Sayer. At least he still remembers how to be an American."

"Erin!" He grasped her shoulders, and her wrath bubbled within her uncontrollably.

She tried to wrench from his grasp but found it firm. "Let go of me"—her palm worked free and rose, coming across his face—"you dictator! You—"

She broke off abruptly, stunned as he returned her slap, his palm delivering a stinging blow across her cheek. Her fingers moved instantly to her sore flesh. She realized somewhere in a far corner of her mind that his eyes were picturing a pain deeper than her own. He opened his mouth, an apology forming, but she spoke out first. "I despise you."

His mouth clamped shut, then opened once more. "Yes, you do make that quite evident." All the safeguards had slipped over his eyes once more. He spoke again with bitter mockery. "I do apologize. That was unforgivable." He turned, only to halt immediately.

Sergei Alexandrovich was standing in the open doorway. How much he had heard or seen was impossible to fathom.

Erin felt her entire body tense, and she realized she was holding a weak breath. But for his own reasons, Sergei seemed determined to ease the situation, pretending he had walked in on nothing.

"Good morning, good morning! Erin, you are truly a delight among women. Beautiful even in dawn's dishabille!" He caught and kissed her hand. "I'm glad to see you awake, my dear. I would like to request your company for luncheon, after I see this husband of yours off at the airport. Would that be convenient to your plans?"

She couldn't seem to speak. It was all too ridiculous. She and Jarod were both wearing the red marks of one another's hands and now this Russian was charmingly asking her out to lunch after

probably having heard her taunting Jarod with degradations aimed at his associations with the Russians. On top of all that, she had just been told she would be lugged back in if she attempted to leave the apartment. She should tell Sergei that, Erin thought. I'm so sorry, Mr. Alexandrovich, my husband doesn't allow me out of the apartment, and I really didn't mean all those things I said, about Jarod, or in general. You're a very nice man, Mr. Alexandrovich. And Tanya is lovely. I know that there are wonderful Soviet people.
. . .

Her thoughts were racing, but all she could actually manage as an answer was an "Ahh . . . ahhh . . ." And to her ultimate self-disgust, she found herself looking to her husband for guidance.

"Go to lunch with Sergei," Jarod said. "He'll see you home safely." He addressed the other man. "We'd better go. I don't want to miss this flight."

Jarod made no pretense at kissing her good-bye, Sergei spoke to her gently, then both men were gone. The door was closed.

Erin stared at the closed door numbly for several seconds. Then she sank to the floor and sat there and cried.

She wore a cape suit to have lunch with Sergei. It was both proper and conservative, and yet eye-catchingly fashionable. That had been one of the differences she had noticed in the U.S.S.R.: the clothing worn was much more drab than that worn in the U.S. She wanted to dress to please the Russian man, and she felt she had done just that with a perfect compromise between attractiveness and utility.

She had wondered a bit bitterly why Jarod had been unconcerned about handing her over to Sergei when he had—in no uncertain terms—restricted her from the company of a fellow American. But she had to admit that she didn't object to Sergei. He was constantly charming, and although she knew she would be a fool to think him any less intense than Jarod, she also felt an instinctive trust.

She was a bit mortified over the scene he had witnessed, but she was also eager to get away from the apartment, and she was very eager to quiz Sergei. Perhaps she could draw some of the answers from him that Jarod refused to give her.

Erin was glad she had showered and dressed as soon as she had managed to pick herself up from the floor, because Sergei returned promptly at eleven. He complimented her on her appearance with both words and sparkling eyes, then ushered her into his car.

"Where are we going?" Erin asked.

He smiled. "Leningrad."

"Leningrad?" Erin gasped.

"Umm. Don't worry, Mrs. Steele. I am not planning a clash with your husband. I shall never tell him about our little trip—we shall keep it a secret."

Thoroughly confused, Erin began to stammer. "But Sergei—I can't go to Leningrad! I wind up in trouble every time I move! I don't dare try to hop a flight—"

"We won't be hopping a flight—we will be taking my plane. And unless you step on a guard's foot at the Hermitage, it will be impossible for you to get into trouble in my company."

This was crazy, Erin thought. She had no good reason to trust a Russian, but she did. And suddenly she was laughing. "Don't ever tell that one to Jarod—he would be convinced that I would manage to step on a guard's foot!" She sobered. "Sergei, I don't get this. We're going to take your private plane and fly to Leningrad. Why?"

Sergei glanced at her with an easy grin and then returned his gaze to the road. "Because I think you have a few questions you wish to have answered. If I am going to answer them, I wish to do so correctly. So if you will bear with an eccentric man, you will return home this evening a far wiser woman."

He was a conspirator, Erin realized. Why? She sighed. Apparently she would discover soon enough. She fell silent for a moment and then asked, "Sergei?"

"Yes?"

"If . . . if Jarod should call home and I am not there until late, won't he worry?"

"Nyet! No, no, he will know that you can be nowhere except with me."

Erin settled back into the comfortable seat, glad of the companionable silence. They reached the airport a few moments later and were ushered to an amazingly plush private plane with deep, soft beige carpeting, engulfing beige seats, and the utmost in oak tables and bars.

Sergei smiled as the jet arced into the air and said that she could release the seatbelt. "I have been watching you, Erin. You are thinking that we are not at all a 'classless' society, that many of us live with far superior conditions."

"I didn't say anything, Sergei—" Erin protested with a flush. That had been exactly what she had been thinking.

"Ahh, my dear Erin, you are not good at deceit. I only wish to draw to your attention that I am a public servant. Your White House is a mansion, and your president has many such niceties at his disposal as this plane."

Erin nodded, not entirely accepting his words, but sorry for the things she had said that he had surely overheard.

"Sergei," she murmured. "I . . . I really don't . . ." She lifted her hands helplessly, then grimaced. "For one, I really don't know how to say this. I know you must have heard some of the things I said to Jarod this morning. I am an American; I will always think my system best. But I've learned a great deal about people on this trip, and I . . . well, I think you're an exceptionally fine man, and that fine people come in any nationality."

Sergei half smiled, reached for her hand, caught it, and squeezed it. "Thank you. You need say no more. You did not offend me this morning; I was just sorry to see you tear at one another. That is why we've come today. But for now, shall I get you a drink?"

Erin smiled gratefully and nodded. "Vodka and tonic?" she inquired hopefully. "With lime?"

"Certainly."

He fixed the drink himself and handed it to her, shrugged, and mixed the same for himself. Then he sat, watching her and smiling at her again.

Erin sipped her drink, brooding for a moment. But he had promised to answer her questions, so she might as well begin asking them.

"Sergei—please explain my ring."

He chuckled. "You must bear with me. You will get your answers in Leningrad."

It was just after twelve when they reached the city, and Sergei was determined to take her on a whirlwind tour. He gave her exactly two hours to taste the treasures of the Hermitage, the one-time Winter Palace beloved by Catherine the Great. Next he took her outside the city to the fabulous Summer Palace—and she marveled at the cascading waterfalls that ran free and sparkling clear despite the cold. They picked up sausage sandwiches and warm beer from a street vendor, and then Sergei was guiding the car brought to him at the plane through outer city streets again. She was startled to realize he had brought her to a cemetery. Soft music played, and numerous monuments rose above the thin mist of snow over the endless mounds of grass.

Sergei looped an arm in hers as he led her along a row of the countless mounds. "Leningrad was held under a terrible siege in World War Two," he told her. "You have probably studied this. I tell you now only because I wish you to realize what the terrible devastation of war did to us—and why it remains with us to this day." He swept an arm out to encompass the row upon row of mounds. "Two thousand are buried to a mound. Men, women, children. In the war all told, Erin, twenty million of our people died. We are actually made up of fifteen nationalities, you know. But all suffered. The Belorussians, the Ukrainians, our Mongol people; those of our European cities the worst, of course. Leningrad, terribly. My mother is buried here, Erin."

"I'm sorry," Erin said softly.

"The war was long, long ago, but it is good that we do not forget that all suffer in war. I brought you here because I wanted you to see the fate of most of my family." He paused, smiling kindly at her, his hazel eyes offering that unique warmth she had sensed from the beginning. "My mother had a younger sister, and she survived the siege and the war. She met and fell in love with an American war correspondent, and after the upheaval of war she was able to marry her American lover and receive permission to leave with him. She even managed to return to the U.S.S.R. with her husband years later. They were both well respected and liked—and trusted by their own government and ours." He laughed suddenly. "Erin, you are so lovely. You listen so politely to the rumblings of a middle-aged man, far too courteous to ask, What has this to do with me? Well, I will tell you. That ring you wear belonged to my mother's sister. She meant for my daughter to have it, but we lost Sibia when she was but an infant, and now I have only a son. Not one to care for diamonds. I have intended for many years to give it to Jarod—yet he had no need when he met Cara because they were both so impetuous—he purchased a ring in the States for her the day after he met her."

"Sergei," Erin murmured shaking her head, "wait, you're losing me. I still don't—"

"I do get ahead of myself, eh?" Sergei sighed an interruption. "My mother's lovely younger sister was your husband's mother. Jarod and I are first cousins. He has not told you? No, I thought not."

"But . . . but . . ." Erin felt the draft of the cold seeping around her as she stuttered blankly. "Jarod . . . is . . . half Russian?"

Amusement touched Sergei's eyes, a kindly, twinkling amusement. "Yes, and no. Yes, by the land, by blood, he is half Russian. No, he is an American, as all immigrants to your country become American. His heart and his soul and his beliefs are all American. He was conceived on Russian soil, but born on American. But like many Americans, he cannot completely throw away his past. He has ties to many old customs and ways. He speaks our language with his mother's accent. And he plays the balailaika as few can." Sergei paused. "You can see why Jarod is so excellent for his position. He knows the subtleties of both peoples, the temperaments, the desires, the fears. If there exists a man who can control a negotiation, that man is Jarod Steele."

"He never aspired to be the president. . . ." Erin heard herself murmur.

"No," Sergei agreed. "It would be unlikely he could ever be elected president of your country. But secretary of state? Who knows? I believe many hope that it will be in the cards for him."

Erin was shaking miserably. It was so cold out here. There was nothing especially morbid about the cemetery; it was even peaceful. But she was filled with the pain of knowing what she had inadvertently said. "You should be a Russian . . . the head of the KGB . . . " And all the while, he was a Russian . . . but an American. . . .

"Come." Sergei took her arm again. "We will have a lovely dinner, and then I will fly you home."

It wasn't until he had fulfilled his promise and wined and dined her elegantly and returned her to the apartment late that night that he paused to speak seriously again. "Erin, I know that this engagement and marriage was a foil on behalf of my cousin. But I would also tell you that he would not have taken the step if he didn't care. He is a little lost in the clouds now. Jarod is a man who does nothing lightly. He lives intensely, he loves intensely. When he lost Cara, he was devastated. He is afraid to love again; he will not even admit to himself that he does love you. Give him time."

Erin compressed her lips and lowered her lashes. He doesn't admit it because he doesn't love me, she thought, but she didn't wish to say so to Sergei, not after all he had done to try to set things straight.

"Sergei—" Erin hesitated just a moment, chewing her lip. "Do you know what happened last night? Why Jarod was in such a terrible mood this morning?"

Sergei hesitated in turn. He didn't wish to tell her the whole truth, and still he had no wish to lie. He hadn't the emotional involvement with Erin that Jarod had, and therefore he was free to work on his instincts, which assured him Erin was as entirely innocent as she appeared of any wrongdoing. And yet keeping her in the dark was the thing that could leave her susceptible to being used.

He hesitated no longer. "I am sure Jarod has mentioned Project Midnight to you. That it exists is no secret to anyone. We Soviets and Americans can be alike in certain ways. When secrets are offered, we are like little children grasping for candy—even when we know we will be sick. We never know when we might get the edge. But we have both been betrayed—and we no longer know the truth from the lies.

"This double spy we seek has no loyalty, no nation. We seek a mercenary who looks for top dollar only. We know information is passed at midnight—and I, like Jarod, believe the action takes place on Red Square. There is someone who laughs before the very nose of the Soviet seat of power.

"I am a Russian, Erin. This is my country, my power. But like my American cousin, I dread war. I was a child when I saw my city of birth razed to the ground, the carcasses of horses lying with those of men—and children. Like Jarod, I wish to put a stop to this rubbing raw of possible negotiations.

"We know of a man who was involved in this razor-edged double-dealing. He was with the American embassy—a great embarrassment to the Americans. And we have all seen fit to allow his death to be forgotten. But before he was killed, he had begun to fear for his life. He fed certain clues into a computer—cryptic clues about who he was dealing with. That is why we are so close. We know this spy is American by birth, we know he was taking over operations himself—or herself—about the time you entered the Soviet Union. People are used, paid well sometimes, duped at other times. But the chain is an excellent one. No one ever knows who is at the top. Ivan could tell us nothing when he was arrested, but Ivan will still spend his remaining days in Siberia.

"Someone is afraid that Jarod is coming too close to the truth. Last night, warning shots were fired at him. I can only assume that you knew where he was going; that is why he was angry."

She was sinking; her legs were refusing to hold her. Sergei grasped her arm and led her to the staircase, where she allowed her legs to buckle and sat on the second step.

She had become pale. Sergei sought to reassure her. "You must not worry, Erin. Jarod knows what he is doing. And"—Sergei winked—"whether he always knows it or not, he has me. He will be fine. We are different men, but we are also blood. Trust me, Erin."

Erin nodded and tried to smile, though she was feeling very ill.

"And you must not worry about what you might have said or done. Jarod could easily have been seen by anyone heading for the square. He made no attempt to hide his movements."

She tried to smile again. It was a better effort. Sergei left her and moved into the kitchen, returning with a snifter of brandy. He handed it to her. "Drink."

Automatically, Erin obeyed. The liquid heat spread through her, and her color slowly returned.

"Erin . . ." Sergei said slowly. "Will you be all right?"

She nodded again.

"Yes, I believe you will be. You are a strong woman. Now, you must promise me you will not tell your husband how much I have told you! We will keep that a secret, like our trip to Leningrad. Jarod is a touchy man when it comes to interference in his private life!"

"I . . . promise," Erin said weakly.

"Good."

Erin was silent for several moments, her mind whirling with reproach and then guilt and then reassurance. She had spoken only to Gil, and she knew he was innocent. He had to be. No one could be so caring and giving. Sergei had said that anyone could have seen Jarod leave the house. If she had mentioned Gil to Jarod, she would have created new tensions for nothing. Her husband was simply contemptuous of Gil, and that was no reason to hound him.

Erin mentally stiffened herself, and the effort straightened her spine.

"Sergei," she said. "I would like to apologize for some of the things I said to him. May I tell him that you did tell me you are his cousin? I'll say you merely mentioned it at lunch."

Sergei paused a minute and then gave her his typical shrug, hazel eyes dancing. "Yes—you may tell him I told you. It is not a great secret. Now I must get home, or I will have my wife shouting similar things at me!"

Erin managed a small laugh. She was able to stand and see him to the door. "Sergei—spa seeba. Thank you so very much. And— Do sveedah nyah."

"Yes, Erin," he smiled, warmly clasping her hand. " 'Til we meet again."

When she had closed the door on him, she walked into the kitchen and made herself a cup of tea and sat before the cold fireplace. If Jarod were here, she thought, the fire would be burning.
. . .

She pressed her fingers to her temples. All the information of the day kept shooting through her head, like shouts growing louder and louder. She simply couldn't cope with it at the moment, and she had to learn that if she made a decision, she had to stick with it—not reproach herself for it hours and days after.

Jarod could take care of himself. He would be fine, and soon she would be gone, the entire, confusing nightmare would be over for her, and Jarod would no longer be a part of her life.

That hurt, even if she would be free from the endless web of deceit and confusion of her stay in the U.S.S.R. It hurt so badly it was like a knife twisting into her. But she couldn't change anything. She could try to apologize for this morning, they could become civil acquaintances again, but the magic she had grabbed for fleeting moments was gone.

As she slowly mounted the staircase for bed, she prayed that Jarod would be fine. Because if she didn't at least know that he was alive and well somewhere in the world, she didn't think she could bear it.

The phone began ringing just as her head hit the pillow. She jerked up, racing into the den for the extension on Jarod's desk.

"Erin? I've been trying to get you all day. Is everything okay there?"

"Yes—yes, fine. I was . . . out with Sergei."

"Oh?"

"We kind of made a day of it."

He was silent on the other end. "I wanted to apologize for my behavior," he finally said stiffly.

Erin took a deep breath. "I wanted to apologize myself. I . . . Jarod, why didn't you ever tell me that Sergei was your cousin? That . . . that your mother was Russian?"

Again she was met with silence. Finally, he said, "It didn't seem necessary—"

"But I never would have said all those terrible things. I . . . I didn't really mean them. . . . I wanted to hurt you."

"Well, it doesn't really matter. It's done, it's over. I provoked you. I'm sorry. I'll still be in about noon tomorrow."

There seemed to be painful constriction in Erin's throat. There was so much more she wanted to say but couldn't. He had called with an apology—nothing more.

"Okay," she said, trying to sound light.

He told her good-bye and hung up. She went back to bed, glad he had called her, but feeling unbearably empty.

At least tomorrow he would come home, and they had apologized for the scene that had left her in such abject misery. They would at least be able to talk.

She awoke in the morning with new thoughts and doubts nagging at her. The whole thing had become a boggling, impossible puzzle. She kept trusting Sergei, but was she an idiot to do that? The man was a Russian. Apparently he had been on the square with Jarod, and blood was not always thicker than water.

Her head seemed to be pounding, and she was no longer happy simply because Jarod would be home. What good was it going to do? He had lost his perfect control and slapped her. Was he sorry for hitting her—or for losing that perfect control?

She was getting too damned tired to know if she cared.

198

Erin made a pot of coffee and mechanically checked the mail. Besides the batch of business letters Jarod received daily, she was pleased to discover two for herself, from Casey and Mary.

Exclaiming with pleasure, Erin took her letters into the living room to read while she sipped her coffee. Casey's was pure Casey. Her long scrawl went on and on about how lucky Erin was, about the miracles of fate and destiny, and about how "wickedly, wickedly wonderful" Jarod surely had to be.

"Oh, Casey!" Erin murmured aloud. "You are a jerk! But a sweet one."

She picked up Mary's letter next, allowing it to flutter to her lap in shock after she read the first line.

Dear Erin:
   Oh, honey! Congragulations! Ted and I are on our way . . .

"Oh, no!" Erin groaned. "Oh, no . . ."

She forced herself to pick up the paper again, only to read that matters were worse than she expected. To get her trip booked quickly, Mary had had to say she would be staying with friends. She had been assured she could quickly transfer to the Rossia once she and Ted had arrived, but did Erin think her new husband would mind tolerating her friends for a night or two?

"Oh, no!" she repeated aloud. "Oh, no. Oh, no."

If there's any problem, Mary's letter read, let me know and we'll cancel. If not, will be arriving on the fifteenth.

The fifteenth . . . the day after tomorrow. Oh, dear God, the confused Russian post had taken days and days to get the letter to her.

"Oh, what the hell am I going to do?" Erin groaned. "Call her—I have to find out a way to call her . . . stop her. I have to think of something. . . ."

She couldn't put through a phone call herself. She bit her lip, and then called Gil. "Anything for you, Erin," he assured her. "You do know that I'm in love."

"Thanks," Erin laughed.

Gil rang off and returned her call a half hour later. "Sorry, Erin

199

a tape machine answers. Mr. and Mrs. Theodore Leary will be out of the country for the next several weeks."

"Oh, Jesus . . ."

"Pardon?"

"Nothing, nothing. Thanks, Gil. I appreciate the help."

Erin smashed out the cigarette she had been smoking and lit another. If Mary were to discover the truth of this marriage, she would worry herself sick. She was worse than a mother. She would feel more pain than Erin. She and Ted were so very dear, so caring. She couldn't let them know, not now.

Erin closed her eyes and swallowed. At least she and Jarod were now on speaking terms. She would simply have to abandon pride for the moment and ask that he play out a certain role for the next few days.

"Oh, please, Jarod," she thought out loud. "Please try and behave 'wickedly wonderful' while they're here."

She crushed out her cigarette and began to pace nervously, trying to plan what she would say when he returned. She looked anxiously at the clock. Two more hours . . .

The phone started ringing. Erin swooped upon the receiver, praying that it might be Gil, and that he might have managed to get through to Mary after all. But the voice on the other end of the line was Russian. She couldn't understand a word that was being said, until she heard a pronunciation of her own name and then recognized the name of the Soviet doctor she had seen the other day.

"Wait—wait," Erin pleaded. "I don't understand . . . ummm . . ." How the hell did you say "please" in Russian? She had been picking up certain words in the language, but at this moment they were all deserting her. "Please . . . uh . . . pazhahlsta!" Call. If she could think of the word for call—"Pazavanee te! Pazhahlsta pazvanee te Tanya!"

She heard some muttering, then a comprehending "Da!"

Breathing a sigh of relief, Erin hung up the receiver, wondering why the doctor had needed to get hold of her while also being grateful that the call had come before Jarod had gotten home.

What a mess, what a mess, her mind kept repeating. Everything had been a mess since she had first stepped into the Soviet Union. But not like this, not this bad, her mind countered.

The phone rang. It was Tanya. "Erin?"

"Yes! Oh, Tanya! I'm so glad they understood me! What on earth did he need to call me for?"

"He doesn't want you taking the pills he gave you."

"Why on earth not? That's what I went for."

Tanya hesitated uncomfortably. "He doesn't want you taking them because you're already pregnant. Erin? Erin? Erin?"

XI

It was ten in the morning, but she was going to mix herself a drink. She wanted a drink, needed a drink, deserved a drink.

A drink! She needed endless hours of laughing gas. Because it really was hysterical.

No, she shouldn't have a drink, and she had to stop smoking like a chimney and swilling coffee. None of her habits would be good for the baby.

Good for the baby! There couldn't be a baby; it had to be a terrible mistake. A mix-up in the doctor's office. Really. It was impossible. You couldn't trust the Russians. . . .

Erin went into the kitchen and started rummaging through the liquor supply. To feel less guilty for drinking so early she filled the glass with a generous supply of tonic and loaded it with lime. There was vitamin C in that lime, she told herself. That much would be good for the child.

What am I thinking? I have gone insane. There can't be a child. I don't feel anything, not a thing. They must have made a mistake.

No, I made the mistake! she quickly admitted to herself. I let my needs outweigh my logic! But that wasn't really true either. She had tried to control her needs, and when she couldn't she had taken precautions—inadequate now, to say the least.

She took a long gulp of the drink she had fixed and returned to the living room in a daze. She lit a cigarette, looked at it, and crushed it out.

Her nails went automatically to her teeth. Realizing what she was doing, she withdrew her hand from her mouth.

Great, Erin, she admonished herself. I can just see it. The world's first high-fashion and commercial model with stubs for fingernails. . . .

Then she pictured herself doing another sixty-second spot for the famous bath oil group. Instead of her knees rising above the tub and a long leg stretched out to be rinsed by a sponge her belly could rise just above the water level.

"Or diet soda! I'll be able to do great commercials for the diet-conscious," she blurted.

"I'm talking to myself. I'm babbling aloud like an idiot. It's happened. I've really gone over. Mary can come and help Jarod get me back to the States to be committed."

Stop, Erin, a saner voice pleaded silently. You're getting hysterical.

Hysterical! Hysterical! Oh, no, hysterical was steps ago. . . .

She sighed and closed her eyes, rubbing her temples with both hands. Then she slowly opened her eyes again. She saw the half-consumed drink and rose tiredly to take it into the kitchen and dump the remainder down the sink.

There might have been a mistake. Tanya had made her another appointment for next week; surely she would discover that they had made a mistake. It was so early to tell—but she knew there were tests you could buy off drugstore shelves that were reliable after ten days. Surely a doctor would be more reliable. No! she would just have to wait for next week, and until then this was all a horrible mistake.

She would deal with things one step at a time. Even if she were pregnant, she couldn't be more than three weeks. She'd be back in the States in plenty of time.

For what? A voice charged scornfully. You never believed in abortion for yourself.

That's not true, she thought defensively. I've always believed it was the only answer in certain circumstances.

But this isn't one of those circumstances, and you know it, the voice insisted.

But she couldn't have Jarod's child. When she left him, he had to be gone, entirely gone, out of her life. She would remember the good that he had given her and then forget that she had ever known him, ever loved him.

She thought about telling Jarod but realized that would be insane. She knew nothing about the medical procedures here and she had to remember there might have been a mistake. There would be plenty of time to worry later about what to do.

"What are you doing?"

Erin glanced up from the sink, horrified to see Jarod standing before her. He had come in without her even hearing him. She wasn't prepared to see him, she still had so much to sort out.
. . .

He was frowning. The blue mist of his eyes was probing as he slid out of his coat; he was watching her far too closely.

"I . . . uh . . . nothing," she murmured. "I was going to put on some coffee. You're earlier than I expected. Would you like some coffee? Did things go well in Leningrad?"

He slightly arched a brow as he tossed his coat over the counter. "I was able to leave earlier than I expected. Things went fine in Leningrad—it was a small clash between Finnish and Russian authorities. And yes, I'd like some coffee."

"Fine." Willing herself not to appear unduly nervous, Erin lowered her lashes and went about the business of brewing a new pot of coffee. Jarod finally stopped staring at her and picked up his coat. She heard him hanging it in the hall closet, then he came back to speak to her over the counter, his briefcase in hand.

"I have some paperwork to catch up on at home today," he said. "I'll be in the den—would you mind bringing the coffee up?"

"No," Erin said hastily. "I don't mind."

She breathed a sigh of relief as he headed for the staircase. She had been granted a few minutes grace. But she found herself chewing a nail again. The news from Tanya had swept all other thoughts from her mind and she had to get herself under control and handle things one step at a time. And the immediate step was Mary.

She had to broach the subject of her friends' arrival with Jarod, had to ask him to continue in their cordial and pleasant manner. Thankfully, he had come home in one of his politely distant moods. Things should go well.

She stared at the coffee as it began to perk against the clear glass dome. When it became a deep, dark color, she poured out two cups and set them on a tray and determinedly climbed the stairs.

The door to the den was closed. Out of purely feminine impulse she detoured to the bedroom, set the tray down upon her dresser, and picked up her brush. She vaguely noticed that Jarod's suitcase had been set upon the bed. Sonia came to clean tomorrow, and she would sort out his laundry for the cleaners. Conscious of their supposed newlywed status, Jarod was careful to keep the bulk of his clothing in the bedroom, slipping in and out during the day with his wardrobe for the next day.

Funny, she thought, it looks as if we really are a couple. Her nightgown lay upon the foot of the bed near his suitcase. And her purse lay below the pillow where she had left it after checking her cache of rubles and kopecks that morning.

Erin realized she was driving through her hair as if she were studiously giving it a hundred strokes. She set down the brush and picked up the tray—aware that she couldn't put off the confrontation forever. The sooner she swallowed her pride and spoke with him, the better it would be.

She tapped on the den door and opened it to his absent "Come in."

He didn't glance up; his silver-tipped jet head was bent low over a form with the impossible Russian characters. "Thanks," he said briefly as she placed the tray on his desk.

Erin took a breath, feeling her determination waver. She could talk to him later today, after he had finished with business. She could make lunch, start their truce without asking. It would be easier to speak to him then.

But before she could run, he suddenly sat back, impaling her with his blue stare. He glanced at the extra coffee cup, then gazed at her again, his arched brow lifting a shade.

"You wanted to talk about something?"

Caught by his eyes she nodded, then made herself speak. "Yes," she said clearly, taking the chair opposite his desk and leaning one elbow on the oak as she fingered the edge of her cup.

"Good, because I wanted to talk to you too," he said dryly. Erin frowned as she watched him. His dark lashes lowered a moment over his high bronze cheekbones, his jaw twisted slightly. Then he raised his intense gaze to her once again. "You go ahead, please."

Great, Erin, thought, he makes me even more nervous, then he tells me to begin. She blinked. What the hell, take the plunge.
. . .

"I've got a bit of a problem. I have a very close friend who is actually more like family. When I knew I would be here longer than

I expected, I wrote her. You mailed the letter. I didn't want her to worry about me, so I skimmed over the facts. I just told her that I had gotten married and would be here for a little while."

He was simply staring at her—not a lot of help.

"As I said, Mary—and Ted—are really like my family. A big sister and brother if you like. They've been there for me through all my catastrophes and they're . . . well, they're just very, very close. I got a letter from Mary today and they're on their way over here."

His lashes half lowered over his eyes again. "Go on."

"I don't want Mary to know that I—about the circumstances of our marriage—not until she has to. She worries about me enough already because of my marriage to Marc. She . . . uh . . . she doesn't know what went wrong, just that I made a severe mistake."

His eyes were upon her again; his mouth was slightly curled in a subtle grin. "Keep going."

"Oh, stop it!" Erin snapped. "You know what I'm getting at! And I've certainly played things your way for your convenience! I'd appreciate it if you were to—to give Mary and Ted the impression that we're a nice, normal married couple."

His lips were compressed against his grin, his eyes still shaded. He leaned back in his chair, hands folded prayerlike against his chin. "And when will we be seeing Mary and Ted?"

"They come in the day after tomorrow."

"Quick visas," Jarod observed.

"Yes, well . . ." This was the part she had been dreading. She wondered if he could see the blood that felt as if it were flooding to her face, that she was squirming inside. "They got by some of the red tape because they're coming here."

"Here?"

"To this—your—apartment. Only for a day or two—just until you can get them into the Rossia."

He didn't say anything, didn't show any emotion except that touch of sardonic amusement. Yet he wasn't as amused as he might have been; there was a grim quality to his features she wasn't sure she liked.

"I tried to call them and stop them, but it was too late. They've already left home—"

"You tried to call? How?"

"I—ah—through the U.S. embassy," Erin faltered.

"Oh—Mr. Sayer, I presume?"

"Yes."

He grimaced dryly and reached for his cigarettes. "Want one?" he inquired.

Erin started to accept and then vaguely remembered that she shouldn't be smoking. But she had already half convinced herself that a mistake had been made—and looking at Jarod, living, breathing granite, she thought again that it had to be entirely impossible. No warmth existed between them at all. She couldn't possibly be carrying his child. And she couldn't quit smoking cold. A few drags would soothe her ruffled nerves and then she could put it out.

She leaned slightly to accept the light he offered and then eased back, watching his unreadable eyes. He inhaled deeply on his cigarette, then smiled a chilling smile.

"Let me get this straight. Mary and Ted are arriving here the day after tomorrow. They are going to stay here, and we're going to convince them that our marriage was created in heaven rather than out of necessity."

"Not amusing," Erin said dryly, "but yes, you've got the general gist of it."

"Ah hah. So where do you propose we put Mary and Ted?"

She sipped her coffee and nervously crushed out the cigarette he had just lit for her. "We'll have to put them in the den and both sleep in the bedroom."

He laughed, and it was a dry sound. "I see. You're inviting me back into my bedroom after you've thrown me out of it."

Erin compressed her lips and said nothing.

"Erin?" he persisted relentlessly. "Have I got another 'general gist of it'?"

"Yes!"

"Hmmm, very interesting." Suddenly he tensed, leaning over the desk, and the glacial twist of his eyes became sizzling. "When did you find out about your friends arriving?"

Erin frowned, confused by his startling, terse pounce. "Just this morning. Why?"

He reached into the top drawer of his desk and tossed a packet toward her. Erin colored as she saw it was the container of pills she had just acquired from the Soviet doctor.

"You went through my purse," she hissed tensely.

He shrugged eloquently. "We Russians are known to do things like that," he drawled. "Actually, it didn't take much going through —they were sitting right on top, and your bag was open."

Erin didn't say anything. Her eyes seemed glued to the plastic packet.

"Well?"

"Well what?"

"These were prescribed two days ago. Before you had any intention of inviting me back into my own bedroom. Certainly not for my benefit, Mrs. Steele. So for whose?"

Oh, God, Erin thought sickly, what a stupid waste. She was going to pay the price for pills the doctor had said were useless anyway.

"Dammit, Erin, I want to know why. I think I stated very clearly that you'd best consider yourself a loyal wife—unwilling or not." His voice lowered suddenly and she felt the heat behind it—and every instinct within her warned that she'd better come up with an answer quickly.

"Erin!"

"I am 'loyal,'" she said acidly, "and I'm quite sure you must realize I couldn't be anything else but. You've informed me you have people watching me." She didn't like the way his eyes narrowed, and so she continued. "I had asked Tanya to get me an appointment right after we were married, when . . . when . . . The other day was the first appointment she was able to get, and I couldn't tell her then that I didn't really need to go . . . "

He watched her for a few minutes more, then picked up a pencil and glanced back down to the papers on his desk. A moment later he glanced back up and lifted his brows as if he were slightly surprised to see her still sitting there.

"Don't worry, Mrs. Steele," he assured her mockingly. "We'll do our best to convince your friends that you're married to a pure gallant and that your life is a bed of roses."

Erin stood and left him.

Sonia had just been in to clean, so the apartment was spotless. But desperately needing something to do to keep her mind occupied, Erin began cleaning again. She made a list of extras to pick up, since they were to have guests, and made little notes to herself about supplying the extra upstairs bath with towels and soap. The one bright spot on the horizon was that Mary would be there, and if she forced herself not to think of other things, she could find pleasure in thinking of how she could play the tour guide for a change.

Jarod appeared while she sat at the dining room table making up a list of things she wanted to do with her friends.

She glanced up at him warily, but his smile was disarming. He had changed into a beige pullover sweater and stretched broad shoulders as he looked at her, working stiffness from his neck and back.

"Are you busy?" he inquired.

"Umm . . . not really," Erin replied, still wary.

"Good. I need to get out. How about a late picnic?"

"Picnic?"

"Umm. We'll go out to Lenin Hills. I don't believe you've been there yet, and the view is breathtaking. Moscow Lomonosov University is there, I'm sure you'd enjoy seeing it. And there are acres and acres of gardens and recreational facilities. A lake surrounded by busts of Russian scientists. Of course, it is kind of cool, there's snow on the ground, but the sun is out and we can find a bench and then sightsee."

This is crazy, Erin thought. We're snapping at one another one minute, and he's inviting me on a picnic in the snow the next. But crazy or not, she couldn't control the rippling thrill of anticipation that riddled through her with the thought of being with him in his curiously light mood.

"Well?"

Erin nodded slowly. "I'd enjoy going out," she said, lowering her lashes so he wouldn't see just how much she would enjoy it.

"Good. I'll run out and pick up a bottle of wine. See if you can throw some sandwiches together."

Thirty minutes later they were following the Vorobyovskoye Highway and the hills were in sight. Jarod had taken on the role of guide, and he spoke casually and informatively as they drove. Since it was growing late, they found benches near the lake and ate, then Jarod amused her with tales about the various scientists whose sculpted heads they assessed. She was sure he invented half the stories, and was surprised to discover that he had her laughing like a young girl out on a first date.

His arm was around her shoulder as he took her to the main

building of the university. One of thirty-seven structures, he told her, it was the largest. Its beautiful spire rose twelve hundred and fifty feet. She believed him when he told her the main campus building was one of the world's most beautiful; its chandeliers and white marble columns certainly impressed her.

It was dark when they left the university. Erin leaned back against the headrest of the car, half closing her eyes while she covertly watched Jarod drive. He was marvelous when he chose to be; his knowledge as a guide seemed to be limitless. But then, he was a Russian. No, not a Russian. An American with a Russian heritage; a man, like any other, aware of his past, knowledgeable about the customs, language, and history that had been a part of his family.

My child would be part Russian, she thought, somewhat incredulously, and then hastily reminded herself that it had all been a mistake, there was no child. But if she ever were to have one, she would like it to be a boy, and she would like to see him grow to be a man like Jarod, with a firm, responsible jaw, and rugged facial contours that were not beautiful, but etched with unyielding strength and character.

Erin closed her eyes completely. I am really in love with him, she thought sadly. I'm in love with a brick wall. And he is capable of a certain giving, but not of loving. In less than two months' time I will be leaving him and he will very politely say good-bye and forget that I existed as a convenience or inconvenience.

She wondered just for a moment what his reaction would be if she were to knock on his den door and announce that despite the fact that he had become her jailer and that she was aware he still harbored suspicions that she might be a spy, she was in love with him. He would probably be annoyed, maybe even politely annoyed. "Oh, Lord, Erin, don't be ridiculous. I had assumed you were more sophisticated than that."

"Are you awake?"

Her eyes flew open. Thank God she had been only dreaming, because it had been a rather humiliating dream.

"Yes, I'm awake," she said quickly. A brief glance showed her that they were home. At least he was home. No matter how comfortable it was becoming, it wasn't her home.

She jumped out of the car before he could come around. He shrugged as she emerged without his aid and walked on toward the apartment door. He twisted the key, pushed the door inward, and motioned Erin ahead of him.

"Thank you for the afternoon," she murmured with stiff nervousness, very aware of his presence behind her. "I did enjoy the university very—"

The ringing of the phone cut her off, and she turned to glance at Jarod. He shrugged and strode toward the kitchen extension. After he answered, he seemed to be doing most of the listening, but when he spoke, it was in Russian. All Erin could make out were a few *da*s and *nyet*s.

"Trouble?" she inquired as he rang off.

He nodded vaguely but his eyes were already opaque; his mind elsewhere. He slipped his arms back into the coat he had just begun to shed. "Nothing big," he said. "I won't be late."

The phone began ringing again before he could leave. He went back into the kitchen to answer it once more and Erin idly followed —just in time to see his gaze become piercing upon her, his features darkly tense.

"Yes, she's here. Just a moment."

He passed the receiver to her.

"Who is it?" Erin inquired with a curious frown.

"Your friend." His velvety deep voice held the rough edge of a growl. "Mr. Sayer."

For a moment, Erin was sure that Jarod would hover by the phone to hear her conversation, but he didn't. He thrust the phone into her hand and walked away. She heard the slamming of the front door before she could say hello. She winced at the sound. It had hurt; it had been a cruel twist within her stomach.

"Hello, Gil."

"Hiya, gorgeous. I just wanted to let you know that I tried your friends a few more times just in case they had made the phone tape early. But they are gone. And I checked their flight. They come in at nine thirty-five on the fifteenth. If you need a ride to the airport to meet them, just let me know."

"That's very nice of you, Gil," Erin murmured. "I'll talk to Jarod and let you know."

"Fine. Give me a call one way or the other. I like to hear that sultry voice."

Erin forced a chuckle. "Sure, Gil. Thanks again."

She hung up the phone feeling slightly unnerved. The day had been so pleasant, and it had all been ruined with the phone call. She sighed. There was no help for it. Gil was just trying to be nice.

Erin shed her coat and trudged her way up the staircase. It had been cold out once it had turned dark; she could still feel the chill. A warm bath might in some way help.

With time on her hands, she soaked a long while, then washed her hair and studiously dried it. It was near nine when she finished, and she thought she would hurry down for a cup of tea. In the mood in which Jarod had left, she didn't want to take a chance on being up when he returned.

With the tea running warm in her veins, she hurried back upstairs and doffed her robe to slide between the sheets in a long satin gown. But of course she couldn't sleep. It was barely nine thirty. Even when she had five A.M. calls, she didn't go to bed this early.

But she wanted so desperately to sleep. It had been an ungodly confusing day. The trauma of the morning she still refused to accept, and then the pleasantness of the afternoon had been shattered by Gil's simple phone call. She wanted to forget for a while, forget that she was forcing herself not to think while also telling herself that soon she would have to face facts.

She had fallen asleep, because the sound of the door swinging open and banging against the wall was sharp and startling, tensing her with fear. From a comfortable field of soft and easing mist she came to instant alertness.

For a moment she could see him silhouetted in the doorway, tall, his shoulders broad, filling the space as he stood braced in the rectangle of dim yellow. Then his arm moved, and the bedroom light flared. Erin blinked furiously at the cruel intrusion upon her eyes while fumbling to sit up in the bed. He stared at her a moment while she watched him, his features fathomless, his eyes both searingly intent and shielded by that infinite blue frost flame.

Erin frowned as he left the doorway and sauntered into the room, casually pulling his sweater over his head. Every nerve within her seemed to jump with both fear and anticipation. A clamp seemed to have formed over her throat as she struggled to speak.

"What are you doing?" she demanded a little breathlessly.

He arched a brow high and then dropped it; he loosened first the buttons on his cuffs and then started on his shirt. "Undressing," he stated dryly, sitting at the foot of the bed to doff his boots and socks. A mercurial chill of lightning and fever raced along Erin's spine in dancing rivulets as she held the eyes that refused to release her. He lifted his brow once more. "You did invite me back in here."

She kept staring at him blankly, her dismay growing. All he had to do was step into a room and her blood ran hot and cold. She was inhaling his special scent, clean and yet masculine; she should be used to it, and she was, but at this moment it was sending her senses reeling.

"Yes," she murmured, "but—"

Her voice trailed away with his sardonic smile. "But?" he inquired. "Ah, yes, I'm two nights early. There is no one here tonight to witness a show. Sorry, Erin, but it doesn't work that way." He reached out to run the rough texture of his knuckles lightly over her chin. "I'll do my best to compromise, Mrs. Steele, but not at your beck and call."

Again, she was finding it difficult to speak, difficult to breathe with his searching eyes so close.

"You've been drinking," she accused him suddenly.

He seemed surprised. "No, not really. I had two scotches with Sergei and Joe, but not enough to influence my actions. I mean, correct me if I'm wrong, but it was your idea to share a room again." At her silence he laughed and continued. "Oh, Erin, you must have overestimated my finer qualities. Were you assuming I would come in here with you and curl on the floor at your feet like a perfect gentleman? Un-unh, honey. Nor will I continue to have my own door shut against me so that you can carry on a mental love affair with the illustrious Mr. Sayer. This is my room, and you're my wife, and if there are any affairs going on here, be they platonic or physical, I intend to be the partner."

Erin was too stunned to protest. Gil? It was incredulous. He was good-looking, yes, but he was like a flat sepia-tone picture compared to the contrasting brilliant and three-dimensional hues that were Jarod.

Suddenly his arms swept around her, bringing her down to the cushion of the pillow as he hovered over her, balanced by his hold on the small of her back and a knee pressed against the mattress. He continued to search her face with grim features from this closer range, as if he sought the answer to a deep and mysterious enigma.

"The strangest thing," he murmured curiously, "is that I never understood why. I held you, I felt you tremble and quiver, I felt the pounding of your heart, I heard you whisper and moan and call my name. . . ."

Abruptly he rolled beside her, continuing his strange vigil as he propped himself up on an elbow, leaving a hand free to touch upon her shoulder with the gossamer lightness of silk. "Why, Erin?"

She could only stare at it. Because I'm in love with you, idiot! she thought, but she couldn't say so, nor did she think she could have spoken at all. She felt as if a spell had been cast upon her, and all she could do was listen to the drowning beguilement of his voice and fight the sensations sweeping over her in great lapping waves.

His fingers moved up her shoulder to stroke her throat and splay across and cradle the soft line of her jaw. Suddenly anger erupted through the mesmerizing spell; he was here because like a typical male he was feeling territorial. She was his property; in his mind, possession had been threatened.

Erin leaped from the bed and stared at him with her eyes blazing a shimmering silver. "Why? Why? Because I'm not a possession! Because you brought me home like a piece of furniture to be kept for your convenience. You read me the riot act, reminding me that I'm your wife while you set other standards for yourself!"

"What?"

He tensed with his explosion, changing position again so that it looked truly as if he possessed animal agility and could pounce within a second. He still wore his jeans, but his chest was bare, and its dark, coarsely haired breadth reminded her of the sinewed muscles lurking beneath the toned trimness, visibly rippling across the span of his shoulders.

Erin backed off a step but lifted her chin. She had begun something, and now she was committed. "You heard me. My movements are watched and censored. I'm supposed to dance to your tune, while you roam about at will. You leave when you want and return when you want. You spend half your time with this Catherine"—she hissed out the name—"and you have the nerve to resent my phone calls."

"Catherine?"

"Yes, Catherine," Erin spat out heedlessly. "You won't be demanding fidelity from me while you're out prowling—"

He pounced. Standing beside the bed with his hands on his hips, he began to laugh. "Catherine, huh? Well, may I remind you, you locked me out of this bedroom."

He began a lazy saunter toward her, which was terribly unnerving. Erin began to inch slowly backwards.

"Catherine," he repeated, shaking his head as if the name itself were incredibly amusing. "My love," he murmured dryly, "if it is monogamy you desire, it is yours. You little fool. Do you really think I would go elsewhere if you were here . . . waiting . . ."

Erin came to a forced standstill. She had backed into the wall and there was nowhere else to go. But he continued to stalk her relentlessly, bracing his hands against the wall on either side of her head as he leaned close. If she had imagined him the slightest bit inebriated she had been badly deceived. His eyes were sharp and alert and staggering with magnetism as they came ever closer.

His lips touched her forehead, and though they but brushed her flesh, they were like a brand that burned. They continued a butterfly trail over her face, circling her lips, but never touching them. He stood back again, cupping her chin and cheekbones between both hands as he pressed his body against her. Her body automatically adjusted to his, molding sensuously against him.

Then his touch, smooth but rough-edged, wedged a space between them. No longer light, but firm and questing, his hands began a downward exploration, pausing to curve over her breasts and massage them until the nipples responded, shielded by the satin of her gown but hard and taut against his fingers. He followed the line of her ribs, then began a slow and sensual circular caress over her hips and abdomen.

"You little fool," he whispered to her, his voice a stimulating taunt against her ear. "Dear God, don't you know what you do to me? No one feels like you, Erin. No woman has hips and thighs that can meet a man like yours. Move closer to me, honey," he murmured urgently.

I'm going to fall, Erin thought. The gentle grind of his hips against hers was so hungrily suggestive that sensations swamped over her with devastating depth. She moaned softly and wrapped her arms around his shoulders, delighting in his tense heat. He smiled at her and untangled himself momentarily to slip his fingers beneath the satin on her shoulder blades and send the gown sailing sleekly to her feet. Then he crushed against her again, the hair on his chest mercilessly teasing her swollen and sensitive breasts. His mouth found hers and hungrily sought to part her lips; they capitulated completely, her tongue moving urgently to tease with a driving need along with his. And while they clung together with their lips his hands slid urgently over her body again, his fingers slipping beneath the elastic of her lace panties, running along the circumference, taunting and taunting until he pulled his lips from hers to slide between the valley of her breasts and he knelt to slowly ease the last remaining lace from her body.

Her legs were hot and trembling, and they couldn't hold her up any longer. She gasped and caught at his shoulders as he ran his fingers along her inner thighs, teasing in the aftermath of his long fingers with tiny, burning touches of his tongue. Her fingers clawed unwittingly into his muscles; they moved and tugged upon his hair desperately.

He slowly came back up to face her, holding her securely with the power of his arms. He kissed her long and deeply, then nibbled against the soft flesh of her neck and shoulder blades. "I need you, Erin," he murmured tensely. She nodded. She wasn't really aware of anything—her desire had grown too ardent. She clung to him while she fulfilled her need to touch him, run her fingers with fascination across his shoulders, feeling the suppleness of his muscles. She touched his male nipples with her fingertips and leaned to touch one with her tongue, grazing it with her teeth as she allowed her hands to explore lower. His belly was like a drum. She wanted more. She began to run her fingers beneath the band of his jeans and when he inhaled sharply she became bolder, searching out the buckle of his belt and loosening it, sliding the zipper down with her trembling fingers. He groaned deeply as she slid her hands inside the material below his hips, forcing both jeans and briefs to give and slide down over the shapely columns of his legs. Like him she followed the material until it hit the floor, and spurred by the resonant and labored breathing that came from him, rising and falling in his sinewed chest, she taunted him in return, feathering her nails over his thighs, rendering tiny, nipping kisses all along them. She felt even their strength quiver. She knew fully what she did to him, and that power was a beautiful, soaring triumph. She knew, too, how he did need her, desire her; the throbbing evidence was hers, as was the guttural assurance he gave her in a throaty, deep rough velvet, as his fingers twined through the gold strands of her hair. A maelstrom swirled within her, a soaring of passion and need so deep it was all-consuming. Wantonly she continued to taunt him to a fury, boldly taking him, reveling in the feel of him, touching, feathering, teasing. . . .

"Damn, woman, you're driving me wild," he suddenly exclaimed, catching her wrists and pulling her to her feet to sweep her into his powerful arms and carry her back to the bed. He had given her dominance; now he was taking it back. He pinioned her arms above her head as he came down over her, holding her as she writhed beneath him in protest. He held her firm. She had flinched only slightly as he gripped her wrists, but he firmly persisted. Even with him, her emotional scars would take time to heal. His gentle, firm persistence was rewarded. Although she struggled against him, it was not with panic, but with the desire to touch him in return.

"Tease me to insanity, would you?" he queried her, blue fire clashing with pure shimmering silver as he caught her eyes. And then he proceeded to inflict a series of alternately light and demanding kisses over her breasts with mouth and teeth and tongue all moving sensuously until she shrieked out a plea.

Jarod wedged a knee between her thighs and rubbed his body against hers, savoring the undulation of her burning flesh. "Oh, Lord, what you do to me," he breathed, fitting his hand beneath her to raise her buttocks and hold her firm against him as he gave way to the rampant fever that riddled him and entered her with an explosion of burning hunger. They groaned out together with the deliciousness of that intimate contact, and he held still for a minute, cradling her against him, tenderly cherishing her hair as he buried his head against her neck. They both needed that split second to savor the instant of filling, and being filled.

And then the passion began to mount wildly, the maelstrom swirled full force. The world was dark and misty all at once, ethereal and primitively real. Spirit and the basic needs of flesh and blood made beautiful by the deepest hunger, the deepest giving.

Their passion mounted, tender and savage, slow, and then in tempestuous rhythm that seemed to soar above and defy even the stars that stretched across the heavens. The explosion was blinding white sunlight, so agonizingly good that it left Erin breathless, motionless, powerless, not sure if she were conscious or unconscious or even still alive. Time was at a standstill as she waited to drift back to reality.

She didn't mind drifting back to reality because he was still beside her. She was held in the strong security of his arms. She would sleep beside him, able to wake and marvel at the length and breadth of his hands, explore the coarse dark curls that thrived over his chest and created new fields far below his waist.

His hand rested now just below her breast, his muscled thigh and knee cast haphazardly over hers.

She was still dizzy with the delight of having made love with him. As she drifted into a satiated and comfortable sleep, her head rested against his chest, her cheek touched by the pound of his heart and the steady rise and fall of his breathing, she didn't care that her life was a shambles.

He stirred slightly and brushed a kiss against her temple. "You've bewitched me, my golden angel," he murmured. "I am a man beguiled and bewitched."

And I, Erin thought, am afraid that I am yours . . . purely your possession.

INTERLUDE

He whistled softly as he walked down the long white hall. When he sat and gained admission to the computer, his fingers flew across the keys.

GOOD MORNING, CATHERINE. IT IS A BEAUTIFUL FIFTY DEGREES OUTSIDE. IT LOOKS AS IF THE SNOW IS ACTUALLY MELTING, AND THE SUN IS BLAZING ACROSS THE SKY LIKE A BANNER OF GOLD.

The computer whizzed for a moment, as if confused. Computers, Jarod assured himself, couldn't be confused. But, he was about to discover, they could be wise-asses.

HAD A NICE NIGHT, HUH, JAROD STEELE?

"Pity that the guy who programmed you is in New York," Jarod muttered aloud. "I'd like to throttle him."

YES, I HAD A NICE NIGHT. BUT IT'S REAL SPRING NOW, CATHERINE, IT'S FINALLY BECOMING SPRING. YOU SHOULD SEE NEW YORK IN THE SPRING. THE HARBOR . . . CENTRAL PARK . . . GRASS JUST TURNING GREEN AND FLOWERS COMING OUT IN BRILLIANT COLORS.

"What the hell am I doing?" he groaned aloud. "Telling a damned computer about spring."
Catherine whirred and printed a line across the screen.

YOU ARE HOMESICK, JAROD STEELE.

He stared at the words pensively. Yes, he was homesick. He loved much of the land that had been his mother's, he understood her problems as few as other men, he sometimes even understood the minds of the men that ran her. But she was an adopted land. And right now, with the mounting tension of petty problems that demanded his time while he sought the answer to a crucial dilemma that ridiculously eluded him, he couldn't help but ache for a sight of *his* home, *his* land. The harbor. The World Trade towers, the beach out on Long Island with the wind and the salt spray and the eternal hot dog vendors. . . .

He would be going home soon—to see Erin home. Strangely, that thought was giving him little comfort. In fact, it gave him a tearing pain in the gut. He was growing accustomed to her being there. And face it, he was eager for night to come again, and damned grateful to the friends who were coming and forcing them to maintain close living quarters.

He heard the sound of his teeth grating together before he realized he was grinding them. It was incredible how he wanted her, again and again and again. It was even more incredible how he enjoyed her in the house, her beautiful blond head lifting from a task that interested her to curiously meet his gaze with those fine, silver mercury eyes.

But she could hardly wait to leave. Return to New York, to the fascinating world that held her with the esteem due a queen. Her first trip once she stepped off a plane would probably be to a lawyer's office to seek a divorce. Which was fine with him. He had no room for a wife, he didn't want a wife. Still, sometimes, when he thought of the word, he would feel a cleansing pain and he would remember that "wife" had meant Cara.

But Erin was his wife, and he wanted her. Waking beside her had made the sun brilliant. The orb in the sky had streaked a flow of gold through the window and touched upon her tangled tendrils of hair to highlight them to spun filigree. Her eyes had half opened with lazy contentment when he had kissed her good-bye, her lips had curled sweetly. He'd needed a great deal of control to force himself to walk out the door rather than start shedding clothes to crawl back in bed beside her and explore the fascinating prospect of teasing her fully awake.

A buzzing sound suddenly permeated his thoughts. He glanced back at the computer's screen and scowled.

NICE NIGHT IS OVER, JAROD STEELE. COMMAND, COMMAND, COMMAND, COMMAND, COMMAND?

OKAY! COMMAND: INFORMATION FEED TO PROCEED CONVERSE, PROBABILITIES AND LOGIC.

Catherine whirred for a second, and Jarod shook himself. He had to get his personal life under control.

Jarod began to fill in all recent facts. Ivan had known nothing, but from his lack of knowledge they had still learned that none of the underlings ever knew with whom they dealt. One-strip messages —or sometimes just verbal numbers, ciphers that put together the halves of a code—passed from stranger to stranger—strangers who would never see one another again. Ivan didn't know the key codes, or how they were passed.

And yet Ivan had given them a great deal of information that pointed strenuously toward the clearing of Erin McCabe, code name Mc. She had been an intended victim of complicity, a decoy. Ivan admitted suggesting that Erin be at Red Square at midnight, but nothing had been intended for her that night. With everyone watching Erin, they would be too involved to catch the real action.

Ivan hadn't known whether anything involving Erin was still in the workings or not. But a celebrity such as Miss McCabe . . . well, it seemed logical that she would pass through customs easily, while her baggage could be handled without her ever knowing it, codes and secrets transferred with no one ever the wiser.

Except that Ivan had been caught and no one had been able to use Erin for anything except a shield. Which they had all fallen for!

The espionage had gone on. The U.S. had recently purchased information about a nuclear buildup in the Mongolian desert, luckily proven fictitious in time. Sergei had informed Jarod that equally agitating information had recently been sold to the Soviets about bombs being planted in the chambers of the Supreme Soviet. The chambers had been emptied, the rulers had waited anxiously, planning retaliatory action, and then nothing had happened. They had felt like fools. They had hastily and desperately called off reprisals.

And we both keep believing the information, Jarod thought with disgust. But he knew the information sold to both sides was taken because it always came to them with other little tidbits that were known to be true—things one diplomat might say to another. They

221

all knew there were certain games to be played, and beyond the official, diplomatic barrier they admitted to themselves they were game players.

Jarod stopped typing and stared at the screen. Erin was innocent, and had always been innocent. Unless she were in with someone. He didn't believe that, but his instincts had been correct. She had been involved. Long before he had seen her name on the visa list, someone else had been planning to keep a sharp eye on Erin McCabe.

At least he had thwarted the agitator thus far. Erin McCabe had become Erin Steele. Under his protection she was no use as a carrier—but possibly useful again as a source of information about his own whereabouts and movements.

Useful, Jarod thought. Useful only. She hadn't given him away knowingly the night of the shots. He was sure of it; he wanted to be sure of it.

Several people might have known. After all, Sergei had found him. And an offhand word spoken in any company could have alerted any number of people who might have spoken another offhand word—until the word reached that one person who needed to know.

OKAY, CATHERINE, WE'RE NARROWING THE FIELD. I KNOW WE'RE STILL LOOKING WITHIN THE EMBASSY ITSELF. BROKEN CODE SHOWS INFORMATION HAD TO COME FROM INSIDER. THAT MAKES PRIME SUSPECT GIL SAYER. HE IS THE

Catherine interrupted.

NOT SO. JOE MAHONEY IS ALSO TOP EMBASSY. AND THERE ARE ALSO OTHERS. YOU MUST BEAR IN MIND THAT YOU DO NOT LIKE GIL SAYER.

Jarod narrowed his eyes and compressed his lips.

THAT MAY BE TRUE, BUT IRRELEVANT. JOE MAHONEY IS A CAREER DIPLOMAT. HE IS NEAR RETIREMENT. WHY WOULD HE . . .

YOU JUST HIT UPON IT, JAROD STEELE. NEAR RETIREMENT. A LIFE OF SERVICE AND MAYBE NOT ENOUGH REWARD.

Jarod typed stubbornly.

222

I STILL SAY GIL SAYER.

AND WHAT ABOUT YOUR WIFE? DID SHE, OR DID SHE NOT, WILLFULLY CARRY THE INFORMATION? SHE CALLS HIM: DATES AND TIMES ARE LISTED IF YOU WISH.

No!

Could he be having an argument with Catherine the Great? Yes, of course, that was partially why he had come. Catherine would force him to face the facts he wanted to ignore.

He closed his eyes, remembering the night he had gone to the square, felt the bullets whiz by close enough to create a breeze that lifted his hair. She had known where he was going. She had been whispering to Gil in the kitchen, but she had denied talking to him.

He printed almost absently:

IT'S SAYER.

Catherine promptly responded:

OR MAHONEY.

They were running in circles.

CATHERINE, THANKS A LOT. IT WAS A BEAUTIFUL DAY.

SORRY, JAROD STEELE.

I WILL CATCH GIL SAYER IN THE ACT.

SURE.

CATHERINE, YOU'RE A PAIN . . .

He stopped printing and smiled dryly, remembering Erin's face suddenly, the haughty tilt of her chin as she told him he could hardly expect tremendous loyalty from her when he spent all his time with Catherine. She had actually sounded jealous, and he had enjoyed the blazing shimmer of silver mercury in her eyes.

SCRATCH THAT, CATHERINE. I THINK I DO LOVE YOU!

YOU'RE INSANE, JAROD STEELE.

YEAH, CATHERINE, MAYBE.

He stared at the screen blankly for a minute, sighed, and started to check out, then paused as he saw Catherine printing out another message.

HAVE ANOTHER NICE NIGHT, JAROD STEELE.

Suddenly, he was laughing.

THANKS, CATHERINE. I INTEND TO.

XII

"Your nose is going to permanently flatten against that pane if you stare out that window any longer!" Ted affectionately teased his wife.

Mary drew her head away from the window to make a face at her husband. The Aeroflot plane which had brought them in from Paris had just ceased the hum of its engines, and all around them the other passengers were busily gathering their belongings.

"We don't even know that they're meeting us," Ted said gently. "I mean, after all, you didn't even give Erin a chance to tell you that it might be an inconvenient time for us come."

"Oh, Ted!" Mary whirled back to her husband. "I couldn't give her a chance to say no! We need to be here! I can't believe that Erin has married again—and so quickly! I have to be here in case something goes wrong. Ted, you didn't see her the night she left Marc. If something goes wrong now, she'll be shattered, she'll need me."

Ted caught his wife's hand. "I think you're wrong, Mary. I think Erin is much stronger than you realize."

Mary turned back to the window. "And I know Erin—she will be here to meet us." Mary's voice trailed away as her eyes lit upon Erin and the man beside her.

They were easy to find, incredibly easy, both so tall and trim and magnificently handsome. Erin looked great; her golden hair was loose and waved over the shoulders of her trenchcoat. There was an anticipatory smile on her lips, and that sleek air of elegance and sophistication that she always wore.

She really looks just fine, Mary thought with a little surprise, and then her eyes were pulled and riveted to the man upon whose arm her friend's delicately slender fingers rested.

He was tall, very tall, she noticed; he stood several inches above

Erin. His physique was lean and trim, but she immediately noted the breadth of his shoulders and astutely ascertained that his trimness was all muscle, toned as tightly as stretched canvas. Then she realized that she was no longer noticing his physique because her eyes had been riveted to his. Mary entertained a small shiver. She had never seen such eyes. Even from this distance she could tell that they were blue . . . the blue of the sky after a snowstorm . . . piercing, direct. She had the strange feeling that they could also sizzle with all the thunder and tempest that preceded a raging storm.

He bent his head suddenly to listen to something that Erin was saying, and in that small gesture Mary saw something that she liked: a natural courtesy, a protective quality. He straightened again, and she thought that the two of them together were as handsome as a king and queen from another time, larger than life, a little more elegant, taller, stronger, more royal, more lithe, more superbly formed and created . . . the ethereally lovely woman and the man who was not beautiful but rugged and alert and compelling.

If she were a psychic, Mary thought fleetingly, she would be seeing an aura of power and assurance about him that encircled him with the tenacious rays of a blinding sun.

George suddenly elbowed her arm lightly. "Think we might get off the plane?" he drawled with amusement.

"Oh, shush!" Mary wailed. "See—I told you Erin would be here to meet us!"

And they were well met. The dazzling smile which had made Erin famous streaked across her beautiful features, and she shouted and waved until she had crushed them both with bear hugs amazingly strong for one so slender.

An hour later Ted sat with Jarod in the den discussing the pros and cons of socioeconomic differences between the U.S.S.R. and the United States while Erin enthusiastically helped Mary hang things in the den.

"I can't believe you're really here!" Erin exclaimed happily, adjusting the collar on one of Ted's jackets. "Honestly, sometimes I'm so homesick I can barely stand it!"

Mary chuckled. "Casey wanted to come too; luckily, she couldn't get the time out of work. I'm afraid she might have been quite a shock to the entire Russian system. She's going crazy because you haven't written; she's dying to hear 'the most intimate little details about the wickedly wonderful man you've married'!"

Erin blushed slightly. "You're right—I think Casey might have been a bit of a shock!"

Mary suddenly sobered. "He is magnificent, Erin—he's made Ted and me feel right at home, and I know we're intruding. But I still can't believe this, Erin. I mean you were refusing even to date, and you take off on a trip and—presto!—you're married in Russia to a man you bumped into in a New York bar!"

Erin averted her eyes and laughed uneasily. "Things did happen quickly."

"Are you happy?"

"Of course!" It wasn't such a terrible lie. There were times when she was happier than she had ever been in her life.

Mary seemed to accept her answer. She sighed softly. "Then I'm glad, Erin. Very happy for you." She grimaced ruefully. "I really didn't need to rush over here. I can see that you're insanely in love and you've found yourself one heck of a man"—Mary paused with a dreamy quality to her eyes—"virile, rugged, incredibly sexy, the stuff heros are made of." She broke off suddenly and glanced at Erin. "Good, Lord, I need help! I'm starting to sound like Casey!"

Erin laughed and picked up the shirt Mary had crumpled in her enthusiasm. "Heaven help us. I love Casey, but one of her is definitely enough! Besides, you have a virile, sexy man of your own down there."

"Ted?" Mary said thoughtfully. "Ted is a gem among men! He tolerates me! But Jarod . . . oh, Erin! It gives me delicious shivers just to see how he looks at you with those astounding blues! He reeks of tension and danger and sensuality and—oh, hell, there I go again! But he must adore you! He seldom takes his eyes off you, and there is fierce possession in those eyes, honey!"

Erin lowered her lashes. Her fingers were trembling, so she hurriedly reached into Mary's suitcase to pick out more clothing to neatly stow away. She picked up the shirt again, absently running her fingers along the collar. "You think so, Mary?" she managed to murmur idly. Was Jarod fiercely possessive? Yes, that was probably true. But she was quite sure Jarod didn't adore her. Still, a warmth spread through her with a tingling of what she refused to describe as hope. *He seldom takes his eyes off you.*

"Erin, honey, you've fixed that collar so many times it's going to turn to cement!" Mary laughed. "I can't wait to see you with children. You're going to make a fabulous, finicky mother!"

Erin dropped the shirt and the hanger and then hastily bent to pick up both. She tried to recover her composure before she rose and shrugged to Mary. "I'm sorry—I don't believe I've wrinkled it."

"Don't be sorry—it doesn't matter in the least. You're doing all the work and I'm sitting here sounding like Casey! Besides, I've never seen you drop a thing or appear the least bit uncoordinated! I love it!"

Erin grimaced. "If you want to hear about my coordination, talk to Jarod. He's convinced I'm the world's greatest klutz. Come on—let's leave the rest of this till later. Jarod says he has the afternoon free, so we'll start your sightseeing at the Kremlin with him."

"I always thought it was marble," Erin said as their group stood before the Kremlin wall and Lenin's tomb. "But actually"—she glanced at Jarod with her eyes twinkling—"it is faced with black and gray labradorite and red Ukranian granite."

Jarod grinned and inclined his head slightly in acknowledgment. "Very good, my love. I'll let you proceed. We'll just have time to do one museum today—so you pick."

Erin picked the Armory, or Oruzheinaya Palata, sure that Mary and Ted would enjoy the vast exhibits of jewels and gowns and carriages from the days of the czars. Ted, however, had a few too many questions for her to handle and Jarod once more took charge. When Mary marveled at the intricate depths of his knowledge, Jarod shrugged and explained that his mother had been born in Leningrad.

Erin eyed him thoughtfully and curiously after his casual announcement, but she wasn't able to quiz him on it until Mary and Ted were safely shut behind the door of the den and she lay upon the bed in their room, watching as Jarod shed his clothing.

"Jarod?" she asked tentatively.

"Hmm?" he replied absently, sitting at the foot of the bed to pull off his boots.

"Why didn't you simply tell me from the beginning that your mother was Russian? When I asked about the ring?"

228

He stood without answering and turned out the light, hiding his features from her as he answered, leaving her in the dark as to the emotion with which his answer was stated. "From the things you had to say, Mrs. Steele, it didn't strike me that you were particularly fond of the Russian people."

She felt the heat of his skin as he slipped in beside her, circling an arm around her midriff and pulling her close. She wanted to keep questioning him, but there had been an air of finality to his reply. She nervously sought for something else to say.

"I want to thank you," she murmured, moistening her lips and attempting to control the writhing that shuddered through her as he drew gentle patterns along her back with his fingertips. "You've been wonderful to Ted and Mary. They're so impressed with everything."

"Go ahead, then."

"Pardon?"

"You wanted to thank me. Go right ahead."

She was glad it was dark. The timbre in the devilish amusement of his tone still brought a flush to her face.

"We aren't alone in the apartment," she murmured.

His voice dropped to a husky whisper. "Then thank me very, very quietly."

Erin hesitated only a moment. Then she raised herself over his chest and bent low, touching the line of his lips with the tip of her tongue and circling it slowly. His arms shot around her and she was pressed close until she taunted him further by sliding her body against his to taste more and more of his salty bronze flesh.

He was careful to groan very softly. Erin didn't make out so well. When he began to make love to her, everything was erased from her mind except for the feel of him.

Erin felt very cold and tired and stiff when she left the doctor's office for the second time. She could no longer deceive herself. It hadn't taken a vast knowledge of the Russian language to realize that the doctor was very positive and very efficient—and not the type to make mistakes.

She had come alone today, having begged Tanya to keep her secret and escort Mary and Ted to the circus with the excuse that she needed to do some shopping at GUM and had just been to the circus.

Erin stood upon the outer steps of the office for a long time. She had been abiding by her decision to handle things step by step, but the time had come to take the step she had been dreading. She had to tell Jarod, and now was the time to do it.

They had talked little since Mary and Ted had arrived, but neither had they argued. They had been alone only at night, and by mutual agreement there was no pretense. To Erin it was a wonderful time of release—and strangely tempestuous peace. In the abandon of their love making she could give to Jarod all the tender love and care she normally had to carefully hide from him.

He remained unerringly gentle to her around Mary and Ted, and for that Erin was grateful. But she didn't try to deceive herself. She was dryly aware that her nights of sweet loving were not the same to Jarod. To him, their sexual relationship was merely a normal, healthy and pleasantly shockingly passionate one.

She did believe that he cared for her, and she cherished the knowledge that he truly found her the most provocative and sensual woman he had ever known. Yet she would have given all that to have a fraction of the love he had apparently granted his Cara.

Erin sighed and stepped to the curb to resolutely hail a cab. Things were going well—as well as they were going to go between the two of them. Now was the time to talk. Mary and Ted would still be at the apartment tonight, so they would be forced to be pleasant to each other. And she wanted to talk to Jarod before she had to think any more about what to do.

She had no difficulty instructing the driver to take her to the embassy, and no difficulty locating Jarod. A pleasant secretary buzzed a number and she was immediately led down a long corridor to a handsome office with carved oak furnishings and a typically Russian chandelier. Jarod rose from his desk with a curious frown and greeted her with a quick kiss on the cheek before closing the door on the secretary and seating her in the chair, throwing a leg over the desk and sitting there himself as his brows lifted in query.

"This is Mary and Ted's last day," he said, crossing his arms over his chest. "I would have thought you would have been with them."

Erin shrugged. It had been stupid to come here. In this political world he was more unapproachable than ever; his eyes held their relentless, unwavering quality.

"Your office is very nice," she murmured.

"Thank you. Now, why are you here?"

Erin folded her hands in her lap and crossed her legs. *I have to say this entirely emotionlessly. I have to be on guard and watch for his reactions. Be dignified, Erin.*

But when she first tried to talk, the simple two words she needed wouldn't come. She noted a silver samovar on a wall case and heard herself say, "Could I have some tea, Jarod?"

His frown deepened but he rose, poured her a glass of the Russian tea, and handed it to her in a typical filigreed holder. Erin took a sip of the hot tea and without looking up from the rim of the glass blurted, "I'm pregnant."

"You're *what*?"

"Pregnant," she repeated weakly.

She finally looked up, amazed by the depth of anger in his eyes.

"How?" he demanded harshly.

She was tempted to laugh hysterically. Surely he knew how! Then she became terrified that he would ask her if she was sure the child was his. If he said something like that, she would shriek and literally fall apart, limb by limb, in front of him.

"I don't know what you mean," she said aloud.

"You were taking pills."

"I—not soon enough."

He was silent for a moment and then exploded. "Good God, Erin! You're twenty-eight years old. How could you have been so careless?"

Erin stared at him for a minute, blank and incredulous. What reaction had she expected from him? She didn't know, but certainly not this . . . this cold fury. Suddenly a burning rage ripped through her and she was standing, lashing out at him in return with a deadly hiss.

"How dare you accuse me of sexual irresponsibility! I had no reason to take precautions when I crossed this border. I was leading a celibate life, which I don't suppose can be said of you! And then I"—she was still furious, but suddenly floundering—"I . . . I tried . . . something, but apparently it was either too late or not good enough." That she was floundering suddenly increased her wrath to

231

where she was shouting out anything that came to mind. "I had no intention of forming any liaisons until you assaulted me."

"Halt right there!" he snapped out, eyes blazing a warning despite the fact that he hadn't moved from his tensed position.

"Assaulted, seduced—what difference does it make?" Erin continued, too wound up to stop. "I—"

"What difference does it make?" Jarod thundered in interruption. "A world of difference—as you of all people should know!"

Erin swallowed sickly, knowing she was sounding like a foolish child. She couldn't stop her tirade, but she had to control her words. He was right; there was a world of difference. She had come so close to the first that it had taken his gentle use of the second to teach that extraordinary difference.

"You knew you were dealing with a woman who had not been involved in sexual relations! You were more responsible than I! You should have cared to take the precautions! This is absurd! I've never believed it was supposed to be the woman's responsibility rather than the man's."

"It is the woman's responsibility," Jarod interrupted dryly, "because it is the woman who becomes pregnant—not the man."

"Oh, Jarod!" Her voice suddenly went low with disbelief. "That is the lowest excuse—"

"All right—I'm sorry," he interrupted harshly.

Erin bit her lip and lowered her lashes. There were men who might really think that way, she thought bitterly. But not Jarod. She knew him better than that. Jarod would always be responsible.

His voice, still harsh, seemed to lash out at her. "But tell me this, Erin—why didn't you say anything to me? Perhaps I was wrong, but you never said anything to me, and I assumed you knew what you were doing."

"I . . ." She moistened suddenly dry lips, desperately wondering herself why she had been so afraid to speak to him. He could have gotten her to a doctor, she could have been on pills all along. But it might have been too late anyway.

"I thought I did know what I was doing."

"You wouldn't talk to me—but I'm to blame?"

Hurt, confused, and miserably aware that she had made a mistake —how did you explain sleeping with a man night after night and yet being afraid to bring up an intimate subject because he was still a stranger?—Erin fell silent. Jarod hopped from his desk and walked around to the chair on the other side. He picked up a pencil and idly tapped it on the desk as he watched her through shielded, narrowed eyes.

"So what do you propose to do?"

"What do *I* propose to do?" she repeated with a wash of new anger cascading over her and her voice grating tensely. Looking at the granite of the man's face and body suddenly convinced her she had made a tremendous mistake. If she had ever tried to deceive herself into believing she had married a man composed of anything but ice and brick she had been a fool.

"Yes," he said, brows lifting sardonically. "I mean—we're speaking about the great Erin McCabe here. Symbol of beauty and sensuality for the western world. I find it difficult to believe you would give up that kind of excitement for the monotony of motherhood." He reached calmly into his jacket for his cigarettes and lit one, still watching her through half-slit eyes.

Erin did her best to conceal her hurt and shock, an effort aided by the heat of fury that trembled through her in continuous waves. He wanted her to get an abortion, she realized sickly, admitting to herself for the first time that she wanted the child she carried within her and that with all the loss she had sustained in her life, she would never, never give up the life of this child.

She smiled at him coldly and bitterly and walked around the desk to face him. "Forgive me, Jarod, I'm really sorry for bothering you. I was mistaken—I thought that maturely and responsibly, I should give you the right to know. I won't trouble you again."

She was very agitated, and her hands were trembling. Her eyes lit upon the cigarette pack on his desk and she automatically stretched her fingers toward it.

His hand came down upon hers and he pulled the pack away, his eyes open wide and starkly demanding as they knifed into hers.

"You didn't answer me." He stood, catching both her wrists. "What do you propose to do?"

She didn't want him towering over her, holding her with his grip of steel, raping her soul with his eyes. She was terribly, terribly afraid that she was going to cry and make a complete fool of herself.

"*Erin!*"

She wasn't fond of the use of feminine wiles, but at the moment she was going to try and use a few. It was easy, because a sob was rising in her throat, and because she still knew that Jarod would never willingly inflict harm upon her . . . upon any woman . . . but that didn't matter now, she couldn't let it hurt because she simply had to get away from him.

She let her head fall back and feigned panic filled her eyes. "Jarod!" she gasped, and the pain in her heart brought agony to her cry. "Please . . . please . . . my wrists . . ."

As she had hoped, he immediately dropped them, concern flooding to his eyes. He moved to hold her, reassure her, but she had the advantage of knowing exactly what she had planned to do.

Before he could touch her she had sped around the desk, jerking the chair after her so that his immediate rush to recapture his hold was thwarted by a collision with the piece of furniture. "Erin!" he lashed out. "You lying little bi—"

She didn't hear the end. If she didn't take every advantage, he would be upon her—she was well aware of his strength and speed. She pulled the door behind her and took off through the halls, heedless of the startled looks of the office staff.

Some god was smiling upon her. She was able to hail a cab in front of the embassy—and see only for a second his furious face as he appeared not ten feet in her wake.

"Kremlin," she told the driver, blanking on anything else to say that he might understand.

Ten minutes later she was staring at the Kremlin wall and the spot where the revolutionary leaders had been buried into the brick.

He didn't want the child and he didn't want her. No, it was worse than that. He didn't even want her having the child. He had actually been furious.

She didn't know how long she stood staring at the walls, those agonizing thoughts spilling in grinding repetition through her mind. Every once in a while she would think that it had been stupid to run, that she would have to go home. And that now he would be ready to kill her and that he would think anything fair game after the trickery she had used to elude him.

Oh, God, she thought, was I ever so foolish to believe that it was like a fairy tale, and that though he never said it, he loved me all the time as I did him. Fairy tale. Romance. Surely she couldn't have been so foolish. He had enjoyed her, that was it. That was the way it often was; she simply hadn't wanted to believe it. Not her. Other women could be used by men, not Erin McCabe . . . Erin Steele. That was a laugh. He had never wanted her to have his name. And he didn't want her to have his child.

"The wall will not change, you know. It has stood so for centuries."

Startled, she turned to see Sergei Alexandrovich with gloved hands stuffed in his pockets, his eyes gently upon her.

"Sergei . . ." Erin murmured. "I—I like to come here. St. Basil's is really so beautiful, and the Kremlin wall never fails to amaze me. I understand it is over twenty feet thick in places."

"And you couldn't care less about the wall at the moment," Sergei finished for her, coming closer and slipping an arm through hers. "I have just spoken to your husband, and he is half insane. What a temper! He is now out in the city looking for you, my dear Erin, so I thought it might be best if I found you first. And I am pleased with my instincts. I knew you would be here."

Erin found herself being turned and led toward a car beyond the square on the street. "Sergei—"

"We will have some afternoon tea," Sergei interrupted before she could continue, "and when you are rested and ready, only then will I take you home."

She was tired, very tired, and too dispirited to argue and Sergei didn't press her. They rode silently down the side streets of Moscow to a building that looked like a hole in the wall but proved to be a small hotel with an elegant and intimate cafe. Sergei ordered them bread, sausages, cheeses, tea, and little rum cakes, telling her that the building had actually been there since the time of Peter the Great and that the crystal chandeliers that graced them with their dim light were also from that era. Erin listened vaguely, sipping at her tea.

Sergei's hazel eyes were very warm, his voice gentle. He paused in his monologue to gaze at her for several seconds. "Come, come, Erin, you must eat something. That little child within you that you attempt to starve is also my cousin, you know."

Erin glanced from her tea to Sergei with horror. "He told you?"

Sergei shook his head. "I keep tabs on you, Erin. I know where you have been."

She should have been outraged, but she wasn't. She merely

235

shrugged. It was no great surprise these days to find her movements easily monitored.

"Don't be angry, Erin. I watch you because I am concerned, not because I think you guilty of anything." He fell silent for a moment, then sighed. "Like my cousin Jarod, Erin, you are a private person. You do not talk. So I will talk to you. And you will understand Jarod."

"I do understand Jarod."

"Maybe not." Sergei savored a piece of cheese and took a sip of tea as if they were discussing the weather. "Ahhhh . . . this is good! It is made from the milk of the hearty cattle of the Ukraine. You must try some." Suddenly his demeanor changed. "You know about Cara, yes?"

Erin nodded numbly. "Jarod's first wife." His only wife, she added bitterly to herself.

"I will ask you to answer me nothing else, my American cousin," Sergei said. "I will only tell you what I presume, and then you must think things through for yourself from there. I presume, Erin, that you told your husband today that you were expecting a child—and that his reaction was not the joy one would expect from a man offered his first child."

Joy. Oh, Lord, it certainly wasn't joy, Erin thought, but she said nothing.

"He hurt you very badly, judging by his temper. But I will tell you why, Erin. He still lives with a certain pain, a natural pain, but an unnatural guilt. His Cara was to have a baby. She was a very tiny, gentle creature, not made to have children to begin with. But they were very much in love and very happy about the baby they expected. When Cara did not feel well, she would not tell Jarod. And so when she went in labor very, very early, he was working. She called him but did not tell him what was wrong. Consequently, he finished his business before leaving work. Things were very bad when they reached the hospital. The doctors could not stop the bleeding. Jarod lost both his wife and his daughter."

Erin was stunned by the story she didn't for a minute doubt. She was horrified, but felt vaguely like another person, one not involved. And then she trembled, thinking that Jarod must be wishing that she didn't exist, that he would be bitterly wondering why Cara and the child he had wanted lay dead while she walked about in perfect health with an unwanted child growing within her.

"It is strange in this day and age, Erin, but Jarod is afraid of childbirth. He has lost once—"

"But Jarod doesn't love me," Erin heard herself say.

Sergei shrugged. "Who is to say exactly what love is? Jarod needs you, he cares for you, he wants you to a distraction. Perhaps there is love in that, maybe a love deeper than he would ever care to acknowledge. Love can be a painful thing, Erin. Maybe the only thing that can create vulnerability in a man like my cousin, Jarod Steele."

They both fell silent, sipping tea. Again, Erin felt too overwhelmed by all the events and emotions of the day even to think. Her mind and heart both seemed numbed and cold. She hurt for Jarod, but she also hurt for herself, and all the hurting couldn't solve a thing.

"Shall I take you home now?"

Erin nodded. She had to face it some time.

Jarod was home when they returned, stalking the living room with tense, pantherlike treads. He stood still as she entered the hallway, glaring coolly at her first, then Sergei.

"Ah, cousin, I see that you are here," Sergei said affably, ignoring the static in the air. "I have been caring for your wife."

"I'll take care of my own wife," Jarod interrupted. His voice was quiet but still a whiplash that brought silence in its wake.

Sergei shrugged and turned to Erin, taking her hand in his and smoothly kissing it. His eyes rose to hers with a bit of a twinkle, as if he wished to convey a message of reassurance. Jarod's attitude was amusing Sergei, and for the life of her Erin couldn't understand why.

"Do sveedah nyah, Jarod," Sergei waved. Bowing slightly with his hat in his hands, he turned and left. The click of the door in his wake seemed deafening.

Erin and Jarod stared at each other for moments of tension that felt like eternity.

Finally he spoke. "You worried me sick."

Erin shrugged, wondering why she trembled. He wouldn't hurt

her, what was it she was so afraid of? Still, she felt as if she were being stalked, the tension building higher and higher.

"I don't know why you worried. I'm hardly the type to go jump off a tall building."

"Don't be absurd. This is Russia. I don't like you wandering the streets."

"Don't *you* be absurd. I've been here a long time now. I know the main streets of the city, and no tourist is under lock and key! Were I to find myself lost, I would still have no difficulty; the Russians civilians are very nice people, not beasts."

"What a generous observation."

"Oh, stop it! If someone around here has a hangup on Russians, it's you, not me."

His lids flickered for a second, and she saw the twist of his jaw. Hands in his pants pockets, he stalked a line in the living room that made Erin feel as if she could actually see a coiled wire twist tighter and tighter. It would have to give, it would have to spring. But he was keeping his distance from her. He was probably afraid he would strangle her if he came too close, she thought ruefully.

"Whether I had cause to worry or not," he said bitterly, "I don't appreciate your running out on me—or the method by which it was accomplished. I don't like being duped."

"I don't like being held against my will—I don't consider it particularly fair that you are the stronger—but that is the case, so if my methods don't seem fair to you, I'm sorry."

"Are you?" he murmured. "Just remember what happens to those who cry wolf. And those who behave childishly. I think we had something to talk about—it was ridiculous for you to run away in the middle of it."

"I didn't run away in the middle of it. As far as I can see, we were quite through talking."

"Erin—" The coil was springing. His pacing turned determinedly toward her.

But she was to be saved before he reached her. The door swung open and Ted and Mary and a laughing Tanya entered, all in the best of spirits from the antics of the circus.

Erin closed her eyes for a single instant in desperation, then opened them wide, meeting Jarod's with a naked plea. She saw him pause, take a deep breath and stiffen, then exhale slowly, tensing and then loosening his fingers as he did so. Please, Erin kept silently pleading, don't make a scene before these people.

He understood. He was the first to speak. "So how was the circus?" he inquired of Mary and Ted, moving with apparent ease to the doorway to greet them. "Tanya," he smiled, bending to kiss the woman's cheek in greeting.

Mary went into a speech on how wonderful the show had been while Ted stood silently by with his small smile hovering over his lips—a smile that etched eternal affection and tolerance for his wife. When he had a chance to get a word in edgewise, he too quietly praised the performance.

"Glad you enjoyed it," Jarod said, bringing his guests into the living room. "Drink anyone? Ted, bourbon?"

"Sounds good," Ted agreed.

"Mary? Tanya? Erin, the usual?"

Erin nodded mutely, breathing again with gratitude. He might still be intending to throttle her, but he was going to do it later.

Jarod announced after mixing the drinks that since it was Mary and Ted's last night, they had planned to have dinner out. Tanya was cordially invited and happy to accept, and they were shortly dining at one of the city's elegant tourist restaurants. Erin couldn't find fault with his behavior for the entire evening—but she couldn't relax, because his touch was an inferno. Even his thigh, pressed against hers in the booth, seemed to burn through fabric to scorch her flesh.

It was a long night—naturally. Mary and Ted were leaving in the morning, and they all stayed late in the living room talking. When the conversation finally became more yawns than words, Ted stood and profusely thanked Jarod and Erin for their hospitality. "We really didn't mean to intrude in your apartment this long," Ted said, "but I did appreciate being in a home rather than the Rossia."

"No problem," Jarod assured him. "We've enjoyed having you."

Not a problem at all, he thought. He had been the one to insist Mary and Ted spend their entire time in his apartment rather than transferring their belongings over to the Rossia. Neither of them would ever know how grateful he had been for their arrival, the event which had returned him to his own bedroom . . . to Erin.

. . .

A lot of hugs went around the room, and Tanya left, insisting that she was fine, had the company car Sergei had insisted she keep while assigned to Erin, and really didn't need Jarod to see her home.

Erin found herself walking Mary and Ted up to the den. She glanced at Jarod with a nervous question in her eyes.

"I'll be right up," he told her, and a glance in his eyes informed her that he certainly would be right up and that there would be no running away and no interruptions.

In the bedroom Erin changed into a gown and robe and sat at the foot of the bed. She had considered feigning sleep, but that would be childish, and besides, it wouldn't work. In his present mood he would rip the covers off and drag her back up.

When he finally entered the room he closed the door behind him and leaned against it, crossing his arms and staring at her. He unnerved her so with his glacial eyes and terse stance that she began talking, which she hadn't at all intended to do.

"I'm grateful, Jarod," she said regally, "that you curtailed this discussion until we were alone, but I sincerely feel that we have finished with all we have to say. There is nothing further to discuss."

"There's nothing to discuss?"

He felt a crippling fury and confusion as he watched her. The fury because she spoke as if she were a queen deigning to speak to a subject, the confusion because his emotions were in a turmoil he couldn't understand.

Pieces of memory he had locked away in a guarded shell came now too easily, too vividly. The love with which Cara had once given him the news of the child she had prayed so long to conceive . . . the uncanny uneasiness that he had felt from the beginning, the fragility of the tiny wife who so dearly desired a child and cherished the life within her.

Cara was dead, their child was dead. He had accepted it, he had lived with it. But now here was this slender, remote, and haughty blond goddess informing him they had nothing else to discuss. Even her weaknesses emerged as strengths. For all her slender agility she possessed radiant health, the ability to conceive immediately.

Now she didn't even want to speak to him. She, who had everything necessary to bear and love a child, obviously found her pregnancy nothing more than an annoyance. She had told him, but then just as smoothly informed him that it was her business, not his.

He believed she intended to abort the child, and that inflamed his

240

heart and fury more than he had ever deemed possible. She had a life she was anxious to get back to, and that life couldn't include a child. The careful control he had exercised and nurtured all his life seemed to be slipping away from him like the shedding skin of a snake.

Because there was something else there. He didn't want to let her go. He had come to expect her to be a part of his home, a part of his life. He wanted her in his bed at night, he wanted to hold her, to care for her, to speak to her over coffee in the morning, to sit down to a meal she had prepared and compliment her eager efforts as a chef. He liked to watch her brush her hair, to see her eyes in lazy, shimmering half slits as she luxuriated in the aftermath of love making, to watch her stretch luxuriously in satiated drowsiness when he dressed to leave in the mornings.

The bitterness, resentment, longings, and needs suddenly exploded. He took a step toward her which was indeed a pounce, grasping her wrists and wrenching her to her feet and hard against his chest. A startled cry escaped her, but he was beyond caring. The soft, feminine feel of her body against his was channeling the storm-swept turmoil of his emotions into a savage desire that demanded release.

"So we have nothing to discuss?" he demanded darkly, crushing her against him and forcing her chin to tilt back so that her wide silver eyes met his. "Accidents do happen?"

"Jarod, please." She began to work at the wrists he held within his grasp, pinioned behind her to the small of her spine.

"Jarod . . ."

"Ahh, yes, your wrists, my sweet. Funny, but I find it hard to believe that they're bothering you." His lips suddenly came down on hers hard, unscrupulously parting them, bruising them with the demand of the kiss. His teeth commanded a further parting, his tongue sought hers in an undeniable primitive duel.

She couldn't fight him. She was held within the vise of his body, unable even to twist her head, unable to deny that despite his ferocity she was being swept up into it. A weakness was stealing over her, a loss of breath that robbed her strength, a trembling that left her gasping against his chest when he finally released his brutal hold on her lips.

His hands moved swiftly to her shoulders to slip beneath the fabric of her gown and robe, pulling them roughly down. Erin shuddered. This wasn't Jarod's touch. This was cruel in its strength.

"Jarod," she protested again. Stupidly, she wanted him; she was accustomed to sleeping with him, joyfully exploring the range of fire and heavenly delight he had given her. She loved him, pathetically. Even if he did not return that love, she couldn't stop loving him. But this was wrong. Jarod could be fierce, his passions could rage like a thunderstorm, but there was no cruelty in the man she had come to know. "Jarod, please." How stupid her protests sounded when she hung weakly against him.

"The way I see it," he murmured bitterly against her ear, "the accident has already happened. Abstinence at this point would be rather absurd, don't you think? Consenting adults . . ."

She felt his anger when the gown and robe she wore were torn and drifted in pieces to her feet. Then she was in his arms, being bounced onto the mattress. He followed her down, his body pressing hard against hers. This time she managed to twist her head from his lips, and her cry of his name permeated the boiling turmoil of his mind.

Her eyes were tightly clenched when she felt him go still. She kept them closed, gasping for breath and fighting the tears that threatened to slip from beneath them.

Seconds suspended into timelessness. Then she felt his weight lift from hers. She lay still, breathing, and then the bedroom door opened—and closed in his wake.

The tears slipped from beneath her eyes. She turned and stared at the door. His name escaped her lips once more. "Jarod . . ." It was a plea, a sobbed out plea, and he might have understood it had he heard it. But he was already out of the house, his footsteps unconsciously guiding him toward Red Square.

XIII

Erin lay staring at the door in a daze for a long time. Then she pulled her body from the bed and walked into the bathroom, feeling as if she had grown very old, as if her legs had grown hard and stiff. In the mirror above the sink she surveyed her reflection. Her tears had dried against her cheeks, her eyes appeared absurdly swollen.

She closed her eyes against her appearance and took a shower, standing beneath the spray of the water in hopes of revitalization. She wanted to sleep, but she couldn't possibly sleep feeling so terribly tired. It didn't make any sense.

Where had he gone, she wondered listlessly. He would come back, he had to come back, it was his apartment, she was the intruder.

Depression swamped over her. He would come back, then so what? There was nothing to say, nothing that could be done.

She wanted him to come back, she just wanted to know that he was there.

Erin turned off the water, stepped from the tub, dried herself thoroughly with a rough shaggy towel, and then wound the towel around her body. She sidestepped her torn gown as she returned to the bedroom and sat listlessly at the foot of the bed. The apartment was silent. Thankfully, Mary and Ted seemed to have slept through the slamming doors.

Tears started to sting behind her lids again and Erin stood, impatient with herself. She had to stop crying. It was stupid, it got her nowhere, and it drained her of the strength she needed.

She ripped open the closet door and stared numbly at the contents. Then she exchanged the towel for one of Jarod's velour robes. She decided to make herself a cup of tea, and try to separate her thoughts and feelings and the facts of the situation.

As the water in the kettle heated to a boil, Erin glanced at the kitchen clock, amazed to see that it was still shy of midnight. They had gone up to bed at almost eleven thirty.

The kettle whistled. As Erin reached for it, she felt again the burning pain behind her eyelids. She wanted to go home to the busy streets of New York, to the spring beauty of the park, to the towering buildings, the people like cattle streaming through the streets. She laughed dryly despite the fear that the laugh would cause her to cry; she wanted to see the Statue of Liberty rising high on her pedestal, welcoming the weary home.

Home. Oh, God, how she wanted to go home . . .

She began humming "America" as she fixed her tea, a little startled to discover how patriotic she could find herself on the shores of another land.

Then her humming ceased. She wanted to go home, but she wanted to go home with Jarod. But in a way, Jarod was home. A part of him belonged to these people. He was Russian, he was American. . . .

But none of that really mattered, because he was also anxious to no longer be her husband.

The shrill ringing of the phone startled her so badly that she sloshed her freshly poured tea all over the counter. Dabbing fruitlessly at the mess she had made while also reaching for the receiver, she simultaneously hoped that the ringing had not awakened her guests and that the caller would be Jarod. It would be so like him, she thought, shivers of prayerful anticipation making her weak. He was quick to anger, but just as quick to apologize.

"Erin?"

Her bubble of hope burst. The caller was Gil. What the hell is he doing calling at this hour, she wondered, her annoyance increased by irritation.

"Sorry to call you so late, but I have to talk to Jarod. It's important."

Erin frowned, her fingers tightening around the receiver. "At this hour?"

"I am sorry, Erin, but if he's sleeping, please wake him."

Erin bit her lip. "Gil, I'm sorry, but he isn't here."

She was met by a moment's silence, in which she could almost feel the agitation of the man on the other end.

"Where is he?"

"I—I'm not sure. He just went out."

"Damn!" Gil muttered.

"Gil, what is it?"

"Ah—nothing. I'll find him. Good night, Erin."

He hung up before she could say any more. For a second she stared at the receiver, her frown furrowing more deeply between her eyes. Then she slowly replaced the receiver and picked up her tea cup, only to put it back down.

"I'll find him," Gil had said.

A wash of cold bolted through her as if she had been subjected to an instant freeze. She closed her eyes, remembering Jarod's anger with her the morning after he had gone to the square, how he had demanded to know who she had spoken to, how she had denied speaking to anyone, how Sergei had told her someone had been shooting at Jarod because he had come too close.

Then she remembered how it had been Gil who had made the arrangements when she had tried to leave the country and then had found herself held in her hotel room instead of Paris.

"Oh, dear God!" she gasped aloud.

Jarod was out walking the streets; Gil would be out looking for him. Her eyes moved to the clock. It was just minutes before midnight. Jarod was always looking for something on Red Square at midnight.

She knew that, and Gil knew that. But Jarod didn't know that Gil had known where Jarod was on that particular night when the shots had been taken at him. Because she had lied.

Her cup clattered and spilled across the counter. With her hands shaking so badly she could barely control them, Erin rummaged through the counter drawer below the phone, searching out Jarod's phone book. She found Sergei's number, but had to dial it twice.

She was answered by the gentle voice of his wife. Every Russian word she had learned fled her mind. "Sergei, please, I know I've wakened you, but please, this is Erin Mc—Steele. Erin Steele. Please, this is Jarod's wife, I need to speak with Sergei . . ."

Mrs. Alexandrovich's English was not plentiful, but her tone was soothing. Erin slowly ascertained that her call had been a waste of time—Sergei was not home either.

"You call back tomorrow, Sergei happy to talk to you then."

The phone went dead in Erin's hands.

Erin stared at the receiver only a brief moment before bolting into action. She had to reach him, she had to warn him that he was right, that Gil was not to be trusted, that Gil was looking for him.

She raced upstairs only long enough to pull on a sweater and jeans, then she tore out the door and into the night. The wind was cold, but she didn't feel it. Even as she tried to reassure herself that her feeling of panic was absurd, it increased. She was desperate. If he were only with her now, she would tell him that she would be there any time he wanted her, even if she understood that he couldn't love her.

His car was parked on the curb, but it only served to frustrate her further. The door was locked. As far as she knew, Jarod kept only one set of keys, and those keys would still be in his pocket.

She began to run. The streets were empty at that hour, her feet clattered against the sidewalk loudly, each sound seeming to pierce her heart. Her labored breathing swirled around her like the gasping wail of a dying windstorm. The thudding of her heart against her ribs was so thunderous she feared it would explode but she kept running because if anything happened to him, she didn't think she could bear it. And it was all the more terrible because her pride had kept her from telling him that she loved him, that with or without him she wanted his child, and she wanted to cherish the child because it was his.

How far had she gone, she wondered, pain streaking through the legs she forced to keep going. A patch of snow melted to an ice slick sent her spinning to the ground, but she rose again with a small sob, dusting herself off and running again. Then, out of the moon-streaked night, she saw the globed spires of St. Basil's rising high against the night. She was almost there . . . she had made it.

The memory of a long kiss on Red Square at midnight raced through her mind, the memory of lips that burned, the memory that she had known, somehow, somewhere deep inside, that his kiss had been dangerous because it had so compelled her, dangerous because she was destined to fall in love with the man who was a part of the blazing red splendor.

The square was dazzlingly lit against the darkness of night. Erin reached the gates of St. Basil's and paused, doubling over with the effort to breathe as she strained her eyes to see across the square.

At Lenin's tomb the guards stood stolidly, and then the clock began to chime.

The guards began their awesome, terrifyingly strict goose step. Then, as Erin stared at the square, dark forms began to move across the red glow. There were three figures, three men. A shot rang out, a figure fell.

Erin's scream tore out across the square, but it was followed by a flurry of action. The regiment of the guards halted. As chillingly choreographed as their walk, they knelt in formation, rifles ready. Whistles shrieked, more men, appearing from nowhere, raced on to the square, and without realizing it, she was racing through them—because one of the figures still standing was Jarod.

And the one lurking behind him was Gil.

And he held a gun.

She screamed Jarod's name, screamed it over and over again until she reached him, hurtling herself into his arms, shrieking and babbling and trying to draw his attention to the man behind him. He caught her in his arms and she closed her eyes, waiting with fear rippling through her, waiting with tears in her eyes, with prayers forming unspoken on her lips. But nothing happened. He was whispering soothing things to her, setting her away from him, and it was then, only then, that she realized they were surrounded by men in uniforms, Soviet guards and police, alert and ready.

Jarod bent down next to the man on the ground. Then Erin watched stupidly as Gil Sayer strode quietly up and knelt beside her husband. "I believe I only winged him," Gil said.

Erin stared at Gil's face for a moment. Then to the ground. The man lying with the ashen face and closed eyes was Joe Mahoney. It didn't make sense.

Sergei came through the crowd of men. He shouted something. The guards returned to their vigil at the tomb; the others disappeared as they had come, melting into nowhere.

"He's alive," she heard Jarod say.

"I'll handle it," Gil said crisply.

"I don't think so," Sergei interspersed, coming between the two men. "This is Russian soil."

"But he is an American," Jarod spat out. "He should be tried in our courts."

Erin kept looking from one face to another. It finally filtered

247

through to her dazed emotions that Gil Sayer had no intention of shooting Jarod. Gil was a good guy. The bad guy was the kindly old gentleman with the graying hair who now lay on the ground, the friendly man with the sparkling blue eyes who had been so very kind to her at that first dinner at Sergei's. He was a traitor. He had betrayed Jarod, and worse, he had betrayed Gil. The pain of that betrayal now streaked through the eyes of the handsome young man who had come through the night not to harm her husband but to help him.

It was too much. The legs which had earlier carried her the mile to the square suddenly gave. The red glow became a mist of black.

She hit the pavement.

It was the disappearance of the sound of the ambulance siren that brought her back to consciousness rather than its arrival to collect Joe Mahoney.

She was warm, Erin noted vaguely, and she was warm because she was wrapped in a blanket. She opened her eyes to see that she was stretched in the rear seat of a car. A woman in a uniform was hovering over her, waving a vile-smelling pellet beneath her nose.

Erin waved her hand away and struggled to sit up, not sure whether she should smile or not to assure the strict-looking matron that she was all right. It didn't matter; the steel-eyed lady in the rigid dress with brass stars upon her shoulders moved instantly, crisply announcing something in her own language.

It was Sergei's face she saw next, and she did try a tremulous smile.

"Little fool," he chastised, "what are you doing out here?"

"I tried to call you," Erin offered weakly.

"Didn't I tell you your husband was a man determined to watch out for himself? And that I would be watching out for him?"

Erin nodded blankly. "I thought it was Gil," she said tonelessly.

Sergei sighed. "So did Jarod. And so now he suffers like a fool, a man plagued by guilt because he let his heart rule his mind. It is going to sit hard with him, he is a proud man. But look—he is also an honest man—ready to admit his faults."

Sergei helped her sit up in the car. She followed his pointed finger and saw that Jarod and Gil were in deep conversation. She smiled slightly, then turned to Sergei.

248

"What will happen to Joe Mahoney?"

"Your voice tremors, little cousin. But do not look at me like that, as if I were a beast. I will allow Mr. Mahoney to be tried in an American court. Betrayal against one's own people is more severe, don't you think? Yes, this one I will let the Americans handle."

Erin started shivering despite the blanket. "I still don't understand—"

"For some men, service to one's country is enough. To others, it is not. Joe saw some easy rewards, he grabbed for them."

"But how? He was with all of us the night I came to the square. And Gil was the one who tried to help me—"

"You forget—Gil was to be replacing Joe. What Gil knew—Joe knew. While your husband was suspecting Gil, Gil was suspecting your husband. Joe was playing the two of them off each other."

"I still don't—"

"It was all taking place here, on Red Square, at midnight. Two of the guards at Lenin's tomb were involved. Such a fine show, don't you think? Easy to drop a tiny capsule of information. A capsule dropped just outside the wall. And so easy to pick up. Even in a crowd, a man could pretend to drop a glove or coin and not be noticed bending to retrieve it. Sometimes microfilm was dropped, sometimes merely numbers to tie into information already in a computer. A lot of the information was distorted—some totally fictitious. But when two giants are wary of one another, they grab at straws."

"But Sergei—how could I have been involved? Or used so? I would have had to know what I was doing to pick up information—"

"On Red Square, Erin, you were a cover. Joe had intended originally to plant some of his information upon your belongings when you returned to the States. But we were too close. Still, Erin—and I will apologize now—I couldn't allow you to leave. I had to hold you until I knew what was going on. I was also afraid you might become a handy instrument in some other way. And at first, I didn't know if you were guilty or innocent. I could only let you go to Jarod because I trusted his honor, and because—if you were innocent—he could offer you the protection I could not. Joe might have been able to make you appear too guilty to be cleared. . . . You must understand this."

Erin nodded weakly. She did understand, she had become accidentally involved in something that allowed no quarter for individuals. And more than that, she knew that Jarod's decision to marry her had saved her from possibly becoming even more involved, caught in the quicksand of the deadly game of espionage.

"But he was selling to your government too—" she began in a daze.

"We don't always know the source of the information we are sold. It was a long time before either country realized she was being duped. Joe had access to a number of secrets. He had only to twist them to make them both believable and highly salable. Most of the contacts he used were like yourself—innocent of the fact they carried information to be picked up by those who would not ask questions but accept money."

It struck Erin again with a terrible stab of pain as she stared at the square—and the guards before Lenin's tomb who stood so strictly they appeared as mannequins—that she wanted to go home. Now she could go sooner than Jarod had promised. It was over.

She heard a crunching against the ground and tilted her chin. Jarod and Gil were both approaching the car.

"How're you doing, gorgeous?" Gil inquired first.

Erin smiled with a weak attempt at cheer. Her eyes left Gil's to focus tentatively on her husband's.

Jarod stretched out a hand and stroked his fingers lightly over her cheek. His eyes were thoughtful and brooding, but she couldn't fathom the emotion that burned beyond their guard.

"You could have gotten yourself . . . hurt," he said admonishingly.

She didn't seem to be able to say much. She merely nodded.

He stepped back from the car; Sergei joined him, and the uniformed matron slipped into the driver's seat.

"Anna will take you home," Sergei said.

At her look of confusion, Jarod added softly, "We have forms to fill out and business to finish. I'll be home soon."

Her door slammed. The car revved into action and moved from the curb.

It was amazing how short the distance to the apartment was. She had felt when running that it had been miles and miles.

"Thank you, spa seeba," she told the rigid Anna as the car came to a halt. But apparently Anna had her orders. She accompanied Erin to the door, bullying her way in when Erin tried to thank her again for the ride. Anna walked into the kitchen and poured a glass of water. She returned to Erin and forced the water and a pair of small white pills into her hands.

"Oh—ah—no thank you," Erin began to murmur.

The pills were more firmly pressed into her hand. "Sergei say that you take. That you must sleep. Pills will not hurt the baby—no sleep will."

Erin colored slightly and began to protest again, but then gave up. If she ever wanted this watchdog out of the apartment, she would have to take the pills. She swallowed them and handed back the glass of water, then opened her mouth wide like a child. "See," she garbled with a sarcasm that was not lost on the other woman. "All gone."

Anna muttered something about Americans that Erin didn't think was complimentary, but she did, at long last, leave.

But I don't want to sleep, Erin thought. I want to wait up for Jarod. I need to talk to him.

She attempted to sit in the living room to wait, but the little white tablets quickly had an effect. Her head drooped, and the urge to close her eyes was so strong that she convinced herself she could wait for him just as well upstairs in bed.

It seemed a terribly difficult task to make her way up the staircase —more difficult than reaching the square. But finally she passed the door to the den—and paused with a smile to think how ridiculous it was that so much had happened while Mary and Ted slept peacefully and blissfully unaware.

She made it into the bedroom and decided to lie down and rest just a minute before finding a nightgown.

She didn't get up. The little white tablets Sergei's guard dog had forced her to take were granting her the blissful oblivion she had just envied Mary and Ted.

It was close to dawn when Jarod finally returned home. He had no intention of going to sleep, because he was afraid he wouldn't be able to wake himself up in the few hours before the time came to take Mary and Ted to the airport. Remembering he had guests in the apartment as well as his sleeping wife, he walked quietly up the staircase. He left the bedroom door open to allow the downstairs lights to flicker dimly into the bedroom. Then he paused in the doorway, watching her as she slept.

She was still clad in jeans and a sweater, and her head didn't even rest upon the pillow. For a moment as he watched her, he was simply struck afresh by her striking beauty, all the more pure as she slept. Her truly fine, aristocratic features were framed by that rich hair that gleamed with natural gold even in the dimness of the room. Her fingers, so elegantly long and fragile-appearing with their handsomely manicured nails, curled near her cheek.

She had come to the square. She had raced across a concrete field of armed men because she had believed he was in danger after he had so cruelly accosted her.

He moved to the bed and touched the silky smoothness of her cheek. "Erin," he whispered softly.

She didn't respond, and he realized how deeply she slept. Thinking her encumbered, he gently released the snap and zipper of her jeans and carefully eased them from her body. She sighed, but curled back into a little ball. Lifting her in his arms, he pulled her sweater over her head, then held her as he pulled down the spread and top sheet, gently laid her upon the cool bottom one, and drew the others back around her. She murmured something, and her fingers momentarily entwined with his before going limp again. He sat beside her then, holding the fingers that had grasped his as he continued to watch her in silent vigil.

It had taken him to this moment to realize that he loved her. And as he sat there he thought of all the things he wanted to say. He wanted desperately to be able to tell her how sorry he was for his brutal behavior, to explain that he had been hurt once, and that he was afraid to be hurt again. He wanted to let her know that her strength was far greater than his because she was capable still of loving, of giving, when he had only been able to take. And if he could just say things so that she might understand, he could ask her if she would consider remaining his wife. If she could give him a chance to learn to love again . . .

He took her into his arms suddenly, holding her tightly against his chest. What a fool he had been. Paradise had been his, and even as he invaded her beauty, he hadn't had the wits to hold her dear.

He clenched his eyes tightly together and held her another moment, then lowered her gently back to the pillow. He touched her forehead reverently with his lips.

She murmured something, then her silver eyes flickered open. They were glazed, opaque with sleep.

"Jarod," she whispered.

"I'm here, my love."

Her lashes closed over her eyes again; she said something else, so softly he couldn't hear her. He leaned closer to her lips. "What, Erin?"

Her eyes remained closed, but she spoke again softly. "I want to go home, Jarod."

"You are home."

"No," she murmured, her brow creasing with a frown as she fought the sleep that overwhelmed her. "I want to go home . . . to America . . . to my home . . ."

His eyes closed again painfully. He stiffened, then set her hand gently on her abdomen and rose.

He went downstairs and put on a pot of coffee.

It was over. The chase of the last months was over, but he couldn't feel victory, only pain. He had been after the wrong man—hell, even Catherine had warned him he was pushing in the wrong direction—but he had been so sure of himself because he had been a jealous fool and hadn't even realized it.

Even Erin . . . he had dragged her into it as surely as Mahoney had done. He had used her, and had forced her into marriage.

She wanted to go home.

The coffee finished perking. He poured himself a cup and glanced at his watch for the time. Almost six thirty. Not too early to begin waking a few people up. He pensively took a sip of his coffee, then moved for the phone. It would only take a few calls to change her departure date.

"Erin. Erin. Erin. Erin."

The urgently monotonous intonation of her name finally woke her. Very bleary-eyed, Erin struggled to sit up. She blinked rapidly to dispel the image, but Mary was still sitting beside her, anxiously staring at her.

"Dear Lord," Mary exclaimed cheerfully, "but you do sleep like the dead!"

Erin blinked again, highly resenting anyone who could sound so cheerful when she was sure she *was* half dead. But then Mary hadn't been in on the catastropic events of the night; she didn't know anything about nuclear secrets or "Midnight" or the drama on the square.

Had it all really happened, Erin wondered? It already felt like a dream. For a moment she wondered if the entire thing *hadn't* been a dream, if she had merely invented Jarod Steele and Sergei Alexandrovich and Gil and Tanya and Joe.

She finally focused on her friend. "Mary, I'm sorry. I know we have to get you to the airport—"

"Not me," Mary interrupted, eyes twinkling. "Us! You're coming home with Ted and me."

"What?" Erin gasped weakly.

Mary nodded strenuously. "Your husband arranged it. He said you were very anxious to get back to the States, so he decided it would be best for you to travel with us."

An avalanche of pain cascaded over Erin, so gripping that she had to will herself not to double over. Of course, she told herself, it *was* all over. Last night had not been a dream; Jarod knew now that she wasn't a spy, nor could she be used by a spy, and so he was sending her home earlier than he had promised. Fast. No more discussions, no more arguments, no more clashes or agonizing encounters. Just a clean split. And how convenient to pass the chance of getting her home on to Mary and Ted.

"Erin, are you all right?"

"Fine," she assured Mary, "just tired. I didn't sleep well last night. Where is Jarod?"

"Loading the car with Ted. He said for me to let you sleep to the last minute, then help you get some things together. And you're not to worry about packing—he'll send whatever you leave."

For a moment she thought she would be sick. She clenched her jaws together, swallowed and nodded, and crawled from the bed, somewhat surprised to find herself clad in only lace bikinis and matching bra. She didn't remember undressing; in fact, she barely remembered making it up the stairs.

"What's wrong, Erin? I thought you'd be happy about traveling with us."

"Oh, I am, Mary!" Erin forced some cheer into her voice. "Very glad. How much time do I have? Enough to jump in the shower?"

"Sure—I'll gather a few of your things."

Twenty minutes later she was ready to go downstairs. She had managed to apply her makeup with enough expertise to hide her sleeplessness and misery while still appearing natural; her hair was swept into a strict and sophisticated chignon. In a tailored spring business suit with a powder blue Gant and wide ascot, she felt as if she could uphold her dignity even when she had to face him.

Which happened immediately following her first sip of coffee. He entered the hallway and caught her eyes across the living room. There was an anxious cast to his eyes, as if he were about to ask her a question. But she stiffened automatically at the sight of him, and the strange, almost tentative cast in the glacial blue disappeared.

"You're ready, I see."

"Most certainly," Erin replied crisply. "I wouldn't take the slightest chance of missing such an opportunity."

He nodded briefly. Hers was the only case not set in the trunk of the car. His broad shoulders encased in a tan spring jacket bunched as he reached for it. Erin noticed with a pang how vividly the silver threaded jet of his lowered head contrasted with and complemented the cool shade of his sports jacket. I've never seen him in that jacket, she thought. He had always worn dark clothing, which had also been a complement to his midnight hair and shocking crystal eyes.

The Soviet winter had hung on so long. Now it was really becoming spring, and she was leaving, going home where she wanted to be.

She had dreamed they would go together, but that had been a childish dream. This was life, reality, and it very often held no happy endings.

Erin followed Jarod out of the door.

She sat beside him as they drove to the airport. It was Ted who kept up a conversation with Jarod, making everything seem smooth even though his replies from his host were monosyllables.

Jarod's hand brushed Erin's as he shifted gears. He gave her an offhand "sorry."

Then they were at the airport. To Erin's surprise, she discovered that Tanya and a young man, Sergei and his wife, and Gil Sayer

255

were all there ahead of them, up and out of bed, apparently alerted to the fact that she was leaving, and caring enough to say good-bye.

"Oh, Erin!" It was Tanya who threw her arms around Erin first. "How I am going to miss you! But you will come back—you must! And you must write—it is allowed. And send me pictures."

Erin hugged Tanya in return, her eyes shimmering with tears. "Oh, Tanya, I will miss you too. So much. And I will write, frequently, I promise."

Jarod had stepped back to watch as his wife said her good-byes to those to whom she had become close. It was a painful procedure. The liquid silver of her eyes was brilliant and open, alive with caring. Her smile was radiant—for Tanya, for Gil, for Sergei.

He had seen her smile like that; he had heard many times the melody of her laughter. The picnic on the Lenin Hills . . . sightseeing with Mary and Ted . . . in the dimness of their bedroom. There had been times when she had been his friend. But she wanted to go home; he could understand the feeling. Perhaps she had learned to care something for him, but that caring couldn't outweigh the life that was rightfully hers, the excitement and glamour she could return to.

Let her go, he told himself harshly. She had taken his name, but she was still Erin McCabe. He was a public servant, unable to offer much against the world that was hers. Let her go back to pretense and the adulation of those who coveted her sterling qualities.

"This has really turned out so well for Erin!" Mary suddenly sighed beside him.

Jarod glanced down at his wife's friend. "Oh? Why do you say that?"

"She's gained so much!" Mary exclaimed, her eyes somewhat misty as she watched Erin with Tanya. Then she gazed up at Jarod. "She wanted to come here in the first place because she hoped to teach political science and history some day—when she can finish her degree. Now she can go back to school and also have all the wonderful experiences with Tanya and Sergei behind her!" Mary's eyes narrowed suddenly. "Surely you knew that?"

Jarod stiffened slightly. "It's my understanding that she will pick up with her career as soon as she reaches New York."

Erin was unaware of the conversation going on near her. When Tanya released her, Gil gripped her next, kissing her cheek. "Don't forget, gorgeous, if that 'steel' hunk of yours over there ever fails you, I'll still be around. A hemisphere away for the time—but I'll take your call from anywhere!"

Erin smiled, guilt overwhelming her at the easy way she, too, had been ready to hang Gil on circumstantial evidence. "Thank you, Gil. I won't ever forget you."

Sergei's wife hugged her and tried to say good-bye in proper English, stuttered, and throwing her hands in the air, spattered out her best wishes in Russian. Erin kissed her cheek.

Sergei would not settle for a simple hug. He slipped his arm through Erin's and began to lead the group down the hallway to the proper gate. "Take great care, little cousin," he advised her. "Do nothing rash, and think on the many things I have told you." He paused for a moment, a mischievous twinkle in his fascinating hazel eyes. "Do you know, Erin, they say that we once had a Romany gypsy in the family. Of course, we don't often admit such things, but I will now, because I believe I have inherited a bit of the gift of fortune-telling. And if you can be but a bit patient, little cousin, I believe you will find great happiness."

Erin lowered her lashes with a rueful grimace. "Thank you, Sergei, you're very kind to me." She stopped in the hallway and hugged him fiercely for a moment. "You have always been very kind to me." She grinned. "My Russian cousin, I thank you with all my heart."

They had reached the concourse gateway; the others were milling close around them, and a voice began announcing the plane. Erin hugged Sergei one more time. "Good-bye, Sergei."

"We do not say good-bye," he told her softly. "Do sveedah nyah, Erin, do sveedah nyah."

"Do sveedah nyah, Sergei," Erin murmured in return, knowing full well control had broken and that her eyes were misted.

Then she felt a wrench on her arm and she was spun around, and held against Jarod's chest. She lifted her chin, her eyes meeting his with liquid silver, the pain and reproach and need shimmering through them. He stared down at her a moment; his mouth opened and closed, then crushed down on hers as he held her close, pressing her fingers against the hammer of his heart as his lips consumed her with a wild hunger that combined passion and tenderness, demand

257

and reverence. Erin shuddered against the moist fire of that desperate duel of tongues, wishing desperately that the moment could stretch to eternity.

But the voice was droning on, passengers were boarding the plane.

"You're not leaving the man forever!" Erin vaguely heard Mary chuckle. "He *is* your husband."

Jarod withdrew from the kiss. "Come on—I'll walk you past the inspectors."

Erin waved a last, painful good-bye to the others, but hurried along with Jarod, eager for any word he might give her.

There was so little time.

"I can't leave right now," he explained in a hush as they stopped at the plane's door. "There are things I have to tie up after last night. But I'll come to New York as soon as I can. Please hold off making any decisions about anything until I get there." His voice was crisp. Stilted. The commander giving an order. But it was an order she would cling to, as she had clung to his kiss. An order issued in the husky velvet she had come to love and need.

Erin couldn't speak. She nodded.

"Promise, Erin."

Her mouth had become too dry. She couldn't possibly utter a sound from her parched throat. She nodded once more. Then tried again and rasped out an "I promise."

And then they were separated. A polite but firm stewardess escorted Erin into the plane, chastising her in no-nonsense language that made its point very clear. She had been holding up their departure.

She hadn't even really had a last view of him to hold on to in her memory. Just his eyes. They would haunt her for the endless nights to come.

She was glad that she was seated behind Mary and Ted. She didn't want to talk, didn't want to pretend that everything was okay.

Soon after the plane took off, she laid her head back and closed her eyes. Tears slipped from beneath the fringe of her lashes unchecked.

Her eyes were still closed when the Aeroflot jet brought them past the Russian border.

She didn't know when it was that she left the Union of Soviet Socialist Republics behind, or when it was that she reached the free world. It didn't matter. It would be another plane, and another long flight, before she would reach home, and that's what mattered. Only home could help ease the ache that not only gripped her heart, but seemed to permeate her entire being with loss and pain.

XIV

The first few weeks hadn't been terribly difficult for Jarod. He had had a great deal to do and had been able to work from dawn to dusk. But things were just about tied up now. There were problems—daily problems—but Gil had proven himself very capable and very efficient, and Jarod could depend on him to handle whatever might arise.

The spying would go on. The Russians would smile over a negotiation table while their cloak-and-dagger agents worked within the United States. Likewise, the United States would have special CIA agents and others probing the sources of the U.S.S.R. There would be more double agents playing side against side.

But generally they would have a loyalty affixed somewhere. And hopefully, the Russians would no longer have access to the files of the United States embassy, nor would the Americans have the ability to burrow into the Soviet side to upset the balance of power with half truths that could block a negotiation table with a wall of sheer ice.

The spying that would go on now would be the respectable type, Jarod thought dryly, the type that had long been accepted and recognized. A type that he and Sergei would never discuss. The Russian would seek out those who worked for the free world, Jarod would again be protecting the interests of his own country and of the mandates of the U.N. It had been a strange and unusual occurrence for his cousin and himself to be seeking out the same man, working toward a joint goal. But then again maybe not so terribly strange. Perhaps he and Sergei, oceans apart in ideology but close by flesh and blood, did continually seek the same goal—a peaceful coexistence between giants who could not be friends but had to be respectful acquaintances were the world to survive.

Project Midnight was over. Mahoney awaited trial in the United States. The Soviet guard who had been in on the microfilm transference had disappeared. Jarod didn't want to think about the man's fate. Sergei—for all his humanity and cultured charm—could be a ruthless man. He had to be. The Politburo allowed no quarter. To hold the vast nation that covered one sixth of the earth's land surface together, men had long been ruthless, from the czars to the commissars.

Jarod poured himself a third drink in his empty apartment and sauntered idly into the music room. He drained half the bourbon, loosened his tie, and sat down. He picked up the balalaika, a treasured remembrance of his beautiful, soft-spoken but strong-willed mother. He thought of his parents as he strummed a chord. They had defied the laws of man to love one another, and they had carried that love through their lives.

His mother had been an expert musician. His talent was a gift from her. Strange that he had such a way with the instrument. Sergei would give his eye teeth to play half so well.

The apartment was empty without Erin. . . .

He began to play an old Russian folk tune, hoping the music would drown out his thoughts, but nothing could.

He should have gone home a week ago. There was nothing holding him here, and he had promised Erin he would be there soon so that they might settle their lives.

He stopped playing abruptly and drained the rest of his bourbon. He looked at the glass, shrugged, and went to the kitchen to refill it. Maybe the liquor could drown out his thoughts. He hadn't been good and drunk in years. Strange, but when one was young, liquor could take away sobriety all too easily. Now, when he wanted to fuzz his mind and blot out the world, it seemed impossible to do so.

It seemed to be growing stuffy. He shrugged out of his jacket, threw it haphazardly over a chair, and picked up the balalaika again.

Erin had cared deeply about Tanya, and Tanya was Russian. She even seemed to have created a damned good relationship with Sergei —and hell, one couldn't be more Russian than Sergei. Did she care what his ancestors had been? He never attempted to hide his parentage—why had he been so elusive each time she had questioned him about the ring? Because she had called him a Red and he had been

261

afraid that if she had known the truth she would have believed her own wild accusation.

Or was it maybe that still, to this day, he felt that he had to prove his own loyalty to the country he had chosen over and over again? No. Hell, he was never going to be president. Look how long it had taken to get a Catholic into the White House. A divorced man had strikes against him; a Russian would never, never be acceptable to the American public. But he loved his land. He had served in any capacity possible and then he had been chosen by the U.N.

He had been determined to prove himself—not to others, but to himself. Well, he had certainly accomplished that.

But had he done so with Erin? Why the hell didn't he go home?

I am afraid to go home. I am afraid that I will discover that she has already started divorce proceedings, that she has rid herself of the child, that she will not be pleased to see me, he thought grimly. And she will be on U.S. soil. I will have no way to hold her. No fierce enigmas to deceive her into believing she needs me.

When, exactly, he wondered, had he fallen in love with her? He had been so determined not to love again.

It was the first night he had held her, the night he had learned what she had faced before, the night she put her trust in him to guide her away from the past and the fears that haunted her.

He had fought the love—loving again had seemed disloyal to Cara. Wanting a child again had seemed disloyal to Cara.

How wrong I was, my sweet, Jarod thought. If I were to really honor the love between us, I would not betray it by closing my heart. I do love Erin. I need her, I want her, I love her and I'm scared to death to try and tell her. . . .

He struck a harsh chord on the balalaika and grinned coldly to himself. "What a coward you are, Steele," he said aloud.

"I'll second that."

Startled, Jarod glanced up. He must be drunk, he told himself. Sergei stood in the doorway to the music room, and Jarod hadn't even heard him enter.

He grinned and lifted his glass to the intruder. "Hello, cousin. Have a drink with me."

"You're drunk, cousin," Sergei replied dryly.

"No, not yet. But I'm trying."

Sergei entered the room, staring harshly at Jarod, his hands planted on his hips. "You are a fool, cousin," he said softly.

Jarod nodded again. "Yep."

"You have a wife who carries your child and who loves you awaiting you, but you sit here like a child sulking in the dark."

Jarod shrugged. "I have a wife, Sergei, but she doesn't love me." He hesitated a moment. "And I don't know about the child," he said softly. "I said things that were harsh . . . that were cruel. I—" He began playing strident chords on the balalaika in self-interruption, which he just as abruptly ceased. "Never mind, cousin. This isn't your affair."

"Straighten up, Jarod!" Sergei hissed scornfully. "You are my blood, so I will help you—because you dishonor our family with such foolish thoughts. Your wife will forgive you—because she loves you. And she knows about Cara and the baby."

"She knows?" Jarod thundered furiously, casting the balalaika aside to stand and face his cousin. "Why you interfering commie! How dare you involve yourself in my affairs?"

Sergei sighed. "It seems, cousin," he said dryly, "that someone has to. You're a good man, cousin—one of the best I know, capitalist or communist. But you are also an idiot."

"I ought to break your face, cousin."

Sergei started laughing at the threat. Jarod was lithe and agile and powerful—in a fight his younger cousin could tear him to pieces. But he also doubted that Jarod could aim a blow at the minute. "Threaten me at another time if you wish to see me alarmed. Face it, cousin: if you lifted a fist sideways at the moment, you would follow it to the ground and break your own face."

He watched his cousin's face. The pain. The fear that was such a terribly difficult thing to swallow and accept for a man who feared nothing. Jarod was capable of hiding any emotion—Sergei seldom knew what he was thinking. But at the moment his cousin's eyes were naked to him; they might have been children, meeting warily again for the first time while their mothers hugged and sobbed in greeting after the years lost between them.

Jarod had wanted to beat him up the first time they had met too, Sergei thought with a sad smile. They had tangled as children, and he had been shocked at the strength of the young stripling. At that point they had learned they could not best one another. They had known they would take paths that clashed; they had acknowledged a wary respect for one another.

But at Cara's death, Sergei had wept with Jarod—or for Jarod. Jarod hadn't wept. He had bottled the pain. It crippled him still.

"Cousin," Sergei said forcefully, "I will make you some coffee. You will sober up. You will arrange a flight home. You will go home because neither your Russian mother nor your American father was a coward. And you will go home because your wife loves you."

Jarod looked up, the glaze somewhat leaving his eyes. "Cousin," he demanded sharply, "when will you leave off interfering in my life?"

Sergei smiled, undaunted by the growl. "When you are no longer in my country for me to interfere," he said placidly.

"Her child will be part Russian," Jarod suddenly mumbled. "Why would she leave her fame and income for a Russian child?"

Sergei smiled. It was sheer pleasure to see his impregnable cousin in this stupor of insecurity. He had wondered himself at times if Jarod weren't composed of pure brick—or of steel, as his name implied.

"A beautiful woman does not have to prove that she is beautiful, my friend. And you bestow upon the lady prejudices that do not exist—except in the back of your own crazy mind."

The next morning Sergei saw Jarod to the airport. When the flight was announced the men turned to one another. They stared into one another's eyes for a long moment. And then they embraced.

"Thank you, Sergei," Jarod said a little stiffly as they withdrew.

Sergei shrugged. "The world has decreed us enemies, cousin, but we are blood. Not even the world can change that."

They embraced once more. Moments later Jarod Steele was in a plane that would take him to Switzerland—and then home.

"No," Erin said flatly as she sat in a plush beige chair in her agent's Park Avenue high-rise office. She was staring through the plate glass window. It was no longer spring in New York, but summer. The tiny ledge garden was in full bloom; insects buzzed around the multitude of carefully cultivated flowers.

Jerry Armstrong didn't seem to hear his favorite client's soft-spoken negative. Enthused, he walked about the airy office space, arms waving, his handsome young face alive with the plans that ticked through his mind. He had originally greeted the news of her pregnancy with a certain horror, but now he had geared himself into acceptance.

"We haven't a problem in the world, Erin! The diaper manufacturers will go crazy for a chance to have Erin McCabe endorse their products—as an expectant mother! And then there are the maternity boutiques, and the creators of all those skin lotions—Erin, it will be fabulous! A whole new world will open to us! I'll get on it right away."

"Jerry," Erin interrupted, "you're not listening to me! I don't want to model through my pregnancy. I don't want to capitalize on this—and I don't want to share it with the world. And my name is Steele, not McCabe anymore."

"McCabe . . . Steele . . . what's the difference! Your husband can join in, Erin, after the baby's born! The two of you discussing the baby food you've chosen for your very special child."

"Jerry—please!" Erin wailed. The thought of Jarod consenting to discuss baby food for a commercial was so ludicrous she would have laughed aloud if she weren't so tired. She wasn't getting anywhere with Jerry and she was too tired to laugh and too tired to sit and argue any longer. Besides, it wasn't really funny, it was tragic. She could explain to Jerry that her husband didn't want the child—she didn't even know if he would be around when the child was born. But she couldn't bring herself to say such things. A certain hope was still alive within her—even though it had been over a month since she had left Russia and in that time she hadn't heard a word from the man who was legally her husband.

She should have filed for a divorce. That was what he wanted. But she couldn't make herself do it. She was clinging to that picture of his eyes upon her and the fact that he had made her promise to wait.

"Jerry"—Erin folded her slender fingers staunchly together and faced him stubbornly—"I am retiring. I mean it. I have ample savings, and I want my life back. That's it." Apparently her tone finally permeated the fantasies in his mind. He looked at her, crushed.

Erin laughed. "Oh, Jerry—the world is full of beautiful girls—younger than I am, fresher—and not pregnant! You'll find yourself a new star attraction! Probably this afternoon if I'm not mistaken!"

Jerry argued awhile longer and then gave up. There was no one quite so stubborn as Erin when she set her mind to something. With dire warnings that she would regret her decision, he finally let her go, hugging her fiercely before she left the room. "We'll always be friends, though, huh?" he queried, so piteously that Erin did laugh.

"Of course, Jerry, and if I ever do decide to model again, you know I wouldn't dream of having another agent."

That seemed to mollify him somewhat. But Erin was laughing again as she left his office. A young and exotically sultry brunette had been awaiting an appointment with Jerry in the reception area, and Erin saw how Jerry's eyes lit up at the sight of her. It had always been a fickle field, Erin thought. She had known she was dispensable!

Erin decided to walk home—the distance wasn't long, and although hot, it was a beautiful summer day. Her steps started out springy, but she hadn't gone too far when a wave of depression engulfed her. What's the matter with you? she demanded of herself bitterly. Bright girl—but you can't read the writing on the wall. The man wants nothing more to do with you. He sent you home the first possible second. You haven't had a word—not a single word, not a letter, not a note, not a call—from him. That's rather clear, isn't it? Salvage some pride, Erin; be ready to give him what he wants if and when he returns. Get hold of your lawyer. Plan an easy divorce.

She had already done lots of planning. She had rehearsed and rehearsed all that she would say about the child. She would be very controlled and very cool and completely logical. She would tell him she still considered it his right to know what she was doing, that she wanted the child and had fully considered all the responsibilities and was still determined to raise it herself. She knew how he felt, expected nothing from him, but should he ever be interested, now or in the future, she would, of course, grant him visitation rights.

Oh, Erin! she mocked herself. How logical, how giving, how mature. If I have everything down so pat, why don't I just write him? It would be so much easier for the both of us. He won't even have to return to the States. I can do everything from here and he'll have his freedom.

Tears started welling in her eyes, but she brushed them impatiently away and bit down hard into her lip. Maybe she had been a fool to stop working. Now she would have hours and hours to brood. And if she were falling apart already, how would she manage as time wore on?

I have to manage, she told herself blandly. But as she approached her apartment house, she was wincing, praying that Casey would be out. Erin hadn't found it in herself to explain the truth of her marriage to anyone, and Casey drove her crazy about Jarod. Good old Casey—going nuts because she couldn't get any "juicy intimate details" out of Erin.

She stiffened mentally and physically as she approached her building and smiled out a greeting to the dignified doorman. She kept her smile plastered to her face as she rode the elevator up; in fact, she kept smiling until she almost reached her door. Then her smile crumbled.

She became convinced that she had finally broken, that lunacy had set in, because she could have sworn she was hearing the softly played chords of a balalaika. . . .

The music stopped. She shook herself; she had imagined it. She brought her knuckles to her mouth and bit down hard on them, and then fumbled in her purse for her key. But she didn't need her key—the door was unlocked.

Fear touched upon her for a moment, but as she began to open the door she heard the drone of Casey's voice from the living room, going on and on in her nonstop fashion. Curiously Erin pushed the door the rest of the way open and stepped into the apartment.

She saw him immediately. He was standing, staring out her floor-to-ceiling window. His back was to her; she could see the rear of his ebony head with the silver threads, the square set of his broad shoulders. His hands were idly clasped behind his back and she thought as she had a hundred times before how well he wore his tailored suits, how they complemented the masculine breadth of shoulders and trim waist and hips.

She wanted to say something but she couldn't. Her heart had begun a pounding within her breast that was deafening. She wasn't sure if she were actually breathing or not, and her mouth suddenly felt parched, top and bottom and tongue all glued together.

The balalaika, she noticed absently, was situated in the corner of the room. She might be paralyzed, but at least she wasn't crazy. She had been hearing the soft tune; evidently he had played for Casey, probably to shut her up.

"Erin!" Casey exclaimed. She was seated on the sofa, chatting endlessly. "You're home! Look who made it! I let him in, of course, and fixed him some coffee. Want a cup? It's still on. Or I can make you some tea."

Jarod had turned at Casey's exclamation. Erin met his eyes, not hearing another word that Casey babbled. They stared at one another for countless seconds, an electric current seeming to charge the space between them. Erin blinked, wondering at the deep cobalt color of his eyes. There was no frost to them, she realized slowly. They were guarded, they were wary, but there was also something else to them, a pensive question, a look she didn't really understand.

It was Jarod who turned to Cassey. He gave her a charming, disarming smile as he interrupted her.

"Casey, would you mind? It's been a while since Erin and I have seen one another . . ." He let his tone run out with a touch of insinuation which Casey obviously thought to be rivetingly sexual. She actually colored, and her return smile was dazzling with the deliciousness of the innuendo.

"Oh, of course! Let me get out of here! See you all later . . . much later, I guess!" She walked by Erin, who hadn't yet been able to shake off the paralysis that held her.

Casey brushed against her, and that finally put her into motion. She managed to give her friend a smile of thanks as she walked with her to the door.

"Oh, Erin," Casey whispered in a rapid hush. "Is he something! I can't wait to hear all about your afternoon. He must be gorgeous naked, absolutely gorgeous!"

"Casey," Erin mumbled in admonition, praying Jarod hadn't heard the excited whisper. She opened her mouth to say more, but then sighed. Casey would always be Casey. "Thanks again, Case," was all she said, but she voiced the words firmly as she ushered Casey into the hall. "Talk to you later." Erin closed the door even as her friend's mouth opened to keep on going. With the door firmly shut behind her, Erin turned and leaned against it, drawing support as she once more faced her husband. He seemed towering at the moment, smoothly assured and sophisticated as always in his handsome suit with his striking granite features.

She had to say something. Where were all her practiced speeches? Where was the cool she had promised herself when they faced one another again?

"You, ah, should have written or called," she murmured, wincing as she stammered out the words huskily. "I would have arranged to be home so that you wouldn't have to waste any time. I . . . uh . . ."

"I have lots and lots of time," he interrupted her quietly.

A silence fell between them, as wide as the space that separated them. It was Jarod who broke the silence. "How are you?"

Erin lifted both hands with a shrug and forced a small smile to her lips. "Fine, thank you."

He blinked, and then his eyes gazed down to the floor for a moment before he glanced back up to her. "I mean," he said, smiling slightly himself, "how have you been feeling?" I'm groping, Jarod thought. I sound like an idiot. Why don't I just come out and ask her if she still wants the baby, if she's done anything . . . I can't even think it, he groaned inwardly.

She answered him in an uneasy rush. "I'm really fine, just fine. No sickness, no tiredness, nothing. I—I really wouldn't believe it if I hadn't been assured by two doctors. Doctor Hanson—he's here in Manhattan—he, uh, he says I'm just very lucky and that everything is fine. I think I will have a cup of tea. Can I get you some more coffee? I'm sure Casey made a very large pot. Did you have a good flight over? How are Sergei and Tanya and the rest of the troops? I wrote Tanya, but I haven't received anything back yet." As she spoke, Erin hurried into the kitchen and set the kettle on to boil. She was unnerved as Jarod followed her, hovering near. That marvelous scent that had haunted her memory overwhelmed her so that if she didn't keep talking she would fall over.

He stood near the counter, a brow slightly arched with gentle amusement. "Sure," he murmured. "I'll have some more coffee. And everyone is fine." Erin kept her eyes on the cup while she poured more coffee from the pot. Her fingers were shaking badly, but what was worse, as she took a step closer to hand the cup to Jarod, she tripped. The coffee ran all over Jarod.

"Oh, no!" Erin gasped in horrified apology. She glanced down to see what had caused her to trip. Bill—Casey's scrounging Persian—had not made it out the door with his mistress. Funny, Erin thought, she hadn't even noticed the cat. But then she hadn't noticed anything but Jarod, who was hastily slipping out of his jacket before the coffee soaked the material and scalded his flesh.

"Oh, Jarod!" Erin wailed, but he was laughing.

"I feel like I've really come home," he murmured, tossing the jacket on the counter and ripping quickly at his tie and shirt, which a second later were also on the counter. Erin stared at his bare chest, thinking how badly she wanted to reach out and touch the crisp curling hairs that stretched across the muscled breadth and disappeared into the waistband of his pants. Then she thought, Oh, yes, Casey, he is gorgeous naked, he is trim and wired and hard as a drum and wonderful to crush against.

"I, umm, I tripped," she stammered, swallowing and taking a step backwards. "Bill was beneath my feet. Bill is Casey's cat, but he thinks he lives here half the time. I didn't see him in the kitchen. He's a bit of a pain, but he really is a beautiful cat. Nice company. I am so sorry about your suit—I didn't burn you, did I?"

He planted his hands on his hips. A broad smile touched his lips, his eyes sparkled with the beauty of crystal. "You didn't burn me, Erin, any more than just seeing you ever burns me. As to the suit"—he shrugged—"maybe we should move to Texas. Or California or Florida. I could probably get away without dress shirts in those climates—much more economical with you around."

Erin stared at him blankly. She felt as if she had lost all control of her breathing once more.

Suddenly he took a step toward her, and his arms came around her. One hand held the small of her back, pressing her close against him, close against the heat of his hips; the other held her nape; his fingers raked through her hair, and her head was tilted to his.

"My interfering but sometimes uncannily perceptive cousin told me that you loved me, Erin," he said huskily. "Is that true?"

She stared at him, at the deep warm cobalt in his eyes. She felt his chest so hard against hers, the coarse jet hairs she had longed to touch touching her flesh through the soft knit of her summer dress. His hands held her firmly, pressing her to him, to the desire that she could feel growing against her.

Anything that she might have planned to say to this man entirely escaped her. She closed her eyes for a second, but nothing helped. She inhaled his scent deeply, and she gasped out a yes that turned to a sob, and despite his hold on her hair she buried her face against his neck and repeated her broken yes.

"Erin," he murmured, and his arms held her even closer. "Oh, Erin . . ." It was a reverent murmur, a brush of velvet that whispered through her hair and touched her cheek as he nuzzled against her bent head. For several moments, lost to time, they stood that way, as if afraid to let go and clinging to something infinitely precious in the determination that it not be lost. But then Jarod untangled himself from her arms and took her hands and she saw that his eyes held no guard as well as no ice; they were open and giving and more gentle than she had ever seen them, and they were filled with the tender love she could barely believe could be for her.

"We need to talk, sweetheart," he said softly. "Could you handle getting me another cup of coffee?"

She nodded. Trembling, she poured more coffee and removed the whistling kettle—which neither had noticed—from the stove. How can I be doing this, she wondered, when I am not sure how I am standing? He loves me, and I can't believe it. Oh, dear God, don't let it be a dream.

He carried his coffee and her tea into the living room, seated her on the sofa, and stooped before her. "You have a lot to forgive me for, Erin."

"No," she protested, but he stopped her with a finger to her lips.

Then he rose, sipping from his mug as he moved about the room. "I love you, Erin, I want to live my life with you, I want not only this child, but perhaps one or two more. I want to sleep with you, wake to your beautiful silver eyes every morning . . ."

"Oh, Jarod," Erin murmured. It was all she could think of to say. His words were all she could ask of God for a lifetime. Why did he keep talking, she wondered in a daze. What else could matter? He was here, all she wanted to do was bury herself within him.

"Erin," he said softly, "you have to listen to me—I want you to understand. I believe I have loved you for a long time. But I didn't want to love you. I did love Cara, very much. When I lost her, I couldn't handle it. I was afraid to love. The only relationships I could have were those in which I could do nothing but take."

He came back beside her again, taking both their cups and setting them on the small coffee table before the couch, and then taking both her hands between his. "Erin, I didn't mean to be so cruel the day you came to me about the baby. All I could remember when you told me was the way that Cara had died. And then I assumed that you didn't want the child—couldn't possibly want my child—and that you, who were beautiful and healthy and alive, would abort the child. I don't think I knew it at the time, but I wanted you to tell me that you did intend to keep the baby and that we would have to give our marriage a real chance."

"Jarod," Erin murmured, "I did want the baby all the time, I would have never . . ."

"I believe you, darling, I believe you. That's why you have so much to forgive me for! Oh, Erin! You thought you were the cripple with nothing to offer because you were terrified to make love. But Erin, you were never the one lacking. I could take you, I could make love to you, but I was the cripple. You never lost the capacity for love itself—I had. But I think it was really from that night, from that very first night we lay together, that I began to love you. Erin, you gave me so very much. . . ."

Erin opened her mouth to speak, to assure him, to tell him that nothing mattered any more except for the incredible fortune that he had come to love her, but he wasn't done. He set her hands down firmly and began to stalk the room again, and she found herself thinking just what a magnificent man he was, with his handsomely toned, cat-graceful body and rugged features, remarkable eyes, and fine, sound character.

"I was jealous of Gil," he said with self-contempt. "With no real right. Oh, I think he would have gladly had an affair with you—but half the men in the world probably feel that way. I should have known I could trust you." He fell silent for a minute, looking out the glass unseeingly. "I misjudged Gil pathetically—and we all paid for it. I've apologized to him, but . . ." He shrugged, and Erin saw again how strong a man he was to recognize his own faults and be pained by them.

He looked back to her suddenly. "Erin—I did use you. I knew you couldn't be a spy—and you could have left the Soviet Union long before you did. I simply couldn't let you go."

Erin was no longer able to stay seated. She flew from the couch, sliding her arms around his neck and holding him as her eyes sought his and her words spewed out vehemently. "I don't care, Jarod! Oh, don't you see, I don't care about anything that happened in the past!

You're here, Jarod." She broke off abruptly and stared at him with confusion misting the silver of her eyes to a charcoal gray. "Oh, Jarod! Why did you send me home? Why did you let me go through this month of thinking you didn't care?"

"Because," he said softly, "I couldn't believe that you really loved me. That you would want a life with me. That you could give up all the glamour of your life to have our child."

Erin tilted her head back and started to chuckle throatily. "Jarod —you do need to be forgiven—for the torture my life has been all this time! I couldn't care less about my career! I was busy retiring while you were sitting here getting acquainted with Casey."

He took her by the shoulders and held her away from him, searching out her eyes. "Really, Erin? I have to admit that I'm too selfish to allow you in any more bubble baths! The only man I want seeing you clad in soap is me!"

Erin chuckled again and lowered her eyes demurely. "I was always dressed in those commercials!" she murmured chastely.

"But not in enough!" he charged. But then he was pulling her back against him and adding gruffly, "Mary said you always wanted to teach. Is that true?"

"Ummm," Erin nodded against his chest. "But that doesn't even matter . . ."

"It does matter," he said softly. "And one day, we'll see that you get to teach. But God, honey," he added, inhaling deeply of the soft perfumed scent of her hair, "I never had a teacher like you. We'll have a pack of adolescents falling in love with . . ."

"I doubt it—I'll be too old to them!"

They laughed together, and the sound was wonderful to them both. It made them gaze at each other with a new shyness. And then a guarded mist shrouded Jarod's eyes once more. "Do you realize, Mrs. Steele, that your child will be a quarter Russian?"

Erin sensed both the pride and the insecurity in him. "I know that," she said softly, a beautiful smile curving her lips. "And I insist that you teach him—or her—the language. And how to play that beautiful instrument. And all the history and heritage. . . . We tend to lose so much of our pasts, Jarod. I want our child—or children, but I warn you, I think three will be quite sufficient!—to know all about both sets of grandparents! And to value their ancestry. I want them to know all that went into making their father such a fabulous man."

"Erin. . . . My God, sweetheart," he said, a husky timbre to his voice, "how I do love you."

Erin smiled. "Can you think of anything else?"

"Yes, lots of things. I'll need to go back to the U.S.S.R., but I can arrange to be here for the next year. I want to make sure that our child is born on American soil. And I'm afraid we can't really move to California—the United Nations is headquartered here. And—"

Erin placed the tip of her forefinger over his lips. "Jarod, I know we will have a great deal to discuss. I want to know more about your parents, and I want to know more about Cara. I know you will always love her a little, and that's okay, Jarod. I'm glad you had such a wonderful love, I believe that that wonderful love is the same that we will share. . . . And I also want to know about Catherine, Jarod, even if knowing will hurt me."

"Catherine?" he queried, a devilish tilt to his eyes. He half closed them lazily. "I'll introduce you to Catherine—tomorrow."

Erin swallowed suddenly. "Catherine is here? In the U.S.?"

"Ummmm," Jarod teased. "One of her is."

"One? You mean there are two Catherines?"

"Ummmm, but you love me and trust me, right? So for the moment, we can forget all about Catherine and Catherine."

Erin pouted for a second, but he was right. She loved him, and right now they had been apart a little too long. A fire was raging within her, and being next to him was like trying to put that fire out with gallons of gasoline.

"Yes," she murmured, her half-closed silver eyes luminescent as she tilted back her head. "We can forget Catherine if you'll just make love to me. . . . Oh, Jarod! It's been so long!"

He swept her into his arms and easily found the bedroom. But as he touched the zipper of her dress, the doorbell began to ring. "Don't answer it," he murmured, and with his whisper deliciously searing the lobe of her ear, she was tempted to obey.

But the bell kept ringing. "I have to get it, Jarod, I'm sure it's Casey to pick up Bill, and she knows we're here so she'll just keep ringing."

He lifted a brow in autocratic query, then scowled. "Okay—but get her out quick!"

"Yes, sir," Erin complied, laughing as she scampered out of his reach. She grabbed the indignant Bill off the sofa where he had made himself comfortable after tripping her and walked to the door.

It was, indeed, Casey. Her eyes were alight with her insatiable curiosity, but before she could speak, Erin stuffed the protesting Bill into her hands. "Here he is, Case—and as to Jarod"—she dropped her voice to a conspiratorial whisper—"I'll tell you two things. He is absolutely gorgeous naked, and he is . . . wickedly . . . wickedly . . . wickedly wonderful!"

For the second time that day, she closed the door on Casey's open mouth. And then Erin chuckled—wickedly—and hurried back to the bedroom door. She paused as she looked in. Jarod had already stripped and was waiting for her on the expanse of her bed. Erin's smile deepened as she thought two conflicting thoughts—one, that her white ruffled bedroom set was way too feminine with Jarod sharing the room—but also that his powerful bronzed body looked wonderfully rugged against the sheer white.

"Is she gone?" Jarod demanded.

Erin nodded, suddenly discovering she had lost her voice again.

Jarod scowled at her with the brilliant, compelling blue of his eyes taking the lash from his next command. He patted the bed beside him. "Then come here, wife, and do it quickly!"

"Certainly," she replied, lowering her thick lashes sweetly, and pretending to comply. But she moved toward the bed very slowly, shedding her clothing with infinite grace as she took tiny steps. She watched as his eyes narrowed and roamed over her.

And for several seconds he *was* content to *watch* as the still deceptively slender form of his wife was bared inch by inch before him. He breathed in deeply as she stood naked before him, savoring the high rise of her breasts heaving slightly in anticipation even as she taunted him, loving with his eyes the tiny waist that flared to full hips . . . to the long, shapely length of silken thighs and calves. She stood just out of reach, and for a second he allowed it, letting his eyes have the first touch of her assets, allowing the blue of his to meet and clash with the suggestive, sultry silver of hers.

And then he snaked out a hand, jerking her so that she fell on top of him with a little gasp of surprise. "Think to torture me again, eh, wife?" he teased, drawing provocative little trails over her buttocks as he pressed her against him, allowing the pressure of his own full arousal to further elicit hers. "Thank God you're a klutz!"

"A klutz!" Erin protested in a panted shriek, pressing her palms against his chest in an effort to confront him with blazing eyes.

"Ummm . . ." he murmured, taking the advantage to lean up and encircle his mouth tenderly around a nipple that had provoked him beyond reason by jutting hard and impertinently in front of his face. "An . . . exquisitely . . . beautiful . . . klutz . . ."

By the time he finished his words, spoken brokenly as he savored first one breast and then the other, she could protest no more. Her breathing had become very ragged. The strength had gone out of her arms and she was above him only because he held her.

Then she was lifted, dragged beneath him, and accosted from head to toe with burning, fevered kisses and hands that caressed and fondled and teased, and her strength returned along with the delicious weakness so that she could tease and touch him in return.

His hands roamed everywhere, and she gasped when they eased her thighs apart, subtly teasing until she whimpered and cried out when his fingers touched the core that burned so for him. He whispered how much he wanted her, and she writhed insanely with the wildfire need. His kisses covered her again, and then she was begging him, and then refusing to beg, touching him until he stopped torturing her with that incredible magic because she had caused him to groan his own need out in guttural demand.

Tears escaped her as he moved within her. She shuddered, opening to him, locking her slender legs around him in feminine surrender that created, that gave and demanded in return.

Similar thoughts struck them both as the world evaporated into a red glow that eclipsed the magnificence of that upon Red Square at midnight. They were together, they were home.

Jarod caught her lips as he escalated his rhythm with the rising spiral of his flaring desire. How he loved her, how he loved the tempestuous passion that met and matched his own. Deep within her he knew not only the ecstasy she gave him, but the love.

When the red glow shattered into blinding rapture, he held within her still, knowing that even now they were together, and that this lethargic delight that gently brought them back to the world was also a form of rapture. Touching her, holding her, being near her. It was all rapture. It was home. It was love.

He refused to pull away from her, but held them locked together. He lifted his head to meet her silver eyes and to see if her need to be together so intimately matched his own.

Her eyes flickered open. They half closed, beautiful, lazy, sensuous with satiation. She smiled, her lips a moist, lazy, half curl. And then she allowed her eyes to close, answering his unspoken question. Her words were richly husky. "My dear Russian American husband, my darling, my love, you *are* wickedly, wickedly, wickedly . . . wonderful."

EPILOGUE

The hallway was long and white, white walls, white tile flooring, evoking complete sterility.

The man and woman who walked the corridor were a vivid contrast, he so dark, she so vividly fair. Both tall, lithe, statuesque; something about them as a couple was very beautiful, arrestingly stately.

Her silver eyes flashed with confusion and sparkling curiosity and she demanded in a hushed whisper that well fit the sterility of her surroundings, "Jarod, where on earth are we going?"

His blue eyes flashed back a teasing amusement and assurance. "You'll see."

Seconds later they reached the end of the hallway and the awesome mass of silver-gray machinery—the floor-to-ceiling memory storage, the multitude of drives, disks, modems, and controls.

She stared with wonder at the machine, but then turned to her husband with her eyes narrowing in further confusion and a smile that clearly indicated she thought he was crazy playing at the corners of her lips.

He smiled and bowed dramatically. "You wanted to meet Catherine. *Voila!* I give you Catherine."

Erin glanced from Jarod to the computer and back to Jarod, then started laughing. "A computer! I was jealous of a computer!"

"Ahhhh . . . not just any computer!" Jarod explained generously. "This lady is top of the line. She is programmed to think—and she is equipped with a marvelous sense of humor."

"A sense of humor?" Erin queried dubiously.

Jarod nodded. "Umm. A sense of humor."

Erin stared at the computer a minute and then frowned again. "But how could Catherine be here and in Russia?"

278

"Easy, my love—she has a counterpart. This lady is Catherine I—in Moscow we have Catherine II—or Catherine the Great as we call her. Both Catherines are sheer works of genius, true tributes to the brilliance of the human mind."

Chuckling ruefully, Erin continued to gaze at the extensive keyboard. "My rival!" she murmured. Then she glanced back to her husband. "Jarod—should I really be in here?"

He smiled. "Access to this corridor is not easy—access to Catherine is even more difficult. She accepts commands only when she has been properly entered—and one enters her through an infallible system. She has special lights that pick up on fingerprints. See."

As he explained, Jarod slipped by Erin and sat in the chair, setting his hand into the pit. Catherine whirred into action.

GOOD AFTERNOON, JAROD STEELE.

Jarod answered:

HELLO, CATHERINE.

The computer whirred again.

THE DATE IS JUNE 4. TIME, 3.02.48 PM. THE TEMPERATURE OUTSIDE THE UNITED NATIONS BUILDING IS A PLEASANT 80 DEGREES FAHRENHEIT, 26.7 CELSIUS. SLIGHTLY CLOUDY, 20 PERCENT CHANCE OF RAIN.

Erin laughed delightedly. "She's wonderful!"

"Umm," Jarod agreed. His laughing eyes met his wife's. "Actually, Catherine introduced me to you."

"Oh?" Erin lifted a brow.

"Oh. Yes." Jarod pushed a number of keys, and she saw a file on herself suddenly appear across the screen. She was astounded by the things the computer "knew." Details she had half-forgotten herself.

Erin set her hands delicately upon Jarod's shoulders and then pinched him. "That isn't fair!" she exclaimed. "You knew my whole life—"

"Ouch!" Jarod murmured, catching her hands with his and pulling them over his shoulders to kiss them. "No, sweetheart, I didn't know everything. There was a lot I had to learn from you. And the learning, that marvelous sense of trust you gave me, was a part of

279

my coming to realize how much I needed you to be a part of my life."

Erin dipped low and brushed a kiss on top of his head. "Then I guess I'll forgive you—and Catherine," she said huskily, before frowning and stiffening once more.

"Jarod—you were watching me all the while, weren't you? That night I collided with you in the bar . . . in the airport . . . on the train—"

"The bar," Jarod interrupted, "was purely accidental! I'll admit to the plane and the train." He sighed a little sheepishly. "You see, Catherine knew that you were somehow involved—but not how. As soon as your name had appeared on the roster of those entering the Soviet Union, Joe had planned to use you as a carrier. 'Mc' was the code name for you in the computer." He hesitated for a moment, then explained. "You see, Erin, there was another embassy man who had gotten involved with Joe. His name was Samuel Hughes." He paused again as he saw her brows raise. "Yes, the man I told Gil about that day in my apartment. Sam wasn't such a terrible man, just weak. Service to the government doesn't always pay much, but espionage can. Anyway, Sam got involved with Joe, then started to get panicky. He wanted out. And he was in a business a man couldn't just quit. He had access to Catherine—so he started planting little clues in the computer. Your code name was one of them. He planned to have a fail-safe system for himself—and I suppose he must have told Joe that he wanted out—and that if anything happened to him, Catherine would be there to tell the world. But apparently Joe knew that Sam hadn't given Catherine too much information—too much would have cooked his own goose, because the Catherines link up and someone with access would be sure to catch on."

"Joe tried to make it look like the Soviets had gotten Sam. The U.S. couldn't have said much if he had been caught in the act of espionage. And there was a while when I believed it might have been possible. Except that Sergei denied it. And under the circumstances, Sergei definitely wouldn't have lied. By the time they found Sam, I knew he hadn't been killed by the Russians, but by whoever was running Project Midnight."

Erin shivered and closed her eyes. She had come close to a little too much, and been such a fool that she had fought the man who had always been trying to save her, even when logic had told him she was a suspect.

She felt her husband kiss the palm of her hand tenderly. "Forget it, Erin," he said softly. "It's all over now." He was silent for a second and then changed the tone of his voice. "Anything you want to ask Catherine? You can think of her as a mystic! She does great things with the laws of probability."

"Hmmmmm," Erin murmured, thinking for a moment as she tried to join his lighthearted attempt to ease away from the past. "Of course! Ask her if we're going to have a boy or a girl!"

Jarod ran the Probability Program and then typed out the question.

Catherine whirred.

PERCENTAGE OF MALES BORN IS SLIGHTLY HIGHER AT THIS DATE THAN FEMALES. HOWEVER, PERSONAL PERCENTAGE IS THAT OF ANY EXPECTING PARENTS.

50-50

Erin chuckled softly. "Well that certainly tells us!"

"I'm glad," Jarod said softly. "I kind of like the element of surprise. I mean, the father gets to call everyone, and the exciting part is announcing a son or daughter, right?"

"I suppose!" Erin laughed. "But which would you prefer?"

He paused a second. "A healthy child," he said softly.

Erin touched his cheek tenderly. "We will have a healthy child," she promised quietly. She placed both her hands lightly atop his jet head and tilted it upward so that she could bend to nuzzle his forehead with her lips. From that angle she held his eyes, her own rich with understanding. "I love you," she said.

"And I love you."

They held together for a moment, then Jarod once more clutched her hands. "It's a pleasant day," he announced, "or so Catherine says—if you don't mind a small probability of showers. You and Catherine have now met, and I think it would be a shame to waste a pleasant day."

"I get your drift!" Erin chuckled. "Let's get out of here!"

She turned and started to retrace her steps down the sterile white corridor. Jarod watched the natural sway of her hips and grinned as he turned back to Catherine to check out.

But before he could touch a key, Catherine whirred, and Jarod smiled as he read the message.

HAVE A NICE, NICE LIFE, JAROD STEELE.

Jarod glanced back to his wife, who had turned to wait for him, her silver eyes filled with dazzling mischief, her lips curled into a secret, tempting smile. He typed out a final message.

THANKS, CATHERINE. I BELIEVE I WILL HAVE JUST THAT!

He checked out of the computer and followed the blond beauty with the stunning silver eyes, catching her with an arm about her waist. They left the building and walked out together.

The sun was shining through the clouds.

Yes, he thought, we will have a nice . . . nice . . . life.

LOOK FOR NEXT MONTH'S
CANDLELIGHT ECSTASY SUPREMES

$2.50 each

Candlelight
Ecstasy Romances™

$1.95 each

At your local bookstore or use this handy coupon for ordering.

DELL BOOKS
P.O. BOX 1000. PINE BROOK, N.J. 07058-1000

B160C

Please send me the books I have checked above I am enclosing $_____ (please add 75c per copy to cover postage and handling) Send check or money order no cash or C.O.D.s Please allow up to 8 weeks for shipment

Name _____

Address _____

City _____ State Zip _____

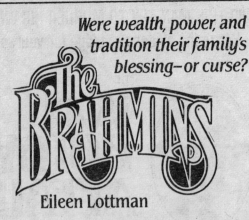